ARKHAM HORROR

It is the height of the Roaring Twenties – a fresh enthusiasm for the arts, science, and exploration of the past have opened doors to a wider world, and beyond...

And yet, a dark shadow grows over the town of Arkham. Alien entities known as Ancient Ones lurk in the emptiness beyond space and time, writhing at the thresholds between worlds.

Occult rituals must be stopped and alien creatures destroyed before the Ancient Ones make our world their ruined dominion.

Only a handful of brave souls with inquisitive minds and the will to act stand against the horrors threatening to tear this world apart.

Will they prevail?

T0020599

ALSO AVAILABLE IN ARKHAM HORROR

Wrath of N'kai by Josh Reynolds
Shadows of Pnath by Josh Reynolds

In the Coils of the Labyrinth by David Annandale

Mask of Silver by Rosemary Jones
The Deadly Grimoire by Rosemary Jones
The Bootlegger's Dance by Rosemary Jones

Litany of Dreams by Ari Marmell

The Ravening Deep by Tim Pratt

The Last Ritual by S A Sidor
Cult of the Spider Queen by S A Sidor
Lair of the Crystal Fang by S A Sidor

The Devourer Below edited by Charlotte Llewelyn-Wells
Secrets in Scarlet edited by Charlotte Llewelyn-Wells

Dark Origins: The Collected Novellas Vol 1
Grim Investigations: The Collected Novellas Vol 2

ARKHAM HORROR™

SONG

of

CARCOSA

JOSH REYNOLDS

ACONYTE

First published by Aconyte Books in 2024

ISBN 978 1 83908 286 3

Ebook ISBN 978 1 83908 287 0

Cover art by Daniel Strange

Distributed in North America by Simon & Schuster Inc, New York, USA

Printed in the United States of America

9 8 7 6 5 4 3 2 1

ACONYTE BOOKS

An imprint of Asmodee Entertainment Ltd

Mercury House, Shipstones Business Centre

North Gate, Nottingham NG7 7FN, UK

aconytebooks.com // twitter.com/aconytebooks

*For Joe Pulver, who showed me
the wonders of Carcosa.*

PROLOGUE
A New Game

"Monsieur? Thorne is here."

The man who called himself Cinabre sighed theatrically and looked up from his book. His servant, Lapp, stood primly in the doorway, dressed in his usual gray suit and vibrant red necktie. Lapp was young and handsome, the way Cinabre preferred his companions. At the moment, however, his expression was one of distaste.

Cinabre set his book aside and gestured curtly. "Show them in, dear heart, show them in. Gods alone know what they might pinch if left unattended."

Lapp turned on his heel. He moved too smoothly to be entirely human; something else Cinabre preferred in his companions. A touch of the strange kept one on their toes. He sat up on his divan and adjusted his dressing gown over his scrawny frame. He was old and felt it; today was one of the rare days that the royal jelly and yoga couldn't mask the weight of years, nor the nagging reminders of a life lived hard.

But it was a life lived in service to a higher cause. Or so many of the disparate members of the Red Coterie told themselves.

It was why they had come together, not as an organization, but rather a loose alliance of individuals with similar goals. They traded information, aided one another when it benefitted them, and came together in quorum rarely, and only when matters of great import lay before them. Then the Congress of Keys assembled and deliberated on what course of action they were to take. Inevitably, these deliberations devolved into arguments; one of the reasons he'd stopped attending.

Some of the members, like the Claret Knight, were idealists. Others were more concerned with earthly pleasures. Cinabre counted himself somewhere between an idealist and a decadent. The world suited him as it was, and he worked to preserve it when needed. But such efforts took their toll, even on him.

"You look like hell, kitten," Thorne said, as Lapp ushered them into the room. Thorne was tall and pretty, in an androgynous fashion. Like Lapp, they wore gray, save for a red cravat tucked into the front of their jacket. Pale skin and platinum blonde hair completed the image. "Age catching up with you?"

"It catches up with all of us, dona," Cinabre said, reaching for his cigarettes and the big, brass lighter that sat on the table beside his divan. Thorne smiled thinly.

"Speak for yourself, Cinabre. Age is just a number as far as I'm concerned." Their eyes flicked to Lapp, who'd bristled slightly at their irreverent tone. "Still collecting pretty faces, I see. Got any other skills, kid?"

Lapp frowned. "I am happy to show you, if you like," he growled. For an instant, the thing inside him stirred, and Thorne's insouciant grin faded.

"Call him off, Cinabre, or I will be forced to discipline your puppy."

Cinabre smiled indulgently, and dismissed Lapp with a request for coffee. "You'll have to forgive him, Thorne. Got an old soul, that one. Pretty face though, as you said."

"Yes, but what's underneath?" Thorne looked at him. "A little birdie mentioned that you have some information for me. Care to gab?"

Cinabre selected a cigarette and lit it. He didn't offer one to Thorne. "Right to it, then? Don't even want to wait for coffee?"

"I'm busy."

"Still searching for that little glass of yours?"

Thorne sneered. "If that's your way of asking if I'm still in the game, then yes. Unlike some people, I'm not inclined to retire. After all, there's a war going on … or had you forgotten?"

Cinabre stiffened. "No. I am well aware of the stakes that the Red Coterie plays for. Nor have I dealt myself out of the game, whatever you seem to think. Indeed, I am making moves all the time."

Thorne looked him up and down. "Really?"

"One doesn't have to gallivant across the globe to contribute to the struggle," Cinabre said, loftily. "I play my part, the same as you."

"Oh, no doubt." Thorne picked up the book Cinabre had set aside. "Poetry?"

"Justin Geoffrey. Know him?"

"Intimately. We shared a few fraught days in the Balkans once upon a time. Or was that someone else? I forget." They tossed the book onto a nearby couch and looked around. "This place is still a mess, I see."

Cinabre followed their gaze. The room, like the rest of the little house in Saint-Bertrand-de-Comminges, was crammed full of things. Grotesque statuary lurked in nooks and crannies; books vied for space with canopic jars and unidentified fragments culled from craters and tombs; decorative palm fronds, dyed red, covered walls, artfully drawing the eye to the murals on them – scenes straight out of Burroughs and Poe. Standing in the doorway and looking in, one no doubt had the impression of peering into a red-tinted kaleidoscope. He smiled. "I am comfortable," he said.

Thorne grunted. "Well, ain't that just ducky," they said, as they turned back to their host. "The Claret Knight said you wanted to talk Ys. You've located it then?"

"The Key of Ys, you mean? Yes."

"Where?"

Cinabre rose to his feet, tightening the belt of his dressing gown as he did so. "Why should I tell you? Perhaps I'll add it to my collection, eh?" The Key wasn't one of the most important pieces in the game, but it was still a piece worth possessing. Various members of the Coterie, Thorne and Cinabre among them, had sought it over the centuries since its disappearance sometime after the fall of Trebizond.

Thorne frowned. "Did you invite me here just to gloat? If so, bad form. Rest assured I will take it up at the next lodge meeting…"

"Oh get off the cross, dona. I could use the wood. I was merely having a little joke at your expense. Yes, I know where the Key is."

Thorne grimaced. "Where?"

Cinabre pointed his cigarette at Thorne, like a teacher

singling out a recalcitrant student. "Patience, poppet. I'm going to need something from you first."

"Now we come to it," Thorne said, with a sly smile. "A favor for a favor, kitten?"

"If you like. An… associate of mine will require your aid. In Venice."

"Venice," Thorne repeated. "Why not ask the Cavalier? That's his patch."

Cinabre frowned. "He is… unpredictable. Mercurial. He may not wish to help." *Il Cavaliere Cremisi* – the Crimson Cavalier – was one of the idealists in the group, though no one was quite sure what, exactly, those ideals might be. Most of the others couldn't stand him, regardless. Like Venice, he stood alone.

"The same could be said of me," Thorne countered.

"Yes, but I have something you want. No one knows what he desires, not even him. Besides, this is a matter which requires your… unique talents."

"You flatter me," Thorne said. "What's the sitch, then?"

Cinabre drew a certain shape in the air with the tip of his cigarette. The ash flared and held its form briefly, before dispersing and fluttering to the carpet. Thorne cursed.

"Them?" Then, "*Him?*"

"Perhaps. In any event, it's worth seeing to… just in case."

Thorne ran their hand through their hair, looking momentarily out of sorts. "Bugger and blast. You really intend to make me work for it, don't you?"

"The game progresses, Thorne. They make their moves, we make ours." Cinabre paused. "In this case, I fear we've only seen the tip of it. A little crack, hinting at bigger problems."

"And you think our man in Venice is involved," Thorne said.

Cinabre frowned. "I don't recall saying any such thing." Despite his words, he had, in fact, been thinking of that very possibility. Venice had always been a battleground of one sort or another. It was a thin place – a threshold. Reality did funny things in those tangled canals, and the unwary could find themselves lost in a world at once familiar and horribly, hideously alien. And, of course, there was something awful sleeping in the lagoon, but that was to be expected. Cinabre himself, sensitive as he was to such things, made it a point to avoid the city. Most of the other members of the Red Coterie did as well.

"You didn't have to. Why else come to me and not him? You say it's for my talents, but let's be honest – you and I have never seen eye to eye in these matters."

That was true as well. Thorne was regarded by some of the others as the *enfant terrible* of the group. It had nothing to do with age; Thorne was at least as old as Cinabre himself, if not older. But Thorne was... troublesome. They had their own agenda, as every member of the Coterie did, but all too often that agenda brought them into conflict with their fellows. Cinabre regarded himself as a collector; Thorne was a magpie.

Cinabre sucked on his teeth for a moment, but was saved from having to reply by the return of Lapp, bearing coffee. "Ah, Lapp – deliverer of ambrosia," Cinabre murmured. He glanced at Thorne. "Coffee?"

"You didn't answer my question."

"No?"

"No," Thorne said.

"Well," Cinabre said. "Does it really matter why? The

situation requires attention. And you are an attentive individual. Besides, Venice is lovely this time of year."

"I hate Venice. It smells like fish and skullduggery."

"I wouldn't bandy that opinion about, were I you." Cinabre poured them both a coffee. "Venetians take such things seriously. I'd hate to hear of you turning up, floating face-down in a canal."

Thorne gave a light bark of laughter. "So would I, come to that." They looked around again, as if calculating the value of the room's contents. "Do you still have it, by the by?"

"Have what?" Cinabre asked, all innocence.

"Your Key, old thing. No one is quite sure, you see, so I thought I'd ask."

Cinabre grunted. "I do."

"Where?"

"In a safe place."

Thorne smiled, mockingly. "That's good to hear. I'd hate to see you lose it. I know you're probably getting forgetful in your old age." They paused. "If you ever want to... pass it on to someone more... energetic, my door is always open."

"And your hand outstretched, eh?"

"In friendship." Thorne paused. "You haven't yet told me who I'm supposed to be helping. They have a name?"

"Zorzi," Cinabre said. "Alessandra Zorzi." He blew a plume of smoke into the air and smiled faintly. "And do hurry, *kitten*. I expect time is of the essence."

CHAPTER ONE
Shadows Lengthen

She awoke to the touch of soft fingers on her cheek. She could hear the monotone thud of water against a boat's hull, and the crying of something that might have been a bird. She looked up at the woman in whose lap she lay. The latter's face was hidden behind a colorless veil of damask, yet somehow, she thought she knew her. She wracked her brain, trying to stir a name from the sludge of sleep. It came slowly. Reluctantly.

Cassilda.

"Cassilda," she began, but a gentle finger to her lips silenced her.

"Along the shore, the cloud waves break," Cassilda murmured, softly "The shadows lengthen but Carcosa stands firm in the light of twin suns. Look, song of my soul... *look...*"

She looked. They were in a long, narrow boat the color of the second sun. Its prow, carved to resemble a galloping horseman, parted the misty waters of an immense lake that stretched as far as her eye could see. The mist that lay across it was so thick that she could not make out the shore from which they'd departed. But ahead of them, it had begun to thin and part, revealing... what?

Carcosa.

"Carcosa," Cassilda said, and there was a familiar yearning in her voice. Carcosa. The sound of it reverberated across the water like a bell, and the circling birds – were they birds? – screamed in accompaniment.

The city clung to the far shore with all the still desperation of a wary beast. It was a great city; a place of looming towers and vast, serpentine walls; of turreted redoubts and marble pillars. But ancient... so ancient. Like all old things, the weight of time sat heavily on it, and she could see places where the walls had crumbled and the towers had begun to lean.

"See, my love... Carcosa still stands," Cassilda said. "Though all the cities of Aldebaran should fall, Carcosa will remain. From here, we will fight him, Camilla..."

Camilla blinked. Her name wasn't Camilla, was it? Then, perhaps it was. It did not feel right, but nothing about this felt right. She – Camilla – sat up, and the boat swayed at the sudden motion. At the rear, the pilot murmured something unintelligible, but Cassilda calmed him with a gesture. "Easy. We are almost there, my love. Soon it will be done."

"What will be done?" Camilla looked down at herself. The hauberk she wore was familiar, the glinting scales as hard as those of a dragon, but supple. The sigil of the dynasty of Carcosa – two suns guardant – was upon her breast. She paused. Something was missing; something important. Her eyes widened in panic. "My sword! Where is my sword?"

Frantically, she began to search for it, until Cassilda calmed her with soft murmurs and light touches. "Your blade is here, my love. It awaits your touch." The other woman motioned to a silk-wrapped bundle at her feet. "But you will not need it. He cannot touch us here." Her voice grew firm. "Let the black stars cast their evil light across the world. Carcosa yet stands unbowed, as it shall for so long as I am queen." She looked across the misty waters toward the turrets of the city that rose from and sprawled across the far shore of the lake.

Cassilda's proclamations agitated the birds and their cries came louder and nearer, as if they were gathering somewhere above. Camilla looked up, but saw nothing save darting shadows in the rising mist. The light of the suns had not yet burned it off, nor were they likely to. The breath of Hali resisted all efforts to disperse it, and in the past its refusal to fade had often stood between Carcosa and invasion.

But not against the enemy that was coming. "I need my sword," she said, hoarsely. Fear gripped her; pulsed in her veins. The crying of the birds seemed to be a single voice, calling out to her, or perhaps to Cassilda. Calling for them to return and cease this foolish act of resistance. The living god could not be resisted, and woe to those who dared make the attempt. "Can't you hear him? He is coming now… the king without a throne. The phantom of truth. He is on the far shore, watching us…"

Camilla felt certain of this, though she could not say how or why. They had escaped him once. They would not do so again. She grabbed her sword and fumbled at the wrappings, fear making her fingers clumsy. She looked at Cassilda and for a moment, an instant, her lover was someone else. As if her veil hid a secret face. "Cassilda," she said.

"My voice is dead," Cassilda intoned absently, clutching her hands together. She was not looking at Camilla now, her eyes fixed on Carcosa. "Die thou unsung, as tears unshed shall dry and die…" An old prayer of the imperial Hyadaen families.

"In Carcosa," the boatman said, in a voice like crushed glass. Camilla's gaze darted to him, and she saw that he was taller than she'd realized. He loomed over them, in robes that were not black as she'd first thought but yellow. A yellow the color of plague. Of sin and sickness. His hands – too thin, those hands, horribly so – were swaddled in a leper's rags. And his face was concealed beneath a pallid, featureless mask.

Her sword slid free of the rags and she rose, despite the bucking of the boat. "Unmask, sir," she demanded, raising her weapon until the point touched his breastbone. The boatman let his pole sink into the water and tapped a finger against the blade. She felt the blow, light as it was, reverberate through the hilt and into the bones of her arms.

"I wear no mask," he hissed. "But the same cannot be said of you."

At these words, she froze. The world itself seemed to halt and shiver, like a glass on the verge of shattering. She saw… another place, another time. Another world? She heard a woman's voice, and a man's laughter. She squeezed her eyes shut as her world threatened to slip away. Behind her, Cassilda was speaking but Camilla couldn't make out the words. There was a roaring in her ears and her limbs ached, as if weighed down by chains.

Then, silence.

Camilla opened her eyes. The boatman hadn't moved. He watched her as if he had all the time in the world. But it wasn't a man's eyes that were fixed on her. No, that dreadful yellow stare belonged to something else. The strength of it gnawed at her soul, and made her weak. His hand fell to his waist, and he drew a rust-pitted knife from the frayed rope belt that held his robes shut. With his other hand, he pushed aside her sword and took her by the throat. She did not resist him – could not.

"Take off your mask," he croaked, as he lifted her with one hand and drove his blade into her stomach... again and again...

and again and – Pepper Kelly sat up with a gulping scream, thankfully muffled by the blanket someone had placed over her. She was on a boat; not a gondola, but a steam ferry. Several other passengers, perched on their luggage or awkwardly crammed on damp benches, clustered near the prow. A few of them gave her hard, disapproving looks. She stuck her tongue out at them and they hurriedly turned away. Behind her, the engine chuntered grumpily as the pilot aimed them toward their destination.

Trembling, she looked out over a soft, gray distance where the towers of Venice rose, repeating themselves in the surface of the water. The city seemed to rise out of the deep sea – *as Carcosa rose from Hali* – and, to her eyes, was nothing more or less than a kingdom out of a fairy tale. "Gosh," she said, softly. Then, recalling her dream, she immediately checked her midsection with trembling fingers. Finding no injury, she sighed audibly in relief.

"Another nightmare?" Alessandra Zorzi asked, in gentle tones – *like Cassilda* – as she lit a cigarette. Pepper glanced at the other woman. Alessandra was neither tall nor short, and was dressed to the nines in a pair of wide-legged trousers the color of mint and a silk top that put Pepper in mind of a pirate. Like Pepper, she also wore a coat against the evening chill.

"I'm fine," she said, the lie making her mouth feel funny. The dreams had been getting worse. Not a night went past now without one and she was starting to feel as if she hadn't slept in weeks. Sometimes she couldn't tell the difference between dream and reality. From the way the other woman frowned, she knew Alessandra had seen right through her.

"That was not what I asked," Alessandra said, smoke wreathing her features. For an instant, Pepper thought she saw another face superimposed over that of her mentor and friend, but the sensation quickly passed and she turned away.

"I know." The last tatters of the dream were slipping away from her, back into her subconscious. As far as she was concerned, they could stay there. "So, that's Venice, hunh?" she asked, hoping to change the subject. "How do they get it to float on the water like that?"

"Magic," Alessandra said. Behind them, the boatman laughed. Pepper glared at him and he gave a little bow of apology, but continued to smile. Still feeling the knife in her guts, Pepper turned away with a shiver. She had to keep reminding herself that the dream was just that. But it was getting harder, and down deep in the back of her mind she was starting to worry about what might happen if she didn't wake up.

Cassilda. Camilla. Carcosa. The names stayed, though all else faded. At first they hadn't but, as the dreams went on, they'd stuck in her head. She couldn't get them out, no matter how hard she tried. Who were they? What were they? Not her, that was for sure. She wasn't Camilla and Camilla wasn't her; it was more like she was living something that had happened to someone else. Sometimes, she found herself remembering a place she'd never been and people she'd never spoken to. It was unsettling, and that was putting it mildly.

She looked down at herself, imagining a coat of mail where her clothes were. Remembering the weight of a sword she'd never held. "Magic, hunh?" she muttered. "I could do with some of that about now." In the distance, Venice wavered in the golden light of early dusk. Its towers elongated, its shape stretched and skewed, and on the surface of the water its reflection moved like a thing alive. She blinked, and all was as it had been.

Alessandra leaned over and patted her knee. "That is why we are here, Pepper. And one way or another, we will get to the bottom of whatever malady afflicts you." She sat back and gave Pepper a confident smile. Pepper smiled in return, feeling as if her fears were momentarily allayed. If there was one thing Alessandra was good at, it was that.

Alessandra blew a plume of smoke into the air, and let the sea breeze take it. Her smile widened as her eyes fixed on Venice.

"But in the meantime, we shall have some fun, eh?"

CHAPTER TWO
Pallid Mask

Jan Znamenski sat at the window of his room and watched the sun set over Venice. It painted the towers and domes a shade of bloody gold, despite the gray of the afternoon. He studied the city with an artist's eye, imagining the stories and legends. Venice accreted myth. Every temple, monastery and monument had been adorned with myth from inception. And those layers of story deepened with every century.

Story upon story. Legend upon legend. Venice was a city shrouded in fiction. And, unsatisfied with their own, they'd acquired those of Egypt and Greece among others, weaving them into the gaudy, vibrant tapestry that was the City of Masks.

Now, a new story waited to be added… one written by him. He smiled and looked down at the book in his hand. A deceptively slim thing; a play, written nearly a half-century prior, by an unknown author of moderate talent and uncertain fate. It was said to drive those who read it to madness.

Znamenski had read it many times. As far as he knew, he

was still sane. Then, what was sanity, save an acquiescence to the prevailing madness?

He'd flirted with lunacy more than once in his life. He'd sought inspiration in chemical stimulation. He'd chased dragons and fairies; dope and drink and other, less quantifiable entertainments. In Paris, he'd plumbed the most illicit enjoyments the city offered to the erudite hedonist. But always, there was something lacking.

He'd noticed it during the war. He'd found his first muse on the battlefield, in the reds and blacks and browns of the trenches. He'd sculpted idols out of the mud of the Somme, and made death-masks for his fellows. He'd painted on canvas, depicting the scenes he saw in his head; an illusion of a better world than the one he was trapped in.

When the war had ended, he'd sought a new muse in the hospitals, among the influenza patients. He'd sketched and painted and shaped the many stages of death, and found patrons who were interested in his oeuvre. Granted, he'd been forced to subsidize their generosity with a sideline of smuggling, but that had been no hardship. Indeed, he'd enjoyed himself immensely, playing the criminal mastermind.

But the time for such games was over. He had new patrons now. Ones who could help him make his dreams a reality at last. He leaned back, momentarily lost in the fantasy. To finally visit that place he saw when he slept, not simply translate it via the earthly mediums of canvas and paint and clay. To see it and be there, to smell the mists of Hali, and taste the sweet fruits of Yhtill. To climb the mountains of Aldebaran and walk the streets of Carcosa.

Behind him, he heard a whisper of displaced air, and knew

that someone was observing him. His smile faded and he said, "You, sir, should unmask."

"No," the intruder replied. The tone was colorless, the accent nonexistent. A flat voice, affectless and empty. A blank canvas upon which a listener might paint any emotion that suited them.

Znamenski grunted. "Forgive me. I am sure you must get the joke often."

"Less than you might imagine," the intruder allowed, as he sat down beside Znamenski and joined him in his study of the city. "An ugly place. Like a dead fish, stinking up the shore."

Znamenski raised an eyebrow. "I am sorry you dislike it so. Would Paris have suited you better, my friend?"

"We are not friends, artist. Merely fellow travelers."

Znamenski studied the other man – no, not a man, something else – as he'd studied the city. Average height, average build, average suit… not too expensive, just enough to imply a man of quality and care… yellow tie, yellow pocket square. Brown, swept back hair. The only interesting thing about him was the mask he wore; utterly featureless, save for two holes for eyes and a raised part that hinted at a nose. Not even a slot for the mouth, though his voice was never muffled; always clear.

The gaze behind the mask was tawny, but lifeless. Color was nothing without life, and the Man in the Pallid Mask was utterly lifeless in all the ways that mattered. He might as well have been stuffed and mounted.

Yet the mask always drew his eye back. Featureless, yes, but there was something there nonetheless. A hint of color, of design. He'd never seen one like it, though he'd become something of a connoisseur of masks in recent months. It fascinated him.

"You are staring, again," the Man said.

"I am and I make no apologies. I am an artist; I stare. I perceive, produce and perform. What do you do, sir – save interrupt my thinking time with baleful commentary?"

"I clean up your messes, Znamenski. I clear obstacles from your path."

"That is your function, is it not?"

"My function is beyond you."

"Perhaps I should ask my patrons. They are the ones who hold your leash, no?" The Marquis of Avonshire and his cronies in the Avonshire Trust were nominally the ones behind this venture. The Man was their factotum, at least as far as Znamenski knew. A jumped-up servant, though a dangerous one.

The Man didn't reply to Znamenski's jibe. Instead, he looked out over the canal again. "You have drawn attention to us," he said, finally. "All our efforts might be undone because of your sloppiness."

Znamenski slapped the play against the table, rattling the empty cups and plates he'd stacked up over the course of the afternoon. "I thought that was the point, *friend*. We are making history – a new history, to replace the current tired version."

The Man stared at him, his flat gaze betraying neither anger nor annoyance. Even so, Znamenski could tell he'd irritated his companion. He smiled, pleased with himself. "Fine," he said. "Whose attention is it that unsettles you so?"

"A woman."

"Venice is full of women. What's special about this one?"

"Her name is Zorzi."

Znamenski stared at him. "Ah. Oh. Well, that's unexpected." Alessandra's face swam to the surface of his thoughts and he found it still filled him with a frisson of pleasure. What a Cassilda she would make – a queen by any other name!

"You know her?"

Znamenski hesitated. Had that been a hint of accusation in the other man's tone? "I… might? That depends. How do you know her?" he hedged.

The Man turned away. "We have had dealings with her in the past, though always through intermediaries. Of late, she has found new employment."

"Good for her." Znamenski smiled. He'd always liked Alessandra, though you couldn't trust her with your valuables. Or your virtue. Not that he'd ever had much of either. "I always thought she needed a proper job."

"She serves those who would see us fail in our great task."

Znamenski winced. "Oh, well, that's a shame. I still don't see what that has to do with me…" A lie, but a calculated one. He'd suspected something like this might happen when that Scarborough woman had come to him in Paris, and offered him a trip to Milan. He'd heard on the grapevine that Alessandra had turned over a new leaf; that she'd started reacquiring certain objects she'd previously procured.

Now she was here. A coincidence, possibly. Or maybe not. He glanced toward the closet where some of his luggage sat. Inside a leather case was a cloth-wrapped bundle containing one of a dozen pieces of black jade, inscribed in hieratic Naacal. For a time, it had been essential to his work. Now it was simply a souvenir. He had a new obsession. Such was the curse of the creative mind.

The Man followed his gaze. "You believe she is after the Zanthu Tablet?"

"A very determined woman, Alessandra. Stubborn. If she wants it, she'll find a way to get it. It is as inevitable as the tides." Znamenski paused. "You say she is working for someone – who?"

"It is of no matter. If they are here for the tablet, give it to them. Do not arouse suspicion. Not when we are so close…"

Znamenski huffed. "I think I deserve to know, especially if there is a chance of… unpleasantness?"

The Man was silent for several moments. Then he lunged across the table and fastened one hand across Znamenski's face, as if to rip it off his skull. Znamenski yelped and grabbed at the Man's wrist, but his grip was like iron. "What you deserve is not for you to decide, artist. You have seen the Yellow Sign. You are His servant, and servants do as they are told… or they are punished."

Znamenski was wrenched up from his chair, and found himself swung out over the balcony. His feet kicked wildly above the canal-side below. The Man dangled him over the water and continued to speak, as if to a recalcitrant pet. "Shall I punish you, artist? Shall I break you, or drown you? What is the best way to remind you that you are not as important as you believe?"

Anger warred with terror in Znamenski's mind. How dare this – this *puppet* – question his importance? Without him, there would be no grand undertaking. Without him, none of this would be possible! A growl burst from deep in his throat as he clutched for the mask, to tear it off and dash it to pieces on the stones below. The Man, startled, jerked back, dragging Znamenski back inside. The table fell over with a crash and then Znamenski was tackling him backward into the room.

It was not a fight. The Man was stronger than he appeared and, while Znamenski had spent his time in the trenches, he'd never been a fighter. The struggle was lopsided and over in moments. Znamenski bounced off a wall and fell to the floor as the Man stood and straightened his tie. "Arrogant fool," the latter said.

"Yes... arrogant," Znamenski coughed. He hauled himself to his feet and laughed. "I admit it, and what is more – I proclaim it!" He spread his arms, trying to ignore the fear that nestled in his veins, the blood pounding in his temples. "I am arrogant, but it is arrogance which propels me to heights undreamt, and you know it. I am creating a masterwork for you and all the rest of my oh-so-generous patrons. Show more gratitude, I beg of you."

"Gratitude?" the Man said. "It is you who should show gratitude, artist. By our master's beneficence, you are part of a great undertaking. Were it up to me alone, I would have stripped the flesh from your worthless bones and cast them into the canals to feed what resides there."

Znamenski snorted. "And how shortsighted such an action would be. Here I thought you had more patience than that." He brushed a speck of lint from his sleeve and carefully righted the table, before carelessly depositing what had fallen on the floor back atop it. No sense making more work for the maid. "How would you like to deal with Alessandra, if it comes to it? Shall I leave the task with you, or…?" He let the question linger.

The Man stared at him. "If she comes to you, you are to give her what she wants and send her away. If you cannot, she will be dealt with in a more permanent manner. We need no more complications."

Znamenski shivered. "As you say. But I am sure it won't be necessary. Whatever else, she's always been a practical one, Alessandra."

The Man was silent for a moment.

"For her sake, and yours, let us hope you are right."

CHAPTER THREE
Grand Canal

Alessandra paid the pilot for the trip, and added a tip. He grinned, taken aback by her generosity, but nonetheless pleased. Steamers were frowned on by most Venetians; loud and smoky, they took up too much room and made the older gondoliers cross themselves and spit. But it was a quicker ride from the station to the Grand Canal, and sometimes fast was better. Especially given the circumstances.

She looked at Pepper. The young woman seemed dead on her feet, though she'd slept most of the journey from Padua. Her dreams were getting worse. It was like a sickness she couldn't shake, and it was beginning to eat away at her. Alessandra frowned, but turned it into a smile when Pepper glanced at her. "Busy, is it not?" she asked, trying to provoke a conversation.

"You can say that again," Pepper said. Alessandra followed her gaze. The quay was crowded. Holidaymakers jostled for gondolas to take them into the city, to their hotels. The gondoliers whistled and sang, trying to elicit fares. Tradesmen loitered at the edges of the crowd, offering guided tours, or waiting their turn to board a vessel for the station and home. Past the motion and confusion of the quay, the city rose in lucid stillness. It was poetry writ in stone; faerie castles, perched along silver roads of water.

"I don't see Selim," Pepper went on.

"He will be here," Alessandra said. "Be patient."

Pepper snorted. "Easy for you to say." Then, more quietly, "How long since you've been back, again?"

Alessandra's smile faded. "More years than I care to recall, if I am being honest." There had always been a reason not to come. The war, her job, others. All important, or so they'd seemed at the time. In truth, home hadn't truly felt like *home* in a long time.

"The way you talk about this place, I figured you'd be back every chance you got," Pepper pressed, as she hopped out of the way of a hotel porter carrying a load of luggage across the quay. Alessandra followed the porter's route, noting the individual who trailed after the young man. It was the bright red cravat that had drawn her eye.

Said cravat was tucked into an expensive coat, beneath an androgynous face. Impossible to tell gender at that distance and angle, nestled as they were in the crowd. But something about them caught her eye and held it, and more – sent a chill along her spine. But only for a moment, until a sudden convulsion of the crowd swallowed them up.

Shouts danced along the quay, and Pepper caught her sleeve. "Hey, get a load of that guy," she said, in a worried tone. Alessandra followed her gaze and saw a spindly, scarecrow figure lurch through the crowd and dance along the edge of the water.

The man was dressed in evening wear – black tie and white jacket, fashionable... or it had been; now it was almost yellow with filth, and his trousers and collar were frayed. He wore no shoes and skipped lightly across the wet stone, hands reaching for the darkening sky like those of an eager child. He was babbling as he spun, half-singing and half-shouting, shoving through the crowd where it was too slow to give him space. A woman yelped as he knocked her onto her rear. Her companion swung for the offender, but missed and nearly fell into the canal as his target slid past him.

The whole affair would have been ridiculous, if not for the unpleasant spinning of the man. It was as if he were a puppet, yanked along on invisible strings. As he pirouetted across the quay, his singing became more forceful. Alessandra couldn't tell what language it was supposed to be in – not Italian or French or English... Russian, maybe, or German. She could only understand snatches of it... something about black stars and long shadows, before it dissolved into gibberish.

"Think he's blotto?" Pepper asked. She sounded almost hopeful.

Alessandra shook her head. "Perhaps, but it is none of our affair." Despite her words, she thought the man's issues stemmed from something other than alcohol. But that wasn't their concern, not now. Let the city take care of its own. She had other business.

She turned her attentions to more pleasant sights. The sun was sinking into the Adriatic, painting the city in royal hues of purple. The city was full of promise, illicit and otherwise. It offered itself up to its visitors like a courtesan, and the sea breeze was like a kiss of invitation.

"*Venetia, Venetia, chi non ti vede non ti pretia,*" she murmured. Whoever doesn't see you, doesn't pay you. An old proverb, as true today as when it had been coined. Venice was spectacle and fantasy, offering riches in one hand as it picked your pocket with the other. It was a con artist, a trickster spirit.

It was just as she remembered, right down to the crumbling stonework and the green staining on the quay. Then, Venice didn't change. It was as it had been and always would be, the Most Serene Republic. Immune to revolution and progress alike.

It was she who'd changed. When she'd left Venice, she'd been a young woman, eagerly embarking on a life of crime. And now she was… what? One of a few who knew the truth of the world and what was needed to keep the sun in the sky, and the nightmares at bay. For her, that meant undoing the wrongs she'd unwittingly committed.

Though she'd called herself an acquisitionist, in reality she'd been a thief, and a good one. She'd stolen all manner of curios – everything from grimoires bound in human skin to cursed statuettes; none of which she'd believed in. At least not then. Then had come a visit to a Massachusetts town named Arkham, and the horrors she'd endured there.

She pushed the memories of that time back down into the underside of her mind. She had other worries to distract her. She looked again at Pepper. The younger woman was still watching the distressed man and his madcap dance. She wondered if anyone had summoned the authorities yet.

"He is not the first I have seen," a familiar voice said. Alessandra turned and smiled at the new arrival. He was a big, bald man, heavy with fat and muscle and sporting a handlebar mustache so black it looked almost painted on. He was dressed in a fine suit, but she privately thought he'd have looked more natural clad in mail and silk, with a sword in his hand.

"Hello, Selim. And not the first what?"

"The first madman," Selim said, without preamble. He greeted Pepper with a nod and looked around, tugging awkwardly at his necktie. He glared balefully at the dancing man, who was now heading away from them, much to the relief of everyone on the quay. "I have seen too many since I arrived last week. It seems the city is rife with them at the moment. Just the other day, a woman threw herself into the canal, screaming something about cats. I do not like it."

"No, well, I can see how that might spoil the ambiance," Alessandra said. Then, more intently, "What is the good word, otherwise?"

Selim reached into his jacket pocket and produced a folded theater flyer. Alessandra took it and heard Pepper hiss in recognition. The flyer had been illustrated with a garish city skyline – all crooked towers and unsightly angles. Twin suns rose overhead and a single, lonely figure stood atop the central tower, arms raised as in triumph… or perhaps surrender.

"This is what you see?" Alessandra asked, glancing at Pepper. "This is the city in your dreams?" Pepper nodded and looked away, her arms wrapped around her. Alessandra looked at Selim. "Where did you find this?"

"Someone was handing them out. They're all over the city."

According to the dates on the flyer, the first performance was in a week's time. "Is it him? Is this Znamenski's work?"

Selim's smile was sharp and cold. "Yes."

Alessandra smacked her fist into her palm. "I knew it!" Jan Znamenski had been one of her clients, in her previous life. He'd been in search of inspiration, and had sought it in odd places, mostly old books, and esoteric objets d'art. The Zanthu Tablet had been something of both; a tablet of black jade, inscribed in a language she didn't recognize.

Znamenski had insisted it held the key to something he'd been working on. At the time, she'd thought little of it. These days, she thought of little else. While Znamenski was no Comte d'Erlette, she was nonetheless determined to retrieve what she'd stolen for him, and turn it over to people who knew how to best deal with such things. More, she believed that he might know something about Pepper's dreams. They'd started after a visit to his Paris studio, after all – though he hadn't been there at the time.

That had been before that bad business with the Comte and the *Cultes des Goules*. Word was, Znamenski had gone to Milan. Selim had followed his trail from there to Florence to Padua and then to Venice. As soon as he'd run the artist down, he'd sent a telegram alerting her. That sort of efficiency was hard to find these days. "You did well, Selim," she said.

Selim inclined his head. He'd been the Comte d'Erlette's right-hand man before turning over a new leaf and swearing allegiance to her. She'd saved his life, and he felt he owed her. More, he'd saved Pepper's life more than once, at no little cost to himself. That alone made him trustworthy in her books.

"He is staying at the Hotel Danieli, on the Riva degli Schiavoni," he said, rubbing thumb and forefinger together in the universal sign for 'expensive.' Alessandra nodded and slid the flyer into her coat pocket.

"I know it. Just off St Mark's Square. Far pricier lodgings than I expected of my old friend. Then, he was always a fiend for Ruskin."

Both Selim and Pepper gave her looks of incomprehension. She sighed. "An artist. English. Jan was quite taken with his studies of Venetian architecture when last we spoke. Ruskin stayed at the Hotel Danieli when he came to Venice." She looked at Selim. "I assume you booked us rooms in the same hotel, as I asked?"

Selim bowed. "But of course. They claimed to have no rooms free, but the Comte d'Erlette has – had – a suite held for his occasional visits to the city."

"Yes, Henri always did love his debauched weekends in the city." She said it airily, but shivered a little as she thought of the man. Henri-Georges Balfour, the late Comte d'Erlette, had not been a saint by any measure of the word, but sometimes she found herself wondering if even he deserved the fate that had befallen him. She'd been pleased, at the time. But now, some months after the dust had settled, she felt a flicker of regret… one that she swiftly quashed. "Well then, let us go before Pepper here falls asleep on her feet, yes?" She took Pepper's arm in her own, and pulled the younger woman close. "We shall take tonight to recuperate from our journey, and mustache Znamenski tomorrow."

"Mustache?"

"Yes. As in challenge."

"Beard," Selim corrected, with a discreet cough. Alessandra glanced at him.

"Is it?"

"Yes."

"That makes no sense."

"But mustache does?" Pepper asked.

Alessandra threw up her hands in mock exasperation. "Nothing about English makes sense! It is a language fit only for magpies." She smiled as Pepper laughed. It was good to hear Pepper laugh. She'd done it so rarely of late. "But I suppose you are the expert."

"Damn right," Pepper yawned. "How are we getting there? Not walking, I hope."

As if on cue, one of the nearby gondoliers called out, "Good evening, signoras! Might I interest you in a ride?"

Alessandra glanced at him, about to answer with a polite refusal; the hotel wasn't far, after all. But something in his tone and his expression made her reconsider. "Of course. Lead the way," she replied.

He sketched a brief bow and led them across the quay to a mooring post where a covered gondola sat, black and dour. Golden vines etched the prow, and the covering was of red damask. The edges of the curtain twitched slightly, and she realized that there was already someone aboard. Something about the craft put her ill at ease, but she couldn't say why.

"What is it?" Pepper asked in a low tone. The young woman didn't look tired now. Tense, rather. She'd noticed Alessandra's disquiet. So had Selim.

"A trap?" he asked.

"I don't know." Alessandra forced a confident smile. "Shall we find out?"

CHAPTER FOUR
Thorne

The *Libreria Leone Scarlatto* sat away from the main drag of the Grand Canal, nestled in the crook of a side-street. A single, lonely window looked out at the street, and a wooden, iron-banded door with red-daubed doorknocker in the shape of a lion's head, provided entry. It was an unassuming little place, but appearances weren't everything.

It had taken Thorne nearly twenty minutes to find it, even though they knew exactly where it was and had been there before. The rumor was it was never in the same place twice; that it somehow floated from one *sestieri* to the next. One day it would be in Cannaregio, the next San Polo.

Thorne knew this to be an exaggeration. It was hard to find, true, but not because it moved. Rather, the shop had a number of spells of concealment woven about its tidy frame, in order to hide it from the hoi polloi. The Red Lion chose its customers, rather than the other way around. If it felt like doing no business that day, it would simply... vanish.

Then, bookshops, especially old ones, were curious things. They accreted magic, and became *genius loci* of sorts.

No place was safer – or more dangerous – to the unwary. Thorne stopped outside for a cigarette. The porter they'd beguiled – why pay when you can charm? – waited nearby with ensorcelled patience. The poor boy stared at nothing in particular, humming softly to himself.

Thorne glanced at him, smiling slightly. These Venetian men were mercurial; one was never quite sure how they'd react to being captivated in such a fashion. Still, done was done and that was that. They gestured, and the young man snapped into awareness. He blinked and looked around, as if uncertain how he'd got there. Thorne paid him, and sent him on his way before he started asking questions that they didn't feel like answering.

Thorne lived and breathed magic. It had been the singular pole of their existence for as long as they could remember. They used it the way rich men used money and poor ones used pity. Their time in the Red Coterie had taught them more than they'd ever once thought possible, but there was always more to learn. One could never have enough power.

They easily hefted their luggage – a set of high-quality valises purchased at no small expense in Paris – and entered the lion's den. The smell of cigarette smoke, mingled with the unmistakable odors of decaying paper and *acqua alta,* greeted them. A bell over the door signaled their entry to the proprietor.

"Matteo, my sweet," Thorne crooned. They looked around, taking in the heavy shelves to either side of the entrance, the slightly sagging floor, the watery yellow lightning that seemed to only make the shadows deeper. At the front counter, stacks of ledgers and old books tottered like the Alps. There was no reply. Thorne, impatient now, called out, "Matteo!" Their voice echoed oddly among the cramped stacks, as if the interior were larger than it appeared.

Matteo appeared a moment later, shuffling out of the back. He was small and balding, bent like a gnome and dressed in a red waistcoat over his grubby white shirt. He adjusted his glasses as he took in Thorne. "Oh," he said, in accented English. "It is you."

"Is that any way to greet an old friend?" Thorne purred, in Italian.

"We are not friends."

"That's right, my mistake. You're not one of us. You just work for us." Thorne dropped their bags with a thump. "I need a room. Is the flat above your shop available? Silly question, of course it is."

Matteo sniffed and took a seat behind the counter. "I was not informed you would be coming, signori," he said, in a reproachful tone. Thorne looked down their nose at the little man, wondering how best to reply. Matteo was a servant of the Coterie, true, but he was also a force in his own right, if a somewhat enigmatic one. The Red Lion had chosen him to be its proprietor; that spoke to a certain amount of power.

"How unfortunate. Lines of communication, what? Regardless, I am here and you are bound by our covenant to render me all due aid in my task."

"And what is your task, signori?"

"The same as always. I am here to add something to my collection."

"Does he know you are here?"

Thorne sighed. Another obstacle, but not an insurmountable

one. "If he doesn't yet, I'm sure he will, as soon as you tell him. Now, are you going to show me up to my room? And would a bite of lunch be out of the question?"

Matteo frowned. "Why do you wish to stay here? Surely you could have your pick of hotel rooms." He opened one of his ledgers and began to peruse it. Thorne sighed again. The truth was, they had considered a hotel. But there had been an unpleasant frequency in the air… a hint of something watchful and nasty. It was all over Venice, in fact. A bad smell, like something rotting on the vine. There was definitely something amiss in Venice.

"That's my business," Thorne said. "The room is still warded, I trust? Protected from those powers and principalities of darkness that haunt this fair city?"

Matteo frowned, but nodded. "Of course, signori. Neither hag nor spirit can enter this place. Not without invitation." The last was said in warning. Thorne smiled. The last time they'd come to Venice, there'd been a bit of trouble. Things swooping down from the starless dark and all that nonsense. But that was in the past.

"I promise – no summoning."

"I will hold you to it." Matteo paused. "The city… is not as you remember, signori. The old nightmares still prowl, but there are new ones as well."

"Yes. And how do the old ones feel about that?" Thorne asked. "Now… going to help me to my lodgings?"

Matteo gestured toward the rear of the shop. "You remember where it is. And there is a bacari down the street. You can get food there."

Thorne snorted and retrieved their bags. "How hospitable."

As they headed toward the back of the shop, Matteo cleared his throat.

"He will be angry, you know. When he finds out."

Thorne paused, then they laughed. "Good!" They weren't worried about the Cavalier; at least not in the way that Matteo thought they should be. The old gentleman was a prickly sort, true – and mad, besides. But who among the Coterie wasn't a little mad? Thorne was certain that they could sweet talk the Cavalier, eventually. After all, who wouldn't want a bit of help in dangerous times?

The flat was upstairs; it sat at the top of a narrow set of wooden steps that creaked and hummed as Thorne climbed them. The flat itself hung slightly over the canal, and it was a small space, reminiscent of a closet... or a coffin. The bed was sumptuous, however, and took up most of the available space. An armoire decorated with carved ships loomed against the far wall, and a water basin beneath a gilt-edged mirror completed the furnishings. There were books stacked against the walls in an untidy heap, and faded murals depicting the exploits of Saint Theodore, and his many struggles with darksome spirits, ringed the room.

Thorne studied one of the murals, noting the curious beast that the Saint was engaged in banishing – a many-armed creature, with a serpentine body and a vaguely equine head, albeit with the beak of a squid. "Hello, you old ugly thing, you," Thorne murmured, as they lit a cigarette. Cnidathqua was its name. Or at least the name someone had given it.

Legend had it, the entity had been bound into the lagoon by Saint Theodore; in reality, it had happened much earlier, and Theodore had only prevented it from escaping. The thing was still down there, as far as Thorne knew. Asleep in the silt, awaiting it's time to rise, just like the rest of its nauseating brethren. Thorne made an obscene gesture in the creature's direction. "And long may you slumber, old thing."

They turned to the window. It looked out at the canal below, and across to the wall on the other side. The narrow embankment there was crowded with watercraft and deliveries awaiting the journey to their final destination. But there were many closed shops as well. Shuttered and boarded. Where had those people gone, they wondered? On the street, pigeons and gulls made noisy war, fighting over scraps of food dropped by passersby.

Thorne peered past the birds, to the corner of the next street, where a slight form lurked surreptitiously in the long shadows of dusk. They smiled. That hadn't taken long. Then, they hadn't exactly tried to hide their arrival. Thorne plucked the cigarette from their mouth and touched the red tip to the air, drawing it around in a wide circle. The air turned watery as they stepped through, and out onto the street, directly behind their observer.

The man, lean and dark-haired, whipped around with a startled hiss. He was a gangly fellow, all knobs, and knees. But there was a feral strength in those noodle limbs. He was dressed like a common laborer, but Thorne recognized him – and the mark he bore stamped on his soul. The man made to push past them, no doubt hoping to flee. Thorne spat a single word, and waved their hand. The man stumbled and hunched, as if beset by cramps.

"Hello, Savio. Come to pay your respect?" Thorne gestured sharply, tightening their fingers into a fist. The dark-haired man grimaced, as the pain increased. Thorne smiled. The spell was only a little one; a child could learn it. But it was useful, in certain situations. "Hurts, don't it? But only if you struggle."

Savio bared teeth that were too sharp, and too strong, to be altogether human. A dog's teeth – or maybe a wolf. Savio's genealogy was the sort of thing to make researchers tear their hair out. He was an anomaly, and an altogether unpleasant one. But he had his uses. "Wh – what do you w – want, Thorne?" he panted. "Why are you here?"

"That's my business, kitten." Thorne spread their fingers and Savio whimpered. "Unless… you're not asking out of curiosity, are you? No. You're not smart enough for that, Savio. Where is he?"

Savio bared his teeth, and his deep-set eyes blazed with fanaticism. "Not far. Never far. This is his city, after all."

"I know a few people who might argue that point."

"The Cavalier is weak!"

Thorne leaned close and smiled. "But I'm not the Cavalier, sweetie. And I am not weak." They twitched their hand, and Savio collapsed in a shuddering heap as pain danced along his nerve-endings. Thorne had a quick look around and then sank to their haunches, dismissing the spell with a whisper. "There's a new player in town, Savio. I can't imagine your master is happy about it. I'm of a mind to help, if he's of a mind to listen."

Savio rolled over and got shakily to his feet. Thorne rose smoothly with him. Savio wiped his face. "Don Lagorio needs no help. Especially not from a creature like you."

"I don't think you're in any position to say what Don

Lagorio needs or doesn't need, Savio." Thorne straightened Savio's collar, and brushed a speck of dirt from his cheek. "So, be a good dog and go tell your master that Thorne wishes to meet him."

"Where?"

"Here will do. Neutral territory, as it were. Matteo will ensure his safety – and mine."

"Don Lagorio needs no protection."

Thorne clucked their tongue. "There you go again, making assumptions. Pass along the message, kitten. I'm sure you'll be well rewarded." They watched Savio stagger off and smiled. Things were off to a good start, thus far.

Now, they just had to hope Zorzi was as sensible as Cinabre claimed.

CHAPTER FIVE
Cavalier

Alessandra's sense of foreboding only increased as they drew near to the black gondola. "I am not entirely certain that this is a wise course of action," Selim said, in a low tone. "Even if it is not a trap, it is not good practice to climb onto strange boats."

"Nonsense," Alessandra said, patting his arm. "Climbing onto strange boats is half of what we do. Besides, if they wanted to kill us there are easier ways." She glanced at Pepper. "Though if you two would rather stay behind, I entirely understand."

"Not likely, sister," Pepper said. "Where you go, I go. Ain't that right, Selim?"

Selim nodded. "That is correct, yes."

"Then come along, by all means." Alessandra smiled. Though she endeavored to put on a mask of confidence, she was glad to have them both beside her. Selim had proven himself a doughty pugilist, and wasn't frightened by the sight of unnatural things. And Pepper had more than proven her abilities in the year or so since they'd first met in Arkham.

"Just the ladies, I fear," the gondolier said suddenly. He blocked Selim's path with one arm. "The Turk was not invited," he added, with visible distaste. Selim's expression darkened, and he appeared ready to toss the gondolier in the canal until Alessandra touched his hand.

"We will be fine. We will meet you at the hotel, yes?" Whatever this was, she felt certain she could handle it. Indeed, she'd been half expecting something like it. Cinabre had mentioned that someone from the Coterie would be meeting them in his last letter to her. She simply hadn't expected it to be so soon.

"Yes," Selim agreed, after a moment's hesitation. He stepped back, turned on his heel and stalked away through the crowd. Alessandra turned back to the gondolier, who was grinning insouciantly.

"Next time I will let him throw you in the water," she said, idly. The gondolier's smile vanished as if he'd been slapped. He hurriedly drew back the curtain and gestured for them to climb aboard. They did so. Beneath the covering were two cushioned benches, one of which was occupied by a masked figure, clad in red robes threaded with gold.

He – and she thought it was a he – wore a Bauta mask, complete with concealing hood and the traditional tricorn hat. These were as red as his robes, save for the hood which was black, as were the gloves that concealed his hands. A ruby-tipped cane lay across his knees. "Good evening," he greeted in a mellifluous voice.

"Is it that season already?" she asked lightly, as she and Pepper made themselves comfortable. "And here I am without a mask. How embarrassing."

The masked man grunted in evident amusement. "I was warned you thought yourself amusing. Thankfully, you are lovely as well."

"Such compliments, signori … ?"

"You may call me the Cavalier, if you like. Insofar as names go, it is suitable enough." He knocked on the side of the gondola and the craft lurched into motion. "Allow me to escort you to your hotel."

Alessandra looked around. "There seems to be plenty of room. Surely Selim could have joined us," she added, pointedly. The Cavalier made an apologetic gesture.

"You must forgive my man, Giovanni. He bears a grudge against the Turks. They killed his brother in the war."

"Many people's brothers died in the war. It is no excuse for rudeness." Her tone was light. She thought she already had some measure of the man before her. She knew his allegiance, if only because of the predilection for red. "Tell me … do you know a man named Cinabre, in Saint-Bertrand-de-Comminges?"

"I might be familiar with such a gentleman, yes."

"And he told you we were coming, did he?"

"Perhaps." He seemed amused by the question. "Then, perhaps I am here for myself as opposed to the whims of another."

"And are you?" she asked, more sharply than she intended.

"Yes, I am an associate of Monsieur Cinabre." He thumped the floor of the gondola with the end of his cane. "Though I must admit I am not always happy about it."

"My apologies," Alessandra said, smoothly. He hadn't quite answered her question, which was an answer in and of itself. "Though I do understand, I assure you."

The Cavalier studied her for a moment. "Yes, I expect you do."

She smiled. "From your regalia and your pseudonym, I assume you too are a member of the Red Coterie."

"You know us, then?"

"Something of you, yes."

"Then you know we are not to be trusted." He waved his finger chidingly. "You should know better than to climb aboard a stranger's gondola. Why, I could be taking you anywhere, and you without your imposing bodyguard."

Alessandra cocked the revolver, still in her pocket. The Cavalier tensed. She smiled. "We are not without our defenses, signori."

"Would you shoot a man in broad daylight?"

"It is almost night."

He laughed. "Yes, so it is! Good. You have spirit, I see." An instant later, so swiftly the movement nearly escaped her notice, he'd twisted the head of his cane and drawn a hidden blade from within the stick. The tip of the blade came to rest against the hollow of her throat before she could even think of pulling the trigger. "But spirit is not enough, sadly."

"Holy–!" Pepper began, halfway to her feet, fists balled. The gondola rocked at the sudden motion. Alessandra gestured with her free hand for the younger woman to sit back down. Pepper did so, but reluctantly.

"I take your point, signori," Alessandra said, through gritted teeth. Angry as she was, she was also puzzled. Something about his voice, his laugh, was familiar. Had she met him before? She wondered what face was beneath his mask.

"I do not think you do, but I will allow you the lie." He

lowered his blade, and she caught a flash of silver, and writing – in Latin, she thought.

"A silver sword?" she asked, lightly. "I thought such things only superstitious fancy."

"Superstition serves us well, at times." The Cavalier held up the blade, so that she could see the writing etched into its length. "It is from the Book of Psalms," he said. "*Tu distinxisti mare virtute tua; Tu confregisti capita draconum in aquis.*"

Alessandra frowned, trying to recall her Latin. "You… divided the sea by your strength and broke the heads of the dragons in the waters?"

"Very good. Fitting, no?" He slid the blade back into the cane. "This blade was forged for Saint Theodore, the original patron saint of Venice."

"Did he kill many dragons, this guy?" Pepper asked. The Cavalier nodded.

"Oh yes. And worse things besides." He leaned forward. "Venice is dangerous. More dangerous than Paris or London, though its dangers are more subtle in their nature."

Alessandra sat back, slightly insulted by his condescending tone. "I am well aware of the dangers of this city, signori. I grew up here, after all."

"Yes. Your father was a most interesting fellow – an exceptional gambler." The Cavalier studied her. "I was much saddened to learn of his passing, and that of your mother. I counted them as friends." She sensed some hesitation in his tone, even as his words struck her like a fist. She hadn't thought about her parents – or the circumstances of their death – in some time. She was careful to keep her expression neutral, however.

"You … knew them, then?"

"Oh yes." He adjusted one of his gloves. "Very well indeed."

"Is that why Cinabre sent you to meet us?"

The Cavalier paused. "Did I say that he had?"

Alessandra paused. "No. You did not, as a matter of fact."

"I told you we weren't to be trusted."

"If Cinabre did not send you–" she began, but he waved her words aside.

"I am not the only member of the Coterie in the city at the moment. You might have glimpsed them in the crowd when you arrived. They were watching for you, even as I was. But I made my move first, so that we could talk in peace."

Alessandra glanced at Pepper, who looked as confused as Alessandra felt. She looked back at their host. "Talk about what, exactly?"

"I do not know why you are here, Alessandra Zorzi, but I do know that you should leave immediately. That arrogant ass, Cinabre, was wrong to send you here."

"Why?" she asked.

"Venice is not safe."

"So you said."

"And you should listen, girl," the Cavalier said, leaning forward. "You cannot conceive of the danger you have walked into, all unknowing."

"We came to find a… friend. Rest assured that once we have done so, we will depart."

"It may well be too late for that. You should leave now."

"No. I do not believe that we will, signori."

"I could make you," the Cavalier said, softly.

Alessandra glanced at Pepper, and they both laughed. "I

think you would try," she said. "But we are hard to dissuade, Pepper and myself." It was bravado, true – but well-earned. Together, they had faced horrors that would shake the sanity of most people, and come out the other side relatively unscathed.

The Cavalier sighed and sat back. "So I see. Fine. But I wish you to know that you make my task infinitely more difficult by your presence here."

"And what is your task? What do you seek in Venice?"

"I seek nothing. I safeguard the city and all who dwell within it." The Cavalier drew himself up proudly. "Venice has many enemies and I stand alone against them all."

"And would one of these enemies be named Znamenski?" Alessandra asked. It was a risky gambit, that. There was no telling what Znamenski had gotten himself involved in since he'd arrived. Selim's telegrams had been bare bones in that regard.

The Cavalier paused, eyes narrowing behind his mask. "How do you know that name?" he asked, with obvious suspicion.

"He is the old friend I mentioned. He has something that belongs to me. I want it back. Help me to get it, and we will be gone with the tide."

"What does he have?"

"Does it matter?"

"Very much so. As does the reason you want it."

"Hard to trust a guy when you can't see his face," Pepper piped up. "Take off the mask and we'll see, hunh?" Alessandra nudged her in warning, but the younger woman ignored her.

The Cavalier peered at Pepper. "You first, girl."

Pepper blinked. "What are you talking about? I ain't wearing no cockamamie mask." She seemed shaken by his comment, far more than Alessandra thought it warranted.

He gestured airily. "We all wear masks, child. The only difference is whether we wear them on our faces, or on our hearts."

"Very pithy, sir," Alessandra said. "If somewhat condescending." She paused, considering. "The Zanthu Tablet. Just the one, rather than the full set. Znamenski has it. I want it back."

"Why?"

"To deliver it to someone who can keep it safe."

"Cinabre?"

Alessandra laughed. "God no!" After a moment, the Cavalier joined in.

"Good! Very good." He paused. "After you get the Tablet, you will leave?"

Alessandra cut her eyes toward Pepper. "Perhaps. There is another matter."

The Cavalier followed her gaze. "What do you mean?"

"Have you ever heard of something called... Carcosa?" Alessandra asked.

The Cavalier fell silent for a moment. "And what do you know of Carcosa?"

"Nothing. That is why I asked."

"There are some things it is better not to know. And some names it is better not to say, especially in Venice of late. If you are wise, you will forget ever having heard of it." He leaned toward them suddenly. "Leave it be, girl. Be wiser than your parents were."

"My–" Alessandra began, but faltered as the gondola thumped against something solid. Giovanni whisked the curtain aside a moment later.

"We are here, signoras... the Hotel Danieli, as promised."

"Wait, what was that about my parents?" Alessandra said, half-rising from her seat. Pepper scrambled past her, apparently eager to be off the craft and away from the Cavalier. Alessandra followed, albeit reluctantly.

The Cavalier thumped the bottom of the gondola with his cane. As Giovanni pushed the craft away from the hotel quay, the Cavalier called out, "We will speak again later, signora. In the meantime, remember what I have said!"

"So what the hell was that about?" Pepper asked.

Alessandra frowned and shook her head. As she did so, her eyes drifted upward. The stars were coming out and, for just a moment, they'd seemed to gleam black against the canvas of the sky. She swallowed and looked away. She felt uncertain; as if the stones of Venice were shifting beneath her feet, and the waters rising to pull her down.

"I do not know," she said, finally. "But I intend to find out."

CHAPTER SIX
Cassilda

"Where are you, my love… what do you see?" Cassilda murmured into her lover's ear as she gently stroked her hair. Her touch brought Camilla awake with a start. She was in a walled garden, filled with yellow jasmine, lavender, thyme, and purple salvia.

"Where?" she said. Her mouth was dry, as if no water had passed her lips in days. She could hear the crying of the gulls, somewhere out over the cloudy waters of Demhe. Blinking sleep from her eyes, she sat up and looked around.

"You are safe," Cassilda said, with a sad smile. "We are safe. In Carcosa."

"Carcosa," Camilla repeated. The word tasted foul, though she could not say why. Decorative masks and softly seeping censers hung from the branches of the ornamental trees that hunched and loomed around the garden. There were flashes of color in the highest branches, where lemurs jostled for perches. "How did we – the boat…?"

Cassilda frowned, her expression uncertain. "We are safe," she said again, but she sounded as if she were trying to convince herself as much as Camilla. "We are in the lemur-gardens of Carcosa. You always loved them so, I thought… I…" She broke off. "You spoke a name, my love. A woman's name. One of your soldiers?"

Camilla shook her head. "I- I do not recall." Flashes of dream passed across the surface of her mind in fits and starts. A city on the water, like Carcosa but very different. A man in a mask – not pallid, but crimson like blood. She cradled her head, as the weight of these strange images threatened to knock her flat. "My – my sword," she asked. She saw the weapon laying nearby and snatched it up with unseemly haste. Cassilda reached for her.

"You do not need it here. Carcosa stands inviolate. He cannot find us."

Camilla turned. "He will. He always has." Above her, a bird cried out as a lemur caught it and wrung its neck. She saw a flash of yellow feathers among the green. A loose one drifted down on the breeze, and for a moment, as it twisted on the air, it resembled a tatter of filthy silk. Heart thudding, Camilla stepped back. She turned away, clutching her sword to her, seeking strength in the meteoric iron. It had slain many beasts, that sword. But it could not slay him.

Nothing could.

Cassilda was still talking. "There is to be a masquerade ball, to celebrate his inevitable defeat and the coming of the rightful heir to the throne," she said. Camilla looked at her.

"You."

Cassilda nodded. "Yes. I will be anointed queen, in Carcosa and Aldebaran. The noble families of the Hyades will bow before me. Before us." She reached out, but Camilla avoided her touch. It reminded her too much of something else. Someone else.

"No," Camilla said. "It is too dangerous. We do not know that he can be defeated."

Cassilda drew herself up. "If he is not, he soon will be. Carcosa is mine. *Ours.* With the Hyadaen families behind us, we will muster an army to retake those lands that have fallen to the Tattered Banner–"

"No!" Camilla turned away, cradling her sword as if it were an infant. "No. I have fought him, and seen the futility of that fight. How can you make war on something that lives in men's minds? Are we to burn every village where his word is spoken?"

"Carcosa will prevail," Cassilda said, with regal firmness.

"Who are you trying to convince?" Camilla said, in what was almost a whisper. Cassilda paused, looking as if she'd been slapped. Camilla turned to face her. "You insist that he cannot find us, that we are safe, but you know that there is no safety from him. That Which Follows cannot be outrun." She felt a flash of pain from her abdomen and looked down. There was blood there, staining the cotton of her garments. Cassilda stared at the seeping redness in horror.

In the trees, the lemurs began to scream.

Camilla staggered back and slumped against a tree. The world twisted in on itself, and the suns rolled across the ground as the trees emptied their branches into the sky. Lemurs leapt from one tree to the other, their high-pitched cries almost like prayers. But to what god did they pray so fervently? She did not think she wanted to know the answer.

The wind whipped up, and her blurring vision caught the

yellow tatter spinning on the breeze. Dancing. She slumped, sliding to the soft ground. The lemurs were silent now, watching. Waiting – for what?

She heard Cassilda call out for someone – guards, perhaps. Doctors? Her voice blurred and merged with the wind, and when the words reached Camilla's ears, they were not those of her lover, but those of someone – something – else.

She could not understand what they said, only the meaning behind them. He was coming. And not all the masquerades or armies in the world would stop him. He could not be stopped here. Not anywhere. She looked at her lover with tear-blurred eyes. "Carcosa has already fallen. We simply do not realize it."

She closed her eyes as pain thrummed through her. Not the pain of her injury, but from a deeper well. It echoed through her like the reverberation of great footfalls, striding across a vast distance but drawing – Ever – *Closer*.

Pepper gasped, sucking in a lungful of air, and nearly choking on it. She rolled over, coughing and felt a strong hand swat her back helpfully. "Breathe, Pepper."

"I *am* breathing," Pepper choked out.

"Breathe correctly, then," Alessandra said, firmly. "None of your lackadaisical American breathing. Do it properly."

Pepper swatted the other woman's hand away, wheezing. She glared at Alessandra, who sat beside the bed. "What does that even mean?" she demanded.

"Just as I said. I want you to do it correctly." Alessandra leaned over and took her by the chin, turning her head one way and then another. As she did so, Pepper took in her surroundings. The room was small but elegant; lush. At least in the dim light of the lamp on the bedside table. She pried Alessandra's fingers off her chin.

"Where…?" she began.

"The hotel. Do you remember checking in?"

"I remember the guy in the mask and the gondola ride, but after that – pfft."

"Are you hungry? You missed dinner."

Pepper shook her head. For once, she wasn't hungry at all. She tried to sit up, and Alessandra pushed her back down gently, but firmly.

"It is the middle of the night. There is no reason to get up. In fact, from the look of you, I expect you will fall back to sleep any moment now. I heard you crying out from my room, so I came across to check on you. How do you feel?"

Pepper ran her hands through her hair. "Like somebody tap-danced on my skull. And they're coming back for an encore." She looked at Alessandra, trying to articulate what she felt. She remembered… a garden? Monkeys? But the dream was already fading. She didn't like the feeling; it was like losing pieces of herself. "That's twice in a day. That ain't fair."

"Yes, the frequency is increasing," Alessandra said, and though she tried to hide it, Pepper could hear the worry in the other woman's voice. She'd heard Alessandra worried before, but it never failed to give her a sick feeling in her stomach. She was too used to Alessandra being in control, even when it looked like she was anything but – especially then. She swallowed and decided to change the subject.

"Did I – did I say anything? A name, maybe?"

"Cassilda," Alessandra said.

Pepper blinked, and released a slow, shaky breath. "Anything else?"

"Not that I understood."

Pepper flumped back onto the bed and stared at the rococo molding on the ceiling. "I hate this. I thought being a thief was going to be fun, but this is anything but. I feel like I'm waiting for the other shoe to drop – right on my head."

"The sword of Damocles," Alessandra said.

"Yeah, that too."

"What do you remember?" Alessandra asked, as she rose and went to the room's small sideboard. "Places, people, things... anything might be of use."

"It's always the same," Pepper said, still studying the ceiling. It wasn't very high. If she stood on the bed, she could touch it, short as she was. More and more, she was finding the only difference between a swanky joint and a cheap one was age. Thirty years might make a roach motel, but three hundred? You could charge what you wanted, and the swells would fight each other for a room. "It's like... it's happening to someone else, and I'm just along for the ride. But I'm only getting part of the story, you know? Never the whole thing. It's like when a radio program stops the action to hawk cigarettes or something."

"Yes, very irksome. But what do you see?"

"A – a place." It was hard to focus on the image. Rounded towers like gherkins, arched bridges spanning the space between them; a spider's web of stone, rising all the way to the suns. Walls that rose and fell like mountain ranges, riddled with holes that were windows and dwellings. An anthill, built by men.

"A city? The one on the flyer?"

"Carcosa," Pepper said, and shuddered. The name hung on the air, like the tolling of a bell. It faded slowly, leaving her wrung out and empty feeling. She closed her eyes. "I don't think it's a nice place."

"No, something tells me you are right about that. Our friend the Cavalier seems to agree." Alessandra brought her a drink, and the young woman sat up and gulped it down greedily. The alcohol had a pleasant burn, and she relaxed. Part of her, the curious part, wanted to go back. To see how the story was going to play out. But the part of her that had been a cabbie in Arkham knew better. Some stories, you didn't want to know the ending; and if you did, you wished you didn't.

"You think he knows something?"

"I do."

"Maybe we should beat it out of him," Pepper said, only half-jokingly. "I miss anything other than dinner?"

"Not much. We are one floor above Znamenski's room. He is not there, however. I already checked. Oh, and this was waiting for me in my room." Alessandra produced a red square of card from inside her dressing gown. It had a stylized golden lion stamped on it. Pepper tried to sound out the writing on it, but it defeated her.

"What is it?"

"An invitation. To a bookstore, of all things. The *Libreria Leone Scarlatto* – the Red Lion." Alessandra smiled thinly. "I wonder who might have sent it."

"The Cavalier?"

"I do not think so. I believe it is from whoever Cinabre was sending to help us."

"Oh, ain't that just ducky. Where were they today?"

"It does not matter. I will pay them a visit in the morning."

"You mean we will," Pepper mumbled. Sleep, real sleep, was pawing at the edges of her consciousness. One good thing about being exhausted, the dreams didn't come. She set her empty glass aside and lay back down.

"Yes. But for now, we will sleep. Tomorrow, we will begin our hunt for answers." Alessandra leaned over and tenderly stroked Pepper's hair, the way the latter's father had always done when she'd had a bad dream. Alessandra leaned close, whispering now.

"We will find the answer, Pepper. I promise you. Even if I must tear it from Znamenski with my bare hands."

And with that promise, Pepper fell into a thankfully dreamless sleep.

CHAPTER SEVEN
The Abbess

Abbess Allegria Di Biase sat in her office in the Church of San Zaccaria and looked over the morning's reports from her subordinates. The day-to-day running of an abbey, for so the church was, required a great deal more paperwork than she'd originally envisioned.

While she was entrusted with the spiritual well-being of her flock, she was also responsible for the upkeep of the church itself, as well as the local hospices under the care of the Order of St Benedict. In practical terms, it meant that mornings once spent in quiet contemplation of the divine were now largely given over to book-keeping.

Perhaps that was God's way of keeping her humble. She was the youngest abbess in the history of her order, barely into her thirties, in a position of authority over fifty nuns. All part of God's plan. Before taking holy orders, she'd been something of a hellraiser; parties, trouble and affairs. At least four of the seven sins on a daily basis. But those days were long past, for better or worse.

She picked up a flyer, one of thousands cluttering up the city's gutters. It depicted a wretched skyline, a doomed figure, but had no title or announcement to identify it. It made her feel vaguely ill to look at it and she set it aside, taking a sip from her already-cold coffee at the same time. She grimaced at the taste, but gulped the rest of the tepid cup before starting with the next ledger.

"You could have them bring you a new cup," someone said, with mild amusement. Allegria glanced up in some surprise and saw a black robed shape looming in one corner of her office. A startlingly crimson bauta mask studied her from beneath the brim of a tricorn hat. A cane tapped against the floor as the intruder moved toward her desk.

"A senseless indulgence," she said, pushing aside her annoyance at the interruption of her morning routine. "It will only get cold again." She peered at the intruder. "I will not insult you by asking how you got in here, but I will ask that you announce yourself next time."

Her guest bowed. "Forgive me. I thought it best that your subordinates remain unaware of our… relationship."

Allegria snorted. "Do not make it sound sordid. We are allies, not lovers."

"Once, I might have taken that as a challenge."

"Need I remind you that I am wedded to God?"

"Even more of a challenge," he said, with a chuckle.

She sighed, pushed her books aside and gestured to the single chair before her desk. "Sit, Cavalier. I am certain you have much to tell me."

"That depends on what you already know," he said. It was hard to tell, with his mask, but she thought he was smiling.

Like many men, he thought he was amusing. She sighed and shook her head.

"Precious little. I have not left the confines of the church in days."

The Cavalier grunted, his eyes on the flyer. "Lagorio has been quiescent of late," he said, referring to the city's homegrown cult of demonologists. It was through their activities that she and the Cavalier had first met, and found a shared purpose, in freeing Venice from the shadows that entangled it. Don Lagorio and his clique were behind much of what plagued the city of late, but even they had been stymied by the arrival of a new player to the old game.

"Are they planning something?" she asked, indicating the flyer.

"I do not think so. Lagorio is waiting."

"For what?"

"For whatever is going to happen. Maybe he is waiting for us to solve his problem for him. That would be like him." The Cavalier's tone was caustic. Allegria couldn't bring herself to blame him. Lagorio was a fiend, but a slippery one. He had taunted and teased his opponents for years, evading God's justice with the grace of a serpent. Every astrological confluence, every eclipse, brought he and his followers closer to their goal of awakening that which slumbered in the lagoon.

But the arrival of the mysterious Marquis of Avonshire had thrown certain elements of Venetian society into an uproar. The Englishman had married the daughter of one of the oldest noble families in Venice, and thus carved himself a firm place in the hierarchy of the city. But he was not simply some expatriate looking for a new place to call home. He was a monster, or maybe just the harbinger of monsters.

"There was a man on the Grand Canal yesterday," the Cavalier began.

"Yes. The Carabinieri took him into custody. He was one of several new admittances to our hospices… all driven mad within the last few days, with no previous sign or family history of mental illness. It is almost as if the city is caught fast in the grip of some plague of lunacy." She looked at him pointedly, hoping he might disagree. Instead, he leaned back.

"I fear that is exactly what it is, Allegria. A phantom of truth stalks the city, and few can withstand what it forces them to see."

Allegria frowned. "What does that mean?"

"It means that things are getting worse. People are beginning to notice. The Fascists are blaming foreign elements, the Socialists are blaming the Fascists and those in authority are hoping no one blames them." The Cavalier twiddled his cane idly. "What is it that English poet said? The center cannot hold. Venice is cracking at the seams."

"At least the tourists haven't noticed yet," Allegria said. She knew that what he was saying was the truth. Her contacts in the Carabinieri told her that much. Crime was up, and incidents of violence. Most of it was kept out of sight of foreigners, but soon enough it would be impossible to hide. In a week's time, maybe less, the city would be on fire.

The Cavalier chuckled. "Ah, Allegria. You always did have a sense of humor."

"Little good has it done me," Allegria said.

"You are young yet." The Cavalier paused. "Too young to

be an abbess, according to some. I wonder what they would think to see us here now?"

Allegria paused. She wondered much the same herself. Her superiors would definitely frown on her dealings with the Red Coterie, if they learned of them. She didn't particularly care, of course. Not when the salvation of Venice was at stake. "I am sure they would commend me for the sacrifices I undertake in the name of holy necessity."

The Cavalier laughed. "An optimistic view."

"And what would your own comrades say, if they learned of our bargain?" she asked. "From what little I know of your group, they do not welcome outsiders into their affairs... save as dupes. Am I a dupe?"

"Perish the thought," the Cavalier said. He paused. "You have not asked why I was on the Grand Canal, yesterday."

"That is your business," Allegria said. But she already knew. Her contacts among the gondoliers had brought word of Alessandra's arrival. She hesitated. "Is she staying?"

"I fear so."

"It is too dangerous." Allegria cast her mind back, to youth and childhood, before God had called her to serve. To days running along the canals and picking fights with the children of the gondoliers. And of her friend, who'd been right with her every step of the way.

Alessandra Zorzi.

Alessandra's face danced in her mind's eye, and for a moment she lost herself to the past, recalling her friend's laughter and the way she'd seemed to fly across the campo, ill-gotten gains stuffed into her pockets. A thief from a family of thieves, but that had only made things more... exciting.

Allegria's fingers twitched; the instinct to cross herself was strong, especially when it came to thoughts of Alessandra.

It was the laughter that had kept them close. But that had ended the day Alessandra's parents had died – not in Venice, but Paris. Why they had been in Paris, only the Cavalier knew. And hadn't that been a surprise to learn? She still wasn't certain whether that slip had been intentional or not.

She shook her head and dismissed her thoughts of the past. It might as well have been in another country. What was really important was the here and now, and how Alessandra's presence complicated things. "Will you tell her about the house?" she asked, knowing the question would startle him.

"Which one?"

"The one she used to live in. The one you bought from her grandfather. The one that is hers by right, that you have been keeping for her all these years."

He shifted uncomfortably. "Is that what I have been doing?"

"Yes, and I have never asked why. I assumed you felt guilty somehow over the circumstances of their deaths. I assumed that was why you revealed that to me. You knew we were friends as children. You knew what she meant to me."

"And then you chose to serve God," he said, with a faint air of judgement. She smiled thinly. Let him judge. God had spoken to her, and shown her the true path. It was a thorny one, but she walked it nonetheless.

"And would I be as good an ally to you as I am, if I did not?" She leaned forward, across her desk. "Why did you keep it, then?"

He didn't reply. She sighed. "Why is she here?" she asked. "Does it have to do with *them*?" She'd kept tabs on Alessandra as best she was able in the years since they'd last seen one another. She'd followed her exploits with a sort of horrified fascination. The amount of trouble Alessandra was able to get herself into had always been nothing short of impressive.

"She says not. But even so, she asked about Carcosa."

Allegria hissed softly. "Oh Alessandra... that is unfortunate." She knew more than she liked about Carcosa and all that went with it. And what she knew told her it was no wonder Lagorio was keeping quiet. Her people had seen the Yellow Sign painted on too many boarded over windows and abandoned boats left to sit forgotten on the quays. The lunatics in the hospices screamed about a nonsense kingdom, ruled by a nonexistent king, or black stars wheeling in an alien sky. All of it, Carcosa.

The Cavalier nodded. "Yes."

"She has no idea what she's getting into." How had Alessandra had the misfortune to come into contact with such unpleasantness? Unless – had Alessandra seen the light? Had God spoken to her, the way he had Allegria? She almost laughed at the thought.

"Are you certain?" the Cavalier asked, in that infuriating way of his. Allegria frowned. There was much he hadn't told her, and much he wouldn't, if he had a choice. They liked their games, the Coterie. Even the ones like the Cavalier, who were less manipulators than idealists. It was almost like they couldn't help it.

"What do you mean by that?" she asked, wondering if he would answer.

"She was sent here by a member of my fraternity," the

Cavalier said, after a moment. "And a third member has come to meet with her. I expect they will do so shortly."

"You weren't invited," she said. It wasn't a question. It was obvious. Over the years, since the beginning of their arrangement, she'd come to suspect that the real reason that the Cavalier had sought her out was because he couldn't trust his own to help him in his fight with the forces arrayed against Venice. She didn't know why that might be, didn't dare ask the question. Maybe it was simply God's will.

"No," he said. "Though the proprietor of the location in question is only too happy to keep me informed of what occurs."

"Matteo," she said, simply. The owner and manager of the Red Lion was another of the Red Coterie's creatures; more, he was bound to the bookshop, which was, in its own way, a player in the great game of Venice. "Do you know the one who is meeting her?"

"I do, sadly."

"Trustworthy?"

"Not in the least," the Cavalier said, harshly. "Do you think she will come here?"

She paused. It was unlikely Alessandra even knew that she was still in Venice. They'd hardly stayed in contact, after all. "I do not see why she would. Why?"

"If she will not leave, I need her to trust me. You are my route to that, I fear."

She frowned. Something in his tone made her wonder if his attempt to warn Alessandra off hadn't been a bit of reverse psychology on his part. "It has been a long time since we last spoke, she and I. She may not trust me either."

The Cavalier stood, ready to depart now that he'd made his case. As she looked up at him, he did not seem the enigmatic paladin she had once thought. Instead, he stood like a tired old man, one weighed down by innumerable cares.

"Let us hope you are wrong about that, dear Allegria. For all our sakes."

CHAPTER EIGHT
The Red Lion

It was midmorning and at the far end of the alley, two gondoliers were quarreling over a rope. It had started as a minor disagreement, but as was the way in Venice, had escalated rapidly into a crescendo of shouting and flexing. A knife flashed, startling nearby tourists, but no blood was spilled. There was an air of theater about the whole thing.

Alessandra signaled the waiter as she and Pepper took seats at one of the small tables outside. The café was, charitably, a hole in the wall. An innocuous nook in a cramped alley, under a sign bearing a black eagle.

She thought it had been part of hostelry during the previous century, but now served fortifying refreshment. She'd spent many an hour here as a young woman, drinking too much coffee and eating too many pastries while flirting with gondoliers and tourists – and picking the pockets of the latter when it came time to pay the bill.

One of the gondoliers stalked away, gesticulating, and muttering to himself. Abruptly he spun and charged back toward the other, shouting at full volume. Several other off-duty gondoliers had gathered to watch and shout encouragement to one party or the other. The affair was growing louder and shriller and fiercer by the moment. Knives were in play, threats bellowed, feet stamped against wet stones.

Alessandra watched the imbroglio with mild interest. Pepper did so with more enthusiasm. "This is almost better than the Arkham docks on a Saturday night!" She looked at Alessandra. "What do you say – two to one that guy gets stabbed?"

"I am more interested in what their children are doing," Alessandra said, lazily. Pepper blinked in confusion.

"What are you talking about?"

Alessandra gestured sneakily to a young girl, more alley cat than child, flitting about through the growing crowd of onlookers. A boy, a few years younger than the girl, prowled the far side of the crowd. "Watch them closely," Alessandra murmured. "Do not take your eyes off them or you will surely miss it."

"Miss what?" Pepper muttered. When she saw it, she stiffened. Alessandra smiled. The young girl had managed to procure a tourist's expensive pocket watch, as well as the chain it was attached to, with the discreet flick of a razor. Pepper glanced at Alessandra. "Should we do anything?"

"Like what?"

"Tell somebody?"

"Why ever would we do that?" Alessandra asked, in bemusement. "Pickpockets are as ubiquitous as pigeons in Venice. A natural hazard."

Pepper sat back. "So the fight's staged."

Alessandra patted the younger woman's hand. "In Venice, nothing is ever what it seems. Remember that, and you and she will get along fine." The waiter arrived a few moments later with their order. The coffee, her second of the morning, expelled steam into the cool, damp air.

Alessandra took a sip and leaned back in her seat. "What is that ditty you Americans sing? Home again, home again, something or other?" She was feeling better now, after coffee. Venice had a certain loveliness at this time of day. Early enough to enjoy the quiet, late enough to get something tasty to eat.

"Close enough," Pepper said, eyeing the pastry before her with undisguised greed. "I already like this place better than Paris."

"I am glad to hear it," Alessandra said. She glanced across the campo, to where the *Libreria Leone Scarlatto* sat. It was already open, according to the signage. But she was in no hurry to go in, as they were still waiting on Selim. He was watching Znamenski's room for her, to report back on how the artist was spending his day.

"So, we meet this guy..." Pepper began, crumbs on her cheek. Alessandra selected a napkin, wetted it on her tongue and dabbed at Pepper's face. Pepper batted the napkin away and wiped her hands on her trousers before continuing. "Or gal, or whoever, at the bookstore... then what? Cinabre wasn't exactly clear on the details, as I recall."

"No, he was not. Then, when is he ever?" Alessandra glanced at the bookstore again. The shopfront didn't radiate menace so much as weary resignation. The paint was fading, the wood peeling. Still, there was something odd about it.

Maybe it was just her. Being home brought back too many memories. The sights, the smells, the sounds; it had all come crashing down on her in the middle of the night and after she'd checked on Pepper, she'd spent a pensive hour or two watching the moonlight dance on the water. Someone, she couldn't recall whom, had opined that the city was best seen by moonlight. That way you didn't notice the crumbling facades, the state of the canals, and the unartistic malaise that afflicted too much of the city in modern times.

She glanced at Pepper. She'd written to Professor Walters and Doctor Armitage at Miskatonic, but as yet they hadn't responded. She'd even checked the Comte d'Erlette's library before they'd left France, or what was left of it, but she'd been unable to make heads or tails of any of it. That left Cinabre, and by extension the Red Coterie, as their best chance to figure out what was wrong. Hence this meeting.

"You think they can help me?" It was the first time Pepper had asked the question. Alessandra did her best to avoid answering it.

"I think the real question is what they are going to want for making the attempt." She paused. "After the Cavalier's warning, it seems only fair to ask you whether you wish to proceed. Perhaps, once we have acquired the Tablet, we should depart. Go back to Arkham. Perhaps Armitage or Walters could help us – help you. It might make more sense than trusting the Red Coterie."

Pepper was silent for a moment. Then, "I don't know that I'd make it back to Arkham." She winced and rubbed her temple. "My mind, it – aw applesauce. Sometimes it's like I'm listening to two different radio programs at once, you know? I'm hearing and seeing what's in front of me, but sometimes there's an – an echo, kind of. Like I'm halfway here and halfway somewhere else."

"Carcosa," Alessandra said, in a near-whisper. Something

made her glance up, toward the irregular rivulet of blue that was the sky overhead. Gulls danced along the rooftops, squalling greedily. She frowned as the light changed; as if something had moved across the face of the sun, if only for an instant. The gulls flurried upward with raucous cries and she wondered if they'd seen something.

Pepper studied what was left of her pastry almost mournfully. "That's the joint," she said sourly, picking at the food. "I don't want to go there no more, not if I got a choice."

Alessandra was saved from having to reply by the arrival of Selim, who snagged an empty chair from a nearby table and dragged it over to join them. "He's left the hotel," he said, signaling the waitress. "I checked his room. It is above the canal. The door is locked.

Alessandra pursed her lips for a moment, calculating variables. "Did anyone notice you?" she asked, after a moment's estimation. Selim gave her a look, and she patted his arm. "Of course, how silly of me. Never mind. Did he take anything with him?"

"Nothing."

"So it's in his room, then," Pepper said.

Alessandra shrugged. "Possibly. Unless he sold it on to finance his stay here."

Selim shook his head. "No. I would have heard. He still has it."

"Then he may well have turned it over to the hotel concierge for safe-keeping. Which, while inconvenient, is not the end of the world."

"My thoughts exactly," he said, then hesitated.

"What is it?" Alessandra prodded.

"There is something off about the city," Selim said, quietly.

"I cannot explain it. It is simply a feeling I have. As if there is something in the air."

"Something to do with the suicides you mentioned yesterday? Or with the Fascists, perhaps," Alessandra ventured. Fascism was on the rise in Italy, and even Venice was not immune to such lunacy.

She'd been startled to see all the propaganda posters everywhere, and couldn't help but wonder how many in the city had embraced what men like Mussolini were touting as the new natural order. Right now, it was all talk, but she feared that organization would follow soon enough. Then would come violence, pogroms… all the vindictive pleasures that such loathsome creatures could imagine.

Selim slowly shook his head. "Perhaps, but – no. Something else. It is on the air. The salt wind tastes… wrong, somehow. The sound of the sea is not right. As I said, I cannot explain it." He looked nervous; something she'd never associated with him. "Perhaps the Cavalier was right, and we should leave." His gaze flicked to Pepper, whose expression was equally brooding.

Alessandra knocked on the table, startling them both. "No. Not yet at least. Now, where did our artist friend go after he left the hotel?" she asked, changing the subject.

Selim grunted. "I followed him to a palazzo not far from here. Some Englishman is renting it. A nobleman."

"Oh?"

"The Marquis of Avonshire, or so the porters claim. I've promised them money if they keep an eye on Znamenski for me." Selim frowned. "Curious, though. I do not believe I have heard of Avonshire. Have you?"

Alessandra slowly shook her head. The name seemed familiar, yet – no. She'd heard of the River Avon, of course, near Bristol. But there was no county called Avonshire. "An alias, perhaps. The English have so many counties, no respectable person can keep them straight." She knocked on the table with her knuckles. "Go keep an eye on this palazzo. Let me know if Jan goes anywhere else." She rose to her feet, and Pepper hastily followed suit. "In the meantime, Pepper and I have an appointment with a lion."

They left Selim to finish his coffee and crossed the campo to the bookstore. As Alessandra pushed the door open, a bell jangled above their heads. Her first impression of the interior was that it was almost obscenely cramped with shelves and books and stacks of papers that twitched alarmingly in time to the creaking of the floor. Pepper sneezed in reply.

Alessandra wound her way to the counter, where a gnomelike individual crouched, regarding the newcomers with a combination of suspicion and eagerness. "Yes?" he asked, in accented English. He'd mistaken them for tourists, perhaps.

"I received this last night," Alessandra said smoothly, in Italian, as she produced the card she'd found in her room. "I assume you are the proprietor?" Though she'd grown up in Venice, she'd never heard of this particular business before. There were rumors of magic shops and spectral booksellers, of course. It was Venice, after all. But this one was new to her, and she found it exciting.

The little man took the card, blinking owlishly as he examined it. "Ah. You are the one, then. And early, besides. They are not yet awake."

"No? Well, we can wait." Alessandra looked around. "Tell me, what would you recommend for a lady such as myself?"

"Got any books on someplace called… Carcosa?" Pepper interjected, scratching her neck. The clerk blinked and then heaved himself off his stool, nearly vanishing behind his counter. When he reemerged, he was holding a broom. He took a menacing step toward Pepper, broom raised. Alessandra bit back a laugh, even as Pepper raised her hands in protest.

"Get out," he barked. "We will have none of your nonsense in here!" He took a poke at her, and she nearly bounced off a shelf in her haste to avoid the bristles. Alessandra's hand snapped out, catching the broom just below the head. The little man gawped at her.

"Is that any way to treat guests?" she purred.

"I will not have that – that *poison* in my shop!" he hissed, eyes narrowed.

Pepper looked shaken. "What's your problem?"

"Matteo, are you being churlish again?" a voice called out from the back of the shop. Matteo, the clerk, frowned and pulled his broom from Alessandra's grip.

"They are awake now," he grunted, sourly. "You may go back, if you like." He glanced at Pepper. "Not you."

Pepper looked at Alessandra helplessly. "What'd I do?"

"Asked the wrong question, obviously," Alessandra said. She hesitated, wondering at the clerk's reaction. It had been more vehement than she'd expected. "Try not to cause any more trouble while I am gone, please."

CHAPTER NINE
Backroom

It took longer than Alessandra expected to reach the back of the shop. It didn't look that large from the outside, but it seemed to fold in on itself in odd ways. There were all sorts of nooks and crannies, odd bends, and tiny off-passages, all of them stuffed with shelves, and the shelves crammed with books. More books than it seemed possible that anyone could read. An infinity of them, complete with the smell of mildew and wood pulp. It reminded her of her old friend Mellin's house, in Angouleme.

The entrance to the backroom was a low door, with a single stone step. There was another door set into the wall just past the entrance, but it was closed. The backroom was a small space, crowded with boxes – full of books, obviously – and a small metal table. A third door occupied the far wall, leading to a portico and quay outside. That door was open, allowing for a breeze in the cramped confines of the room.

The person sitting at the table had a high, thin, androgynous face, and was dressed for a night out. Fair haired and willowy of frame, they might have passed for a young woman playing dress up in her lover's clothes, but for the smooth baritone that emerged from their mouth when they spoke. "Good morning, Countess."

"Good morning," Alessandra said, warily.

"Coffee?" her host asked, indicating the battered steel French press occupying the center of the table. There were two cups waiting, and a small plate of pastries.

"Do you have a name?" Alessandra countered, as she took a seat.

"I am called Thorne," they said, in a mild tone. Slim fingers played with the red cravat at their throat. "Monsieur Cinabre might have mentioned me."

"No, I am afraid not, signori," Alessandra said. She took out her cigarette case and a book of matches and set them on the table. "Then, as you may know, Cinabre speaks often but in the end, says very little."

Thorne chuckled politely. "Indeed. Age has made him voluble. But, as I said, I am Thorne. We serve the same masters, you and I."

"Do we?" Alessandra asked, all innocence. "I was not aware I had a master."

Thorne's smile could have cut glass. "We all serve someone, whether we know it or not." They indicated her cigarette case, and she nudged it toward them. They selected one and gave it a perfunctory sniff. "Turkish?"

"Moroccan."

"Ah." Thorne leaned forward, expectantly. Alessandra lit their cigarette. "I do love that part of the world. Have you ever visited the smoke-market in Marrakesh? I'm told men are not allowed there – only women, and … well."

"I have not had that pleasure," Alessandra said. "You are with the Red Coterie, then. I expected as much when I spied that garish cravat in the crowd yesterday. Cinabre mentioned someone would be here to meet us. Is that someone you?" She decided not to mention the Cavalier. Not just yet, at any rate.

"If it wasn't, I doubt I'd tell you."

"How rude. I expected more manners, at least."

Thorne puffed on their cigarette, digesting this. Alessandra was content to be patient. While she had no doubt Thorne was here to help, she knew enough about the Red Coterie now to expect there would be some ulterior motive or esoteric price. Would Thorne demand a favor, as Cinabre had? Either way, she had no intention of refusing. Not if it meant helping Pepper. Finally, Thorne said, "Point taken, kitten. I believe we've gotten off on the wrong foot. I am here to help, if I can."

"And how do you intend to do that?"

"Ah, ah – first, we discuss the matter of payment." Thorne's smile was mocking. Alessandra was getting the distinct impression that they thought they were very clever. "You may not wish my help, after you hear what I require in return…"

"Then by all means, tell me."

"I'm looking for a fellow by the name of Znamenski. You know him, I'm told."

"And what is your interest in him?" Alessandra asked, wondering exactly what Cinabre had told Thorne about why she was in Venice.

Thorne smiled. "A little birdie told me he knows the whereabouts of something I want. That's my price, before you ask. This particular item, in return for my help."

"Done," Alessandra said.

Thorne blinked. "That was quick. Don't even want to haggle?" They seemed surprised, even, as Alessandra had hoped. It was best to keep individuals like Thorne guessing. She'd dealt with enough shady characters in her life to know that when they got too confident, they started to get creative with the interpretation of agreements.

Alessandra laughed. "Not in the least. I do not care about mysterious items. I care about my friend. If you want me to hand over the Zanthu Tablet, I will."

Thorne paused. "The Zanthu Tablet? Oh my no." They laughed. "Why would I want that old thing?"

It was Alessandra's turn to look confused. "Then what do you want?"

"What I'm looking for is a key," Thorne said. "A very old key. Ornate. Made of something that looks like silver." They gestured for emphasis.

"Looks like?"

"Yes. It's a good deal more precious, though."

"Does it have a name, this artifact? In my experience, they always have names."

"The Key of Ys."

Alessandra paused. "Ys… it seems to me that I have heard of that place."

"I doubt it," Thorne said, dismissively.

"No. No, I have definitely." She cleared her throat and recited, "*Pa vo beuzet Paris, Ec'h adsavo Ker Is.* When Paris is engulfed, the City of Ys will reemerge, or something to that effect. It has to do with a Breton legend of some sort, I believe."

Thorne applauded politely, if somewhat mockingly. "Very good. Though I doubt there is a connection between the two. Or if there is, it is of little importance to me."

"And why do you want it?"

"I was under the impression that your sort of person didn't ask such questions."

"I am not that sort of person anymore," Alessandra said, stiffly. Thorne was attempting to provoke her. She was certain of it, but couldn't say why. Maybe they just enjoyed upsetting others.

Thorne chuckled. "Leopards and spots and all that. But again, no concern of mine. I want the Key. That is reason enough."

"And Znamenski has this Key of yours?"

"So I'm told."

"What does it do?" Alessandra asked, turning it over in her mind. Cinabre's reason for sending Thorne was starting to make sense. Thorne frowned.

"What do you mean? It is a key. It unlocks things."

"What sort of things?"

"Again, the sort of question I'm not usually of a mind to answer, kitten," Thorne said. Their smile was scythe-like; sharp and unpleasant. Thorne was not used to being questioned. Alessandra decided to do it again.

"If Znamenski has it, then it undoubtedly does something unfortunate. Whatever it opens should no doubt be left closed. I ask again, why do you want it?"

"Because I do, that should be reason enough," Thorne said. Then, slyly, "Does it really matter, given the circumstances?" They glanced knowingly toward the door, and the shop. Alessandra followed their gaze, and sighed.

"Can you really help her?"

Thorne took a long drag on their cigarette and then said, "Possibly. Cinabre told me something of her affliction, but was vague on detail."

"Nightmares, mostly. She's dreaming of a place that does not exist."

"Carcosa."

"Yes. Your man outside seemed to know the name."

"I'm told it's become something of a common refrain hereabouts," Thorne said, leaning back in their chair. "Venice is in the grip of something unpleasant, as is your friend, and by my reckoning, this Znamenski chap is at the heart of it." They smiled. "Aren't we the lucky ducks?"

Alessandra waved this aside. "What is this… unpleasantness, then? Does it have a name… a cause? The less cryptic the answer, the better."

"*The King in Yellow*," Thorne said. "Ever read it, kitten?"

"I cannot say as I have," Alessandra said. It wasn't quite a lie; she'd once been asked to purloin that particular work for a former client. But she wasn't the sort of woman who enjoyed reading plays.

"*The King in Yellow* or, rather, *Le Roi en Jaune*, is a two act play that was first performed in Paris some years ago. Everyone there went mad."

"All of them?"

"Even the poor understudies," Thorne said. "Even the ushers. Even the mice in the eaves. All incurably mad. I'm told it's not the first act that does it, but the second. That's where things go off the rails, as they say."

"You have never read it yourself, then?"

"I lack the attention span to go mad," Thorne said. "Has your friend read it, by chance? Is that why she's … ."

"Not that I am aware of. Pepper prefers more muscular reading material. Jack London. The American pulps. She is a blood and thunder sort of girl."

"Lady after my own heart," Thorne said. They blew a thin stream of smoke into the air and continued, "So if not by the play, how?"

"How what?"

"How did she become infected?"

Alessandra frowned. "You make it sound like a sickness."

"It is … in a sense." Thorne tapped ash into their coffee cup.

Alessandra paused. "What does the Marquis of Avonshire have to do with it?"

"Everything and nothing, depending." Thorne looked slightly startled by the question. "He's – was – the figurehead of, well … a cult, I suppose. They have many names and their organization takes many forms. Rather like a strain of influenza … just when you think it's burned itself out, a new one pops up. Suffice to say, they are quite unpleasant. Are they in the city then?"

"Znamenski might be working for them," Alessandra said.

Thorne grunted. "How unfortunate. When I said it was akin to a sickness, I meant it. Carcosa … it infects the mind and soul, twisting them all out of joint with reality as it stands. Right now, it's dreams. Soon, she'll have trouble telling what's real and what's not. Then, as the two worlds begin to slide into one another, she'll begin to change."

"How?" Alessandra asked, her heart bobbing in her throat.

Thorne shrugged. "It's different for everyone, or so I'm

told. Some go mad, some transform physically... some vanish entirely, swallowed up by Carcosa."

"Which doesn't exist."

"Save when it does. The only certainty when it comes to Carcosa is that once it has its hooks in you, it requires a supreme effort of will to dislodge them. Very few can manage it. You have to be tough, or a touch mad already, to even attempt it. A bit of both is better, frankly."

"Pepper is tough," she said, absently. Thorne nodded.

"I'm sure she is, kitten. But is she tough enough? That's the question." Thorne paused. "What say we find out, eh?"

CHAPTER TEN
Avonshire

"It is said that Ruskin hated half the buildings in Venice and worshipped the other half," Znamenski said, a trifle too loudly, as he sipped from his drink. "Byron thought her irredeemably corrupt, and all the more beautiful for it." He was dressed fashionably bohemian, down to the gold hoop in one ear. It helped set him apart from his patrons, who he privately thought of as a singularly dull set of interchangeable bodies in black. Not a speck of color among them. As if they dreaded the very thought of it.

"Myself, I find it hypnotic," he continued. "I lose myself in every speck of mortar and leprous mural. Even the smell of the filth at the bottom of the canals inflames me." He lifted his drink in a toast. "Rest easy, for you will not be a virgin for long, oh Dominante… wedding bells ring, in far Aldebaran, and your husband-to-be stirs…"

"If you are quite finished with your recitation, we have matters to discuss," a young woman called, from behind him. Her accent was softly Italian; she'd learnt English as a girl, and had her speech properly trained at a finishing school.

Znamenski saw no sense in sending children to England to learn anything, but then, the rich had different priorities. He turned and bowed.

"Of course, signora. How rude of me. But once the poetry rises, one must let it vent or one pays for it later." As he spoke, he took in his surroundings, not for the first time. The walled garden was filled to bursting with yellow jasmine and crooked trees pressed tightly against the ancient stonework, at once threatening its integrity and holding it intact. The grass was parched and dying, save in those spots closest to the ancient wellhead that crouched at the far end. Capped now, for more than a century, but still containing potable water, or so his hostess had insisted.

A large, round stone table occupied the flat center of the garden. The table's edges had been carved to resemble crowds of cavorting figures that might have been men or animals, or both. The surface had once displayed an intricately carved map of the world, with Venice at its heart, but was now all but indecipherable thanks to the attentions of time and weather.

Around the table sat half a dozen men, young and old, none of them Venetians. One was a Florentine, by the name of Giocondo. It was he who'd introduced Znamenski to the esteemed members of the trust, including their chairman, the Marquis of Avonshire. The old man sat at the head of the table in a Victorian bath chair the color of jaundiced leaves, looking as if he had no idea where he was or what was going on. Behind him stood his pretty, young wife, Carla ... the only Venetian among them.

"Might I say I am grateful as ever to be invited among you," Znamenski went on, his eyes on Carla. He smiled as he spoke, all charm. It glanced off her, like an arrow from a buckler. She was pale, with hair like midsummer light. Her face might have been carved from marble by some besotted sculptor a century prior, and her lean form was sheathed in black. The dress was fashionable, if a touch too old for her. Like a child playing dress-up in her grandmother's clothes.

"Gratitude is shown, not spoken," Carla said. A ripple of awkwardness went through the seated men. Znamenski chuckled, as much at them as himself. He caught Giocondo's eye, and the Florentine had a pleading look on his face. Znamenski sighed and nodded.

"You are right, signora. I do talk too much, I suppose. What matters do we need to discuss?" He paused. "I do hope it's not about money again. We are supposed to be beyond such concerns, no?"

Giocondo cleared his throat and spoke. "Not money, Jan. We simply wish to know how matters proceed. How is the performance coming?"

"How is it coming? At its own pace, as all great works must." Znamenski snagged an empty chair and poured himself into it. "You cannot force inspiration, my friends. All you can do is step aside and hope for the best."

This elicited a communal grumble, but Carla silenced it with a dismissive laugh. "Inspiration? You are no longer simply an artist, signori. You are a conduit, and conduits have but one purpose."

"To conduct, yes," Znamenski said. "Which is what I am doing. I refuse to… to skimp on such an undertaking. We have a week yet. If this thing must be done, let us do it well."

Carla's eyes narrowed. "That is not up to you. You are merely one part of his story. Play your part, and do not seek to make it about you." Her grip on her husband's shoulder tightened, and he mewled like a hungry kitten. She looked down at him with an expression that was somewhere between disgust and pity, and held his cup to his lips so that he could drink. "Slowly, Hildred, my love," she murmured. "Slowly, else you will choke."

Giocondo and the others all busied themselves looking elsewhere. Znamenski didn't. He watched Carla tend to her paramour with interest. As far as anyone knew, the Marquis was the last of his line and senile besides. How he'd come to be married to a Venetian heiress like Carla Mafei was unknown, at least to Giocondo. She was at least thirty years the man's junior, in Znamenski's estimation.

Znamenski continued watching with mild annoyance. She was too attractive to be chained to such a worthless specimen. A more vigorous match would suit her better. Someone like himself, perhaps. As if she'd heard his thoughts, she glanced at him, and her gaze was sly. He smiled knowingly. Of course she was thinking the same about him. She'd be a fool not to. And he knew she was no fool.

The Marquis finished lapping at his prune juice and sagged back in his chair with a grunt. Carla set the cup down and delicately wiped her hands with a handkerchief. She looked at Znamenski. "Enough foolish posturing. Answer Giocondo's question."

"You will be happy to know that I have found the ideal space for the performance," he said, and paused as if for applause. When none was forthcoming, he sighed. "None of the theaters were quite right. I had to think laterally."

"What do you mean?" Giocondo asked, his tone laced with suspicion. "You have been engaged in preparations at the Teatro San Trovaso for weeks!"

"Yes, but I found some place better. One of the *Isole del Dolore*… an old quarantine island, out in the lagoon. Near Podolo." Znamenski saw Carla shudder at the mention of that nasty little scrap of island. Podolo was cursed, though no Venetian knew exactly how or why or when. There was something there – something old and hungry and wild – but it was not anything of Carcosa. Just another small nightmare in a world full of them.

"Why a place like that?" Giocondo demanded. "The Teatro San Trovaso is perfectly acceptable, and, more importantly, *already ours.*"

"Exactly," Znamenski said. "A pittance. A paltry hovel. Is that the sort of place you wish to welcome our lord into the world? Rather, shouldn't it be a place of meaning and intent? A place from which he can see the city and all the world beyond?" He paused. "The view from the shore is excellent. Venice spills across the horizon like a canvas. Beautiful." He looked at Carla. "You are offering him Venice, signora… a new Carcosa. So let him see it in all its glory. One last time, before it becomes something else entirely."

"Something better," Carla said, doubtfully.

Znamenski inclined his head. "I've already begun painting the backdrops, but I'll need more men to help with setting up the stage, or, rather, building a stage. We'll keep it rustic, of course. They'll pay extra for rustic, you know…"

Giocondo shook his head. "No. This is ridiculous. We can't set up on an island and expect people to come. You will stay at the Teatro San Trovaso." Murmurs of agreement went around the table. Znamenski sucked on his teeth in annoyance. For a cabal of wealthy occultists, the Avonshire Trust was, at times, utterly lacking in imagination.

"And what about my island?" he asked.

Giocondo raised an eyebrow. "Your island? You are our servant, Jan. Do not forget that. As the Marquise said, you are but a cog in the mechanisms of Carcosa."

"Yes, but an important one," Znamenski said, without humility. He gestured airily. "You came to me, remember? I am as much of Carcosa as you, and a good deal more valuable I dare say. What do you provide, save money?" He looked around, challenging them to argue. They had come to him, after all. Something had whispered his name to them in their dreams, and like good dogs they had done as their master bade.

"Money that you need," Giocondo said, pointedly. Good old Giocondo always rose to the bait. "Without us, you are nothing but a smuggler playing at art."

"I have many strings to my bow," Znamenski purred. He was grateful to Giocondo. In a way, the Florentine had made all this possible. But the man was an unmitigated ass. Giocondo flushed and made to reply, but was interrupted by Carla.

"Enough. Giocondo is right. The site has been chosen. Besides, attempting such a rite outside the city is to risk the wrath of our… neighbors."

Znamenski tapped his chin. "Ah, yes. The mysterious Don Lagorio. Can we expect him at opening night?"

Carla grimaced. "Lagorio is a fool. He claims to speak for Cnidathqua, but I suspect there is little truth in that." She looked down at her husband and stroked his withered cheek. "Even so, he is a dangerous man to cross. At least until our king takes his throne."

Znamenski leaned forward. "Yes, about that… in a week, the theater might not be there. The local wildlife is getting restless. My actors are being threatened, my crew bullied. What are we going to do about it, hmm?"

"All earthly obstacles will fall away in time. Already, Venice drifts into the mists of Hali," Carla intoned, with an ease born of practice. It wasn't an answer, but it was as close as he was going to get. He sighed and sat back as she clapped her hands and a masked servant entered the garden, carrying an engraved box. Znamenski felt his heart quicken at the sight. Giocondo and the others fell into a reverential silence.

Carla opened the box, revealing a familiar silvery shape within. Znamenski sighed in pleasure and Carla met his gaze with a respectful nod. After all, hadn't he procured it for her… for them? And no little effort on his part. Seas and messes of blood, indeed.

Carla took the silvery object from the box and raised it up. "Behold… the Key of Ys." Znamenski knew the artifact was magic. He'd grown sensitive to such things of late. It had always been there in him, he thought. Just buried. The war had freed it. All the blood and death and noise… it had shocked something loose in his mind, and opened him up to the true nature of reality. He'd seen behind the curtain, as it were.

Giocondo and the others murmured as Carla continued. "It was once part of the royal jewels of the Empire of Trebizond. It is said that their daughters were so comely because their mothers had come from the Hyades, even as the key itself supposedly came from Brittany. Some of those same daughters married Venetian men, in order to further the aims of both kingdoms. I am descended of one such union, and this Key is my birthright." Her eyes seemed to glow with an awful radiance. "With this Key, we shall open the way to Carcosa. We shall fling wide the gates of falsehood and let loose the hounds of truth upon this ignorant world."

"Amen," Znamenski said, interrupting the spiel. The silvery sheen of the Key was hypnotic; it called to him in some way he could not fathom. He wanted to possess it, to be possessed by it. Instead, he had offered it up as a sign of his devotion to the King in Yellow… and his queen.

Sometimes, he regretted it.

As if reading his thoughts, Carla lowered the Key and looked at him. "Of course, there are those who would claim it for themselves," she said, in a tone just shy of accusing.

Znamenski smiled. "Anyone I know?"

"Her name is Zorzi, I believe."

Znamenski frowned. "Ah. He told you, then?" He wasn't quite certain where the balance of power between Carla and the Man in the Pallid Mask tipped. Was she his master, or was it more of a partnership. Perhaps it didn't matter.

"He tells me everything," Carla said. "Nothing happens in this city that I am not aware of. Including the fact that this woman has come looking for you."

"And as I told our masked associate, I will handle it." As he spoke, his eyes drifted once more toward the Key. It haunted his dreams, and had ever since he'd pried it from the mummified grip of its previous owner.

Carla frowned. "When?"

Znamenski laughed. "Today, if you wish. Tomorrow at the latest." He smiled widely. "Never fear. The play has already begun, and the show will go on."

CHAPTER ELEVEN
Selim

Selim sat in a shuttered doorway, smoking his fifth cigarette of the day. Good Turkish tobacco, these. None of that depressing French weed he'd had to make do with before. He watched the passersby with only vague interest, the majority of his attentions on the palazzo doors across the campo. The front entrance faced the canal, but Znamenski had entered via the rear. Selim suspected he would exit by the same method.

According to Alessandra, the artist was a criminal as well as a scribbler. He certainly moved with the sort of confidence Selim associated with criminals. Like a wolf among sheep. Alessandra moved the same way, though she was better at hiding it when she wished. She was better at many things; more, in fact, than he'd expected.

When they'd first met, he'd pegged her for nothing more than a common thief. The Comte d'Erlette had never spoken of her with anything other than condescension. But in the months since, Selim had come to realize that she was anything but common. In her way, she was far more capable than his previous employer. She had more common sense. At the very least, he was fairly confident she had no plans to invade another world.

He tapped ash onto the ground, and watched the pigeons fight over a scrap of something repellant – a bit of squid, perhaps. More of them joined the fray, until a squabbling gray mass occupied the center of the campo. He'd never seen fiercer pigeons than these here. They thought nothing of attacking each other, or the occasional gull.

Then, perhaps that was simply one more sign of something wrong. The last time he'd visited, it had seemed a sedate sort of place. As if all the fight had been knocked out of it by Napoleon, and now it was simply idling away in its dotage. But there was an angry vibrancy in the air, now. A harsh, metallic echo that accompanied the songs of the gondoliers and danced along overheard conversations.

Alessandra was partially right; some of it was simply down to the new order. Selim caught someone watching him. A sour-faced youth, dressed like a laborer but with pale hands and a complexion that only saw the sun on Sundays. A black armband was visible, over the sleeve of one jacket. He lounged on the rim of a capped wellhead, absently shooing away the cats that came to drink from the bowl-like depressions at its base. He wasn't alone in his loitering. Three others were with him; a proper bundle of sticks, Selim thought.

The Fascists weren't in power yet, but in Selim's opinion it was only a matter of time. There were too many black armbands and posters and meetings going on for his taste. Florence and Padua had been no different. As far as he was concerned, the sooner he and the others were out of Italy, the better.

He studied them carefully, without looking like he was

paying too much. Hard faces, but soft middles. Not academics, but some middle ground between over-educated and under. Two were of an age with the one staring at him. One was a lump, heavy and pouting, while the other was leaner, with a smile that flickered in and out of sight, as if he were full of conflicting thoughts.

The last one was in middle years, and had a face that had been kissed by shrapnel. He muttered to the others, though Selim was too far away to hear what was said. He could imagine it, though. Turks were not well-loved in Venice, even in these modern times. Too much bad blood over the centuries; then there was the war, of course.

Selim had done his share of fighting, mostly in the Balkans. It was where he'd seen the things that had made him amenable to the Comte d'Erlette's offer of employment. He closed his eyes and took a long, shaky drag on his cigarette as he tried very hard not to think of those events. There were things men should not see, not if they wished to sleep well.

When he opened his eyes, he saw the Fascists were huddled together, darting hard looks in his direction. He wondered which of them would lead the charge: the one who'd been staring at him, perhaps. Not the older man. War made men less prone to such foolishness, not more.

Selim discreetly adjusted the weight of the small Belgian revolver hidden in his jacket. There were laws against firearms in Venice, but he had no intention of attempting to confront the sort of creatures he'd encountered over the years barehanded.

He thought about what Alessandra had told him about her meeting with this so-called Cavalier. And the other one she was ostensibly meeting at that bookshop whose address he had folded up in his pocket. He was to meet her there later, at his discretion.

While the Comte d'Erlette had been more than happy to deal with groups like the Silver Twilight Lodge, even he had balked at tangling his fate with that of the Red Coterie. From what Selim had learned, they were an acquisitive bunch... magpies, snatching shiny things that no sane person would get within a mile of. And now he and the others were in Venice, at the behest of such fools.

No, to help Pepper, he corrected himself. The young woman was a trial at times, but he felt a certain paternal fondness for her. She reminded him of his sisters... loud and brash and brave, though lacking in all but the barest modicum of sense. He did not wish to see her come to harm. Not if he could help prevent it.

The pigeons scattered, drawing his attention. Someone was coming out of the palazzo. Znamenski, dressed in his flamboyant best. He'd followed the artist's trail from Florence, never getting very close. It was almost as if something had protected the man, keeping him safe from those who might mean him harm.

Almost at the same moment, the Fascists stood up. Selim sighed as they made their way toward him, advancing like a phalanx of thuggery. Znamenski, who'd paused to light a cigarette, hadn't noticed. That was good. If the matter could be settled quietly, Selim might be able to continue following him unawares. But he didn't hold out much hope.

"What do you think you are doing here?" the one in the lead barked. "You think you are allowed here, eh? Is that what you think?"

Selim rose to his feet, still puffing on his cigarette. Heads were turning throughout the campo, watching the confrontation. That was unfortunate. He made as if to go, knowing even as he did that there was a better than average chance it would simply provoke them further. But it also provided the best chance of not alerting Znamenski.

Unfortunately, he wasn't quick enough. A hand settled on his shoulder. "I am talking to you," the young man growled. Selim spun on his heel and jabbed his cigarette into the accoster's eye. The young man howled and reeled back, hands clapped to his face. Selim didn't waste the opportunity. He was in among them a moment later, fists swinging. A well-aimed knee dropped the big one, who squealed loudly. Stiffened fingers to the throat sent the lean one staggering, clutching at his windpipe.

The older one came forward in a boxer's stance. Selim copied him, and for a moment they circled one another. "Turkish dog," the man grunted.

Selim bared his teeth. "Maybe. And maybe next time, you pick a smaller dog to kick, eh?" They traded jabs for a few moments, neither connecting with much force. Selim was tempted to let it play out, but the others were recovering. They'd be on their feet in seconds, or worse, the police would arrive. He knew they'd arrest him without thinking.

A crowd was starting to gather. He risked a quick glance, but had lost sight of Znamenski. Perhaps he'd already left. His opponent's fist danced across his forearm and Selim seized the opening to drive a punch into the man's gut. His opponent gave a whoof of pain and stumbled back a step, waving a hand for Selim to stop.

Selim didn't. He took two quick steps and flattened the man. One of the others yelled a curse and charged at him. Selim turned, but too slowly. The big one had him in a bear hug. He lifted Selim up and shook him hard enough to rattle his teeth. Selim threw his head back, and felt something crunch. He was released, and dropped to the ground. The back of his head ached but his assailant was staggering like a drunk, blood gushing from his nose.

Then, the big man stiffened – and fell. Znamenski stood behind him, holding a leather sap. He smiled benignly at Selim. "Good morning. Were you waiting for me?"

Before Selim could reply, the thin Fascist lunged at him, something sharp in his hand. Selim leapt back, the tip of the knife barely nicking one of the buttons of his shirt. He cursed and backed away. The knifeman followed, too intent on his prey to notice Znamenski sidling up behind him. The sap rose and fell, and the knifeman fell with it.

The last of the bunch ran, cursing them the entire way out of the campo. "No doubt he's going for reinforcements," Znamenski said. "They're a plague on this city; like rats."

"I required no help," Selim said, stiffly.

Znamenski nodded and flicked an imaginary speck from his sleeve. "No, but I haven't had a good fight in months." He looked Selim up and down. "You work for Alessandra, don't you? I recognize your face from the train station in Padua. You've been dogging my trail since Florence, I believe."

Selim said nothing. Znamenski nodded, as if that were answer enough. "She obviously wants to discuss something. Where is she staying?"

Again, Selim did not answer. Again, Znamenski nodded,

though now a look of annoyance flashed across his face. "Fine." He pulled a flyer out of his coat pocket and hastily scribbled an address on the back. "Here is where I will be most of the afternoon. Tell her to meet me there, if she wishes to discuss the matters that lay between us." He looked down at the dazed Fascists groaning at their feet and smiled again. "A pleasure, signori. I look forward to our next meeting."

With that, he turned and strode away across the campo. Selim watched him go, but only for a moment. The crowd of onlookers had broken up and dispersed, leaving him all but alone in the square. He paused, gave a parting kick in the ribs to the largest of his opponents, and left. Alessandra would, no doubt, meet with Znamenski. Selim hoped that they would leave, soon after.

But something told him he wasn't that lucky.

CHAPTER TWELVE
Magic

Pepper fixed Thorne with a suspicious stare. "Who's this, then?"

"Your knight in shining armor, pet," Thorne said. "You may call me Thorne."

"Well, you may call me Pepper, not pet," Pepper said, pugnaciously. She looked around the bookshop's backroom, and then at Alessandra. "What do they want?"

"To help you," Thorne said. "If I might be allowed."

"Thorne believes that they can… force loose whatever has you in its grip." Alessandra paused. "But only if you are willing to let them. If you do not wish this, we will not force you." She glanced at Thorne, who shrugged.

"No skin off my nose either way."

Pepper frowned. "What, exactly, are you going to do? Like, magic or something?"

"Or something," Thorne said. They rose to their feet and circled Pepper, studying her with narrowed eyes and pursed lips. Abruptly, they darted forward and grabbed Pepper's face, forcing her eyelids up so that they could get a better look at her eyes. She yelped and smacked them away. Thorne said, "Yes. She's definitely seen the Yellow Sign."

"Which means what, exactly?" Alessandra asked.

"I told you," Thorne said.

"No, you gave me possibilities, symptoms… not what it meant. What is Carcosa, Thorne? Is it real, or imaginary? Or is it like Pnath… is it a halfway place?"

Thorne frowned. Finally, they said, "It's all of that. Carcosa might once have existed, or never at all. It might be in the future, or a galaxy away. Or all of those."

"It's a city," Pepper said. Thorne nodded.

"That too."

"They got lemurs," Pepper said.

"What an interesting fact," Thorne said, with a mocking grin. Pepper shook her head.

"You don't get it. It's a real place. It's got real people in it." She looked at them both. "You two are acting like it's a delusion. Like I'm crazy. Only I'm not. I'm… connected. Something bad is happening over there, and I got a front row seat to the show. Maybe… maybe we can use that, somehow."

Alessandra looked at her. "Use it how, exactly?"

Pepper shrugged in visible frustration. "How should I know?"

"You can't use it," Thorne said. "It uses you, not the other way around."

"Maybe we should ask that Cavalier guy," Pepper shot back.

"The Cavalier?" Thorne's mouth twisted into a moue of distaste. "Has the old fool made contact with you, then?"

Alessandra nodded. "When we arrived. Quicker off the mark than you, I must say."

Thorne sniffed. "I was getting the lay of the land. In any event, that's a bit disappointing. I'd hoped to avoid his involvement. He's prone to overcomplicating even the simplest of matters, that one. Flamboyant, what?"

Alessandra looked them up and down pointedly. "And you are not?"

Thorne's expression became indignant. "I'm stylish, darling. There's a difference and you damn well know it."

Alessandra couldn't hold back a sharp laugh. "Fine. You want this Key, and I want to help Pepper. If you can aid us with the latter, I will lend you my expertise for the former."

Thorne smiled. "Excellent. After you get me that doo-bob, I shall–"

"No. Now."

"Excuse me?"

"You will help her now. While we are here."

Thorne hesitated, a look of consternation on their face. They glanced at Pepper. "That... is inadvisable. It takes time to work the hook out of the fish's mouth."

"You calling me a fish?" Pepper asked, hands balling into fists.

Alessandra waved her to silence, her eyes on Thorne. "Then you cannot do it."

Thorne sneered. "There is very little I cannot do, I assure you. It's simply that you caught me a bit... underprepared. It's not as simple as an exorcism, you know."

"I do not know. That is why you are here. So do what needs doing, or find your own damn Key," Alessandra said, prettily.

Thorne laughed. "You drive a hard bargain. Fine." They

tapped Pepper between the eyes, eliciting a muttered curse from the young woman. "Let's see what we can do, eh? Hold still, kitten." Before either Alessandra or Pepper could react, Thorne grabbed the young woman by the sides of the head and began to chant under their breath. Alessandra didn't recognize the language, and it stung her eardrums to hear it.

Pepper arched her back, her body trembling as Thorne continued to chant. The air around them took on a febrile vibration. All the moisture seemed drawn from the air, to orbit the two in a phantasmal typhoon. Alessandra covered her eyes as an eerie shimmer enveloped Thorne and Pepper, nearly blinding her. The shimmer stretched and widened, and within it she saw… something. A shape – a person? A city? She couldn't tell. The shimmer whipsawed like an animal in pain, and she felt the floor bow beneath her feet.

The watery image became clearer – mountains, twin suns and a city of tall towers… was this what Pepper was seeing in her dreams? There was an ugly choleric tint to the sky in that other place; a hideous lemon ache that made her eyes sting and her stomach flip-flop. Something in it put her in mind of sick beds and men choking on gas-blistered lungs.

She could hear explosions – no. A giant's tread. Or maybe wing beats. As if something titanic were approaching. A wind rose from nowhere, perhaps within the shimmer itself and clawed at her, as if trying to draw her into itself. She felt her heels slip on the floor and braced herself against the pull of the wind.

She heard Thorne calling out, but their words were ripped away by the wind. Books and papers hurtled about the room, caught in the maelstrom. She tried to see past the shimmer, to Pepper, but could see nothing but that godawful light. It burned to look at it, and her ears ached to hear the roaring.

Then, something erupted from within the heart of it. It was a mote at first, but it swelled rapidly as she watched, unable to tear her eyes away as it went from a speck, to a splotch and then something foul and leathery came out of the shimmer like a fish out of water. Grotesque jaws spread wide, the thing lunged toward her. It was all that was awful about bats, bugs and dead bodies; all leather hide stretched tight over ugly bones, with thorny sections of carapace clinging to its flesh like barnacles.

She'd seen a picture of something like it once, in Henri's library. Some sort of demon or creature from the outer dark, with a name that she couldn't pronounce. She fired on instinct, the Webley's bark lost in the roar of the wind and the screaming of the thing as it jerked away, black ichor spurting from its bony carapace. She emptied her weapon into the creature, causing it to twitch back.

Its leather wings snapped out, smashing aside boxes as its weight came down on the table, shattering it. The room was too low for it to fly, thankfully. Though, unfortunately, that meant it couldn't leave.

It swiped at her with a talon – leg? – that hissed as it cut the air. She leapt away, rolling across the floor. The door was right there, but she refused to leave Pepper behind with only Thorne to protect her.

Adrenaline warring with terror, she cracked open the Webley, emptying spent shells onto the floor. After her trouble with the Comte, she'd taken to carrying a pair of modified

Prideaux speed-loaders on her person. She scrambled behind a pile of boxes and inserted the first speed-loader into the cylinder, even as she tried to come up with a plan.

The creature was clearly confused; its movements reminded her of a bird that had just flown into a window. Wherever it was from, it clearly hadn't intended to be here – and that was only making it angrier. It reared up, wings smacking the walls, and loosed a blood-curdling shriek. Alessandra flung herself out of the way as it came for her again, fleshless jaws snapping. It had clearly decided that she was a problem – lucky her. But, so long as it was focused on her, it wasn't going after Pepper and Thorne. Not that she could tell where they were at the moment, thanks to that blasted radiance.

Her eyes strayed again to the shimmer. That was where it had come from – that was where it needed to go. She had to lead it back, somehow, preferably without being torn apart. Her opening came when the door leading to the shop burst open and Selim stepped through, eyes wide and gun in hand. He froze, just for an instant, as the creature spun toward him, eyes burning with fury.

To his credit, Selim reacted with commendable swiftness. His revolver snapped up and roared. The creature twitched away, as it had before. Bullets weren't enough to do the job, but it didn't seem to enjoy being shot. But its moment of inattention gave her the opening she needed. She leapt to her feet and headed for the shimmer.

"Selim! Fall back," she shouted, as she planted herself between the creature and the shimmer. It wouldn't do either of them any good if it decided to pursue him. She shot the thing in the back of the head, and it jerked around with a querulous bark. Selim stepped back and slammed the door. He was no fool, at least.

She retreated slowly, drawing it after her, back toward the shimmer. Heat built against her back, as if she were backing toward a roaring flame. She could hear things, more shrieks – were there more of these beasts on the way? What had Thorne unleashed? And what did it mean for Pepper? Too many questions, not enough answers.

All she could do was hope she was doing the right thing. "Come on then," she shouted at the creature. "Come and get me, beast!"

CHAPTER THIRTEEN
Carcosa

Pepper looked around in confusion. "Where…?" she began. The streets swooped up and away in smooth runnels of stone, but like no stone she'd ever seen. It was too smooth, and the colors unlike any she was familiar with. There were people everywhere, but they didn't seem to notice her, or her companion. Overhead, two suns hung in the sky.

"Carcosa," Thorne said, sounding bored. It was a put on, Pepper thought. There was a quaver in their voice; a thready hitch that Alessandra had taught her to recognize. "Or at least the version of it you're afflicted with."

"What do you mean?" She tried to recall when one world had given way to the other, but as with her dreams it was all but impossible. There had been a sudden flash of light, and she'd felt as if she'd been falling… then – poof. Here.

Thorne sighed. "Carcosa is an idea, kitten. A thought-form on a grand scale. Despite what I told matron, it was probably never real. Just a story, like King Arthur. But it forced itself into a twilight reality. It insinuated itself and made people believe, so now it does and always did. But it's not stable. It changes and repeats itself; the same sad cycle over and over again." Thorne glanced at her, their eyes glittering oddly in the weird half-light of the two suns overhead. "Once, it never existed. Now, it has always existed. That's the kind of unpleasantness we're dealing with."

Pepper shivered and looked away, trying to get a sense of her surroundings. It was odd, seeing it with her own eyes. It lacked the familiarity of her dreams, and was more unsettling. The city rose around them like the petals of a flower, or one of those weird German films where all the buildings were built at wrong angles. "So, if it's not real, why can I feel the wind? Why can I hear these people talking?"

"Because you're hooked. Let me guess, when it began you couldn't understand what they were saying, or what you were seeing, could you?"

Pepper paused. "No. Not really."

"But, as it got stronger, it slithered into your brain and made itself understood. Insidious little bug, ain't it?"

She shook her head and looked up. Round towers rose overhead with bridges slung between them seemingly haphazardly. The people around them were uniformly tall, dressed in robes. Something about them was alien; unlike the people she was used to. "Don't worry, they can't see us," Thorne said, noting her growing agitation. "We're not really here. We're in your mind, in the part of your brain that is infected."

"How the hell did you do that?" Pepper asked, touching her head.

"Magic, kitten. The human mind isn't just fat and water; it's also a door into the collective unconscious. Step through, and you can go damn near anywhere. Unfortunately, your parcel of it has some serious mold issues."

"You make it sound like I got the plague," Pepper began, then paused. For a moment, she'd thought she'd heard Alessandra calling her, albeit from a great distance. But the sound faded before she could focus on it. She pushed the thought aside and spotted a procession coming down the street. The crowd was making noise; they were excited. "What is that?"

"Looks like a parade," Thorne said. "Oh look – lemurs."

There were indeed lemurs on leashes, ostriches and other animals, all wearing royal tack and harness. She recognized the insignia, even if everything else was strange. People bowed as the procession passed them, knocking their heads against the ground in a strange pantomime. "It's like a performance, ain't it?"

"What do you mean?" Thorne asked.

"They're moving, but all stiff. Like they've rehearsed it."

"Good eye. Did she teach you that?" Thorne peered at her more closely. "Keen eye, quick thinking – grooming you to be quite the little investigator, eh?"

"She's teaching me how to be a thief," Pepper said, irked by Thorne's tone. "Anyway, why are we here, what are we doing?"

"Looking around. Seeing how strong the infection is." Thorne smirked. "Your prospects ain't the best, kitten."

"So you can't help me."

"I didn't say that."

"So you can," she said.

"Didn't say that either," Thorne clarified. "Think of this as a fact-finding mission." They started toward the approaching procession, their hands clasped behind their back. Pepper hurried to keep up. They threaded through the crowd and she was reminded of a play she'd once been in as a kid. The world around her had the feeling of a backdrop, the people actors. Even the air tasted artificial. Was that what Thorne had been trying to explain to her?

"What sort of facts?" she asked.

"All sorts," Thorne said. "I've never been in the mindscape of someone who's seen the Yellow Sign. That is what happened to you, ain't it?" Thorne leaned over her. "You saw something you shouldn't have and it squirmed in through the cracks."

"What the hell is a yellow sign?" Pepper demanded, even as she recalled the death-masks she and Alessandra had seen in Znamenski's studio in Paris. Something had been marked on them… something she couldn't quite remember, but nor could she forget. Like Thorne said, it had squirmed into her mind.

"It's magic… a bit of this place, twisted up into a sign that gets into the minds of whoever is unfortunate enough to see it and have the sensitivity to recognize it. Most people can look at it a hundred times and have nothing worse than a bad dream. But others see it, and their dreams go from bad to worse. Just like yours."

"Lucky me," Pepper muttered. She glanced toward the procession again and stopped. The woman in the lead was familiar – heartbreakingly beautiful, draped in damask and golden mesh. She walked with servants carrying her train, and lemurs on golden leashes capering ahead of her. "Cassilda," she murmured.

Thorne nodded. "Yes, Queen of Carcosa – at least in some

versions. Daughter of the Hyades, and the reason the King comes to Carcosa. Tell me, in your dreams, are you her?"

"No," Pepper said. "I'm someone called ... Camilla."

"Ah, the handmaiden. Or the queen's lover. Her betrayer – or the one who is betrayed. It's always a bit different, depending on the version. The story changes itself to suit its audience. In some, Camilla vanishes after the first act. In others, she is pivotal to both. I wonder which Camilla you will be."

"How can a story change itself?" Pepper asked, unable to look away from the procession. In her dreams Cassilda was beautiful, but here and now that beauty was odd; off-kilter. Like looking at a department store mannequin. "Why does it look so artificial?"

"Like I said, it's not real. Think of it as a hunter's blind. What you should be worried about is what's behind it." Thorne paused. "There we are – look. At the edges of the crowd."

Pepper followed their gaze and saw a flash of yellow. More than one. "Who are they?" But Thorne didn't reply. Instead, their eyes were on the sky. Something swooped overhead, disrupting the routine of the procession. Heads turned, looking upward. Conversations faltered. Another shape swept along the line of buildings – then a third. A fourth. The air quivered with the thunder of wings.

Thorne frowned in puzzlement. "What are they doing here?" they muttered. "They shouldn't be here. This isn't right."

"What are they? Birds?" Pepper craned her neck. A moment later, she realized they weren't birds. Or bats, or insects. Instead, they were something awful. Her stomach twisted at the sight of them as they drew closer. The crowd was panicking now, running in all directions. But not fast – they were moving like treacle.

"No, Byakhee," Thorne said. "And they're hunting. Why are they hunting?"

"I don't know, why are you asking me?" Pepper asked, as the crowd began to blur into one and the city seemed to smear around her. "What's going on? Who are those guys in yellow?"

Thorne didn't reply. Instead, they were concentrating on the flying things – which were getting closer. A slurred roar of panic rose from the inchoate blob that had been the crowd, as the yellow shapes wove through it. They were men or dogs or something halfway between both; the only commonality between them was the vivid hue of their raiment and the fur on their blistered limbs. Whatever they were, they made her sick to look at them. Where they passed, the ground became pallid and sound became tinny and discordant.

Pepper tensed as one drew close. He – it – was on all fours now, hooded head sniffing at the air. "I thought you said they couldn't see us," she hissed. Again, Thorne didn't reply, their eyes on the sky. More of the creatures converged, closing in from all sides. Pepper looked around, trying to keep them all in sight, but it was impossible. Despite Thorne's earlier words, it was clear the newcomers knew they were there somehow. She felt the first stirrings of fear, and fought against the urge to flee.

The closest one sprang for her, blistered fingers crooked like claws. It came with a yowl and she pivoted as Alessandra had taught her, letting it leap over her. Before it could recover, she leapt on its back and wrapped an arm around its neck.

It felt soft; boneless. Her skin crawled, but she kept up the pressure. It seemed to be working, as the thing staggered under her weight and clawed at her arm. But the others were closing in and Thorne didn't look inclined to help.

Thinking quickly, she leapt off, shoving her opponent toward one of the others as she did so. The two creatures collided and – merged. It was like watching paint splatter; one moment there were two, the next just one. It turned, jaws working soundlessly as its eyes fixed on her again. Its frayed lips quirked in something that might have been a smile. It lurched toward her again and she narrowly avoided its grasp.

She spun and sent a punch thudding across where its jaw ought to have been, trying to keep the others in sight as she did so. The yellow thing staggered back, its indistinct face twisting into a grimace. Pepper threw another punch, and it easily caught her blow on its calloused palm. Its eyes flickered like candles in the shadows of its hood.

"Take… off… your… mask," it gurgled, and she froze. Its voice seemed to drip across her thoughts like acid, and she felt all the strength go out of her as it tightened its grip on her fist. "Take… off… your… mask," it said again.

"You first, sweetness," Thorne said, from behind it. It released Pepper and whirled to face Thorne. It hissed and the others turned to face Thorne as well. They made a complicated gesture and the yellow thing came apart like sand on the wind. The others were still there, still on the move, but whatever Thorne had done, it seemed to have thrown them for a loop. They hesitated, swaying in what might have been confusion.

Then, the Byakhee landed atop one of them, obliterating it. The monstrous being reared up, shrieking in obvious fury. Its wings stretched wide as it made ready to leap again. Thorne shoved Pepper back, out of the way as they made another complicated gesture even as the Byakhee sprang for them. There was a rushing, roaring sound and the monster vanished. Thorne stumbled back, androgynous features coated in sweat.

"We have to run, kitten – now!" Thorne caught Pepper's arm and propelled her away from the street as more Byakhee drew near, circling lower and lower. The yellow things were gone, as if they'd never been.

"What – why? Just magic the rest of them!"

"That's not how it works," Thorne snarled, shoving her along. "The Byakhee should not be here. Someone summoned them. They're not part of your delusion! Now run!"

CHAPTER FOURTEEN
Byakhee

The creature reared up over Alessandra, screeching like a bat out of Hell. And maybe that was what it was. She snatched up a chair and slung it at the beast, but it batted it aside as it dove toward her. She skidded aside, nearly losing her balance in a sludge of spilled coffee and mashed pastries. The creature flapped its wings spasmodically as it pivoted to follow her. It was persistent, if nothing else.

She continued her slow retreat toward the shimmer. She still couldn't see anything within it – not Pepper, not Thorne. Nothing. It was as if they had been swallowed whole. She didn't know what it meant.

"Countess," Selim called, from the doorway. "Do you require assistance?" He had the door open a crack, and his eyes were wide. Alessandra didn't have time to reply as the creature came for her again. She slid under its raking talons and scrambled toward the door. It was clear now that the creature wasn't planning to depart. She needed a new plan, fast.

Selim took her silence for assent and flung the door

open, firing as he did so. The monster wailed and retreated. Alessandra thought it was more surprised than hurt. "A Byakhee," he growled, watching as it crawled up the wall with reptilian speed. "I have not seen one of them in a long time."

"You know what this thing is?" Alessandra asked, climbing to her feet. She had her back to the wall now. Not the ideal position, but at least she could see where it was.

"Sadly. I know too that bullets will not harm it."

"Fire?" Alessandra asked, watching the Byakhee cling to the ceiling. It watched them the way a cat might watch two mice.

Selim shook his head. "Not fire, nor iron. Only sorcerers can harm them." He licked his lips. "If it should escape…"

"It won't," a calm voice said behind him. Alessandra saw the shop's proprietor peering past Selim at the Byakhee with an expression of mild interest. "The shop won't let it leave. Nothing can leave, if the shop doesn't wish it."

Alessandra shared a quick look with Selim. "Well, that is… something," she allowed. As if it had heard them, the Byakhee hissed. But before it could act, its attention was caught by a sudden shout from within the shimmer. Alessandra, startled, saw two figures racing toward her from the other side. As they drew closer, she realized it was Thorne and Pepper. The Byakhee saw them as well, and gave a feral snarl. It dropped to the floor and scuttled toward the shimmer.

Cursing loudly, Alessandra stalked toward the monster, firing as she went. Selim followed, copying her. The Byakhee retreated with every impact, just as she'd hoped. "Back up, you overgrown turkey buzzard," she spat, until her revolver clicked dry. Moving quickly, she snapped open the weapon and reached for her second speed-loader. But before she could reload, a hand caught her wrist. Thorne.

"No need," they said. "No need for any of that." They pushed past her and Selim and raised their hands, as if trying to make themselves look bigger. The creature reared up and drew back, globular eyes narrowing. Thorne kept approaching, but the beast didn't react as Alessandra expected. Instead of attacking, it sank down and made an odd, chuntering noise.

Alessandra lowered her weapon. "Well, there is something you do not see every day." She glanced at Pepper, who looked none the worse for wear thankfully. "Are you–?"

Pepper took off her hat and ran a hand through her hair. "Alright? No. In one piece? Sure." She looked around. "Looks like a hurricane tore through here."

"Well, blame your flying friend there," Alessandra began, even as Selim took aim at the now-calm beast, but Thorne stepped between them.

"Don't hurt it," Thorne said, sharply. "Just… stop. Byakhee aren't monsters. They're just animals, of a sort. Like wild horses or – or hyenas, or geese. Large, unpleasant geese."

"So… geese?" Pepper muttered. Alessandra gestured sharply, and Selim lowered his weapon, if reluctantly. He stared at the Byakhee and shook his head.

Thorne gestured and the Byakhee followed the motion, chirruping softly. "Normally, there's a drink of sorts one must consume to communicate with them. In reality, it's a sort of honey produced by Byakhee dams; ingesting it makes them think you're one of their young or a member of their cavalcade."

"Cavalcade?" Alessandra asked, looking up at the creature.

Up close, it was beautiful in an odd, unsettling way. It was something clearly designed for predation and travel through hostile spheres. Built for function over form.

"What did you think a flock of Byakhee were called?" Thorne said, hesitantly stroking its beak-like muzzle. "There's a sweet girl. It was all just a terrible misunderstanding. No harm meant. We'll have you back with your friends in a moment."

The Byakhee seemed to understand. It gave a soft, trilling cry; much gentler than its earlier shrieks. Those had been hunting calls, Alessandra thought. Meant to cause fear and disorient prey. Unable to help herself, she reached up. The Byakhee blinked slowly, like a cat. Its hide wasn't clammy or cold; rather it was warm, like leather that had been sitting in the sunlight. It nudged her with its beak, snuffling at her clothes. "I hope you like my perfume," Alessandra murmured. "And that all is forgiven for the misunderstanding earlier."

"Byakhee don't hold grudges and they're damn near-unkillable through terrestrial means. It's why they're the mount of choice for sorcerers and travelers to the outer spheres." Thorne stepped back. "Someone sensed my intrusion into the Carcosa-dream and summoned the cavalcade to chase me off, or kill me." They smiled. "Thankfully, I've dealt with Byakhee before. Rather like sending attack dogs after an animal trainer."

"I doubt they will make that mistake again," Alessandra said. Thorne glanced at her and gave a terse nod.

"Next time, they'll send something worse than a Byakhee. Not that there's going to be a next time… at least not until I get that Key." Thorne raised a hand to forestall her protest.

"The Key is the only thing that will give us the slightest chance of helping her."

Alessandra frowned and glanced at Pepper. "What did you find?"

"Bupkiss," Pepper said, flatly.

"What I found was what I expected to find. It's in her mind. The dreams are part of the story. They're leading her down a primrose path to a nasty end." Thorne looked at Pepper. "You saw them yourself… the hounds of Carcosa. They're circling you in your dreams, waiting for the right moment to take you and hollow you out and replace you with… something else."

"What?" Alessandra demanded. None of this was what she wanted to hear. It was somehow worse than she'd expected, and what she'd expected had been fairly awful. If Thorne couldn't help Pepper, what were they even doing here?

Thorne laughed. "How should I know? She might just go mad, like that poor fool on the quay yesterday. Or she might become a mask for something much worse…"

"They keep talking about masks," Pepper said, softly. She looked at Alessandra. "In my dreams, they – they keep telling me to take off my mask."

"Yes, they do that," Thorne said. They looked at the Byakhee and smiled again. "Well, enough shillyshallying. Let's send our girl home." They gestured and murmured a few unintelligible syllables and the air split to their left. Screeches and cries emanated from within it, and the Byakhee gave a grunt and entered the rift without hesitation, as if it had seen one before and knew what to do. Thorne made a second gesture, and the rift sealed itself. "There we go. Off to fly the abysses between the stars, like a good Byakhee."

"We should have named her," Pepper said. Thorne snorted.

"Maybe I'll let you ride one, if we ever get that Key." Thorne looked at Selim. "And who is this burly fellow?"

"Selim – you showed up just in the nick of time," Alessandra said, ignoring Thorne. "Did something happen with Znamenski?"

"You might say that," Selim grunted. "Znamenski wants to meet you." He handed her a theatrical flyer with an address written on the back. He glanced at Pepper. "You are… okay?"

Alessandra spoke up before Pepper could reply. "I asked you to follow him, not have a chat with him!"

"It was unavoidable," he said, defensively. She noticed he was rubbing his knuckles, as if they were sore and she wondered what had occurred. "He did not seem surprised to see me. I believe he has been expecting you to show up."

She frowned. "You think it is a trap?"

"No." He hesitated. "At least not in the sense of armed gunmen. He wants something from you."

"Did he say that?"

"No." Selim ran a hand over his pate. "Just a feeling."

Alessandra sighed. "I trust your feelings." She smiled. "Even so, it would be rude of me not to go."

"Rude is better than dead," Selim said, pointedly.

"Only in France, dear heart," Alessandra said. "Besides, I want to put a question or two to Znamenski and this gives me an opportunity to do so, hopefully without interruption." She looked at the others. "I will go meet him. In the meantime, I suggest you take the opportunity to see the sights, or rest. Or both."

"So, we're on vacation now?" Pepper asked.

"Consider it part of your education. Selim, go with her."

"I don't need a babysitter," Pepper protested. Selim made to argue as well, but Alessandra cut them both off with a sharp gesture.

"I would feel better if Selim accompanied you. As I said, call it educational." She looked at Thorne, who was making a lackadaisical attempt at straightening the room beneath the stern eye of Matteo.

"Wish me luck. I am going to go see if I can find your blasted Key."

CHAPTER FIFTEEN
Insult

"You did what?" Znamenski snarled, turning from the stage to glare at the Man in the Pallid Mask. Nearby, Carla stood primly, her gaze on the rehearsal. But every so often her eyes strayed in his direction. They'd been playing this game for weeks. In public, she was all sharp edges and brittle tones. But in private… well.

The Man glanced at her, as if seeking her approval. "Thorne is dangerous. I took the opportunity to eliminate them." As ever, there was no hint of emotion in his voice. Even so, he sounded slightly defensive which pleased Znamenski to no end. The Man was an annoyance; an obstacle to his rise, and future enjoyment.

"You failed, obviously," Znamenski snapped. "I told you I was going to handle this!"

The Man paused. "You are not in charge, artist. I am the hand of Carcosa."

"If you had killed them, Alessandra would not look kindly on us. In fact, it would have made things worse. We are at a delicate stage, my friend. Any upset now, and things may go dreadfully awry."

That wasn't an exaggeration. While preparations for the performance were going well, there were also the usual headaches. Bribes needed handing out, and the Fascists were no longer taking their payoffs with the same grace as the local criminal gangs. In a point of fact, their window of opportunity was narrowing with every passing day, not due to any ritual concerns but to the political unrest in the country. The very circumstances that made the performance effective at this juncture might soon prevent it from occurring.

"You put much stock in her ability to interfere," Carla said, without looking at him.

"I know Alessandra."

"Do you? I wonder." Carla sighed and indicated the stage. Rehearsals were going as well as could be expected, given the material. Some of the actors looked half-dead; many of them were complaining of nightmares. "You have taken many liberties with the story."

"I have done as my muse advised. Do you not approve?"

"If I did not, you would not be allowed to continue."

Znamenski bristled, but didn't rise to the bait. He forced a smile. "So long as you are happy, then." He looked at the Man. "You, on the other hand, are as shortsighted as ever. You yourself said I was to give her what she wanted…"

"And when do you plan to do this?" the Man asked.

"Today. I invited her here, to watch the afternoon rehearsal."

"Here? Are you certain that is wise?" Carla asked, looking at him for the first time. Znamenski smiled, confidently.

"Of course. Alessandra once did work for your

organization – *our* organization." He paused, then added, slyly, "Perhaps she could be convinced to do so again... on a more permanent basis."

"And what use would she be, in the world to come?" Carla asked. She sounded intrigued. Then, the servants of Carcosa were a rapacious bunch. Nothing they loved more than new members, and spreading word of the King to the uninitiated. He'd seen that eagerness for himself when Giocondo had approached him in Florence.

Znamenski looked at her. "We both know that the world will not change overnight. The King's advance is a slow one. We can but open the door for him. A professional thief of her caliber would come in handy, as the King gathers his power in this world."

Carla and the Man exchanged glances. Znamenski wondered if he'd oversold it. The truth was, they had thieves aplenty in their ranks. One more or less wouldn't matter. But Alessandra was... special. He'd always been able to talk to her in ways he couldn't with others. Even his new patrons lacked her appreciation for his craft.

It would be nice to have someone to talk to.

He shook the thought off and said, "Tell me about this Thorne. Why are you so frightened of them? Are they a sorcerer, then? Or a cult-leader, like the estimable Lagorio?"

"No. Thorne serves the Red Coterie."

"Ah, like that old fool in the bauta," Znamenski said, dismissively. Carla had filled him in on the dangers of the man who called himself the Cavalier. An enemy of Lagorio's, who'd set his sights on the Marquis of Avonshire when the latter had arrived in the city. The Cavalier had prowled around them for months, even prior to Znamenski's arrival, but had yet to make a substantial move. Lagorio had done much the same. Znamenski had no patience for such games. It was one of the reasons he was glad Carla was handling that end of things.

"Thorne is not like the Cavalier," the Man said. "They are dangerous. Skilled and amoral. If Thorne puts their mind to it, they might well destroy this city to eliminate us."

"Destroy…?" Znamenski paused and glanced at Carla. "Hyperbole, I trust."

She looked uncomfortable. "No. Not in the least."

Znamenski grunted, not quite able to comprehend such a thing. He'd seen what sort of destruction man could wreak in the war, of course. But if Carla was worried, it implied something on rather a larger scale than mere gas and bombs. "And this is the person with whom Alessandra has allied herself?" He blew out a breath and grinned. "That makes your attempt to kill her little friend even more foolish."

The Man looked at him, hands twitching as if eager to wrap around his throat. "Do not presume to lecture me, artist. I will do as I must whether you approve or not."

Znamenski laughed and looked at Carla. "This Thorne is clearly dangerous – fine. That makes it all the more imperative that we gain Alessandra's services. With her, we can draw Thorne into a trap and deal with them effectively. Not throw summoned monstrosities at them."

"The Byakhee would have been enough…" the Man began.

"You may go," Carla said, softly. The Man hesitated and Znamenski smiled at him, showing all his teeth in a wolfish grin.

"You heard her, signori. Be a good fellow and listen to the lady."

The Man glanced at him, and Znamenski felt a chill at the emptiness of that gaze. No anger there, no rage. Just a yawning hunger that threatened to envelop everything. But also, a consideration. As if he were unsure of how to proceed. A moment later, the Man was gone.

"I do not care for him," Znamenski said, bluntly. "Wherever did you find such a disagreeable creature?"

"He came with my husband," she said, her tone amused. He wondered what that meant. The hierarchy of his patrons was a confusing thing, even to him. Was Carla in charge, or her husband? Maybe neither. Perhaps the Man in the Pallid Mask was more than simply a servant. It didn't matter, really.

No matter who was in charge, it was Znamenski who was the important one. Without him, there was no play, and no opening of the way. He might need their money and protection, but those were finite requirements. Soon, he might not need them at all.

"Speaking of disagreeable creatures…" he began. She laughed and touched his arm. Her fingers slid down to his wrist and she turned his hand this way and that, as if looking for something.

"Why did you join us, Jan?" she asked. "Giocondo was never very clear on your reasons, I am sorry to say. Just that you had the Key of Ys, and wanted to give it to us."

"I was bored," he said, truthfully. "I wanted to do something that mattered – but more importantly, something that was interesting. You promised both." Sometimes he wondered if he had truly been in control of himself, then. Or if something else had guided him to Giocondo, and then to Carla. If so, he hoped it was pleased.

Carla nodded, and said, "What will you do, if she does not accept your offer?"

"Alessandra has never been one to turn down a good thing," he said, flexing his hand. It ached where she'd touched him, and he felt a sudden thrill of uncertainty run through him. Had it been a seduction attempt – or something else? Carla's smile flickered.

"But if she does?"

"I'll kill her myself," Znamenski said, smoothly. He wasn't sure if he was lying or not. But it didn't matter. Alessandra would see sense. She always had in the past. "Now, why don't you tell me what's worrying you?"

Her eyes flashed slightly at the condescension in his tone and he smiled. Two could play the manipulation game; it was often more fun that way. But the moment passed swiftly. She had amazing self-control, if nothing else.

"Are things truly going well?" she asked.

"Yes," he said. "The curtain will rise in a week's time. It will be exquisite, I assure you." He tilted his head. "Would you like to have dinner tonight? Or tomorrow, perhaps?" He dearly wished to get her alone, to see what might occur between them. He had no real thought as to his reasons for this attempted seduction. Perhaps it was simply that she was there, and he was in the mood to cause trouble.

She smiled, as if reading his thoughts. "This performance must go on as scheduled, Jan. We may not get this opportunity again, given the way things are going in Europe. Italy is not alone in its slide into Fascism. And Fascists are not noted lovers of art."

"Not good art, at least," Znamenski said. "But I take your point." He paused. "Giocondo mentioned that Lagorio has the Fascists in Venice in his pocket. Perhaps he could do something for us."

Carla frowned. "Why would he help us?"

Znamenski shrugged. "Why wouldn't he? We have enemies in common, after all. Perhaps we should invite them to the party tomorrow night. As a gesture of good will, let us say. Make friends, not enemies, that's my personal philosophy."

"I shall take it under advisement." She straightened his lapels and traced the buttons of his shirt. "You are doing well, Jan. I am pleased." As she touched him, he felt a ripple of something inside him – like a hunger pang, or an upset stomach. "You are an excellent servant to him. To us. You will be remembered, when I take my rightful place at his side."

"I live but to serve," he said, smiling.

CHAPTER SIXTEEN
Coterie Business

Thorne tapped a cigarette on the pack and slid it between their lips. They stood on the bookseller's portico, watching the thin river of blue overhead, broken up by fluttering shapes that bobbed and wriggled across the gap. "Venice has too many pigeons, don't you think?" Thorne said, lighting their cigarette.

"I never imagined that you were as much a fool as this," the Cavalier said. The masked man stood at the far edge of the portico. His crimson cloak was pulled close about his lean shape, and he struck the stones with his cane, as if to punctuate his statement.

"I never imagined you were such a pigeon fancier," Thorne countered. "Or were you referring to something else?" They'd known the Cavalier would show up, sooner or later. The bookseller, Matteo, was loyal to the Coterie in general but to the Cavalier in particular. The old man had likely sent word as soon as Alessandra and her ragtag band had departed.

"Cease your prevarication, Thorne. What you have done is dangerous. What are you thinking? Have you completely lost your mind?"

Thorne rolled their eyes. For so flamboyant a dresser, the Cavalier had precious little gumption. "She asked me to help her friend. I was merely obliging her."

"I do not care. I will not allow you to endanger her for your own ends."

Thorne paused, wondering why the Cavalier seemed to care so much about a thief. "Oh? And what ends might those be?"

"You know as well as I what you seek. Do not play the coy innocent with me." The Cavalier prodded Thorne in the chest with his cane. Not painfully, but just enough to make the point. "You came here in search of the Key of Ys."

"Did I?" Thorne wasn't surprised that the Cavalier knew. It was common knowledge that the Key was somewhere in the Adriatic. It had once belonged to the royal heirs of the Empire of Trebizond, but had travelled from the coasts of the Black Sea, through the Golden Horn and to the waters prowled by the Lion of St. Mark. Thorne absently recalled a delightful week in the company of a certain Englishman on holiday on the Black Sea.

"Thorne," the Cavalier said, warningly. Thorne raised their hands in surrender.

"Fine, yes." They blew a thin line of smoke into the air. "And what of it? If you will not become its bearer, why not me?" The Key was a powerful talisman, infused with arcane energies; more, it could open doors that could not be perceived, save by its wielder. Thorne wanted it, if only to keep it out of the hands of the unworthy.

"You have no understanding of the situation here," the Cavalier began.

Thorne snorted. "To which situation are you referring, kitten? Your frankly embarrassing stalemate with the estimable Don Lagorio, or your problems with these Carcosan Johnnies or perhaps your relationship with…" They trailed off meaningfully and drew a crude outline of a woman on the air in cigarette smoke. The Cavalier's grip audibly tightened on his cane, the wood creaking slightly. Thorne wondered how far they could push their fellow Coterie member.

The Cavalier was not quite a stranger, but neither was he a close acquaintance. There were others in the Coterie that Thorne knew better – and liked more, come to that. The Cavalier had always been an odd one. No one was quite sure what he wanted, or what artifacts of power he held in stewardship. He held himself aloof, at least of late, content to hide away in his beloved Venice.

"Do not speak about what you do not understand," the Cavalier said.

"I understand plenty," Thorne snapped, tired of the man's condescending tone. They jabbed a finger into the Cavalier's chest, mimicking the latter's use of his cane. "I understand you're fighting some grand war of shadows against the influence of an other-planet horror; a war, I might add, which you could win if you just asked for help."

"And what would I have to pay for this help?"

"Pocket change, given the alternative." Thorne shook their head and puffed on their cigarette in annoyance. "Why are you so stubborn?"

"Venice is mine."

"Have bloody Venice with my compliments! Enjoy!" Thorne gesticulated wildly, carving a circle of cigarette smoke on the air. "I just want the Key. Help me get it, and I'll leave. Hell, the hounds of Carcosa will probably chase after me to boot. Two birds, *mes amis*. A better bargain you will not find this side of Istanbul."

"And what of Alessandra?"

"What about her?" Thorne threw up their hands theatrically. "Why do you care about that jumped up house-breaker?" Why did Cinabre, for that matter? Thorne couldn't see a reason. Maybe they enjoyed her antics.

"She insists on aiding her friend."

"By all means, let her. We both know there's no helping that ragamuffin. She's seen the Sign. It's just a matter of time until – well." Thorne mimed cutting their own throat. "But until she figures that out, we can put her to use." They smiled. "Maybe we'll even let her live, when all is said and done."

There was a soft hiss as the blade came free of the Cavalier's cane and came to rest against the side of Thorne's neck. Thorne paused, startled. "Did I say something wrong?" they asked. The Cavalier's gaze was cold and flat.

"Neither Alessandra nor her friend will be harmed," he said, harshly. "Not by you or anyone. Not while I live."

"Perhaps I spoke out of turn," Thorne said, carefully.

The Cavalier stepped back and lowered his blade. "You will leave Venice. The Key is not meant for you, Thorne."

"So, you do intend to claim it?" Thorne said, taking a long pull on their cigarette.

The Cavalier grunted, but did not reply. Instead, he was looking at something above them. "We are being watched," he said, in a low voice. Thorne glanced up and saw pigeons perched along the line of the rooftops above. There were at least a dozen of them. The birds watched them with an unusual focus. Thorne blew smoke into the air.

"Well, ain't that a fine how-do. Friends of yours?"

"No."

"Pity. What do they want?"

One of the birds gave a convulsive flap of its wings, shedding feathers. Another twitched, as if ill. A third rotated its head in an unsettling fashion. Then, as one, they began to coo. A ridiculous sound, made unpleasant by its echo.

Something hissed. Thorne and the Cavalier turned. A cat sat on the edge of the portico. An unhappy looking animal, with mangy nicotine-colored fur and patches missing from its coat. It watched them with sickly yellow eyes, idly bathing itself.

"We should go inside," the Cavalier said, softly.

"Scared of the moggy?" Thorne replied, with some amusement. It was clear something was wrong with the animal, but at the end of the day it was still just a cat, and they were members of the Red Coterie.

The portico door opened and Matteo peered out owlishly. "Signori, I–" he began, but didn't get a chance to finish as the cat sprang toward him, arrow-quick. The little man screamed and fell back as the blur of teeth and claws caught him on the head. The Cavalier cursed and lunged, blade flicking toward the animal. Improbably, he missed. The beast sprang away and scampered across the portico toward Thorne, hissing like a steam engine on the boil. It didn't move like a cat, more like a lizard; all scuttling quickness.

Revolted at the thought of being touched by such a foul thing, Thorne swept their hands through the air in a protective gesture. The cat leapt and light flashed. The animal tumbled away, smoking. It shrieked in pain and staggered blindly, tail lashing. Its body spasmed, and its piebald skin split as something moved beneath it.

The Cavalier stomped forward and flicked the animal into the canal with a twist of his blade. "That's not a cat," Thorne said. The Cavalier looked at him, but said nothing. Instead, he gestured for the whimpering Matteo to go back inside and close the door. The bookseller hurried to obey.

The water frothed and churned at the edge of the portico for a moment, before something erupted from it. Not a cat; not anymore. Something worse. At first glance, it reminded Thorne of a child's drawing, with too long limbs and a body that was contorted all out of proportion. Its tail had split, freeing a lashing crimson line, speckled with sharpened vertebrae. Its paws had flattened and spread into simian hands. Its head was the worst; the cat's features had ruptured, revealing something beneath. Its jaws spread like a blooming flower, even as its eyes bulged. Oily tendrils emerged from its clattering maw, slowly twisting about as if testing the air.

The animal – the *thing* – took a step toward them. "Definitely not a cat," Thorne murmured. They took their cigarette from their mouth and touched it to the air. The end of the cigarette flared red, and Thorne drew another protective sigil on the air. This one was a tad more potent than the last.

"It is a beast of Carcosa," the Cavalier said, sidling away so as to catch the creature between them. "The city is infested with them."

The creature hissed and shuddered, its limbs lengthening with an ugly cracking sound. It was still growing. That wasn't good. Thorne grimaced. "I take it this isn't the first of these you've encountered," they said.

"No," the Cavalier replied.

"Any advice?"

"Yes. Kill it before it gets any bigger." The Cavalier stamped toward the creature, blade flashing. It leapt away with a curious undulating motion. Thorne struck while it was distracted. They flicked their cigarette at the creature and muttered an incantation in the ancient Naacal tongue. The cigarette burst like a shot from a flare gun, casting a painful ruby glare across the portico. The creature screamed and fell, mangy fur alight.

As it thrashed about in agony, the Cavalier spitted it with his blade, pinning it to the portico. It stiffened and fell silent. As Thorne watched in fascination, its form began to dissolve into a tarry, foul-smelling mess. Thorne stepped back, already reaching for another cigarette. "Well, that was unpleasant."

The Cavalier cleaned his blade and slid it back into his cane. "Yes. It is getting worse." He looked up and Thorne followed his gaze. The pigeons were still there. But only for a moment. Then, as one, they rose into the air and scattered across the city.

"Message delivered," Thorne muttered. They looked at the Cavalier. "That is what this was, wasn't it? A message, from them to us."

"A warning," the Cavalier said. He nudged the muck with the toe of his boot.

"What did you mean when you said it was getting worse?" Thorne asked, lighting a new cigarette. While the members of the Red Coterie were motivated primarily by self-interest, only the maddest of their number would ignore something like this. Whatever was going on here, it needed to be stopped, post haste.

"Carcosa draws nearer with every passing day."

"There is an obvious solution, if you'd care to hear it," Thorne said.

The Cavalier's eyes narrowed. "You would use her as bait." It wasn't a question.

"Might as well, given that they're already after her. Besides, you said it yourself… she wants to help her friend. This way, we do both. We draw them out, and save her. Easy as pie." Thorne smiled. "Just leave it to me, kitten. I'll have your problem solved in two shakes of a lamb's tail, or my name's not Thorne."

"Your name is not Thorne," the Cavalier said. "That is merely what you call yourself." He drew himself up. "I know your true name, and were I of a mind, I could use it to bind you with a geas that not even you could slither out of."

Thorne paused, suddenly uncertain. "But you won't."

The Cavalier said nothing. He merely turned and strode back into the shop, cane tapping against the stones. Thorne watched him go. Then, they flicked their cigarette into the canal. "Well, hell," they muttered.

CHAPTER SEVENTEEN
Teatro San Trovaso

Alessandra made her way down the narrow, crowded ledge of the Nani embankment. Nearby, music drifted from the open door of a bacari and danced convulsively along the water. She felt a sudden, nostalgic longing for cheap ciccheti – perhaps a crostini, topped with pistachio cream – but pushed it aside. She wasn't really in the mood to eat, just now. Not after what she'd seen that morning.

It wasn't just the Byakhee, but all of it. Her world had gone from one of iron certainties to something nebulous and confusing, all in the span of a year. And now she was back in a place haunted by the ghosts of her parents. She'd been old enough to understand death, when it had happened. Old enough to realize that she'd become an orphan while in a foreign city, alone and with no recourse. Only there had been, hadn't there?

Her memories of that time were dim; scattered. But someone had gotten her home from Paris, hadn't they? Someone had shepherded her back to the care of her grandfather. She couldn't recall their face, or the sound of their voice or... anything. It was like a still-raw wound on the surface of her mind, and she rarely probed it for fear of – what? Remembering something she'd rather not, maybe.

She wondered if, perhaps, she ought to ask the Cavalier about it, should she see him again. Would he answer her questions, or avoid them as he had earlier? She sighed and dismissed the thought with a shake of her head. The past was the past; her concern was the present. She looked around.

She was near Squero di San Trovaso, one of the oldest boatyards in the city, and the faint sounds of hammering and sawing wafted on the breeze. The theater Znamenski had invited her to was in the campo of San Trovaso. The rounded arches of the eponymous church rose over the largely barren square, casting long shadows that flapped and danced as the light wavered. Structures the color of dried clay looked out over the flat, stone square. A single wellhead sat in the center of things, like the spoke of a wheel.

There were no trees, no stalls. Many of the doors were barred and windows shuttered. There was a lot of that in the city at the moment. As if there was a storm in the offing. There were plenty of people around, however. Some were laborers from the nearby boatyard, or tourists. She spied a small congregation of students lurking near the entrance to an osteria, probably discussing politics and trying not to be seen to be doing so. The waters of Socialism had largely dried up in Venice since the March on Rome, but there were still some holdouts.

The rest of the loiterers were clearly stage crew and actors, taking a break from morning rehearsals. They sat in small groups, chatting and drinking. Young men with a whiff of totalitarianism about them watched these groups from the edges of the campo, occasionally scribbling notes in notebooks or muttering to one another.

The Teatro San Trovaso sat north of the church, its face at an angle to the campo. It was one of the smallest theaters in Venice, and often left out of the guidebooks. The front façade was smallish; brittle looking. The canal nearby was shady and cool in the thin light. Greenery hung over the tops of walled gardens, casting strange reflections on the muddy water. Boats navigated the serpentine length, carrying deliveries or passengers.

She made her way around the side of the building, down a short stretch of narrow passage that was little more than a gutter with delusions of grandeur. She felt the eyes of the actors and crew on her, but gave no sign she'd noticed. Let them think what they liked. In most cases, it was better to let the marks come up with their own reasons for why you were there. If nothing else, it saved you some time.

The stage door was little more than a wooden rectangle set into a brick recess. It was old and solid despite that. A holdover from previous centuries. Something had been carved into the brickwork above it… a curious, swooping shape, like a stylized sun or a comet.

Alessandra checked the door, and found it unfastened. She pulled it open and was assaulted by the smell of woodwork, paint and dust. A passage of raw brick walls and wooden floorboards unfurled before her as she stepped inside.

It wasn't La Fenice, of course; then, few things were. The passage split, veering into storage areas and dressing rooms, before continuing its route to the backstage area proper.

Alessandra could hear the hum of voices, and the clatter of tools. The occasional shout as a stagehand dropped something, or had something dropped on them. It reminded her of the few joyous months she'd spent dancing in a chorus line in Marseille.

For all its familiarity, however, there was a strange artificiality to it. The voices of the crew were fevered; snappish. The interior of the building was hotter than it should have been and the boards under her feet were warped and noisy. Boles of buttery-hued cloth were piled in out of the way corners, and the sets under construction made no sense. It all felt wrong, but she couldn't say why with any clarity.

She paused as something caught her eye from one of the storage rooms. It was dark, lit only by a single window set high in the canal-side wall. Crates of props and forgotten costumes littered the floor; dressmaker's mannequins stood arrayed in loose formation, as if awaiting orders. It was one of these that had caught her attention.

It was dressed in loose robes of golden thread, with a sharply-tined crown perched untidily on its featureless head. The robes rustled in the breeze coming through the open window, making it look as if the limbless mannequin were twitching – or dancing. Turning in place, as if to some unheard melody.

Alessandra took a step toward it, driven by some unspoken impulse to knock it over or otherwise disturb its position. But before she could so much as touch the hem of the robes, someone cleared their throat. She whirled, startled.

Znamenski smiled, cheerfully. "Do you like it? The crown's a bit art deco, I admit, but I am inordinately fond of the stitching on the robes." He had a lit cigarette clutched between his fingers, the smoke making a hazy mask of his face.

"Hello, Jan," Alessandra said. "Fancy meeting you here."

"Let's don't play dumb," Znamenski said, without preamble. "You had the big fellow following me from Florence. Might I ask why – or should I hazard a guess?" He grinned. "You know, I distinctly recall your dismissive attitude the day you delivered that tablet to me. Told me it was a waste of money, in fact."

"I was trying to be a good friend," Alessandra said, primly.

"I admit, I often despaired of your inability to perceive the ineffable. And now, you've gone from assured ignorance to some medieval variety of self-righteousness."

"Medieval?" she asked, eyebrow raised.

"You're on a crusade, my love. Medieval is the correct term." He circled the mannequin, fingering the hem of its robes. "Snatching back what you've stolen in order to – what? Balance the scales? Positively Catholic."

"So you have heard, then," she said. She looked him up and down. He looked tired; almost feverish. As if he were gripped by some unidentified malady. Something in his gaze reminded her of Pepper, and not in a complimentary way. "Good. It simplifies things. Do you still have the Zanthu Tablet?"

"I do."

"Where is it?"

"Close." He smiled at her. "I intended to give it to you."

"Past tense," she said.

He shrugged. "You can still have it, if you like. I no longer need it."

"No, you have new obsessions now, or so I hear." She looked

around. "I am surprised this place is not better guarded. Especially when you consider who is sitting outside keeping an eye on things."

Znamenski frowned. "What?"

"The young men lurking outside with their notebooks."

"Oh, them." Znamenski gestured dismissively. "Filthy little Fascists with their filthy little minds," he continued. "They are all Sado-masochists, you know. Or so Freud contends. They long to indulge their basest desires, but fear to be seen as weak. Torn between pleasure and pain." Smoke bloomed from the tip of his cigarette. In that instant, he resembled a satyr out of myth, all shaggy lusts and feral glee. "One might pity them, if one were of a mind."

"I reserve my pity for the deserving," Alessandra said.

Znamenski nodded agreeably. "Well said. They're winning though. Weak as they are, they are winning. They'll break the back of the world, just to see it grovel. You have but to look east, to Germany, to Russia… small men with small minds and even smaller souls, yearning to cut the rest of us down to size. They have a design and they will see us fit it, even if it takes a century."

"But…?" Alessandra said.

Znamenski raised an eyebrow. "But, what?"

"But, because there is always a but, Jan. You have never been particularly political; something has changed."

"Keen as ever," he said, affectionately.

"I make it a point to know things, Jan. Some people collect stamps; I collect information." She paused. For a moment, she'd thought she'd glimpsed someone – something spying on them. Like a shadow on a shadow. But it was nothing. A trick of the light. "Does this sudden political bent have anything to do with the Marquis of Avonshire?"

Znamenski looked startled. "You *are* well informed."

She smiled, pleased to have put him on the backfoot. "Forgive me, but you know there is no Avonshire, yes?"

"Is there not?"

"No."

Znamenski smiled. "Are you certain?"

Something about his expression made her uneasy. "Who is this person really?"

"My patron." He tapped cigarette ash onto the floor, and straightened the mannequin's crown. "I'm sorry about that imbroglio in Paris, by the by. Had I known, I would never have agreed to that Scarborough woman's offer."

"Why did you agree to it, Jan?"

"Would you believe that I had an epiphany?" He took a drag on his cigarette. His eyes gleamed like those of a wolf as he gazed at the mannequin. "I found something – or maybe it found me – and I was… compelled…" He trailed off and, cigarette hanging from his lips, he set about fussing over the yellow robes.

Alessandra studied him for long moments. She thought about asking him about the Key of Ys, but something told her that wasn't the smart play. Then, deciding the direct approach was better than being oblique, she said, "Tell me about Carcosa."

He smiled, and she had the distinct impression that he'd been waiting for her to mention it. "Why don't you tell me?"

Alessandra paused again, wondering if she was making the right play. She and Znamenski were clearly on opposite sides, but she still wasn't sure just what that meant in this case. After all, she only had Thorne's word that these new patrons of Znamenski's were a bad lot. Finally, she decided to try honesty. "A ... friend of mine has been dreaming of it. A place that does not, cannot exist."

"Carcosa is a dream. Utopia. A place where all men can be free." He grinned at her from behind the mannequin, his arms draped over its torso. "Your friend is lucky. Only a special few ever get to dream of Carcosa."

"Lucky? It is making her ill."

"Only because she is resisting its call," he said, bluntly. "I know that much. If Carcosa has chosen her, there is no going back. Better for her to give in, and bow at the feet of the Living God." The words slipped out of his mouth so easily, she almost thought she'd misheard. The Znamenski she knew wasn't the sort to talk of gods, save in the abstract. What had happened to him, to change him so?

"Last we spoke, you were an atheist."

"I was a child, and thought as a child. Much as you do." He gave her a vulpine grin. "Carcosa is the truth, Alessandra. The singular truth of existence. I found it at the Somme, in the red muck that flowed through the trenches. And I will show it to them here." He gestured around them. "With my newest work."

"And does this work have a name?" She looked around, uneasy. It was as if the conversation were not real, as if it were no more than recitation. As if they were acting for an unseen audience. The unease grew and she found herself looking around, expecting someone to get up and join them – or worse.

"*The King in Yellow.*" Znamenski sniffed. "I have adapted it for a modern audience, of course. Trimmed the fat, goosed the berry, as they say."

"Can we not simply let the classics stand on their own merits?" Alessandra asked. She shivered. It had become cold, suddenly. The bricks radiated the chill of sea, and the floorboards felt soft beneath her feet. She cleared her throat. "I have heard certain... rumors about this particular work, you know."

"Have you now? And what might those rumors be?"

"That it drives people mad."

Znamenski chuckled. "They said the same thing about *Don Juan Triumphant,* as I recall. Overblown nonsense; the assertion of small minds. The play is unusual, I admit, but it is no worse than any other work of decadent literature for the time. Indeed, it is a good deal milder in some aspects." He shook his head. "My patron wanted me to make an opera of it, but my musical abilities are somewhat limited."

"You mean you cannot carry a tune in a bucket," Alessandra said. This elicited a smile from him, and for a moment, he was the Znamenski of old. But the moment passed, and so too did the smile.

"*Song of the Hyades* will be remembered as a thrilling adaption of the source material. Gone, the fuzzy staging, the archaic pentameters... instead we will have music and laughter, and yes, a bit of blood." He peered at Alessandra, his face half in shadow.

"Would you like to see a bit of it? Rehearsals are underway."

CHAPTER EIGHTEEN
Bird Market

Pepper and Selim wound their way from the Red Lion down a narrow street toward St Mark's Square. Tradesmen lined the route to the piazza, bellowing to passersby. Pepper paused in front of a fruit stall, admiring the neat stack of dark green watermelons and the print of the Virgin, sat at the back of the stall amid a tabernacle of fresh laurel leaves. Something about the Virgin's face put Pepper in mind of Cassilda.

"You look distracted," Selim said. He'd procured a guidebook from somewhere and was perusing it as they walked. "What did that Thorne person do to you?"

"Showed me something is all," she said. "You ever seen one of those… whatever it was, before?" The sight of the Byakhee had stuck with her, but not in the way it once might have. After what she'd seen in Pnath, a giant bat-insect thing wasn't that scary. Instead, it made her curious. There was a whole level of existence she hadn't known about, and now here it was, practically right at her fingertips.

"The Byakhee? Yes, sadly." Selim scratched his cheek. "Only at a distance. Henri – the Comte – summoned one once. He rode it… somewhere and came back looking disheveled. Frightened. It was a look I had never seen on his face before, and never saw again until… well."

"Pnath," Pepper said. The Comte had had big ideas about what was going to happen in Pnath. But he'd wound up getting swallowed by a giant worm instead. As far as she was concerned, it couldn't have happened to a nicer guy.

Selim nodded. "Such creatures are dangerous, whatever Thorne claims. They do not belong in this world. It is good it is gone."

"I kind of want one."

"No," Selim said, automatically.

"A little one," Pepper went on. "Small enough to sit on my shoulder."

"Absolutely not." Selim resolutely looked away.

"You're no fun," Pepper said.

Selim sighed. "You know, the last time I was here, I was sent to acquire a certain book the Comte needed to perform a certain rite. I had to kill a man to get it."

"Bad guy?" Pepper asked, hopefully.

Selim nodded, after a moment's hesitation. "Very. He was the servant of a cult who see Venice as a holy site." He looked at his hands, and Pepper did as well. They were big and scarred up, and she was reminded suddenly that Selim had probably been killing people for longer than she'd been alive. He was an alright joe, but he was dangerous.

She looked away. "I wish we could leave." She wrapped her arms around herself. Ever since her little trip with Thorne, nothing looked familiar. Even the faint squall of the gulls overhead sounded… alien. Unpleasant.

"We are staying for your sake," Selim said, gently.

"That only makes it worse," she said, shaking her head. "Why's she got to meet this guy alone? That's not smart, is it?" She was annoyed by Alessandra's decision, though she understood. But sometimes, the other woman made her feel like a child.

"No, it is not. But she is the Comtesse, and I am her man."

Pepper looked at him. "You take that sort of thing seriously, hunh?"

Selim smiled. "A man must have standards." He extended his hand. "Shall we further our education, as she advised?"

Pepper laughed. "Lead on, big man." They passed through the pillars that marked the exit to the Bocca di Piazza. He paused there, scanning his guidebook, and she stopped as well, momentarily awed by the sight before her.

The shadows of the passage were banished by a great light, and the tower of Saint Mark reared up over an immense square of checkered stones. Countless arches arranged themselves in perfect symmetry to either side of the square, as if to stand in contrast against the untidiness of the surrounding streets.

Pepper whistled softly. The square was an assemblage of pillars and white domes, clean and orderly. Something about it reminded her of Miskatonic University; all those white pillars and gabled roofs and green ivy. The sea unfurled opposite the square, stretching past the limits of her vision. She took a step forward, her eyes drawn to the two towering, granite columns that braced the sea.

A winged lion crouched atop one, and a warrior atop the other. He had a sword and shield, and his foot was braced atop a dragon – or maybe a crocodile. Pepper looked up at them in sudden confusion. For a moment, it had seemed as if the warrior had looked down at her. Had they moved, or was it just a trick of the light? "Who's he supposed to be?" she asked. "Saint George or something?"

"Saint Theodore," Selim said. "The patron saint of Venice, before they stole the bones of Saint Mark in order to venerate him instead."

"Sounds like he got a raw deal," Pepper said, recalling the Cavalier's claims about his weapon. "Why'd they do a thing like that?"

"Because they are too clever for their own good, these Venetians." Selim paused, his eyes on a group of young men lounging near the sea. Pepper watched them as well.

"You know them?" she asked.

"No. I know what they are, though. Fascists, on the lookout for tourists to bother." Selim sighed. "It is a beautiful city," he said, peering intently at his guide book. He snapped the book shut and tossed it in a nearby waste bin, startling her. "But it is no Istanbul."

Pepper snorted and thrust her hands into her pockets. It didn't look so beautiful here and now. "Don't let Alessandra hear you say that."

Selim chuckled and they ambled across the square, watching the tourists, checking out the sights. Pepper tried to enjoy herself, as Alessandra had advised. It wasn't easy. The afternoon sounds swallowed her up and she tried to lose herself in the noise. More than once, she thought she saw someone keeping pace with them in the crowd, but she couldn't say whether it was a man or a woman … or something else entirely. She thought of the yellow things she'd seen in Carcosa, and shivered.

Names hung like weights in her head, but she couldn't attach faces to them; just emotion. Love and hate and fear were all pumping through her so intensely that it was hard to focus on the here and now. Cassilda, Camilla… others. Dozens. Nonsense syllables that ricocheted around her brain like shrapnel.

She shaded her eyes and looked up. The sun wavered – split. It was getting harder to recall the details of what she'd seen with Thorne. But there had been two suns in the sky over Carcosa, she remembered that much. The thought chilled her.

She blinked and the crowd around her was suddenly full of robed figures and alien accents; she blinked again, and the unsettling forms wavered and burst like soap bubbles, leaving behind holidaymakers and Venetians. She heard someone laugh nearby, and thought there was an edge of hysteria to it. The sound sent a chill through her.

A shadow passed across the face of the sun. She heard a cat's yowl, and saw the animal slink away, winding through the legs of passersby. Was it the same cat she'd seen earlier? Something told her it was. She shook her head, suddenly woozy. The city spun around her. "Are you alright?" Selim asked, and his voice came as if from a great distance. She blinked, trying to focus on him.

"Yeah. Yeah. Just a bit… you know?"

"I know," Selim said, and she believed him. "I saw many odd things, while in service to the Comte. Monsters and worse than monsters." He paused. "This is the latter, I fear."

"You sure know how to fill a girl with confidence, Selim."

He smiled. "Whatever comes, I will be here. You will not have to face it alone, whatever it is." He hesitated. "Unless it is very big, in which case I might well run away."

Pepper blinked. "What?"

"I have a fear of being eaten."

"You'd just leave me?"

"I assumed you would be running as well," he said.

"Yeah, and probably faster than you," Pepper said. She looked up as a flock of pigeons rose into the air with a loud whirring of gray wings. Something about the shape of the flock put her in mind of something else… someplace else? "The bird market," she murmured, without knowing why. Selim frowned.

"What?"

Pepper shook her head. "Nothing. Just… nothing." She looked back. Someone was following them. Her. The woman from her dreams? No. A quick glance told her it was a man. Average height, dull clothes… but his face – indistinct. As if it were always turning away from her. As if it weren't there at all. She stopped, intending to get Selim's attention when suddenly, her pursuer was right there. Right in front of her, somehow.

His face wasn't a face at all, but a mask. A plain, colorless mask, like something that might be worn by an injured soldier. But his eyes were the worst of it; twin yellow orbs that held her in place. She felt as if she had been doused in ice-water, and fire, all at once. As he looked down at her, pigeons rose up like a living shroud, obscuring the rest of the square. "Have you seen the Yellow Sign?" he asked. His voice was soft, but she heard it regardless. It insinuated itself into her mind.

She took a step back, wanting to run, but unable to look away from that awful gaze. "Have you seen the Yellow Sign?" he asked again, more intently.

"Begone," a woman's voice interjected, before Pepper could reply. The man in the mask wavered, like a mirage. Then, he was gone and in his place was a ragged beggar, clad in yellowed wool robes. The beggar shuffled away, accompanied by the shrieking of birds. Not pigeons now, but colorful birds she didn't recognize.

Pepper – no, Camilla, she was Camilla – stumbled back, the great square spinning around her. Her lover's hands steadied her. "What did that foul creature say to you?" Cassilda asked. Camilla shook her head, uncertain as to how to reply. Already, the words were fading, as was the memory of that other city… a city of islands and strange accents.

"Carcosa," Camilla said, cradling her head. "I am in Carcosa…"

"Yes, my love. Carcosa. We are safe here."

Camilla looked at Cassilda, not recognizing her at first. There was another woman's face superimposed over that of her lover, just for an instant. Then the last tatters of dream-memory slipped from her grasp. All save a name – Pepper. Who was she, this woman in her dreams? Camilla saw her, felt her fear and anxiety as her own. "Safe," she repeated, softly. "We are not safe, Cassilda. Not here, not anywhere."

Cassilda frowned and turned away. The bird market was alive with noise. A forest of tall poles, and a cage at the top of each. In the cages were colorful avians of all descriptions, brought from all corners of Aldebaran and the Hyades. They squawked and trilled and shrieked, providing accompaniment to the merchants who hawked their wares below. Citizens of Carcosa wandered through the forest of poles, laughing delightedly at the merchandise available. As if they were not under the shadow of an awful truth.

"How can you say that?" Cassilda asked. Her voice rose, and those nearest tossed startled looks their way. Camilla could hear the murmurs of unease, the envious glances, the gears turning in the minds of the courtiers. Cassilda sat uneasy on her throne. With the fall of the other great cities to madness and plague, her authority was nominal. The quiet whisper of revolution prowled the deep alleys and shadow-streets of the lower city.

"How can you say that?" Cassilda said again, in a quieter tone. "I have done everything I can to make Carcosa safe for us. For them! Here, the families of the Hyades are secure, protected from the madness engulfing the world, protected by the roiling mists of Hali!" She drew herself up, regal and powerful. The last queen of Carcosa.

"The shadows are lengthening in Carcosa," Camilla began, but Cassilda turned away, unwilling to hear it. Unwilling to see the phantom of truth that haunted them. Camilla saw the tall, thin figure of the priest, Naotalba, hurrying toward them, surrounded by his sycophants. They waved censers, filling the air with sweet smoke to banish the demons of plague.

Cassilda waved him back even as he began to speak. "Let them lengthen! I am queen by my right in Hastur, queen because I know the mysteries of the Hyades and my mind has sounded the depths of the Lake of Hali," Cassilda said, loudly. Like an actress on stage, playing to the Gods. "Carcosa is mine! Shadows and all."

But Camilla was no longer paying attention. Instead, her eyes were on the edge of the market where the beggar lurked – and not alone. Others were with him, circling through the crowd, their eyes fixed on the queen. Her guards had not noticed, or perhaps did not wish to. Camilla reached for the hilt of her sword. Was he among them? Was he in the city, even now? "Cassilda," she began, but her lover was not listening, lost in her declaration. Lost in dreams of sanity. But the world was not sane.

The beggars circled like low, yellow curs; like jackals in the ashy desert. When they came for the queen, only Camilla was ready. Her sword sprang into her hand and she met the hounds of Ys, the curs of Aldebaran, steel to steel. They barked slogans of change, of revolution, and Camilla cut them down one after the next. She was the champion of Yhtill and their knives could not touch her.

When it was done, she stood in a circle of blood. No – not a circle. Another shape entirely. She heard Cassilda scream, and saw Naotalba and his servants hurrying her away – to protect her? Camilla took a step in pursuit, but she felt a sudden weakness in her limbs. Her wound was not yet healed, and it was leaking again. She sank to one knee, and glared at the crowd. Panic thrummed through them, and even the birds were silent. Until suddenly, they were not. As one, the birds began to shriek.

It sounded like a name.

She couldn't breathe, couldn't think. Blood welled between her fingers, and she felt the tip of the knife still lodged inside her. The world went gray and then white – pallid. She slumped, lost in a swirling nothing that rose up to claim her like the mists of Hali. She fell and fell and fell – And fell – *Falling.*

Pepper gasped, jolted by a blow on her back, the back of her head. She saw a dark shape swoop overhead. Had someone freed the birds from their cages? She heard a voice, as if from far away – a woman's voice, unfamiliar. Not Alessandra, not Cassilda, but powerful like them. Used to being obeyed.

"Come, quickly – bring her inside, out of the sun. Hurry, man!"

CHAPTER NINETEEN
Rehearsal

Alessandra followed Znamenski down the twisty corridor. In the wavering gaslight, the walls seemed to lean against one another in unsettling fashion. Znamenski prattled on about the performance until she interrupted him with a question. "How big a part does Camilla have?" she asked, recalling what Pepper had told her of her dreams.

Znamenski glanced at her, his expression wary, but tinged with curiosity. "Bigger than she used to," he said, after a moment. "Camilla is an interesting character, largely because she's a cypher – empty of meaning or purpose. She can be anything you want her to be, unlike Cassilda, whose role is largely set in stone." He clucked his tongue. "Poor Cassilda. The protagonist, of course, but also the hardest role. She is at once villain and victim in my version. The queen who sacrifices her kingdom all unknowing, in pursuit of a throne."

He stopped suddenly, and Alessandra realized that they were standing in the wings. The stage was before them, bathed in golden light. "There she is," Znamenski murmured. Alessandra saw a young woman come onto stage, clad in glittering raiment that would not have looked out of place in a painting by Klimt. The backdrop resembled a lush garden, full of odd statuary and yellow-furred shapes that might have been monkeys.

Znamenski crooked a finger at one of the crew, and the man brought him a cloth wrapped bundle. Without looking at it, he handed it to her. "Here. As promised."

She unwrapped the bundle. The Zanthu Tablet shimmered in the light coming off the lagoon. An ugly thing. She quickly rewrapped it and nodded her thanks. "I am somewhat surprised you are so willing to part with it."

"As I said, it served its purpose. Now hush – listen."

Onstage, the actress began to sing, and though the lyrics were nonsensical to Alessandra's ear, they nonetheless hung on the air like the echoes of a drumbeat. Znamenski leaned toward her. "How long has this friend of yours been dreaming of Carcosa, then?"

Alessandra paused, wondering if she ought to answer. But she was here for information, and Znamenski was as good as offering it up. "Since Paris."

"Ah," Znamenski murmured. "Was it … ?"

"The things in your studio, or rather the things in the quay under your studio? Yes." Alessandra looked at him. "What did you do, Jan?"

"Me?" he asked, innocently.

"Yes, you." Onstage, scenery was shifted by bedraggled looking members of the crew. She wondered when they'd last slept. The garden was replaced by a room with high windows. Outside of them, mountains were visible and a vast lake of dark water.

"Hali," he murmured. Alessandra wanted to ask what he

meant, but Znamenski continued before she could get the words out. "You didn't really come just for the Tablet, did you?" He waved her reply aside. "No, no, it doesn't matter. Your friend's… condition is a cause for jubilation, not recrimination. She is chosen. Blessed."

"Like you," Alessandra said.

"Like me." Znamenski turned back to the stage, where the song was coming to an end. "This is a scene from the first act. Cassilda has newly arrived to take the throne of Carcosa. Enemies surround her; she is caught in a web of lies. Only the Phantom of Truth can set her free."

"And who is this… Phantom?"

"Sometimes he is called the King in Yellow," Znamenski said. "He is the true ruler of Carcosa, and of this sad world."

"The Living God," Alessandra said, recalling their earlier conversation. She watched as an actor dressed like an opium addict's idea of a priest flounced onto stage, spouting more inane dialogue. It had the tenor of challenge, but she wasn't sure about the substance. Znamenski liked his dialogue ornate and edging into the purple.

"The very same. I'm a late convert, I admit. But I saw the light."

"What light?"

He answered her question with one of his own. "Have you seen the posters, Alessandra? The bundle of sticks, the righteous fist… the sheep are stirring, and the shepherd sleeps. The only question is which wolf devours them first." Znamenski twirled his finger for emphasis. "I serve a tyrant no less cruel than man would choose for himself. But at least mine doesn't have any particular interest in a person's ethnicity."

"It is a low bar," Alessandra said. Onstage, Cassilda and the priest were having it out as various others in the cast watched in pantomime concern. The actors looked tired, despite their makeup. Frayed. They reminded her of Pepper, and she wondered how many of them were having similar dreams.

Znamenski nodded. "Yes, but it is still a bar and my point stands. You can tell which way the wind is turning as easily as I. In a year, maybe less, the streets of Venice, of all Italy, will ring out with the triumphal march of Fascist boots. How soon before the rest of Europe follows, eh? Germany is a powder keg. God alone knows what's going on in Russia."

"You are talking about war," Alessandra said, softly.

Znamenski waved the suggestion aside. "Not for a few years yet, I expect. The last one is still too fresh. But things are heading that way."

"Perhaps not," she said, but her tone lacked confidence. He was right; she'd seen it herself, in her travels across Europe over the last year. Maybe a change was what they needed. Maybe–

She shook her head and looked at him. He was smiling. "What is the answer, then?"

"Carcosa," he said. "He who reigns there will make of this world a satrapy. Things will change. The old will give way to the new. We will all be happier, in the end." He hesitated, and then took her hand. "I promise you. Your friend will be better-off if she accepts her place in the story. That is the only way she survives what is to come."

"I wish I could believe you, Jan," Alessandra began. She had him, she thought. He was playing the missionary. For whatever reason, he thought he could convert her. Now, how to turn it to her advantage?

"Would a show of good faith help?" he asked.

"It might," she allowed. It wouldn't do to be too eager. Znamenski could flip from accommodation to suspicion quickly. Onstage, Cassilda was singing something saccharine and melancholy. Actors dressed in funereal shrouds wafted about her in a stately gavotte. Alessandra watched them for a moment before continuing, "Have you ever heard of something called the Key of Ys?"

He frowned. "And if I have?"

"I want it."

"And the Tablet as well? Greedy girl." He looked at the stage. "Why do you want it?"

"So you have heard of it."

"Let us say I have. Answer my question."

Here, again, she paused. It was a gamble, mentioning the Key. But sometimes, to win, you had to make a wager. "Consider me something of a go-between," she said, smoothly. "I represent another party who wishes to procure it."

He snorted. "And here I thought you'd turned over a new leaf." He looked at her. "Who is this interested party, then?"

She smiled and tapped him on the chest. "Now Jan, you know I can't tell you that. But suffice it to say, your interests run parallel."

"Their name wouldn't happen to be Thorne, would it?"

Alessandra felt her prickle of unease grow into an itch. It was proof, if nothing else, that he was definitely involved. "And however did you come by that name?"

Znamenski tapped the side of his nose. "You're not the only one who deals in information, Alessandra. I have my own sources."

"Do they wear masks, by chance?"

"Don't we all?" He peered at her. "Why do they want it?"

"I do not ask that question."

"You asked me every time," he countered.

"Well, you are very interesting, Jan."

He preened slightly, as she'd hoped he would. There was still something of the man she'd known left in him. That was good. It gave her hope, and not just for Pepper. Thorne was right; whatever this was, it was like a disease. It was a sickness, infecting and twisting the mind. Hollowing people out and leaving an empty shell behind. Znamenski would take a lot of hollowing. Maybe he could be saved. And if he could be saved, so could Pepper.

"I will give you that," he said. "The Key... well. That's a different matter entirely. I did possess it, for a short time. But now it's in the hands of its... rightful owner. She will not part with it willingly."

"She... not the Marquis, then?"

"His wife," Znamenski said. His attentions were on the stage once more. "A Cassilda by any other name, I fear." He glanced at Alessandra. "What if I could help you get it?"

"Why would you do that?" Alessandra asked, startled by the offer. She didn't trust the artist farther than she could throw him, but she hadn't expected such an offer. Znamenski was clearly playing his own game within the greater scheme of his patrons. Maybe that explained his insistence on getting her onside. Either way, it was an opportunity.

Znamenski shrugged. "Why not? Call it a gesture of good faith." He took a breath. "Listen, there is a do late tonight, at the Marquis of Avonshire's palazzo. Fancy dress, all the trimmings. I want you to come. Consider this an official invitation. Bring this Thorne person, if you like. I shall guarantee that it will be worth your while."

"Can you do that, then? Invite me to another person's party?" Onstage, the cast was dancing as if at a party themselves. The costumes were outrageous, vibrant. Znamenski had always had a good eye for color.

"Technically, the party is to celebrate my achievements so, yes." He smiled, and reached out to take her hand. "Come with an open mind, is all I ask. Let yourself see – really see – what there is to see. I will show you the glories of Carcosa."

"Oh, I will. I look forward to it, in fact."

Znamenski smiled again and clapped his hands like a delighted child. "Excellent." He paused, head tilted, listening. "Ah. Well, we were due, I suppose." Alessandra was about to ask him what he was talking about when she heard it – the crash of wood, and the jolting stomp of heavy boots on the floor. Znamenski gestured back the way they'd come. "You'd better take your friend and go."

"What is going on?" Alessandra asked.

"Fascists, what else? They like to remind us degenerate artistic types of our place; a little citizens' raid, nothing too worrisome."

"That sounds quite worrisome," Alessandra began. "Should we call the police?"

"No, I shouldn't think so. They'll break some props and rough up the crew, but they know better than to cause too much damage. Every dog has its master, and mine is scarier than theirs." He gave her a thin smile. "I am glad to see you again, Alessandra. I hope we can come to an understanding in this matter."

"That is my hope as well, Jan," she said, and was surprised to find that she meant it. She'd always liked him, arrogant and debauched as he was. The world needed artists, even the ones with vastly inflated notions of their own importance.

He gestured sharply as shouts reached them. "Go. I'll see you tonight." He turned back to the stage, looking for all the world like a king surveying his kingdom.

Alessandra quickly headed back the way she'd come, holding the Zanthu Tablet tight against her chest. Her mind felt stretched and full at the same time, stuffed with things she thought she'd seen, but couldn't have. So preoccupied was she that she almost missed a thin whistle from the canal.

She turned and spotted a familiar face lurking unobtrusively aboard his gondola. Giovanni, the Cavalier's man, gave a wave. She quickly made her way over to him. "I expect you have a reason for being here," she said, without preamble.

Giovanni nodded. "Your young friend – she collapsed in St Mark's Square." He had his hat in his hand and he twisted it as he spoke. "I was in the area, eh? I see that big Turk carrying her someplace in a hurry, and I followed him. Didn't realize he was taking her into a church. Then the sister, she grab me and say, 'Giovanni, go find Alessandra Zorzi, eh? Bring her here, *capische*?' And I do not argue with the sisters, not me." He gestured to his gondola. "So we go, eh? I take you there, free of charge."

Alessandra hesitated, but only for a moment. "Yes. Let us go."

CHAPTER TWENTY
Don Lagorio

Matteo peered into the room without knocking. "We have a visitor."

Thorne opened their eyes and sat up on the bed. They were fully clothed, and wrinkle-free. They had not been asleep, but meditating on what had happened that morning, and then later. For the servants of Carcosa to have reacted so quickly was unexpected and disturbing. The desire to depart was tempting, but untenable. If Venice was a front in the war, the enemy had to be stymied – else it was all for nothing. They looked at Matteo. "Who is it?"

"A woman."

"Delightful. Does she have a name?"

"I did not ask," Matteo said, already turning to leave.

Thorne smirked. "Helpful as ever, Matteo. Perhaps you'd like to go tattle to the Cavalier again, eh?"

"You are unpleasant," Matteo said, simply.

Thorne blinked. "That is possibly the rudest thing anyone has ever said to me."

"You deserve worse. That young woman might have been killed – the shop destroyed – all because you were too arrogant to take proper precautions. Just like last time!" Matteo was trembling; not in fear, but rage. "The Cavalier is right about you. You cause nothing but trouble. Venice has an equilibrium and you set it to rippling with every loose word!"

"Maybe a few ripples are just what this city needs," Thorne said, checking their tie in the mirror. "Tell me about this woman. Familiar?"

"Yes."

"Ah." Thorne glanced at the bookseller. "I hear distaste in your tone. She's a rum one, then, I take it?"

"She serves two masters." Matteo delivered this statement as if it were damning. Thorne laughed and turned from the mirror.

"Two is better than one any day," they said. "How do I look?"

"Like an Englishman," Matteo said, leaving the room in a visible huff.

"I had this suit made in Paris," Thorne protested, following the bookseller. Despite their teasing tone, they watched the little man with all due suspicion. Matteo's loyalty was a chimera; neither to one thing nor another, and changeable as the sea.

If the Red Lion decided to leave, or close its doors to Thorne, there would be little they could do about it. Worse, if the bookshop decided that the Cavalier was right, it might take steps to remove Thorne from Venice entirely, and while they were fairly certain they could handle whatever Matteo and his shop could throw at them, there was no sense poking the beast. "Have you heard from him?" they asked, quietly.

Matteo grunted. "He hopes to meet Zorzi tonight."

"Where?"

"He did not say and I did not ask."

"I should be there," Thorne said.

"If he wished you there, you would be." Matteo paused. "The woman – she claims she is here at your invitation."

"Ah," Thorne said. The identity of his visitor was suddenly clear. "She must be a representative of Don Lagorio. I… extended a hand across the aisle, as it were."

Matteo stiffened. "You what?"

Thorne smiled. "We need allies, Matteo. Who better than the enemy of our enemy?"

Matteo took a step toward them, hands twitching as if he was yearning to grab Thorne by the lapels and shake them. "The servants of Cnidathqua are the enemy of all that lives in Venice. We cannot make bargains with them!"

"Carcosa is worse," Thorne said. "At least Cnidathqua is asleep. The King in Yellow is very much awake and prowling. Now, if you would be so kind as to procure some coffee for my guest and myself, I would be grateful."

Thorne stepped past Matteo without waiting for a reply and continued downstairs. They found a young woman with vibrant red hair waiting patiently at the front of the shop. She smiled at the sight of them. "You must be Thorne. Salvatore Neri's description of you does not do you justice."

"Neri is in Venice?" Thorne asked, with a flicker of hesitancy. Salvatore Neri was a sorcerer of no little skill; he also bore something of a grudge against Thorne, for reasons which entirely escaped them. The woman smiled.

"Yes. He is a loyal and true follower of Don Lagorio. As am I."

"And you are...?" Thorne asked, filing this information away for future use. Neri was a potent enemy – but could make an equally powerful ally, should the need arise.

"Elisabetta Magro," she replied, extending her hand, as if expecting it to be kissed. Thorne, never one to upset a lady, took the proffered hand and ran their lips across her knuckles. Elisabetta smiled widely – too widely. There was something eerily vulpine about her; beautiful, but it was a beauty that undoubtedly hid some potent nastiness.

"And you are here to – what? Check my bonafides?"

She laughed politely. "Nothing so forward. Don Lagorio is very aware of who you are, but he has no liking for this shop – and it has none for him. He wishes to meet outside, aboard his gondola." She indicated the door. Thorne hesitated. It was a risk, meeting someone like Lagorio on their own territory.

As if sensing their reticence, Elisabetta chuckled. "I assure you, you will come to no harm. Not today at least." She tilted her head. "Besides, you are the one who wished to speak with him."

"Point taken. By all means, lead on." Thorne extended an arm, and Elisabetta led them outside where a gondola waited as promised. It was open to the elements, and despite the gray clouds overhead, the passenger did not seem unduly concerned. "Looks like rain," they said, holding out a hand.

"Afraid of a bit of water?" Elisabetta teased.

"Not quite." Thorne glanced at the gondolier and saw something flicker behind the man's bland expression – the shadow of a rictus, and the whiff of rotten meat. A dead man then, animated by sorcery. Not the most impressive trick, but Thorne nodded respectfully to the passenger even so. "May I come aboard?" he asked.

Don Lagorio gestured to the bench across from himself. As Thorne boarded the gondola, they studied the man. Lagorio was lean and austere, dressed in a fine suit and carrying a cane. They wondered if, like the Cavalier, Lagorio was a fan of hidden blades. Probably. All these aristocratic Italians fancied themselves swordsmen.

The man's expression betrayed nothing. His eyes were dark, his cheeks hollow and his pallor was that of someone who spent too much time indoors. An academic – or an occultist. "You are Thorne," he said, as he signaled for the gondolier to put the craft into motion. "Neri's description of you was accurate, if somewhat biased."

"So your friend said," Thorne replied. Elisabetta hadn't boarded the gondola. Instead, she stood in front of the bookshop, lighting a cigarette. She looked bored now. They wondered whether she'd still be there when they got back.

"Signora Magro is my associate," Lagorio corrected, watching the buildings to either side slide past. "She pretends to be part of my Order, but in reality, she serves an American named Sanford. We have common interests, he and I, so I allow it." There was a defensive undercurrent to his words, and Thorne wondered if he were sensitive about his ranks having been infiltrated by the Silver Twilight Lodge. These little cults were always so territorial.

"I know Carl Sanford. Not intimately, but well enough to agree that is the wisest course." Thorne recalled Matteo's warning about Elisabetta serving two masters and smiled.

They wondered if the Cavalier knew as well. That might explain his hesitation in putting an end to the Order. "My own organization has had some dealings with him of late. But we're not here to discuss him, are we?"

Lagorio tapped his cane against the bottom of the gondola, and gave Thorne a hard look. "I suspect I know why you are here. But I wish to hear it from you."

"And why should I tell you anything?"

"Because it might be that I can help you."

Thorne tapped their lips with a finger, considering. This was what they'd hoped for, and they'd worked with worse devils than Lagorio, and recently. Besides, fortune favored the bold. "I am here for the Key of Ys. You know it?"

"I do. It is in the possession of a woman named Carla Avonshire née Mafei. How she came by it, I do not know." Lagorio paused. "She is the one to be worried about. Not the artist. He is a pawn of Carcosa, nothing more."

"And this young woman is – what?"

"A slightly more elevated pawn. But hers is the mind and will behind this… offensive." Lagorio smiled thinly. "I once considered marrying her myself, you know. She is from a good family, and wealthy. But in the end, I decided against it."

"Ah. Too young?"

"Too clever. Dangerously clever. She is a woman of ambition and drive. That is a deadly combination in an organization such as mine."

"You mean you were worried she might drop you in a canal one night and take over as the mouthpiece of Cnidathqua," Thorne said, with a crooked grin. Lagorio snorted.

"She would not be the first to try. I am still here."

"Not for long, if she succeeds. Carcosa is a malignancy that not even you could hope to survive. It will brook no rivals, no neighbors. Cosmic fascism run wild."

"And that is why I am here. It is why you tendered your invitation." Lagorio looked up at the clouds overhead. "Venice is mine, whatever your friend the Cavalier thinks. It is mine, and thus it is Cnidathqua's. It does not belong to Carcosa, or to the Red Coterie…"

"Or the Silver Twilight Lodge?" Thorne asked, innocently.

Lagorio grimaced. "No. Nor them either. But Carcosa is the immediate threat." He paused. "Its influence on the city is growing. You can see it in the water – look." He used his cane to indicate the canal, and Thorne saw that the afternoon sun had bifurcated into two faded red orbs. They looked up, and saw that the sun was as it should be.

"The water shows the truth, as always," Lagorio said, in a quiet tone. "It shows what is and what will be. Look. Even the shadows are tainted here."

Thorne glanced back at the water and saw that the reflections of the buildings were… wrong. Distorted, and not in the usual fashion. They hastily looked away. "I have seen the real thing. Shadows don't impress me much."

"You have seen nothing," Lagorio said, sharply. "Only what they wanted you to see. Even one of your skill cannot deny the strength of Carcosa."

"Is that why you've been content to rest on your laurels until now?" It was a risky gambit, provoking Lagorio. But Thorne needed to know the depth of the man's feeling on the matter. To his credit, Lagorio didn't so much as flinch.

"We are old, Thorne. But that does not mean we are foolish.

When the first posters went up, I knew what was coming and I have done what I can to stymie them."

"Your pet Fascists, you mean."

Lagorio inclined his head. "They have their uses."

"I'm sure Mussolini says the same."

Lagorio grunted. "But it is only so much, without openly declaring war."

"And you don't want to do that because – why?" Thorne paused and answered their own question. "The Cavalier. Of course. He would use the opportunity to strike at you."

"As we would use the opportunity to strike at him. We are in a deadlock. But it will not hold forever. We have only another night, maybe two before the King in Yellow makes his triumphal entrance into the city… and then it will be too late for all of us." Lagorio leaned forward. "I want them gone. As do you. Our aims align, in this, and so an alliance is prudent." He peered at Thorne. "I will help you, however I can."

"And what would you want in return for this help?"

Lagorio smiled. "The Cavalier."

"What about him?"

"He is tiresome, don't you think?"

"Oh, quite. He lives to be a source of frustration. What of it?"

Lagorio's smile widened, becoming sharklike. "Make him go away."

"Easier said than done, old thing," Thorne said, feeling a slight chill. "Besides, at the moment he's more useful to me than you. No offense."

Lagorio gestured in a friendly fashion. "He is not the only one who has been at war with the servants of Carcosa. We can be as useful as he – and, might I add, much less self-righteous about it."

"That does get on my nerves," Thorne admitted, turning the offer over in their head. On the face of it, it wasn't much. A promise of aid was just that – a promise. Anyone could make a promise. Thorne had made more than their share over the years, and only followed through on half of them at best. "I am open to your request, but it would have to be at a time and place of my choosing. Agreed?"

Lagorio smiled. "Agreed." He didn't offer to shake hands, for which Thorne was grateful. "Elisabetta will be at your service. She will act as… liaison, for when you wish to enact whatever scheme you are concocting."

"You place a lot of trust in me," Thorne said.

"As I said, you would not have reached out had our aims not been served by alliance." Lagorio leaned, hands balanced atop his cane. "The enemy of my enemy, eh?"

"Something like that," Thorne murmured.

CHAPTER TWENTY-ONE
Allegria Di Biase

Alessandra hurried up the steps of the Church of San Zaccaria, her heart thudding in her chest, the wrapped bundle containing the Zanthu Tablet under her arm. "Idiot," she hissed, annoyed at her own presumption. "Fool. Moron."

She kept the litany going even as she stalked through the entrance to the church, Giovanni trailing in her wake. "Are you talking to me?" he asked.

"No, Giovanni – myself," she said, and fell silent, annoyed that he had seen her anger. She still wasn't sure whether or not they could trust the Cavalier or his man. She didn't truly believe that Giovanni had just happened by at the right moment. No, he'd been keeping an eye on them for the Cavalier. The question was, why?

The interior of the church was a medley of Byzantine and Gothic stylings; lofty, slender columns separated the side aisles from the nave, making it resemble a museum gallery. It was a dim, dreary place, but mild and serene as well. She shivered even so; she'd never been greatly enamored of churches, no matter how well designed.

A nun hurried to meet them. "You are Signora Zorzi?" she asked. Alessandra nodded, and the nun led them into the rear of the church, past the altars. The room there was small, but well-appointed. For visitors, Alessandra judged. Giovanni stayed outside without being asked. Inside, Pepper was laying on a couch, dozing. Selim sat beside her, a pensive look on his face. He rose as Alessandra was shown into the room. "She was fine one moment, and the next–" he began, apologetically.

"It wasn't your fault," she said, cutting him off. Selim flinched, as if struck, then resumed his normal impassivity. She felt a flicker of regret, but instead of apologizing, thrust the bundle with the Tablet into his hands and bent to check on Pepper. The young woman was breathing easily. Indeed, she looked more relaxed than she had in some weeks.

"Do not disturb her," an authoritative voice said. Alessandra turned – and froze, startled. Another nun stood in the doorway. She was of an age with Alessandra, perhaps a few years older. It was hard to tell, in the habit. But Alessandra recognized her even so, as the other woman continued. "By the look of her, it has been some time since she had an undisturbed rest."

"Yes," Alessandra said, as she rose to her feet. She hesitated. "Hello, Allegria." The words came out softer than she intended.

"It has been a long time, Alessandra," Allegria Di Biase said. She paused, as if choosing her words with care. "You look … well."

"As do you," Alessandra said, after her own pause. She tried to recall the last time she'd seen Allegria. "I have you to thank for looking after my friend, then?"

"Your friend is very ill. But I do not think it is a physical malady." Allegria was much as Alessandra remembered. A short, round woman – vibrant, with eyes that were hard and clear and sharp. She'd never imagined Allegria might join the church; for one thing, she'd always had the impression that the Almighty would have a hard time measuring up to Allegria's standards. "What have you brought to my doorstep, Alessandra?"

"Your doorstep? I was under the impression that this was a church."

"It is an abbey, by act of Pope Benedict III. And I am an abbess. Ergo, it is mine."

"God might argue," Alessandra said, with a slight smile.

"He is welcome to try." A bit of the old familiar ferocity flashed through Allegria's eyes. She had a spine of steel, and a heart to match. "Why are you back, Alessandra?" It wasn't quite an accusation, but close enough to bring back the old defensiveness.

"Can I not visit my old stomping grounds?"

"No. Not without some ulterior motive." Allegria looked down at Pepper. "She will recover, in time. She needs sleep. I can have a bed made up."

"We have a hotel…" Alessandra began. Allegria snorted.

"A hotel will do nothing for her soul. Let her sleep here for the moment. This is holy ground, and whatever stalks her will not find her here." She gestured to the door. "Come. We will talk in my office."

Alessandra hesitated, but only for a moment. She left with a parting glance at Selim, who twitched aside the edge of his coat to reveal the revolver holstered under his arm. She nodded and followed Allegria. In the corridor, Allegria was murmuring in low tones to Giovanni. The gondolier hurried off before Alessandra could hear what was being said.

"You know Giovanni, then?" she asked, innocently.

"Is that his name?" Allegria glanced back at the room. "She is not well."

"Pepper is fine. Just exhausted."

Allegria looked at her, and frowned. "You and I both know that is not true."

Alessandra fell silent, as Allegria started down the corridor. "How long has it been?" Allegria asked. "Five years? Ten? Since before the war, at least. The last I'd heard, you were driving an ambulance on the Western Front."

"You sound surprised."

"It seemed uncharacteristically charitable of you, cousin."

"I felt I ought to contribute in some fashion," Alessandra said, off-handedly, though Allegria's use of 'cousin' made her flinch inwardly. She tried hard not to think about family these days… for their safety, as much as her own. "What about you? Get your hands dirty at all, or did you ride it out here?"

"I worked in a hospice tent, doing what I could for young boys coughing out their lungs from gas attacks or bleeding out from bullet wounds." Allegria's tone was even, but Alessandra could read the tension in her shoulders and hips. "As you said, I felt I ought to contribute. Have you spoken to your sisters of late?"

"No. Why, have you?"

"Of course. I write to them regularly. As I would write to you, if you had an address you could be reached at."

"I do not like to be tied down," Alessandra said, somewhat lamely.

"No. Then, you never did. Here we are." Allegria opened a heavy wooden door to reveal a startlingly modern office. There was even a typewriter. Alessandra stepped inside and looked around warily. Allegria shut the door behind them and chuckled. "What were you expecting? A rack? An iron maiden?"

"One can never tell, with you religious types. By the way, how did this happen?" Alessandra gestured to Allegria's habit. "You used to be quite the pagan, as I recall."

"God called to me."

"Asking for some help, was he?"

"In a manner of speaking." Allegria seated herself behind a modest desk, and gestured for Alessandra to take the chair in front of her. It was all very conservative, and very unlike the Allegria that Alessandra recalled. "Why are you here, Alessandra?"

"You invited me."

"I mean in the city."

"Why does everyone keep asking me that?" Alessandra asked, with mock indignation. She studied the woman before her, searching the mild features for some trace of the wild young aristocrat she'd once known. In those days, Allegria had been quite the daredevil – leaping from moving gondolas and climbing rooftops. It was hard to recognize that young she-wolf in the somewhat plump, matronly figure sitting across from her.

"Because we are familiar with your habits, obviously," Allegria said, with a faint trace of amusement. "Are you working for someone?"

Alessandra sat back in her chair and flung up her hands,

even as she wondered just how much Allegria knew about her career of late. "Again, why does everyone assume I am working for someone else? Am I not my own woman?" She decided to go on the attack. "Speaking of which, when did you become a nun, Allegria?"

"God called to me not long after you left Venice. And in time, I became abbess here."

"A quick rise through the ecclesiastical ranks, Allegria."

"God saw my merit, Alessandra," Allegria said, with a slight smile. The expression faded as she said, "He sees yours, too, though you hide it well."

Alessandra frowned. "What do you mean?"

"Are you a servant of the Red Coterie, cousin?"

"You know of the Coterie?" Alessandra asked, in some surprise. Allegria knew more than expected. Obviously someone had been keeping tabs on Alessandra. The thought was not a pleasant one.

"I know many things, Alessandra. Venice has ever been home to shadows, and it is my sacred duty to bring light to the dark places."

"Meaning what?"

Allegria waved the question aside. "Are you still a thief, then? Still taking what does not belong to you on behalf of wealthy fools?"

"You *have* been keeping an eye on me," Alessandra said, grudgingly.

"Someone must."

"I am no one's servant."

"Have you told them that?"

Alessandra glared at her. "Perhaps you should do it for me.

As I recall, you were always quite adept at speaking for others, and then claiming it was for their own good."

Allegria was silent for a moment. "Are you still angry about that?"

Alessandra looked away. "You would be." Even now, the memory of the last time they'd spoken was unpleasant. Allegria had taken it upon herself to act in what she thought was Alessandra's best interests, and the results had been... predictable.

"No. I would have forgiven you," Allegria said, primly.

Alessandra laughed. "You have never forgiven anyone in the entirety of your existence, *cousin*."

Allegria grimaced. "Perhaps it does not matter." She hesitated. "Have you heard of a place, or perhaps a person, called Carcosa?"

Alessandra sat back, the sinking feeling in the pit of her stomach growing harder to ignore. Giovanni's presence definitely hadn't been a coincidence. "Why do you ask?"

"Because your young friend was murmuring the term in her delirium."

Alessandra paused, wondering how much she ought to share with Allegria. Then, she seemed to know a good deal already. Alessandra was beginning to wonder just how coincidental this all was. "She is... dreaming of this place."

"She is not the only one," Allegria said. "There are many in the city of late afflicted in a similar fashion. Fits and bad dreams. A few have gone mad, and been sent to asylums by their relatives."

"I am not sending Pepper to an asylum," Alessandra said, firmly. It all seemed to come back to Carcosa. She was beginning to feel as if they'd walked into a trap, all unknowing. Had Cinabre known? Is that why he'd sent them here? Or was it all simply a coincidence? She doubted she'd get a straight answer out of anyone.

"Nor would I recommend it. What afflicts them cannot be exorcised in such a fashion." Allegria paused. "Is this why you are here, Alessandra? This affliction of hers?"

"And if I am?"

"Then I will help you." Allegria was silent for a moment. Then, "God moves in mysterious ways. You know who Giovanni works for."

"Yes," Alessandra said, slowly. "Do you?"

"Of course. It was no accident he was watching your friend. Nor was it by chance that I happened upon them. I was looking for them."

"You? Why?" Alessandra asked, startled.

"Because Matteo told me where they would be, and I needed to speak with you. Given our… history, I thought it best to approach your friend first," Allegria admitted, reluctantly. "Thankfully, I arrived in time to help."

"Or maybe your friend the Cavalier caused it, so I would have reason to trust you," Alessandra snapped. She regretted the words immediately. Allegria didn't flinch.

"Perhaps. For what it is worth, I do not think he possesses that sort of malice."

"You know him well, then?"

"As well as anyone can." Allegria paused. "What was the young woman's name again? Chiara something, wasn't it?"

"Chiara Santin," Alessandra said, grudgingly. "She is a dancer now. In Vienna."

"Her family was quite upset, as I recall."

"Which is why you should have kept your mouth shut," Alessandra snapped.

"If I hadn't, they would almost certainly have killed you. The Santin were not to be trifled with. Your parents knew that." Allegria sighed. "I did what I thought best. But I am sorry, cousin."

"You are only saying that because you want me to trust you."

Allegria nodded. "Yes. Do you?"

Before Alessandra could reply, someone knocked on the door. Allegria went to the door, opened it, and admitted Giovanni. He glanced at Alessandra. "Is she…?"

"She is listening," Alessandra said. "What did he want me to know?"

Giovanni grinned. "He wants to speak to you, eh?"

"Then why not come speak to me?" Alessandra looked Giovanni up and down. The gondolier grinned insouciantly and twirled his straw hat around his index finger. "Why send his… chauffeur?"

"He thought maybe you might be mad."

"So he sent you to take the brunt of my anger, did he?" She let an amused smile dance across her lips. "How courageous of him."

Giovanni shrugged. "I do not question. I just do what he says."

"How professional of you."

He glanced at her and sniffed. "I ask some of the others about you, you know. They say you were a thief, eh? Little girl, snatching purses. Old Fidel? He knows you. Marco. Carmen, at the American restaurant. They speak highly of you."

Alessandra raised an eyebrow. "Fidel is still alive? I would have thought he would have gotten drunk and fallen into a canal by now."

Giovanni laughed. "He has! Always climbs out, though." He put his hat back on and smiled at her. "The old man, he wants to see you, at your convenience. Before you do anything rash, he says."

"Like what?"

Again, Giovanni shrugged. "Who am I to say, eh? I just do what I'm told." He paused and handed her a scrap of paper. "He said you'd know the address."

Alessandra took the paper and glanced at it. Froze. Looked at it again. She looked at Giovanni and then at Allegria. "This – it is…"

"I just do what I'm told," he said, tapping his hat. "I am to take you there when you are ready, signora. I'll even bring the Turk, if you like."

Bemused, Alessandra glanced at Allegria, who nodded. "Well then," Alessandra murmured. "I guess one can go home again."

CHAPTER TWENTY-TWO
Inner Light

Pepper awoke groggily. Tatters of dream slipped aside, taking with them fragmented memories of Boston and Arkham, all jumbled up with Carcosa. In her head were images of a hot dog stand, only it was selling some sort of food she didn't recognize... a train station, but the trains were yellow-scaled serpents whose hisses sounded almost like singing... a dog, yellow-furred, its red jaws clamped around a child's rattle... and her father, singing a soft lullaby in a language she couldn't understand from behind a colorless mask.

None of the images were especially pleasant, especially that last one. It made her think of other things. She felt disembodied and disassociated, like she was trying to climb into a too-small space. Her hands, her legs, they didn't feel like hers. She forced the sensation aside and sat up, adrenaline flooding her. Panic followed. "Where am I?" she burst out. Selim caught her, gently, and stopped her from hopping to her feet.

"Safe," he said, simply. "In a church." His collar was undone, his tie loose. He looked relieved and anxious in equal measure, and she felt a quick stab of guilt for the trouble she'd caused him. He had a cloth bundle on his lap. She was about to ask about it until his words percolated through her grogginess.

"A church?" She looked around. It looked more like an office to her, if you ignored the religious prints on the wall.

"Technically, it is an abbey," Alessandra said, crouching beside the couch Pepper was seated on. "How do you feel?" Like Selim, she looked concerned; but that wasn't anything new these days. Guilt turned to annoyance; neither was appropriate, but she was more comfortable with the latter.

"Tired," Pepper said, running her hands through her shaggy hair. "Like I got a crowd doing the Charleston on my medulla oblongata."

"Do you even know what that is?" Alessandra asked, with a smile.

"Yeah, it's a dance," Pepper said. She looked around. "How did I get in a church?"

"Selim carried you," Alessandra said. She caught Pepper's chin, and peered into her eyes. "How are you really feeling? The doctor said you just fainted."

Pepper swatted the other woman's hand away. "Better. Did you talk to Znamenski?"

"Yes." Alessandra sat back, looking pensive.

"Well?"

"He's invited me to a party."

"There's a shocker. You going to let me go with you, this time, or what?" Pepper tried to keep her tone light, but she could tell Alessandra heard the accusation nonetheless. Alessandra frowned.

"I am sorry, about earlier. I was simply trying to – to keep you safe. After what happened with Thorne, I... overreacted slightly." Pepper figured that was as close to an apology as she was going to get, and decided to be satisfied with it.

"Thorne? Thorne is here?" a new voice interjected. Pepper peered past Alessandra and saw a nun looming in the doorway. She was young, but stern looking. "You said nothing of this earlier, Alessandra."

"Does it matter?" Alessandra asked, in visible annoyance.

The nun fumed. "Yes! I knew there was another member of the Coterie here, but – Thorne? Things are worse than I thought. They cannot be trusted."

"Preaching to the choir, sister," Pepper said. She looked around. "Where's my hat?" Selim produced her cap and handed it to her. She beamed at him and looked at Alessandra. "You never answered my question."

Alessandra stood. "We will talk about it later."

"Now's good," Pepper said, reclining on the couch, her hands behind her head. "You've been treating me like a kid this whole trip and I'm getting tired of it. I thought we were partners. So maybe we act like it, hunh?"

Alessandra stared down at her, as if unable to comprehend her words. The nun covered her mouth, but Pepper knew she was smiling. Alessandra turned on her. "What are you laughing at, Allegria?"

"Nothing. Just – well." The nun came over to the couch and sat down beside Pepper. "In any event, I must check Miss Kelly before she leaves." She smiled at Pepper. "Let me hold your hand, dear."

Pepper hesitated. "You don't look like a doctor."

"I am not. But then your malady is not physical, is it?"

Allegria took Pepper's hand and held it. Her grip was firm; warm. Warmer than Pepper had expected. She looked into Pepper's eyes, and her own gaze seemed to flicker like an open flame. "It is an affliction of the spirit. I can see it hanging on you, like a shroud."

Pepper winced. The warmth was deepening; becoming real heat, just on the edge of painful. "Yeah, so can you do anything about it?" she muttered.

"No. Nor will I pretend otherwise. But I can ease the effects." Her voice came as if from far away. It echoed strangely in Pepper's ears, and she wondered if the others could hear it as well. She wanted to look away, to ask, but couldn't break the hold Allegria's gaze held on her. "It makes you tired… irritable."

"Maybe I got good reason to be," Pepper said.

Allegria chuckled. "Maybe. Or maybe she simply cares for you."

"Yeah? Sounds like you two know each other."

"We are… old friends. Relax." As she spoke, the warmth flared into real heat. Painful heat. It crept into her bones, driving out the aches and pains she hadn't even realized were there. It felt like something was being shaken loose from her, and she glanced back and saw something yellow clutching tight to her shoulders. The sight startled her.

"What–?" she began, instinctively trying to turn around.

"No," Allegria said, softly, in warning. "Do not look at it. Do not acknowledge it. It is not real. Not unless you give it reality."

"Looks pretty damn real to me," Pepper hissed. It had no shape she could discern; just a wavey mass, like a bunch of rags or an animal skin. It seemed to stretch away from her, as if it were connected to something just out of sight. "Is – is that what's in me?"

"Yes. All who see the Yellow Sign are connected to Carcosa. Once it has a hold of you, it is all but impossible to shake it loose. That you have lasted this long is a testament to your strength of will."

"This ain't anything like what Thorne showed me," Pepper said, forcibly tearing her gaze from the mass. "I saw a – a city. People. This is – is worse…"

"Then Thorne showed you the illusion. The mask. This is what is under it. Rags and tatters." Allegria's voice echoed through Pepper's head. "It is a spiritual wound, kept open so that the thing that made it might sup upon your mind and soul. The city, the people, the things you see are not real. They are simply fever dreams."

"They feel real enough," Pepper said, touching her side. She could feel the ache of Camilla's wound as if it were her own.

"That is the trap it has laid for you. The more you believe, the tighter its hold."

"That's what Thorne said." Pepper looked at her fingers, half-expecting to see blood. "Only neither of you has explained how I'm supposed to stop that."

Allegria tightened her grip on Pepper's hand. To Pepper's eyes, her face shone almost like the sun. "Because we cannot. All we can do is give you the tools by which you might defend yourself. Imagine yourself with a–"

"A sword," Pepper said, softly. She closed her eyes, trying to envision the blade. Camilla's blade. Old. An heirloom, she'd called it. The memories were there, just beneath the surface of her mind. She remembered – Camilla remembered – how it felt to hold it. She saw… felt… something; a great serpent, coiling and thrashing in a black forest. She felt the jolt in her arms as she – as Camilla – took off its head.

"Remember, it is not real," Allegria said, her voice a whisper. "What you see, what you feel, it is a performance for your benefit. To lure you in and trap you in a web."

That was what Thorne had said. But something about it sounded false; or at least, not quite right. Trying to pretend a thing wasn't a thing made it harder to ignore. The story was trying to tell her something, or maybe Camilla was. Maybe there was another way.

Maybe…

The warmth faded, and the light with it. Pepper found she was still holding Allegria's hand. She hastily let go and sat back. Allegria smiled tiredly at her. "I have done what I can. The rest is up to you."

Pepper nodded jerkily, still imagining the weight of the blade in her hand. It felt good; familiar. She could almost remember it, but not quite. She concentrated on the feel, trying to hold it solid in her mind. The fatigue she'd been feeling since they'd arrived in Venice was gone, or had at least receded temporarily.

When she looked up, she saw that Alessandra and Selim were watching her. "What? I got something on my face?"

"You look better," Selim ventured. He glanced at Alessandra. "Does she not look better?"

"Yes." Alessandra gave Allegria a somewhat accusing look. "What did you do?"

"Helped her to help herself," Allegria said. She dabbed at a gleam of sweat on her face. "It isn't much, but it might mean the difference between sanity and madness for her. The curse of Carcosa is potent; it burrows in and replaces your thoughts with those of something else. Most people break. That she hasn't yet means that she has a good chance of surviving with her mind intact – if we can find a way to stop whatever they are planning."

Pepper wanted to comment, but the words wouldn't come. She knew she was strong; you couldn't be a cabbie in Arkham and not be tough. But the thought she might falter had never seriously crossed her mind until now. She'd heard the screams coming out of the sanitorium windows on stormy nights. That wasn't the sort of fate she'd ever imagined for herself. She clenched her fists, trying to drive the thoughts back. "Maybe we should go find that Cavalier guy. He might be able to help."

"Interesting you should mention that," Alessandra snorted. "First he wanted us gone; now he wants our help. He should really make up his mind."

"What'd I miss?" Pepper whispered to Selim.

He nodded hesitantly. "It seems the abbess is in league with the Cavalier."

Pepper grunted. "Well, that ain't suspicious at all."

Selim nodded. "We also appear to have walked into the middle of a war."

"Great." Pepper stood. Both Allegria and Alessandra looked at her. "The Cavalier didn't strike me as a bad guy... weird, maybe, but not bad. And the sister here helped me. Maybe we should trust them. Like I trusted Selim, remember?"

Alessandra frowned. "It is not the same."

"Thorne said he could get rid of this thing inside me, but

only if we got him that key-thing, right? Well maybe the Cavalier can help us do that." Pepper took a breath. She felt better than she had, but that wasn't saying much. The thought of going crazy wasn't a pleasant one either. She pushed it forcefully aside, consigning it to the place at the back of her head where she put all her fears. She could be scared later. She squared her shoulders and looked at Alessandra. "It's not like we got anything to lose, right?"

Selim cleared his throat. "She makes a compelling argument."

Alessandra threw up her hands in resignation. "Fine! Yes. I will hear him out." She looked at Selim. "I want you to take the Zanthu Tablet back to the hotel. Hide it someplace safe." She looked at Pepper. "In the meantime, how would you like to see where I grew up?"

Pepper grinned. That was exactly the sort of distraction she needed at the moment. "What are we waiting for?"

CHAPTER TWENTY-THREE
Palazzo Zorzi

Alessandra watched Selim cross the square, the Zanthu Tablet tucked safely into his coat. She felt a flicker of guilt at handing the task off to him, but under the circumstances it was likely the wisest course. "He'll be okay," Pepper said, as if reading her thoughts. "He's a tough cookie."

Alessandra glanced at her. The young woman sat nearby, legs kicking over the edge of the wellhead she was perched atop. The afternoon light made her shadow look odd, almost bifurcated. As if there were two of her sitting there. "Yes, well, takes one to know one, I expect."

"Ah, applesauce," Pepper said, dismissively. She watched the pigeons grouped in clusters across the square. "You think this is on the level?"

"Which bit?"

"Your old digs."

Alessandra frowned. "Who is to say? I will not know until I see the place."

"You think it's a trap?"

Alessandra was silent for a moment. She'd been wondering

the same thing. "No," she said, finally. "If you are worried, you do not have to come, however."

"Applesauce," Pepper said, bluntly. "I'm tired of playing tourist. Besides, you don't talk enough about all this stuff. You know everything about me, but what I know about you could fill a shot glass."

"I am an open book. Ask me what you like."

"Okay. So tell me about your pal, Allegria."

"Allegria is not my friend, she is my cousin."

"Sounded like you two were friends to me." Pepper sniffed. She looked around. "Nobody is looking at us. Not even those chuckle-wits sitting over there watching everyone else." Alessandra followed her gaze, and saw a few young men sitting at a nearby bacari. They had that familiar, half-feral look she was coming to associate with the city's newest political agitators.

She chuckled and indicated her outfit. "Fashion is the devil's plumage, yes?"

Pepper blinked. "I – yes?"

Alessandra smiled. "Clothes make the individual. They tell observers a story. The right suit, a man becomes all but invisible. For a woman, it is different. We have a harder time blending in, even when dressed down. My mother taught me to do the opposite – to dress up, rather than down. Bright plumage and shiny talons will make most men hesitate."

"Like you're too good for the bums, you mean?"

Alessandra tapped the side of her nose. "Exactly. If you dress down, men will take advantage. Dress up, they are frightened. Both reactions can come in handy, on occasion. My father always said that class is something one should take no notice of, unless it is of benefit to you."

"Sounds like a smart guy."

Alessandra's smile turned sad. "He had his moments." Her memories of her parents were tainted by their deaths; whenever she thought of them, the fact that they were no longer here rose up to remind her that she still had no idea why they'd been in Paris that night… or why they'd died, ostensibly visiting the home of a friend.

Pepper cleared her throat. "Do you – do you think that the Cavalier is on the up and up about knowing your parents?"

Alessandra frowned. "I do not know. It is certainly possible. They had many friends."

"Do you think Cinabre knows?"

"Almost certainly," Alessandra said, flatly. She felt the urge to change the subject. To think about something, anything else. She was saved from any further questions by the arrival of Allegria. The abbess strode across the campo, scattering the pigeons. The birds didn't go far, of course.

"Are you ready to go?" Allegria asked. "We should do so before it gets dark."

"We? Where do you think you are going?" Alessandra asked, as Allegria joined them.

"I thought it best that you have someone you trust with you."

"How nice. When do they get here?" Alessandra asked, snidely.

Allegria sniffed. "You are tiresome."

"I beg your pardon, I am sure," Alessandra said. She hesitated, then stuck her tongue out at the nun. Allegria's eyes narrowed and for a moment Alessandra thought she might return the gesture. Then, dignity won out and Allegria sighed.

"Childish to the last."

"They will put it on my tombstone," Alessandra said. "Why are you really here?"

"To help, as I said." Allegria looked at Pepper. "How do you feel?"

"Like I got all my marbles, thanks," Pepper said. Allegria paused, as if deciphering Pepper's statement. Then she nodded.

"You are strong, as I said."

Alessandra turned her attentions to the other side of the campo, and the waterfront quay, where a line of vessels was waiting to take on passengers. Gondoliers shouted friendly insults at the steamer pilots and deliverymen, as the sun set over the city and rain clouds gathered. Pigeons fluttered through the air, making weird spirals overhead.

Alessandra watched the birds with a suspicious eye, but they made no attempt to land. Satisfied that they weren't planning to be bothersome, she sought out Giovanni, and saw him lounging against a mooring post, his craft blocking several others from edging past. He ignored the complaints of the other gondoliers, and concentrated on the orange he was deftly peeling with a small knife. "There's Giovanni," she said. Pepper hopped off the wellhead and together the three women headed across the campo.

He grinned when he saw them, and stashed the remains of his orange. "Ah, signoras, right on time! It is about to rain. It would be best if we were on our way before then, eh?"

Giovanni erected an open-sided canvas tent to keep out the rain as they boarded. The gondola bobbed gently as Giovanni pushed them away from the wharf and into the stream of traffic. "He wanted me to tell you that he will meet you there," he said. "You are to make yourselves at home until he arrives."

"How nice of him," Alessandra said. She peered at Allegria. "Did you know?"

Allegria was silent for a moment. "About the house? Yes."

"How did he come to own my parents' home?"

"You should ask him."

"I am asking you, cousin."

Allegria looked at her. "I do not know."

"You never told me how you came to be allied with him."

"You did not ask," Allegria said, meeting her gaze. "Did he tell you of the dangers that threaten this city and its people?"

"Yes."

"That is the reason. God put me here so that I could protect Venice. The Cavalier was called to do the same... and so were you."

"I have what I came for," Alessandra said. She glanced at Pepper, who was staring up at the clouds. "Thorne has promised to help her, if I steal something for them."

"You cannot trust Thorne." Allegria paused. "What do they want you to steal?"

"Something called the Key of Ys. Ever heard of it?" Alessandra studied Allegria with a wary eye. Perhaps the Cavalier was after it as well. That might explain Thorne's reticence.

"No. But then, my experience with this sort of thing is thankfully limited." Allegria frowned. "If Thorne wants it, I advise you not to give it to them."

"Why? What does the Cavalier have against Thorne?"

"I do not know. I know only that the last time Thorne came

to Venice, innocent people died. Neither I nor the Cavalier wish a repeat of that." Allegria peered past Alessandra, at Pepper. Alessandra followed her gaze, and saw that Pepper was still staring upward.

"Pepper? What are you looking at?"

"Pigeons," Pepper mumbled. Alessandra looked up. Pigeons flowed through darkening sky in a formation quite unlike any she'd ever seen. They swooped low over the gondola, as if to get a good look at the passengers.

"Vermin," Allegria said. "They are the servants of the enemy. He co-opted the pigeons first, and then the rats and stray cats. Little minds and souls, easy to twist into servitude. It is only recently that he has started on men."

"He who, Allegria? Who is this enemy?" Alessandra leaned close, one eye still on the pigeons circling above. "What is he called?" She could feel a faint tremor in the air, as of anticipation. From the look on her face, Pepper felt it as well.

"The King in Yellow," Allegria said, softly. Pepper closed her eyes.

Alessandra paused. "Like the play?"

Allegria frowned. "Yes – and no. The play is nothing more than tall grass, and the King is the tiger lurking in it. The truth is, I do not know what he – it – is. I know only that his influence spreads through Venice like plague." She was silent for a moment. Then, "How many shuttered shopfronts did you see?"

Alessandra hesitated. She hadn't thought much of it at the time, but Allegria was right. There were too many shops closed, too few people other than tourists on the streets. It was as if the city were hunkering down and awaiting a storm.

She reached into her pocket and found the flyer Selim had given her. She showed it to Allegria. "Is this the cause, then? Znamenski claims to have adapted the play. Could that be why…?"

A pigeon swooped down under the canopy and snatched the flyer from her hand. She was so startled that she barely reacted until it was too late. They watched the bird vanish into the dusk. The others peeled away as well, as if they had accomplished what they set out to do… or as if something had frightened them.

"We are here, signoras," Giovanni said. The gondola bumped against a wharf decorated with two great pillars that rose to a portico roof. Alessandra hesitated, and then stepped onto the wharf. The sound of the water was like whispers, welcoming her home.

"It has not changed," she said, softly. The inner portico was even as she recalled; pillars of jasper and porphyry, a floor of deep green, dotted with motes of white and the mosaics on the walls slyly peeking out through pergolas laden with vines. But on second glance she saw that the vines were now brown and shriveled, the mosaics cracked. Water gathered on the floor, seeping up from compromised foundations.

"Things do not change in Venice," Allegria said.

"Some things change. You were not a nun, last we spoke."

"But you were a thief. I presume you still are?"

Alessandra frowned. "In point of fact, I have turned over a new leaf."

Allegria laughed. "That I have a hard time believing!"

At the far end of the portico was a set of steps inlaid with marble, leading up to the entrance to the palazzo. Once, her grandfather would have been waiting for her there, arms wide, eyes twinkling. Now, there was only a closed door, with tarnished bronze facings.

"When was the last time you were here?" Pepper asked.

Alessandra sighed. "Just after they... well." Their footsteps were loud in the space, echoing eerily, making it seem as if they were not three but several. "My parents were not aristocrats," she said, stopping at the foot of the stairs. Wanting to go up, but not wanting to, at the same time. "My father was a gambler, my mother a dancer. They were also thieves – something of a family tradition. My father won this place off some dissolute fool of an aristocrat in a game of cards."

"Rigged?" Pepper asked, all innocence.

Alessandra glanced at her, feigning indignation. "What a dreadful thing to even suggest." She paused. "But yes, I assume so." Pepper laughed.

It began to rain at last; a light drizzle, but promising greater fury later on. "We should go inside," Allegria said. She looked at Giovanni, who was tying up the gondola. He waved them inside.

"I will wait out here," he called. "Go in. The doors are open."

"I suppose we must," Alessandra said. Steeling herself, she started up the steps. Allegria and Pepper followed, silent as shadows.

Inside, it was much as she remembered. The tight corridors, the draperies, the pictures. It was as if someone had gone to great lengths to ensure the place was kept as it had been the last time she'd seen it. Pepper whistled. "Swanky," she said.

"Not in comparison to some, but I was happy," Alessandra said, as she led them to the dining room. It seemed smaller than she recalled, but was otherwise the same. Faded murals clung to the plaster walls; lions and tarasques stared down at her with vaguely disapproving expressions. "Hello, old friends," she said, quietly. She'd wiled away many an hour in this room, counting beasts of legend or weaving stories about them for her sisters.

Her fingers traced the murals on the walls. The family who had owned the place before her parents had been old by the standards of Venice. They had proudly counted two doges and one infamous murderer among their lineage; a paltry number, given the centuries they'd resided in the city. Her own family line was less staid; murderers and magicians; alchemists, healers and witches; artists, gamblers, thieves and assassins. Or so her grandfather's stories had made it seem.

She ran her hands along the piscine carvings that decorated the edges of the table. Even now, it was in good condition, if a trifle dusty. Everything was as she remembered. Someone had seen to the upkeep of the place, at least. Perhaps the Cavalier himself, though why and how he'd come to do so she could not imagine. He'd claimed to have known her parents but there was no way of telling if that was true. She could imagine any number of reasons why a man like that might lie about such a thing.

Cinabre had warned her, in his own oblique fashion, not to trust the other members of the Red Coterie. Not that she trusted him, either. If Cinabre was helping her, it was for reasons of his own. "It is as I remember," Allegria murmured.

"Have you been here since…?" Alessandra began, and stopped.

"No."

"Since what?" Pepper asked.

"Since they died," Alessandra said. Outside, the rain had begun to slacken and the first stars peered through the clouds. The rising moon painted the canals in cold silver. She could hear the sounds of the city now. Long shadows slid along the walls of the buildings on the opposite side of the canal. Laughter reached her ears, and drunken singing.

"Venice dances while the world sleeps," Allegria murmured.

"Once, we danced with it," Alessandra said, looking at her. "Do you still dance?"

"Only with God."

Alessandra laughed. Then stopped, as she heard the creak of the water door below. She glanced at Allegria, and the other woman nodded. She'd heard it as well. Alessandra set her revolver down on the table and took a long, steadying breath. "Pepper… get the door."

Pepper did so, revealing the Cavalier. He stood in the doorway, as imposing as he had been the day before. Rain slid off his cloak, and dripped from the brim of his hat. "Signora," he said, doffing his tricorn in a show of old-world respect.

"Welcome home."

CHAPTER TWENTY-FOUR
Carla

Carla Mafei poured herself a drink. She did not offer one to her guest; to her knowledge, he did not drink. Or eat, or sleep. He simply... was. "She took it, then?" She stood in the drawing room of the Palazzo Mafei – no, Avonshire now. The new name still tasted odd. She had grown up here, but these days it felt unfamiliar. As if it were changing around her. Becoming something far grander than any of her ancestors could have imagined.

"Yes," the Man in the Pallid Mask said. He stood as if at attention, hands clasped behind his back. His tone was even, his eyes flat and empty. The perfect vessel. She did not know who he had been, before he had claimed the mask – or it had claimed him – nor did she know where he had come from, before he had made himself known to her.

"And where is she now?"

"Palazzo Zorzi."

Carla raised an eyebrow. "Are they connected?" The windows were open, and she could taste rain on the air.

"Yes."

She frowned. Another thing Znamenski had forgotten to mention. The artist was handsome and clever – too clever. If she had not been surer of herself, she might have suspected him of plotting something. "You followed them?"

"For as long as I could. The house is… protected. My servants could not get close to it." He sounded almost perturbed by this. She wondered if that was arrogance talking, or simply bewilderment. "The Cavalier is there."

"Our enemies do not trust one another," Carla said, sipping from her drink. "They plot and scheme behind one another's backs. The King sews dissension in their ranks." She smiled and looked out at the dusk. Despite the clouds, the sun's reflection floated in the canal like a ship… the ship of a king, sailing into a newly-conquered port. She turned and glanced at her husband. The Marquis of Avonshire sat silently in his bathchair, his rheumy eyes fixed on a better world than this.

He had been so vibrant when first they'd met. So full of life and power. The holy throne of Carcosa, his to claim. He had told her stories of lost kingdoms… of Trebizond and K'n-Yan and Ys. Of kingdoms fallen and forgotten. Of Carcosa, the greatest of them all. The city which all other cities were but sad reflections.

Hildred, her dear husband, had intended to claim Carcosa, and make himself emperor of all the world. But he had failed. His mind, his will, had not been up to the task. He had crumbled away in pursuit of his obsession and left her with the ruin of a kingdom to rule. And so she had. She had risen up and made herself queen. Her generals obeyed her orders, and now all that remained was to throw wide the gates of Ys, and allow her new lover inside.

Her king.

The Man in the Pallid Mask was his emissary. She looked at him. "What of the one called Thorne. Did your… display frighten them?"

"No."

"Ah." Carla set her cup down. "A shame. They are… unpredictable."

"Yes."

Carla gestured dismissively, banishing her moment of worry. "The party tonight… I expect Jan invited her. Zorzi, I mean. I do not wish her to come."

The Man was silent. She could not tell whether he approved or not. Finally, he said, "Why? Zorzi is no threat. Znamenski warned us not to provoke her…"

"We have already done so. She is a threat. So I would like her to vanish." Carla met his gaze. Once, she'd been unable to do so. These days, it was easier. The emptiness in his eyes was no longer frightening. Instead, it held a promise – of love, of power. Everything a young woman could want.

"Znamenski will not like that."

"Znamenski's use to us is coming to an end."

The Man made a sound that might have been a chuckle. "He will not like that either."

"He is an artist," Carla said, sharply. The Man tilted his head, studying her the way a hawk might study a particularly fierce mouse.

"Art is in the eye of the beholder," he said, after a moment. He swept out a hand, and the room behind him changed, as if the world were a curtain and he had pulled it aside. She saw shining towers rise over the misty waters of Hali. They blazed like the twin suns overhead, and she heard the jubilant horns of her people as they welcomed their rightful king. The skies rippled like curtains, the clouds skidding across them like things alive.

The Man stood behind her, his hands on her shoulders. No, not his hands – the hands of the King. "Do you see, Carla? Do you see the beautiful thing that awaits us all?"

"I do," she murmured. She felt light feather touches along her arms and face – the tatters of the King. The wind rose, splitting the mists that obscured the lower parts of the city. She saw wildly cheering throngs awaiting her arrival on the quays of Carcosa. "Will I rule well, my love?"

"As only you can, my love," the King said, in a voice at once impossibly deep and soft as silk. The rumble of a panther, the whisper of a lover. "You will be queen in Carcosa and of all the world, when I am upon my throne."

Hildred gave a rattling moan, and she glanced at him in annoyance. He reached for her with a palsied hand, his eyes bulging. How dare he intrude upon this moment! "You had your chance," she hissed. "Your will faltered. Mine will not. Now be silent in your misery."

"Do not judge him harshly," the King whispered in her ear. "Not all who bear the blood of the Hyades are fit to rule. Not all who see the Sign understand the glory it promises." His voice changed as he spoke, becoming something harsh. The clash of swords, the rattle of guns. The snapping of an animal's teeth. "Carcosa is only for the worthy. For those who understand the cosmic truth. All others will but pave the route with their bones."

Carla shivered as he loomed over her, impossibly tall, as

vast as the night and as cold as the depths of the Adriatic. She wanted to turn, to look up into that immortal – impossible – gaze, but knew that to do so before she was made ready was as good as suicide. One could not simply look upon a king without being struck blind or driven mad. That had been Hildred's mistake. A long finger caressed her jaw and she purred in satisfaction.

"You will make a fine queen, my love. And all will be well when I have come into my power. We will make a beautiful garden of this sad world. All waters will be Hali, all cities Carcosa. And we shall rule in power and glory forever…"

As if from far away came a dull boom, and she shook her head as she realized someone was knocking at the door. She flung up a hand and tore her eyes away from the grandeur of what was to be. It hurt, but the here and now was where she must be. "Enter," she called out, her voice barely more than a croak. The King was gone, and only the Man stood in the room now, looking as placid as ever.

A servant opened the door, admitting the Florentine, Giocondo. He stopped when he saw her guest and stared at the Man in startled silence. Carla smiled. "Never fear, he was just leaving. Weren't you?"

The Man inclined his head. "As you wish." A moment later, he was gone, as if he had never been there at all. Or perhaps he had merely stepped behind the curtain. Carla poured Giocondo a drink. "I assume you have news."

"Y- yes," he said, looking around. He gratefully took the drink and knocked it back. "The dress rehearsal went well today. Jan seems… pleased. Annoyed by the limitations of the theater and the – the interruptions, but otherwise pleased."

"And what did you think?"

"It is… magnificent," Giocondo said. He paused. "He's made some… alterations to the script since the last rehearsal. Nothing major, but I thought it best you knew ahead of time."

"What sort of alterations?"

"New dialogue, a new scene, clearly improvised on the fly. Connective tissue, he calls it. I call it giving a pretty actress additional time on stage. You know how he is…" He trailed off as he noticed her expression. "Not that I think anything is going on. He has been quite the gentleman with the cast."

Carla smiled thinly. "Yes. He has his eyes on other prey."

Wisely, Giocondo kept his thoughts to himself. Carla didn't care for the Florentine. He was a devoted servant of Carcosa, as they all were; but he was arrogant. He saw the coming of the King not as a great change, but as a simple switch of rulers.

More, he fancied himself a replacement for Hildred, and not just as leader of their organization. The way he looked at her when he thought she was distracted was revolting. He saw only the mask, not the power beneath. In his foolishness, Giocondo imagined himself as a regent-to-be, not as a servant of the King. Time would disabuse him of that notion. But that was a concern for later.

He cleared his throat, and she dutifully refilled his glass. "There was something else," he said, after a moment. "The Zorzi woman." He hesitated. "I think we should–"

"It is already taken care of," she said, pleased with her own foresight. "She will be dead soon enough."

"I take it she won't be attending the party tonight,"

Giocondo said, with some amusement. Carla smiled and went to refill her own glass. Giocondo followed her. "Of course, Jan will be unhappy. He is quite taken with our thief."

"So I noted," Carla said, in a warning tone.

Giocondo ignored her and pressed the matter. "Any fool can see that he is also taken with you." He leaned close. "The question is… do you feel the same?" He reached for her. She froze for an instant, astounded by the impertinence of the gesture. She caught his fingers – and twisted. Giocondo blanched and stumbled.

"My feelings are for my King, Florentine. And only for him. Jan Znamenski is a useful pawn in this great game of kingdoms, as are you and the others. We all serve him in our own way, and we are all rewarded as he sees fit. You and the others are destined for greatness. Do not let foolish ambition thwart your destiny."

He whimpered as she increased the pressure on his fingers, bending them to the point of breaking. To her eyes, his face flickered – as if his pale features were but a mask, concealing something within. Something yellow, that snarled piteously as she held its paw. She leaned close to him. "Can you hear them, Giocondo? Do you hear their howls in your dreams? If so, rejoice… for your reward is a great one indeed."

He looked up at her in confusion. But that bewilderment became something else – awe or perhaps terror. He wailed and she released her grip on his fingers, allowing him to fall and scramble backward, weeping like a child. He had seen something in her eyes, and it had unmanned him utterly. The thought pleased her to no end.

She wiped her hand on her dress and turned to the

windows. "Do get a hold of yourself, Giocondo. The time for weeping will be here soon enough." She lifted her cup and drank deep, her eyes on the setting sun and the water.

"Besides, we have a party to get ready for."

CHAPTER TWENTY-FIVE
Cavalier

"Allegria, I did not expect you," the Cavalier said, his tone laced with admonishment. From what Alessandra could see, Allegria didn't seem bothered. Then, she'd never let the opinions of others dictate her mind.

"Yet here I am," the abbess said. The Cavalier circled the table.

"Yes, here you are."

"And where were you?" Alessandra asked, her hand resting on her revolver. The Cavalier looked at her. There was a smell clinging to him – acrid, rancid. A sickly sourness emanating from the black tarry substance splattered on his boots and the hem of his robes.

"Something unpleasant was lairing in the arsenal. A beast." He took a chair and sat heavily. "I sent it back to where it came from."

"Which was where, exactly?" Pepper asked, looking interested. The Cavalier met her gaze and tapped on the table.

"You know where, child. You can hear them howling in your dreams, I expect."

Pepper sat back, a queasy expression on her face. When she didn't say anything, Alessandra gestured and caught his attention. "Why did you want us here?"

"I wanted you here. These others..."

"Are here on my invitation." Alessandra sat back. "If that bothers you..." She let the implication hang. The Cavalier studied her with calm eyes. Was that a spark of amusement she saw there, or frustration? Perhaps both.

"You always were a stubborn child."

Alessandra frowned. "Forgive me, but I do not recall you being around when I was a girl. And I think I would remember a face like yours." She'd been wracking her brain since they'd first met, trying to recall him, but – nothing. It was as if something had splattered acid on the surface of her memory, eating gaps in it.

The Cavalier guffawed and slapped the table. "Do you think I wear this mask all the time?" The bauta mask twitched in such a way that she thought he might be smiling. "These days, perhaps. But then – ah, then I saw no reason to hide my face. Your parents knew my features well. Indeed, your mother often complimented me on my nose."

"On your...?" Alessandra paused. Men and women of all persuasions had come in and out of the house. Some were criminals, like her parents. Others were marks. Which had the Cavalier been? Maybe neither. Maybe something else. "Were they – did they work for the Red Coterie?" It seemed ridiculous on the face of it, but... what if?

The Cavalier threw back his head and laughed. "By the blessed saints, no. Your parents were too smart for that." He peered at her. "No offense."

"Some taken," she said. "But I will find it in my heart to forgive you." She looked around. "I thought my grandfather would have sold the old pile, after I left."

"He did. To me." The Cavalier turned his gaze to the window. "It was a good investment. Or so I told myself. In truth, I think I simply missed them. Memory accretes in this city. It overlays itself and makes it hard to forget anything." His eyes flicked toward her. "You can have it, if you like. The palazzo, I mean. I will make a gift of it to you."

Allegria gasped. Alessandra paused, taken aback by the offer, as well as what he'd said about her parents. She wondered what he'd meant by that. "Why?"

"Why not? Do you not want it?"

"I…" She hesitated and then shook her head. She glanced at Allegria, who was frowning as if upset. "Perhaps this is a conversation best saved for later. Once matters before us have been settled."

He sighed. "If that is your wish." He tapped on the table for a moment, then said, "You met your artist friend, then." It was more an accusation than a question.

"I did."

"He is not to be trusted."

"No. Then, one might say the same of you."

He grunted. "You also met with Thorne."

"Let me guess – they are also not to be trusted?"

The Cavalier nodded. "No. Thorne is loyal only to Thorne." He paused. "What did they want?"

She glanced at Pepper. "To help, they claimed."

The Cavalier followed her glance, but didn't inquire. Maybe he already knew what had happened at the bookshop.

"In return for what? There is always a price with Thorne."

Alessandra considered demurring, but decided against it. Something told her that the Cavalier already knew the answer to his own question. "Something called the Key of Ys. Do you know of it?"

The Cavalier sank back into his seat, as if fatigued beyond measure. "I do. I also know who has it. Clever, Cinabre. Clever, clever." This last he murmured almost to himself.

Alessandra leaned toward him. "Tell me."

"The Key is currently in the possession of a man called the Marquis of Avonshire. It is a false title. One cannot be a lord of a nonexistent place."

"Unless it does exist somewhere… like Carcosa."

"You know nothing of Carcosa," the Cavalier said, heavily. Harshly. "And you should be glad of it, girl."

Alessandra frowned. Annoyed by his tone, she pressed on. "Allegria here said you were at war with the King of Carcosa. Is that true?"

He glanced at the nun, who didn't so much as flinch. "The abbess speaks too freely."

"Maybe. But is she right?"

The Cavalier sighed and rose from his chair. "I am at war with many enemies. My battles have many fronts. Carcosa, and its servants, are one." He went to the window and stared out into the deepening night. "But there are others."

"What can you tell me about it?" Alessandra gestured to Pepper. "Thorne seemed to think it was real enough. Were they wrong?"

"No."

She paused. "Can the Key be used to help her?"

"If used properly."

"By Thorne?"

"No."

"By you?"

The Cavalier hesitated. He looked again at Allegria, who gave a terse nod. "Yes, but Allegria would serve as well. She has certain... gifts."

"I can vouch for that," Pepper said, softly. Alessandra looked at her and Pepper added, "She... did something to me, earlier. It's like she – she turned down the volume on it. It's not gone, but it's not eating at me anymore."

"A temporary reprieve," Allegria murmured.

The Cavalier nodded. "When – if – the King manifests in this city, you will be overwhelmed, as will all others who have seen the Yellow Sign. Which is why we cannot allow it to occur... no matter the cost."

"Leave that aside for the moment," Alessandra said sharply, reaching over and taking Pepper's hand. The younger woman looked tense; the Cavalier's words had clearly bothered her. Too many people of late had been telling her she was doomed; that only made Alessandra all the more determined to help her. "If these enemies of yours have it, that implies that they need it. Yes?"

The Cavalier hesitated. "Yes."

"So, we get it, we stymie them and we help Pepper. Simple, no?" She decided to leave aside the fact that Znamenski had offered to help her retrieve it. She wasn't entirely certain she could trust the Cavalier yet. The Key was, well, the Key. Everyone wanted it. That meant it was her best bargaining chip. If she could get it, she could dictate terms as she pleased.

The Cavalier shook his head. "No. Not simple. It is guarded and not just by men. I have attempted to secure it on more than one occasion without success."

"Ah, but then you are not me," Alessandra said. "I have ways of gaining entrance to places I should not be. Ones which do not require lockpicks or magic or blades."

The Cavalier grunted. "Znamenski."

Alessandra smiled. He was quick to catch on. Perhaps that was why her parents had liked him. "Exactly. Jan, for whatever reason, is trying to woo me. So, I will give him the chance. The Marquis of Avonshire is his patron, and he has been seen by Selim going in and out of that worthy's palazzo. Thus, he has access. If I cozy up to him, he might well grant that access to me." She sat back with a triumphant expression. The rough outline of a plan was already taking shape in her mind.

Allegria snorted. "And if you overestimate your ability to... cozy?"

"Then I will point a gun at him." Alessandra tapped her revolver. "Either way, I will get into that palazzo and acquire that Key."

"And then?" the Cavalier asked, quietly.

Alessandra looked at him. "Then I will give it to whoever can help Pepper. If that is Allegria, so be it. Thorne can ask her for it."

"You never did have a sense of honor," Allegria said, though her tone was almost admiring. "Then, if you had, you never would have become a thief, would you?"

Alessandra sniffed. "Honor is for rich aristocrats. I am a hardworking member of the proletariat." Allegria laughed. So did Pepper.

"Ain't you a countess?" the young woman cackled.

Alessandra frowned. "Only technically." She sat back. "Is that plan satisfactory, Cavalier? Or do you have something to contribute?"

The Cavalier grunted. "You remind me very much of your mother."

Alessandra hesitated. Allegria rose to her feet and gestured for Pepper to follow suit. "Come, Miss Kelly. I wish to see if the chapel is still intact."

"What do you need me for?" Pepper asked, darting a glance at Alessandra.

"Protection, obviously," Allegria answered, already at the door. Pepper hesitated, but Alessandra gave her a shallow nod. She wished to speak with the Cavalier alone, and was grateful, if a trifle surprised, that her cousin had seen that. Pepper reluctantly followed Allegria out of the room. Alessandra waited until she could no longer hear their footsteps and then said, "I would like the truth, signori."

"Which truth?"

She frowned, annoyed by the cryptic wordplay. "The truth about my parents."

"They were thieves and rogues. Your father was a cheat at cards, and your mother was a pickpocket and too quick with a knife. They left some men floating in the canals, and others in the poorhouse." A moment later, he added, "They were my friends."

"Then you must know how they died," she said. She knew the basics; the date, the place, but not the particulars. Not how or why. She had been in Paris with them, had been outside that house on the Rue d'Asueil when whatever had happened… had happened.

"And if I did?" he asked. His tone was almost teasing... but also sad.

She recalled the way the shadows had thickened and the way the birds in the trees had screamed – the smell, like lightning and the air knotting in her lungs. The sound of her father, arguing with someone; of her mother, screaming. An unearthly radiance that she'd once convinced herself was nothing more than gaslight dancing on damp air.

And then, the silence. The dreadful, all-consuming silence.

Moments were all she had. A scattering of images and fragments. All she knew for certain was that it had happened in the night and by the morning, she and her sisters had been orphans. Her grandfather had stepped in, but had refused all entreaties to tell them anything. That mystery had weighed on her for most of her adult life; it crouched waiting at the back of her subconscious, prowling forth when she least expected – or wanted – it. And now here was someone who could answer those questions... if she were brave enough to ask them.

But before she could give voice to the words, he hunched forward, hand pressed to his side. She saw that his coat was wet there, and not with water or the tarry substance.

"You are injured," she said, rising and circling the table toward him.

"It is nothing," he said, waving her back. "The beast got in a lucky blow. I have endured worse, I assure you." He reached up with his free hand and pulled off his mask and hood. Alessandra froze, just for a moment, as she saw the ghastly ruin hidden beneath.

The Cavalier's head resembled a struck match, and the flesh of his face was puckered by keloid tissue. A few wisps of hair were all that remained on his scalp, and his nose was little more than a frayed ridge. Yellow teeth showed through ragged cheeks, and his neck was frilled with old burns. Only his eyes were undamaged; human. "I am very pretty, am I not?" he asked, with a harsh snicker.

"What happened?" Alessandra asked, as she sat back down.

"It is an old injury; an old story." He set his cane on the table beside his hat. His fingers traced the coiling designs that marked along its length. "Your mother saved my life that night. And your father recovered the item I failed to acquire."

"Then it is true, you were friends," she said. It was hard to imagine. Her grandfather must have had a good reason for not mentioning it. Maybe he feared she would follow their path. Then, in a roundabout way, perhaps she had.

"Oh, more than that," he said, with a weak chuckle. "It is not for nothing that your father was known as a swordsman without peer." His eyes twinkled as he said it, and she sat back, bemused by the implications.

"I cannot imagine what my mother thought of that," she said.

"She was quite enthusiastic, as I recall." He chuckled again, at her startled expression. "As I said earlier, I was more handsome then. Not the grotesque wreck I am now." He indicated his burned features. "Oh, those were good days. We made quite the fellowship, your parents and I. We… lived and loved. In this city, that is a sort of magic."

Alessandra was silent for a moment. The question,

interrupted before, came to her lips now. "Were you there when they died, that night in Paris?"

He hesitated. "We had … gone our separate ways by then." His tone was heavy with pain, and not, she thought, from his wounds. "Sometimes I wonder – but no. Such fancies are for lesser men. The past is a different country, and we are well out of it." He fixed her squarely with his eyes. "Even so, I promised your mother I would … look after you," he said, and the bluntness of the statement startled her. "While you are in Venice, you are under my protection."

"I feel better already," Alessandra said, not caring that it came out somewhat acid. If the Cavalier noticed, he gave no sign. "So you tried to chase us away earlier in order to – what? Protect me from this king who wears yellow?"

"More than that, but yes. Him too." The Cavalier sighed. "Venice has been a battleground since the first island was settled. But unless something is done, the tattered banner of Carcosa will flap atop the Doge's palace."

Alessandra scratched her chin. "Znamenski invited me to a party tonight. At the palazzo of his new patrons." She glanced at the walls, with their murals of rearing animals.

"You must be careful," the Cavalier said. "Carcosa is … predatory. It will pounce when you least expect it."

"Then we have that in common," Alessandra said, with a fierce smile. But her bravado faltered as an odd sensation went through her and on the walls, the murals *contracted*. The animals turned, as if suddenly aware of her presence. Their eyes glowed fiercely and she felt a strange pull … or perhaps a warning. At the same moment, she heard a shout from somewhere else in the house. Allegria.

She was on her feet and out the door in moments, the Cavalier at her heels.

CHAPTER TWENTY-SIX
Pale Shadows

"Alessandra! Come quickly!" Allegria's voice echoed from upstairs. Alessandra took the steps two at a time, her heart pounding. Something had happened to Pepper – she knew it, could feel it churning in her insides.

The Cavalier called out something from behind her. Alessandra wasn't listening. Childhood memories flooded back to her; sunlit chases through narrow corridors and the impact of youthful limbs against centuried plaster. She heard her father singing as he shaved in the mornings, and the smell of her mother's perfume.

She swallowed against a sudden wave of sadness and found herself at the door to her old room. She'd shared it with her sisters, but it was empty of everything save a single bed now. The pictures were gone from the walls, the toys. Her grandfather had cleaned it all out, put it away safely somewhere. Or maybe the Cavalier had. Not something she liked to think about, so she pushed it aside.

Pepper stood in the center of the room, holding a rapier in her hand. Allegria had her back pressed to the wall, trying to stay out of the way. "Where did she get a bloody sword?" Alessandra demanded.

"She found it under your bed," Allegria snarled in reply, trying to keep out of reach of the slashing weapon. "One of your old toys, I presume."

Alessandra ignored her and peered at Pepper. The younger woman's dull, unfocused gaze was fixed on the blade in her hand. She muttered something indistinct and lifted it. "Pepper?" Alessandra began. The rapier slashed out, and Alessandra narrowly avoided injury as she leapt back. "Pepper… stay back. I do not wish to hurt you," Alessandra continued, hesitantly. Pepper moaned and lifted the sword. She fell into a stance, displaying far more skill than she ought to have had.

"No mask," she muttered. "No mask!"

Pepper lunged, blade whipping out in a gleaming arc. "Pepper," Alessandra barked, trying to wake her. But the dream – the hallucination, whatever you wanted to call it – held her too tightly. Pepper whipped the blade up and around, cutting a line along the wall as Alessandra ducked aside, mind torn between concern and confusion.

In that moment, she saw another woman's face where Pepper's ought to have been. She looked terrified; mad. Her clothing, her posture, all of it was different. "Camilla," Alessandra said, taking a chance. The woman's eyes widened and she made to speak but only gibberish spilled from her lips.

It wasn't Pepper. Camilla, then. But why was she attacking? Unless…

Alessandra paused, waiting for the sword to dart toward her again. Her hands slapped together, catching the blade. A risky maneuver, and more of a party trick than anything else. But it worked. She forced the blade down and away, until the tip thudded into the floor. "Camilla," she shouted. "Stop!"

Pepper hesitated. That was it! Alessandra booted her in the stomach and snatched the blade from her hands, sending it clattering across the floor. Pepper leapt for it, and Alessandra caught her by the back of her jacket and flung her against the wall. She held her there, with an elbow against her throat. Pepper – or Camilla – cried out in frustration and perhaps fear. It was all Alessandra could do to keep her pinned in place.

"Someone help me, for the love of God," she cried out. Allegria lunged forward and caught one of Pepper's arms as she flailed at Alessandra. The Cavalier entered a moment later, his grisly features twisted in what might have been concern.

"What is happening?" he demanded.

"Pepper is – she attacked me." Alessandra nodded toward the fallen rapier. "She found that somewhere." She winced as Pepper's struggles grew more frenzied.

The Cavalier snatched the weapon up and paused. "I gave you this," he said, absently, as he tossed it onto the bed. Then he turned and made a curious gesture. Pepper stiffened and slumped, like a puppet with her strings cut.

Alessandra looked at him. "What was that? What did you do?"

"A simple enchantment. She will sleep for a few hours."

"Handy," Alessandra said, as she and Allegria got Pepper onto the bed. She plucked the rapier up and extended it in his direction. "What did you mean, you gave this to me?" She recognized the sword now – a gift from one of her tutors, though she could not recall the young man's name and face, she could recall her father had thrown him out one day, after a bitter argument.

"It is of no importance now," the Cavalier said, looking down at Pepper. Allegria stood beside him. She seemed unsurprised by his grotesque countenance. "This is not the doing of our enemies. It is something else."

"A warning," Allegria said.

Something struck the window. Hard. Alessandra whirled. A pigeon sat pressed against the glass. And not just one. They were all but perched atop one another, little pink eyes fixed on her and the others. It was hard to tell how many with all the shifting and fluttering. One of them opened its beak as if to vomit. Something long and twisting emerged, dripping and vile. It was too large, too thick, to have been inside the bird, or so it seemed to her. It quested toward the glass, coiling and twitching. It was the color of jaundice; of illness.

The yellow thing struck the glass with a wet sound, and she flinched back, her heart thudding against her ribs. "What in the name of heaven is that?" she whispered, nauseated by the sight of it.

It wanted in. She had a feeling that wouldn't go well for them if it managed it.

"A thing of Carcosa," the Cavalier said. He drew his sword-cane and tapped the tip against the glass. With a flick of his wrist, he scratched something into the surface of the pane, and the pigeons vanished as if blown back by a strong wind. "Come. Quickly."

"What about Pepper?"

"I will stay with her," Allegria said, taking the rapier from Alessandra. "You go."

Alessandra hesitated, but only for a moment. Her scalp was prickling; something was happening... something was here. She raced after the Cavalier and found that he was already headed outside, down into the courtyard. She paused only long enough to retrieve her revolver and then was out the door. She stopped at the top of the steps, struck by a sudden incongruity.

In the fading light of dusk, the buildings on the opposite side of the canal looked wrong. Not distorted, not exactly, but wrong nonetheless. She flinched as something fluttered past, just out of the corner of her eye. A pigeon?

No.

It was too big, too unpleasant looking. And the feathers...

More of them swooped and dove between the buildings, their unnatural speed making them indistinct. The whirring of their wings was like machine-gun fire. Then – silence. She could no longer hear the flying things, or see them.

Long shadows crept across the stones of the courtyard and she felt as if they were hemming her in. The Cavalier stood below facing the water door, Giovanni by his side. The gondolier was babbling rapid-fire, but none of what he was saying made sense.

Alessandra descended to join them. "Can you feel it?" the Cavalier asked. "The enemy has come to us."

Alessandra didn't reply. Her eyes were fixed on the canal. In the red gleam of the afternoon, the water was the wrong color. Not brown or blue or even green; a hue she didn't recognize.

The surface rippled, as if something were moving beneath it. "What is going on?" she breathed, softly.

"We are under attack," the Cavalier said, flatly. "Gird yourself, child. Trust your instincts, not your eyes." He motioned Giovanni back, and the gondolier made for the stairs without argument. Alessandra wondered how often he'd experienced this sort of thing.

As she made to reply, something like a puffball rose slowly from the water, slick and shimmering. More followed, until more than a dozen hovered over the surface of the canal. Though they made no approach, she nonetheless felt as if they were watching her. A forest of eyes, shining in the dark.

Something low and yellow passed across the edge of Alessandra's vision. A dog? Whatever it was, more of them prowled along the edges of the bank, staying out of sight, not entering the courtyard, but looking as if they wanted to. They moved strangely, at once like animals and windblown rags.

"The hounds of Carcosa," the Cavalier said.

"Is that what they are?" Alessandra lifted her revolver. "And what do they want with us?" But she already knew the answer to that. Had Znamenski betrayed her, or was this something else?

"I want you."

The voice was unfamiliar – and coming from behind her. She and the Cavalier turned to see a man in a light brown suit standing behind them, his hands clasped behind his back. How he'd gotten inside without them noticing, she couldn't say.

He wore a curious mask; featureless, save for the eyes. It was the eyes that truly caught her attention. They were... flat.

Tawny. Flecks of gold floating in yellow. Something about them reminded her of Murano glass.

"Would this be the King I hear so much about, by chance?" she asked, glancing at the Cavalier. He shook his head.

"No."

"Ah. But he is an associate, I expect."

"Yes. I am." The intruder's head tilted like that of a hawk studying a mouse. "You are Alessandra Zorzi. A thief."

"I was." Something about him reminded her of Arkham, and a man named Zamacona. Only Zamacona hadn't been a man. Not really; rather, he'd been something playing at humanity. A monster, wearing a man's face. The thought sent a chill through her and her fingers tightened on her revolver.

"Once a thief, always a thief," he said, in that same emotionless tone.

"Such a cynical outlook," Alessandra said. "You know, I met a fellow like you once. Most unpleasant." She felt something – a rush of air, a damp waft from the canal – and glanced over her shoulder. The hounds were prowling closer.

"Begone from this place," the Cavalier said. "You have no power here."

"I beg to differ," the intruder said. He raised his hands, and the hounds began to yelp and bay. The sounds were like screams, or laughter. As if the gesture were an invitation, the creatures boiled into the courtyard. They were not dogs or men or anything Alessandra had ever seen before, and she was glad that her eyes couldn't focus on them.

The Cavalier lunged to meet them, his cloak swirling, his skull-like countenance grinning maniacally. As he did so, Alessandra whirled and shot the masked man. It caught him high in the chest and he staggered back, but didn't fall. Something oily and dark spilled across his jacket and sleeve from the wound. Not blood; something else. Ichor, maybe. He touched the wound and studied the substance smeared on his fingers for a moment, before his eyes fixed on her. "You shot me," he said, and she heard irritation in his flat tone.

"Let us try for two," she said, and snapped off a second shot. Improbably, the second shot missed. One moment the target was there, the next he wasn't. Instead, he was right in her face, right up close, one hand gripping her wrist while the other reached for her throat. She lashed out instinctively, aiming for where a gentleman was weakest. Her knee shot up but he didn't so much as flinch. Instead, he caught her by the neck and lifted her with hideous ease.

"Tedious," he said. "You are tedious, thief. Why struggle against what is to come? It is a paradise, compared to this dismal place."

"One – man's paradise – is another's purgatory," Alessandra choked out, as she flailed at his face with her free hand. Her fingers scraped the edges of the eyeholes in his mask, and she gave it a quick tug.

He screamed. The sound was so unexpected that she stiffened in shock. He flung her away and clutched at his face, as if she'd injured him somehow. "You – you – you…" he shrilled, in high piercing tones that were utterly unlike his earlier manner. Alessandra glanced at her fingers and saw more of the oily dark. In dawning horror, she realized that the mask wasn't a mask at all. It was a part of him.

She pushed the thought aside as she rose to her feet. She caught a glimpse of strange, tall towers and minarets poking above the neighboring red-tiled rooftops, and she could hear the sounds of battle, or celebration, or both, somewhere in the distance. It was as if it were still changing, moment to moment, becoming someplace *other.*

Fear coursed through her, but she crammed it back down into its hole. There would be time to tremble later. For now, there was only survival.

Her thoughts juddered to a sudden stop as the masked man's hand caught her by the hair, dislodging her hat in the process. He jerked her backward and hissed, "You should never have come here, little thief. The glory of Carcosa is not for such as you."

She slammed the heel of her shoe down on his instep and he released her. She spun and drove stiffened fingers into the hollow of his throat. Her martial skills were a tad rusty; she preferred to fence with words. But she could still crumple a windpipe the way the old English cricketer had taught her, as a child.

He stepped back, gurgling slightly. His eyes bulged behind the mask; fury burned in them now. The rage of a predator unused to the struggles of prey. She grinned defiantly at the thought and felt a rush of adrenaline as he took a wary step toward her. "Come on then," she said, readying herself. "Come and have a go, signori. You might devour me, but I will see that you choke on me all the same, eh?"

At the sound of her bravado, he hesitated. Then, his attention strayed to something behind her. She heard the whisper of silk, the rustle of a cloak, and then something silvery bright slid past her and into the masked man's chest.

His eyes widened to such a degree that she thought the

flesh of his face might rip. A thin, wailing moan slipped from him as he wrenched himself off the blade and staggered away, clutching at his chest.

The Cavalier stepped past her, his robes in tatters, but otherwise unharmed. The man in the mask fell to his knees and rasped something. The shadows seemed to bulge and swell to engulf him – and then he was gone. Alessandra turned, but the hounds were gone as well… save for a few tarry patches on the stones.

The Cavalier panted and leaned on his sword-cane. "Now do you see?" he asked. "Now do you understand what we face?"

Alessandra didn't answer. Things were rapidly spiraling; Znamenski clearly wasn't on the same page as his patrons. Perhaps that was why he'd offered to help her get the Key. Was there some sort of power struggle going on among the followers of Carcosa? If so, what did it mean for Pepper? Too many questions, not nearly enough answers. But she knew someone who might have them.

"I need to talk to Thorne," she said.

CHAPTER TWENTY-SEVEN
Decisions

When Thorne arrived, the palazzo was silent and dark. Even the gulls nesting along the rooftops had ceased their rapacious song as the night came on. The water door was open, and they entered the courtyard unchallenged, save for a brief chill that heralded the palazzo's more subtle defenses. According to some, there was a Mnar starstone embedded in the structure's foundations. Nor was it the only building with eldritch protections in Venice. The old Doges had known what slept in the lagoon, and had made certain that at least part of their city would survive come the beast's awakening.

Thorne brushed such thoughts aside. That was a worry for the future, and likely would never come to pass. Not if the Red Coterie had its way. That which slept would remain sleeping, or dead, or both, whatever Don Lagorio hoped. The sun would continue to rise, the world would keep turning and the myopic inhabitants of Earth would never notice the horrors that lurked just beyond their threshold, and so on and so forth, et cetera ad nauseam.

Inside, it was as silent as out. They'd expected to hear

voices raised in argument, at least. Zorzi struck them as the argumentative sort. But perhaps it was for the best. A few more moments with their own thoughts was no bad thing.

Tonight was the night they had to decide whether to go through with Lagorio's demand and take the Cavalier off the board. Assassination was frowned on, among the Coterie. It happened with greater regularity than any of them liked to admit, but was still frowned on. Thorne wasn't concerned with the displeasure of the others; they might not forgive, but they would understand.

The morality of such an action didn't weigh particularly heavily on Thorne. Rather, the real question was whether it was possible. The Cavalier was old and canny. Like Cinabre, he'd survived an awful long time and that meant only one thing – he was good at staying alive. Thorne was confident in their own abilities, but even so... there was a crumb of doubt. If they made the attempt and failed, well that would be unfortunate. The Cavalier likely wouldn't kill them, but they certainly wouldn't be in any position to claim the Key of Ys. And that would be a real shame.

"Fortune favors the bold," Thorne murmured to themselves as they reached the dining room and found the Cavalier waiting for them. "Matteo said Countess Zorzi wished to see me. Imagine my surprise when he said where."

"You do not sound surprised," the Cavalier said.

"Oh, your little hidey-hole was what they call an open secret." Thorne looked around the room with interest that was only partially feigned. "So this is the infamous lair of the Cavalier, eh? Somehow I expected something... danker. More depressing."

"Quiet. We have matters to discuss."

"Of course, forgive me." Thorne paused. "Where are they?" They raised an eyebrow and looked about, as if searching for the women. "Not abed, I hope. A bit early in the evening, isn't it? They're not children, after all."

"I wanted to speak with you privately, first."

"How very paternal of you," Thorne murmured.

"Enough. Tell me what you have been up to."

"Right to it then. Fine. Lagorio is willing to set aside his differences if you are."

The Cavalier grunted. "Lagorio? You spoke with him?"

"Of course," Thorne said, fiddling with their cravat. "The Order is a power in Venice. They have resources we do not. Resources that they will marshal on our behalf, if we agree to their terms for a truce."

"He cannot be trusted."

"No, he cannot. Nor can we, frankly. No party in this arrangement is trustworthy. But we all want our mutual foe gone, and they are willing to help. Given what I've seen, I am inclined to take them up on the offer. Needs must, eh?"

"Pretty words, but it is still a deal with the devil." The Cavalier shook his head. "Lagorio must be desperate to even propose such a thing…"

"Technically, it was me who made the suggestion. And I stand by it. No one wants an apotheosis event; or, at least in Lagorio's case, not this one. Our enemies are dug in to the very marrow of Venice, despite your best efforts. To root them out we need manpower. Lagorio can provide that."

"And what does he want in return?"

"A trifle."

The Cavalier was silent for a moment, and Thorne began to wonder if they'd overplayed their hand. Their fellow Coterie member was old, but not a fool. Erratic, but not stupid. Thorne had enough self-awareness to know that they often underestimated the intelligence of those they moved in opposition to. It was a failing that they had attempted to correct, but with little success.

"What does he want?"

"As I said, it is of no matter. We can discuss it later."

"Later," the Cavalier muttered. His gaze strayed to the window. "Alessandra believes the Key of Ys is within her reach."

Thorne nodded, pleased. She was as resourceful as Cinabre had implied. "What happened, earlier? Something unpleasant, I gather."

"We were attacked. By the Man in the Pallid Mask."

Thorne hissed under their breath. "That creature has lived too long. Someone needs to put it down for all our sakes."

"I made the attempt, but he fled before I could finish him." The Cavalier tapped his cane with his finger. "Blessed steel does wonders against something so foul."

"I expect it does." Thorne paused. That the Cavalier had managed to injure a being as potent as the Man in the Pallid Mask was impressive, if true. Thorne resolved to be more wary. "That isn't all of it, though, is it?"

"The young woman, Pepper… she is possessed."

"The Yellow Sign," Thorne said, knowingly. They'd expected this. The young woman was as good as dead. Really, killing her would be the merciful option but they doubted such a suggestion would be appreciated. The Cavalier shook his head.

"This is not simply madness, but something else. Something is reaching out from within her, as if trying to make contact."

"That is what it does–" Thorne began. Again, the Cavalier cut them off.

"As I said, it is different. I do not understand how."

"Well, I look forward to seeing it for myself when they wake." Thorne sat back. "Perhaps I can be of assistance, eh? A bit of the old whatsit?" They waggled their fingers but the Cavalier showed no amusement.

A familiar voice said, "I hope it is more effective than last time."

Thorne turned, frowning. Alessandra stood behind them, looking distinctly ruffled. "Hello, Thorne. Took you long enough to get here."

"I came as soon as Matteo informed me of your request," Thorne protested, though it wasn't strictly true. First, they'd sent word to Elisabetta Magro, asking for another meeting. It was always best to keep one's allies appraised of new developments.

Alessandra sniffed. "I am sure. I thought you were sent here to help. Thus far, you have done little of that."

"Oh, I've been very busy on your behalf, I assure you," Thorne said. "Why, I've even secured some allies for the struggle ahead. Which is more than I can say for you two. By the by, heard about your little set-to." Thorne clucked their tongue in what they hoped seemed sympathetic. "You cannot go back to your hotel room, obviously. They will be waiting for you there."

"They will stay here," the Cavalier said.

"Yes, that might be for the best," Alessandra agreed, if

somewhat reluctantly. "Selim is bringing our bags from the hotel." Thorne smiled at her.

"How does it feel, then, to be back in the old homestead?"

The woman frowned. "What would you know of it?"

Thorne raised their hands in surrender, amused by her anger. It was clear her patience was frayed. "Not a thing, kitten. Merely curious. Our masked friend here says you have some way of getting me my Key. Let's hear it."

"I spoke with Znamenski. There's a party tonight, at the palazzo of the Marquis of Avonshire. Jan invited me."

"Ah," Thorne murmured, in understanding. How convenient. Perhaps fate was on their side after all. They paused as a question occurred to them. "But if he invited you, why did this other fellow try and kill you?"

"I think Jan is playing his own game. He offered to help me get the Key. I do not think he would do that if he was totally aligned with the interests of his patrons."

Thorne scratched their cheek. It seemed that they weren't the only one planning a double-cross. Then, artists were a notoriously unreliable bunch. "Znamenski wants you to join him," they said. "It is the nature of the beast. Those who have given themselves to Carcosa wish for others to do so. The more who believe, the easier it is for the thing they worship to manifest. That is why they chose a play as their ritual – what is suspension of disbelief, but a form of belief, however temporary?"

"It does not matter why," Alessandra said. "What matters is that it is an opportunity. You said that you could help her if I got the Key." The last sounded almost like an accusation. "Is that still the case?"

Thorne smiled. "The Key of Ys can close the path to Carcosa, as well as open it." Which was technically correct, if not strictly true. What had been seen could not be unseen. Once you had visited Carcosa, it never left you. At best, you could avoid the attentions of its inhabitants, which was easier for some than others.

"How?" Alessandra demanded.

They shrugged. "A ritual." A simplification. With the right words and tools, a barrier of sorts could be erected between the afflicted soul and the horrors that hungered for them. It wasn't foolproof, but these things never were. Either way, Thorne saw no reason to share that particular downside with the woman. She was already suspicious enough.

"And you know it?" Alessandra asked, dubiously. Thorne felt a flicker of annoyance. Hadn't they said that they could? Who was she to question their abilities?

"Yes, they do. As do I," the Cavalier said. Thorne glared at him.

"So, it makes sense. I will go, get the Key and bring it back here. We will perform whatever ridiculous ritual is required, and that will be the end of it."

"Sounds like a plan. So when do we leave?"

"You say we," Alessandra said. She smiled slyly, and Thorne felt a sudden stirring of unease, as if they'd been baited into a trap. "Are you coming with me, then?"

"I'm quite in the mood for a knees-up," Thorne said, warily. They leaned toward her, grinning like a cat with a mouth full of feathers. "You'll wear something pretty for me, won't you, kitten? Wouldn't want to let the side down, would we?"

Amusingly, Alessandra didn't pull away. Despite their

better judgement, there was something compelling about her. Thorne knew she was attractive, confident – but utterly untrustworthy. Then, the same could, and had, been said of Thorne themself. Even so, when she took their hand, they were startled. They stiffened slightly, eyes wide. "No, we would not want that," she purred. "Definitely not."

"Ah, yes, well, I expect you won't, at that," Thorne said, sitting back.

CHAPTER TWENTY-EIGHT
Revel

Night had fallen and the party was in full swing when Znamenski deigned to make his entrance. He'd come as Pulcinella, and even crafted his own mask just for this occasion. The mask was yellow, of course, as was the rest of his costume. It was at once a statement and an affirmation, though he doubted anyone would notice.

Music washed over him as he entered the palazzo's ballroom. High windows looked out over the canal and the city, and chandeliers swayed in the breeze, stirred up by the movement of the dancers beneath. Everyone was in costume, of course. Masks and capes abounded, though none were so vivid as his own. He took satisfaction in that. He was the resident artist, after all.

The guests were a mixed bag. Old aristocracy and new blood; prominent tradespeople and international guests. All members in good standing of what Giocondo and the others in the inner circle called the Avonshire Trust. A silly name for a powerful thing. Everyone in this room was a servant of Carcosa, or was being wooed by such.

Znamenski closed his eyes for a moment, and in the darkness he saw a flicker of golden light. He'd had some queasiness earlier, but it had passed soon enough. Nerves, perhaps. He opened his eyes and scanned the crowd, searching for Alessandra. Would she come? It had been a risk, offering to help her, but what was life without risk?

"There you are," Giocondo hissed as he pushed through the crowd and caught Znamenski by the arm. "You are late!" He was dressed in high fashion, with a long robe and Pantalone mask. Bought from a local *mascherari*, of course.

"This is my party, Giocondo. It only starts when I arrive, yes?"

"That is not how it works and you know it." Giocondo shook his head. "You are determined to be obstreperous, I see. And after all I have done for you."

"For which I most sincerely thank you," Znamenski murmured. He caught Giocondo's hand and kissed the Florentine's knuckles. Giocondo jerked his hand back with a strangled snarl. Znamenski laughed. "How rude. You enjoyed my kisses in Florence."

"We are not in Florence," Giocondo said. "This is not the time for your japes, Jan. There are people you must meet."

"Must I?" Znamenski said, lazily.

"Yes," Giocondo said, firmly. "Things are coming to a head. Lagorio is here, and his closest advisors. Carla believes he wishes to treat with us, before the coming of the King. She asked us to meet him and bring him to her."

"Get in good with the new management, eh?" Znamenski laughed. "Wise."

"Yes, and it would be wiser still not to mock him. A lot can happen in one day. The ritual could still be disrupted, and our plans ruined. We must ensure that the King's arrival isn't delayed in any way!"

Znamenski grunted. He was beginning to find this business of occult societies tedious. They spent all of their time jockeying for influence and position, just like the rest of the world. It was infuriating. The sooner Carcosa came to this world, the better. In the paradise to come, all would be free to indulge in their innermost desires and ignore the harsh compromises the world foisted on them. Or so the King had promised him.

Even so, he allowed Giocondo to lead him through the crowd of revelers in search of Lagorio. A part of him was genuinely curious about the man. Giocondo and the others in the inner circle – barring Carla and the Man in the Pallid Mask – seemed to be terrified of him. He was a shark in the sea, circling their craft.

But sharks could be hooked – and devoured. That was Lagorio's final fate, if he didn't bend the knee. Znamenski had no intention of pointing that out, of course. That wasn't his responsibility.

"There he is," Giocondo murmured, as Znamenski snagged a drink from a passing tray. All the servers wore black, with black *moretta* marked with the Yellow Sign. A bold, if subtle statement of intent. He wondered if any of them understood what they were wearing, or whether they were simply trying to keep body and soul together.

"Ah, Don Lagorio, a pleasure," Giocondo said, pulling Znamenski toward a lean, saturnine example of the Venetian aristocracy. Lagorio was dressed fashionably, if archaically, and one thin eyebrow arched as he took in Znamenski's flamboyant clothing. He had a *Volto* mask in his hand, but seemed to have no interest in hiding his face. Perhaps he wanted to be seen. "Have you met Jan Znamenski, our artist in residence?"

"Is he an artist, then? I thought he was a juggler, perhaps." Lagorio spoke in deep tones that put Znamenski in mind of the lagoon's bottom.

"I am that as well," Znamenski purred. "Acrobat, singer, painter, sculptor... I am a multi-faceted entertainer."

"Or indecisive," Lagorio said, studying him. Znamenski felt the weight of that gaze on his soul, and suddenly understood the others' fascination with the man. Here was another chosen one, albeit one serving a different god. A smaller god, but still infinitely more powerful than the hollow recitations of the church.

"Well, we artists are known for being flighty." Znamenski glanced at the red headed woman standing beside Lagorio. She was dressed in a rather fetching harlequin outfit, complete with porcelain mask. He gave her a smile, and she returned it with interest. "And who is this vision of loveliness?"

"Elisabetta Magro," the woman said, in silky tones. She extended her hand and Znamenski kissed it. "I once saw your works in Paris, signori. You are quite talented, though I never imagined that it extended to playwriting."

"Have you read it, then? Has Giocondo given you a little peek at my masterpiece?"

"Your masterpiece? I am given to understand that you merely adapted an older work," Lagorio interjected. His eyes flashed with a sea-green light, and Znamenski felt his hackles bristle. Elisabetta tittered, and his annoyance deepened.

"Adaptation is a traditional practice in the performing arts," he began. Lagorio smiled thinly and nodded, as if he had been expecting the answer.

"Theft, too, is a tradition."

Znamenski's hands clenched into fists. The ache in his arm had traveled to his shoulder – his chest – a nagging, throbbing pain that made it hard to concentrate. As he glared at Lagorio, he felt as if something were twisting and coiling in his stomach. Lagorio's smile widened in a way that chilled him.

"Are you feeling ill, artist? A bit too much of the grape, then?"

Znamenski bared his teeth. "You will have to try harder, if you wish to insult me, sir."

Lagorio's smile was that of a wolf eyeing a meal. Before he could reply, however, Carla made her appearance. She strode through the crowd, greeting some and ignoring others, before stopping in front of Lagorio.

She was wearing a costume based on the one he'd designed for the actress playing Cassilda; a floor length gown of gold and black, with a featureless mask topped by a spray of gold-dyed peacock feathers. Her elbow length gloves were fashioned like the gauntlets of a warrior of old, complete with decorative spikes and engravings. Her eyes shone with a feverish light that Znamenski thought only he – and perhaps Lagorio – could see.

Carla removed her mask, revealing her face to her guests. "Good evening, Don Lagorio. I am pleased you could attend." She smiled as she spoke, but it didn't reach her eyes. Those were as cold as the waters of the canals. Lagorio looked down his nose at her. Znamenski hid a smile. It wasn't often Carla was outranked.

"It seemed an interesting diversion," Lagorio said, sipping from his glass. He paused and studied the drink. "I thought the Mafei stock was better than this."

"These are from my husband's cellars in Avonshire. An old vintage, I am assured."

"Given what the English consider old, I am not inclined to give it the benefit of the doubt," Lagorio said, as he deposited the drink on a passing server's tray. "How is your husband, by the way. I do not see him here."

"He is overly tired," Carla said.

"Yes, age does take its toll," Elisabetta murmured, eliciting a glare from Carla. Znamenski traded glances with Giocondo. The Florentine looked nervous.

Carla lifted her chin. "As I said, I am glad to see you here. Perhaps the hostilities between our organizations can now be brought to an end…"

Lagorio loosed a rattling guffaw. Carla looked taken aback. Giocondo grimaced. Znamenski relaxed. So that was it. Lagorio hadn't come to make peace. Hence the insults. The man probably hadn't even read the script. "There is an old Venetian proverb… just because you married a foreigner, it does not make them welcome. Not them, nor the foolishness of their ideas."

Carla frowned. "What do you mean?"

"I mean, your king has no authority here. Venice belongs to another. And his rise will not be superseded by the coming of some cosmic interloper." Lagorio's expression was placid, but nonetheless awful. Like something monstrous peeking out from beneath a silken shroud. Znamenski's hands twitched, and he wished he could make a quick sketch.

"I would like to paint you," he said, suddenly.

The others looked at him. "What?" Lagorio asked, eyebrow raised.

Znamenski grinned. "I would like you to sit for me, when this is done. Your face, your posture – fascinating. Like something growing on a submerged corpse."

Lagorio looked at Carla. "Is he serious?"

"I rather think he is," Carla said, staring at Znamenski. Lagorio grunted and turned away. He paused and glanced back at Carla.

"Thank you for inviting me. The gesture was appreciated... even if it was in vain." With that, he departed, merging with the crowd of revelers. Elisabetta followed, smiling coyly at them as she went. She hadn't spoken much, but he had the feeling she'd been observing it all. Taking notes, perhaps.

"Well, that does not seem to have worked out, eh?" Znamenski said, looking at Carla.

"No. Lagorio is stubborn. I had hoped... but never mind." Despite her words, she looked unsettled. Not worried, exactly. But anxious all the same. Perhaps Lagorio was a greater concern than he'd imagined. Even so, it wasn't his worry. The play was the thing, and so long as that went off without a hitch all would be well.

"And what about the woman?" he asked, trying to change the subject. "Elisabetta. Is she someone of note?" He already knew the answer to that, but he enjoyed the flicker of annoyance that crossed Carla's face.

"She is a busybody and of no importance," Carla said.

"She's a member of the Silver Twilight Lodge," Giocondo said, idly, as he plucked another drink from the tray of a passing server. He glanced at Znamenski. "You flirted with them a time or two in Florence, as I recall."

Znamenski smiled. "It was the other way around, I think you'll find."

"And why were they interested in you?" Carla asked, with suspicious mildness. Was she envious? How delightful. Perhaps she was interested.

"Why were you?" Znamenski said. He finished his drink and set the empty glass down. He was still feeling parched; the alcohol was no help. "The truth is, many recognize my genius. Luckily for you, I am a true believer." He leaned close to her.

"You are attracted to me," Carla said, stepping back. Her smile was not quite a promise; more an insinuation. Giocondo nearly choked on his drink.

Znamenski smiled and shrugged. "Confidence and power are well known aphrodisiacs. I am as susceptible as any man, I admit."

"Were you attracted to her, as well?"

"Who?"

"The thief." Carla lifted her chin. "Zorzi."

"Oh yes," Znamenski admitted. "Of course."

"Is that why you invited her?"

He paused. Was that jealousy in her tone, or something else? Curiosity? "I invited her because I hoped she might be convinced to see sense."

"And join us, you mean?"

"Yes." He frowned. "Why do you speak of her in the past tense?"

Carla sipped her drink, and didn't reply. Znamenski's frown deepened. "What did you do, woman?" he asked, in a low tone.

"What I thought best."

He tensed, rage stirring within him. "She is dead?"

"No," the Man in the Pallid Mask said, from behind him. Carla's eyes widened. Znamenski couldn't resist a smirk as he turned. Giocondo, he noticed, had slunk off with the Man's arrival, like the frightened cur that he was.

"Proved too much for you, did she?" He paused. The Man was wearing a different suit than usual, and he held himself oddly – as if injured. Had Alessandra actually managed to harm him? He would have to congratulate her.

"No. I had her. We were… interrupted."

"By whom?" Carla demanded.

"The Cavalier. He interfered."

"Maybe it was the King's will," Znamenski said, idly.

"You have no concept of what he wants," Carla snapped.

"Why else would Alessandra still be alive, save that divine forces were watching out for her?" Znamenski paused and smiled.

"Why don't we ask her when she gets here and see which it is, eh?"

CHAPTER TWENTY-NINE
Mingling

"You are lucky that your man arrived when he did, with your luggage," Thorne said, as they entered the ballroom of the Palazzo Avonshire. "Else you would have had nothing to wear. How sad that would have been." They were dressed to the nines in a red suit, with a red domino mask over their eyes. They looked like something out of a French pulp novel.

Alessandra sniffed and patted their arm. "I would have managed. I have never yet been found wanting, when it comes to parties." She was dressed in a floor-length cocktail dress, with a fur wrap and a mask that complimented Thorne's own.

Selim had come through for her once again, bringing their bags from the hotel that afternoon. No one had tried to stop him, thankfully. He'd brought the Zanthu Tablet with him as well, and concealed it in the palazzo.

She patted her hair absently. She had lockpicks concealed there and in her garter, files stashed in the lining of her coat, and various other tools of the trade hidden about her person. She hoped some of it might be useful, but you never could tell with this sort of thing.

"Always a first time, kitten." Thorne looked around as they joined the revelry, already in progress. No one had attempted to stop them, or argued with their presence. Some of that was Thorne's doing, Alessandra thought. Some minor enchantment, to grease the wheels. The rest was that they looked as if they belonged. "Look at this lot," they went on. "A well-heeled bunch, no doubt. The great and the good, as they say."

"Neither of which includes you, Thorne," someone stated. The man was tall and handsome, his costume elegant and modern. He wore no mask, perhaps the better to show off his handsome features. He resembled Valentino, in a certain light.

Thorne smiled in a friendly fashion. "Hello, Salvatore. How's tricks, old thing?"

Salvatore frowned. "Do not be disingenuous, Thorne. We are not on friendly terms, you and I. Not after that business in Palermo."

Thorne put on a sad expression. "I can't believe you still hold that against me. The fate of the world was at stake. What was I to do?"

"For starters, you could have not pushed me off a building."

"You landed in the water," Thorne protested. They looked at Alessandra. "You see? People always think the worst of me. Especially Signori Neri, here."

"Because you are a duplicitous serpent," Salvatore snapped. "One for whom I have no patience. Why are you here?"

"You know me, I always like a good party."

Salvatore's eyes flicked to Alessandra. "And who is she? One of your creatures?"

"I belong to no one," Alessandra said, meeting his gaze. He frowned.

"I know you," he began.

"Of course you know her," a woman's voice interjected. "She's the one who stole the Itzamna amulet from that private collection in Amsterdam. Or so I'm told." Alessandra turned and saw a red-haired young woman, dressed in a harlequin's outfit, watching them. She smiled and twitched aside her mask. "When I got word you were in Venice, why I was just tickled to think what hijinks you might get up to, Countess."

"Do I know you?" Alessandra asked.

The other woman shook her head. "No. But we have a mutual acquaintance… a Mr Carl Sanford, of Arkham." She smiled, and there was nothing pleasant in that expression. "My name is Elisabetta Margo. A pleasure, Countess."

"It is all mine, I assure you," Alessandra said, smoothly. She glanced at Thorne. "Who are these people?"

"Remember those allies I mentioned? Elisabetta is one of them. As is Salvatore, I hope." Thorne extended their hand to the man. "Bygones, old chap?"

Salvatore bristled and glanced at Elisabetta. "I told you this was a mistake. Thorne cannot be trusted. They are treachery incarnate!"

"Says the self-proclaimed Master of Illusions," Thorne said. They looked at Alessandra. "He's a sorcerer, you know. Not a very good one, but… adequate in his way. It does not surprise me to see you aligning yourself with Don Lagorio. He's a generous man, willing to overlook the faults of others."

Elisabetta caught Salvatore before he could lunge at

Thorne. She smiled again, at Alessandra, and then at Thorne. "We have done as you asked, Thorne. We have cast down the gauntlet, though you have not fulfilled your end of the bargain yet, I note. Don Lagorio will not be pleased to hear of such… hesitancy on your part."

Thorne sighed. "Don Lagorio must learn patience, I fear. I will do as I've sworn, make no mistake. But in my own time, and at an hour that best suits my needs." They tugged on Alessandra's arm, pulling her away from the two. "Let's mingle, kitten."

"What was that about?" Alessandra murmured. "What bargain?"

"Lagorio is an unpleasant character. Then, he does worship a giant cuttlefish. His lot aren't happy about this lot moving in and trying to take over before they can. So, I reached out and aimed one set of cultists at another." Thorne flashed her a smile. "As you can see, I have been very helpful."

"Yes." Alessandra wasn't quite certain that she wholly bought that. Thorne was clearly up to something; she didn't like not knowing the nature of the bargain they'd made. But now wasn't the time to worry about it.

She looked around, but didn't see Znamenski. Then, he was probably mingling with his guests. That was fine by her. She didn't trust his promise of aid any more than she trusted Thorne's. Now that she was here, it was time to get to work.

But before she could make a move, someone in a Pulcinella costume intercepted them. Znamenski's eyes gleamed behind the mask and she laughed. "Of course, I should have known." Thorne turned, a look of concern on their face. "Thorne, allow me to introduce the man of the hour… Jan Znamenski."

Znamenski glanced at Thorne. "Ah, the famous Thorne. I've heard much about you."

"Have you?" Thorne preened.

"Not really, no."

"Ah." Thorne's face fell and Alessandra bit back a laugh.

"A fine crowd for your coming out party," she said. Znamenski laughed and removed his mask. His expression was odd. Feverish. Strained. As if he were ill… or in pain.

"Any excuse, in this city," he said. "Take a wander, I'm sure you'll see a few things that'll curl your hair."

"My hair is curly enough, thank you." She tugged at her hair for emphasis. Thorne grimaced and turned to address one of the other guests, leaving Alessandra alone for the moment with Znamenski.

"I'm pleased you came. A little surprised, but pleased." Znamenski took her arm. "I need some fresh air, come." She allowed him to lead her to the windows. There was a balcony outside, overlooking the canal. They went to the stone railing, away from the press and heat of the party. The lights dancing on the water reminded her of the eerie puffballs she'd seen earlier and she felt a moment of queasiness. It passed quickly, thankfully.

"Where is it?" she murmured. Znamenski grunted.

"Right to it, then?"

"Right to it. Where?"

"Upstairs. In his private rooms. I don't know which they are, otherwise I'd show you. It is in a small, ornate chest. Old. You will know it when you see it." Znamenski smiled thinly. "You being an old hand at this sort of lark, I mean."

"They tried to kill me, you know."

He swallowed and looked away. "They told me."

"I am hardly inclined to be generous, given such provocation." She pulled her stole tight about her and looked at the lights across the canal. "Once, I might have set fire to this building to cover my escape."

"Please don't," Znamenski said, somewhat plaintively.

Alessandra smiled and patted his arm. "I will refrain, for your sake if nothing else."

"You treat me better than I deserve." He took her hand. "I wish you could see what I see, Alessandra. What your little friend sees. How is she, by the by?"

"Thriving," she said. She wanted to pull her hand free, but his grip tightened. His gaze burned into her, through her. She felt as if she were drowning in it, in a misty, murky lake full of great, serpentine forms that slowly coiled about her in order to draw her down, down. "No," she said, firmly, blinking.

He frowned. "No, what?"

"Whatever you are trying to do to me – no." She pushed him back, not gently. "Have you added Svengali to your list of talents?"

"I'm not trying to do anything but make you see sense," Znamenski said. He sighed and crossed his arms, seating himself on the railing. He glanced at the water over his shoulder. "There's a monster in the lagoon, you know. Venice is built on its back. If it wakes, the city will collapse into the water."

"Nonsense," Alessandra said.

"Truth, and you know it. Reality is but a name for the veil we pull over the nightmare of existence. The world is a corpse, and monstrous maggots gnaw at its vitals."

"How... poetic."

Znamenski snorted. "I wish I could claim credit, but I'm quoting a poet named Justin Geoffrey. A fine poet. A tad high strung for my taste." He paused. "But he was correct. There are worms in the earth and spiders in the stars. They will destroy us. But I say, if we are to be destroyed, let us at least then choose the manner of our destruction. If it is to end, let it be beautiful."

"Carcosa," she said.

"Carcosa," he agreed. He touched his chest. "I can feel the drumbeat of his armies here, beneath my ribs. I can hear the rattle of spears, the flap of banners... the slow, stately tread of his approach. All that is required is that we swing wide the gate and invite him in."

"Like a vampire," Alessandra said.

"In a sense, I suppose. All evils are invited in, even mundane ones." Znamenski winced and clutched at his stomach. "We cannot help ourselves. I saw that, during the war. Man is a broken animal; mad and bloodthirsty. We need a master to bring us to heel."

"The Fascists would agree."

Znamenski laughed, and it sounded like the snarl of a dog. "Of course! But they think our master should be just one more animal. I think he should be something greater – something above us." He bared his teeth. "If you could but put aside your preconceived notions of freedom, I could show you the truth – and then you would truly be free."

"Why?" she asked, simply. The question had occurred to her before, but only now did she see the opening to ask. To yank the mask from his face and see what he was hiding.

He paused. "Why what?"

"Why me? What do you want of me, Jan?"

"I- I…" He hesitated, seemingly at a loss. She frowned. The Znamenski she knew had never been at a loss. He always had an answer, even if it was complete rubbish. She looked into his eyes and saw something yellow flash; it reminded her of the beasts she'd faced earlier. Was that what was inside him? Was he just another hound?

"You do not know, do you?" she said, taking a step toward the doors. "Did you think it a mere impulse; a bit of holdover affection from better days? Is that what you told yourself? Poor Jan."

His eyes narrowed. "Alessandra…"

"I do not know much about what madness it is that possesses you. Ignorance, as they say, is bliss. But I know that you are not the man I knew. You have become nothing more than a mask. Something pretty, drawn over something foul. Worse still, the chains you wear, you forged yourself."

Znamenski stiffened. "Quoting Dickens, now? How pathetic."

"Yes. Pathetic. Deep in my heart, I thought maybe that if I could help Pepper, then I could help you as well."

"I do not need help," he growled.

"Then why did you invite me? Why tell me where the Key is?"

He stared at her without replying. She smiled sadly. "And again, you do not know. You have always been a whirlwind of impulse, Jan. We shared that, once. But I think you are reaching the end of your story… and I am still at the beginning of mine." She turned and went to the doors, but paused to look back at him. "You used to read Dickens to me, do you remember?"

She left him there, speechless, and went back inside. As she closed the doors behind her, she shivered and took a deep, steadying breath. She would mourn her friend later.

For now, she had a key to find.

CHAPTER THIRTY
Handmaiden

"I should have gone with her," Pepper said. She stared out the window of the dining room, watching the moonlight dance on the canal.

Allegria shook her head. "No. She will be safe enough. You must rest." Though she wasn't sure exactly why the abbess had stayed, Pepper couldn't deny that she felt better for the other woman's presence. Selim and Giovanni had gone with Alessandra and Thorne, ostensibly to make sure they got out of the palazzo in one piece. The two men seemed to have come to some accord, at least as far as Selim getting to ride on the gondola went.

"People keep saying that, but I don't feel rested," Pepper said, turning to look at the other woman. "I can feel her, you know? In the back of my head." She glanced at the Cavalier, who sat nearby, a selection of old books spread out before him. "Her name is Camilla. Sound familiar?"

The Cavalier grunted, but didn't look up. "Yes. It is in the play."

"*The King in Yellow*," Allegria said, softly. "You are experiencing the events of the play as if they are real." It wasn't a question.

Pepper nodded. "Except they are real. Just… somewhere else. Who is she? Znamenski told Alessandra a little, but I want to know more, especially if I'm sharing my noggin with her."

The Cavalier sighed. "There are different versions. In most she is Queen Cassilda's handmaiden – or her lover. But her part is always the same. She is the warning, the doomsayer; through her, we are shown the futility of resistance to the influence of the King. It is her scream of realization that closes the innocuous first act, and opens the way to the true horrors of the second."

"So why am I seeing her life?" Pepper asked.

Allegria answered. "The play is a peephole, of sorts. A way to look upon the madness of the King, but in a measured dose. Unfortunately, even a measure of madness is too much. The sign you saw, the one that started all of this – it is from the play." She frowned. "Plays, moving pictures, artwork even… these things can trick the subconscious into feeling something despite itself. To see what is not there, to feel what should not be felt. That is the borderland where devils dwell."

"Careful," the Cavalier mused, eyes alight with amusement. He snapped a book closed and opened another. "Next you'll be burning books in St Mark's Square."

"Some knowledge is too dangerous for unprepared minds," Allegria said, softly. But she looked shaken by his words. Pepper cleared her throat.

"Yeah, well, if I could unsee it, I would, but I can't. So what do I do instead? Can you do whatever you did before and… shake her loose?"

The Cavalier shook his head. "No. The play has you now. The only way is to… suck out the poison, and for that, we need the Key of Ys, or an artifact of comparable power and function. Even then, it will always be with you."

Pepper sat back, disgruntled. She looked at her hands and for a moment they felt like someone else's. Camilla's. It wasn't just dreams now, but echoes when she spoke, when she moved. It was as if she were two people in one body. And one of them was trying to get out, but which one? She could barely recall what had happened earlier, though Alessandra had done her best to explain. Camilla had taken control somehow, had tried to kill Alessandra, but not really. Pepper could feel it. Camilla had been after someone – something – else.

"Was Carcosa ever real?" she asked, still turning things over in her mind.

The Cavalier looked at her. "What do you mean?"

Pepper leaned forward. "The story had to come from somewhere, right? So, at a certain point – these people I'm dreaming of were real."

"Possibly. Or some variation, thereof. Why?"

"So maybe the story ain't all bad."

Allegria frowned. "Meaning what?"

"I mean maybe, she – it – is trying to tell me something."

"It's trying to drive you mad," Allegria said, pointedly.

"No, the thing that took over Carcosa is trying to drive me crazy. But Carcosa itself?" Pepper shrugged. "Maybe not, hunh?"

Allegria looked at the Cavalier, who had paused and was looking at Pepper in what she hoped was a contemplative fashion. "You think Camilla is trying to… communicate?"

"Not exactly, no. It's more like… she's fighting the same guys we're fighting, just somewhere else. In Carcosa. Like a – a resistance movement."

"Ridiculous–" Allegria began, but the Cavalier cut her off with a gesture.

"No. I have heard of similar occurrences. The play is a fluid thing. It shapes itself to fit its container, with all that entails. If someone resists it, it might well react in such a way. It is still trying to trap you, just in a different way… it is offering hope, rather than despair."

"Even more reason to ignore it," Allegria said, firmly.

"Perhaps. But perhaps, with the right preparations, we might make use of it." The Cavalier stood abruptly, thumping his cane against the floor as he began to pace. "Yes. Thorne took you into Carcosa – your version of it, at least. A simple spell, one that I can easily replicate."

"You cannot mean to take her back," Allegria said. "They almost took her last time. She needs to be warded against that place, not sent back."

"They almost took her because Thorne was foolhardy and unprepared. I am neither. She will be safe. Warded against the dangers…"

Allegria shook her head in apparent disgust. "To do what? Speak to the ghost of a woman who might never have existed?"

"Hey!" Pepper said, loudly. They looked at her. "It's my risk, ain't it? It's my soul, so I'm the only one with say in how this goes down. *Capiche*?" She took a breath. "If we do this, if

I can talk to her, do you think I might be able to get her to – to help us somehow?"

The Cavalier tapped the floor with his cane in a thoughtful fashion. "It is possible. Our foe will sense what you are doing, like a spider sensing a fly's struggles in the web. Tug hard enough, and he will come for you. Together, we might be able to trap him … or even banish him entirely." He tossed his cane up and caught it, almost like an excited child. "If we have an opportunity, we should take it."

"And what about the cost?" Allegria asked. She took Pepper's hand. "You say it is your choice – fine. Make an educated one. To do this is to risk damnation, plain and simple. I will not be able to help you … no one will." She paused. "Alessandra will find the Key. This risk you propose to take is unnecessary…"

Pepper hesitated. She was sure the abbess was right, but at the same time something warned her that it wouldn't be enough. Alessandra always said that it was good to have a backup plan for when the first one inevitably went wrong. "Anything that helps us is necessary," Pepper said, slowly. "Alessandra is risking herself right now, for me. Can I do any less to help her?"

Allegria had no reply for that. Pepper nodded brusquely and looked at the Cavalier. "Let's get started. What's first?"

He stepped around the table. "Come. The room you slept in is perfect for such a ritual." He led Pepper upstairs and Allegria followed. The palazzo creaked and groaned around them, as if it were trying to warn them off. Maybe it was. Pepper wondered what sort of ghosts a place like this had.

In the bedroom, the Cavalier shoved the bed against the

wall and flung aside the carpet on the floor, exposing the bare boards. A circle had been burned into them at some point in the past, its rim adorned with sigils that made Pepper's head swim to look at them. "What the hell is all that?"

"Hell indeed," Allegria said, from the doorway. "A circle of invocation. And in a child's bedroom? What foolishness prompted such a thing?"

"Foresight, not foolishness," the Cavalier said. "The Zorzis saw to it that their daughters would be safe from anything that came searching for them, so long as they remained in their room, Alessandra included. The whole palazzo is ringed about with similar protections, some more useful than others. Indeed, it was built atop them. That is why Ferro claimed it from its original owners… on my recommendation." He added this last as if ashamed. Allegria made a disapproving sound, but Pepper barely heard her.

"Pigeons," she said. There were pigeons at the windows. Unhealthy looking ones. She didn't like the way they were staring at her.

"Ignore them," the Cavalier said, not looking up from the circle. "If their master were here, it would be a different story, but without him, they cannot enter. Not while the ancient sigils are in place."

"Yeah, easy for you to say," Pepper muttered. But she tried her best. Allegria came to stand behind her and placed her hands on Pepper's shoulders.

"Even now, you can turn away," she murmured. "You do not have to do this."

"Yeah. I do."

"You have nothing to prove to Alessandra."

Pepper glanced at her. "Is that why you think I'm doing this?"

"Aren't you?"

"Lady, all due respect, you don't know me. I got nothing to prove to nobody. But sometimes, a thing just has to be done and when it does, you might as well roll up your sleeves and get to it." Pepper tossed her cap onto the bed and shrugged out of her jacket. She was suddenly very warm; uncomfortably so.

"Are you ready?" the Cavalier asked, from the circle.

"Yeah." Pepper joined him, and he enfolded her in his cloak. Up close, it was hard to ignore how much he smelled like the city. It was caught in the folds of his cloak, in his clothes. It wasn't a bad smell, just potent. "How are we doing this?"

"It is already done," he murmured. The edge of his cloak fell, and she saw that she was no longer in the room or the palazzo, or Venice. But neither was it Carcosa... at least not the one she saw in her dreams.

"What in..." she began, in a startled whisper. The city that rose around her was a decaying husk; the towers were broken, the walls fallen, the streets broken and covered in silent, swaying grasses the color of bile.

"*Per me si va ne la città dolente,*" the Cavalier said. "I am the way into the city of woe. This is the real Carcosa. A forgotten ruin, inhabited only by shadows. Yet it lives still. Look – see." He flung out an arm, and she saw that he had no substance. Neither did she, come to that. Two more ghosts roaming the streets. The thought didn't make her feel any better about their surroundings.

"I don't understand."

"It is a ghost, haunting itself. The King in Yellow took all that it was, its past and its future and crushed them into a hideous, unending *now*." The Cavalier resembled a shadow, walking alongside her through the crumbling streets. "This is what he will do to our world, if he is allowed in."

"So we got to shut the door, hunh? Easy enough."

He laughed. "Once, I thought the same. Time cured me of that delusion, as it will cure you… if you survive."

Pepper snorted. "Gee, thanks, mister. That makes me feel better."

He chuckled warmly. "You remind me of her, you know. Alessandra. She too has always had an inflated notion of her own invincibility."

"Hey, pal, I'm all too aware of how mortal I am," Pepper said. She caught a flash of something yellow out of the corner of her eye and paused. "You see that?"

"Yes. They caught your scent on the night wind. Come, we must hurry."

She started moving quicker, her heartbeat loud in her ears. "I thought you said this place was dead!"

"That means nothing where these beings are concerned," the Cavalier said. "I can protect you, for a time. But they are stronger here than in our world."

"Wonderful. Wish you'd mentioned that."

"Would it have changed your mind?"

Pepper hesitated. "No."

"Yes, you really do remind me of her." He paused. "There! Look!" A fold of shadow indicated a brick archway to her left. A watery radiance shone within it, and beyond… a garden. Or rather, a painting of a garden. For that was what it resembled.

"Are you sure? It doesn't look real."

"It is not. It is a scrap of a dream. Go – quickly!" As he spoke, she heard a low growl from a nearby doorway. Yellow eyes gleamed within, and something that might have been a hand or a claw, grasped the edge of the doorframe.

Pepper turned and ran. Yellow hounds gave pursuit, their bodies blurring like spilled paint. Eyes rose from their mangy hides like blisters, and their paws had too many toes. Their tails were scorpion stingers... scaly... fiery. Their muzzles opened, disgorging the faces of men and women, and these faces cried out a name... chanting it like a battle-cry. The Cavalier intercepted them, sliding across their path like the shadow of a sundial. His blade sprang into his hand – a shimmering, painful blaze of silver in this un-land. It cut the air, sizzling eerily and a hound tumbled, whimpering.

Pepper had no time to see anything else; the archway loomed and the garden beyond. Without hesitation, she threw herself into it. The moments that followed felt as if she were floating in warm water, but everything was dry. When she came out the other side, she felt as if she had been walking in a fog and suddenly everything was clear.

She turned slowly, surveying the garden, noting the artificiality of it (like being on stage, a part of her murmured), and a woman that might have been her older sister was staring at her. She was dressed in a tunic and mail, like something out of a moving picture. Her hand was tight about the hilt of the sword sheathed at her hip. "Who are you?" she asked, and her voice was unsettlingly familiar. It took Pepper a moment to formulate a reply.

"I think you got an idea, lady." Pepper looked down at herself. She was indistinct; like a faded photo-still of herself.

"I don't think I got much time, so I'll make it quick. You got to fight him. We got to fight him."

From the horrified look on Camilla's face, she knew exactly who Pepper was referring to. "Fight...? No. He cannot be fought."

Pepper sighed. "Yeah, I figured you'd say that. Somebody told me you always say it. That's your role in the play... to show how hopeless it is. Only I think that's boring." She put on her best confident smile, and held out her hand.

"Maybe we should change it up, hunh?"

CHAPTER THIRTY-ONE
Cavalcade

Alessandra found Thorne holding a disquisition on the available wines to a rapt crowd. She caught their attention and pulled them away from their admirers. "Znamenski is mad. Utterly mad."

"But still helpful, one hopes," Thorne said, signaling a server.

"We will see." She looked around. "What do you make of it."

"We are in the belly of a sleeping beast. Things will go properly pear shaped once we make some noise. We'll need a quick exit, if and when you find what we're looking for."

"I will leave that part of it in your capable hands." She nudged Thorne lightly. "Until then, what is it that Americans say? Hold down the fort."

Thorne gave her a suspicious look. "And where are you off to, kitten?"

"To look for your Key. Make sure no one notices I am gone."

"Easy enough. Who's paying attention to you, anyway? I'm here after all." Thorne stepped away from her and loudly greeted someone she didn't recognize. She watched them swan about for a moment, and then stepped back and turned, threading her way through the crowd with casual grace.

Her exit was aided by the fact that the guests had percolated through the palazzo as the night wore on. The English might like everyone to stay in the same room, but Venetians were a bit looser in that regard. Especially for this sort of party. It wasn't a proper masquerade ball; rather, it was more a relaxed affair.

She made her way quickly through the palazzo, heading for the central stairs. They resembled those such as might be found in the grand houses of Damascus and Baghdad. The rest of the house might have been uprooted from Rome or Istanbul; she climbed the stairs and passed through the *piano nobile,* the long central room that ran the length of the palazzo, and entered the warren of bathrooms, bedrooms, offices, and miscellaneous closets. Even the most modest of palazzos was akin to something organic; grown rather than constructed, with each generation of owners adding or subtracting as need and whim dictated.

Some of the rooms were occupied; the balconies as well. Men in masks conversed quietly, while women laughed and gossiped. In other rooms, the guests engaged in rather more amorous activities. That too was to be expected at these sorts of parties. Servants prowled the halls in their unsettling black masks.

She headed up. None of the bedrooms she'd seen so far had been grand enough to belong to the Marquis. No one stopped her. No one even noticed. Even so, she had the distinct and unsettling feeling that she was being watched, if only from a distance. But she saw no one, and detected no shadow, human or otherwise.

It was quiet, upstairs. The windows had all been thrown

open, to allow the heat from below to escape. A chill breeze whistled through the hall, and curtains rustled. There were no servants up here, nor any guests. Just moonlight and shadows and herself.

Then – a soft laugh. A child's laugh. A shadow, moving away from her at speed. She paused. A child – no. Something told her that were no children in this place. At least not the sort she'd want to meet. She shivered slightly and tried to concentrate on finding what she'd come for.

The main bedroom was at the end of the hall, on the canal-side of the palazzo. It was a large room, dominated by expensive furniture, including an old-fashioned four-poster bed and towering armoires that stood like dark sentinels along the far walls. But it was not just the furniture that drew her eye; instead, her gaze fixed on the mural that covered the entire circuit of the room, broken only by the great windows that looked out over the canal.

Looking more closely at the walls, she was reminded of another room, and another mural. That one had been of a red jungle, and something else. Something she didn't like to recall. This one, however, wasn't a jungle, but a city of sorts. She traced the rising and falling of towers, arched bridges, and walkways. In a way, it reminded her of Venice, or perhaps Istanbul. It also put her in mind of Pepper's dreams.

Despite her better judgement, she leaned closer. She could make out indistinct figures, tiny against the immensity of the towers; barely more than smudges. In the dim light, they almost seemed to move – no, not just move. They were running. Fleeing. She could see it now. There was an air of frenzied motion about them, of panic and hysteria. As if the population of an entire city were going mad, all at once and suddenly. But why?

She turned slowly, backtracking the smudges, trying to find the point from which they were fleeing. But it all seemed to blend into one. She heard a rasping cough and snapped around. A bathchair that had not been there before now sat in front of the windows. She had not heard it arrive. She took a step to the side. A shriveled form sat hunched in the chair; a man of advanced years, his chin resting on his chest, his rheumy eyes fixed on the lights that danced along the canal. "The Marquis of Avonshire, I presume," she murmured.

The old man twitched at the sound of her voice. His eyes rolled in her direction, and she thought she heard the rustle of cloth and the snap of frayed rags in a sudden wind. She took an instinctive step back, pity warring with disgust. Something about him was exceedingly off-putting. It wasn't just the air of decrepitude, but something else… like a miasma hovering about him. Part of her wanted nothing more than to roll him into the canal and watch him sink.

"Beautiful, don't you think?" a woman's voice said, startling her. She cursed herself – of course someone had wheeled the old man in. "My husband painted it himself. Sadly, it was the first sign of his… collapse."

Alessandra turned to find a small blonde woman watching her. "And you are…?"

"Carla Mafei. Well, Avonshire, now. For my sins." She stroked the hunched man's scalp, as if he were a beloved pet, rather than a spouse. "He was not strong enough. Men rarely are, whatever they tell themselves. There is a difference between strength of body and mind that many of them do not fully grasp."

"So I have noticed," Alessandra said. She felt confined; cramped. As if the room were closing in on her. The murals twisted and contracted, the tiny figures moving faster now. Speeding away from some unseen horror. It was getting hard to breathe. She could smell something – taste something – on the air. A strange, heady incense that interfered with her thoughts, making it hard to focus.

"You were searching for this, I think," Carla said, holding up a silver key that shimmered with an eerie radiance. "I cannot imagine why else you would have come here, Jan's obsessions aside."

"Is that a hint of jealousy in your voice?" Alessandra asked. Of course Znamenski would have set his sights on her. And from the way her face twitched when she mentioned his name, Alessandra was certain of it. "I assure you I have no interest in him."

Carla straightened. "Nor do I. In fact, I think his use is coming to an end."

"Something tells me that he believes the same of you," Alessandra said, as she stepped back and put the bathchair between them. "Why else would he have offered to help me get that Key of yours?"

Carla hesitated, and Alessandra made her move. She grabbed the bathchair and shoved it toward the other woman. The old man gave a strangled moan as he collided with his wife and they went down in a tangle. The Key fell from Carla's grip and Alessandra snatched it up as she made for the door. It felt warm and alive in her hand, and she almost dropped it when she felt it twitch, like a cat stretching for a scratch. Carla called out, but Alessandra was already out the door and running.

Shadows undulated along the walls, as if in pursuit. There were shapes moving within them – birdlike or batlike, or maybe catlike. All of the above, and then some. She averted her eyes, not wanting to see them if they became more visible.

Unfortunately, they were quicker than she was. They stretched ahead of her, filling the landing, obscuring the stairs. Things like the yellowed jawbones of animals pierced the flowing ebon mass, snapping and emitting hollow snarls. It gave a sudden shiver and split, allowing the Man in the Pallid Mask to step through. He checked his cufflinks, and then glanced at her. "The Thing That Follows cannot be so easily outrun, thief. Not by any mortal soul."

"No, but I would bet it does not want to risk this," she said, holding up the Key of Ys. The shadows quivered around her, and the Man cocked his head to the side. Slowly, he held out his hand.

"You have no idea what it is that you hold, woman. Give it to me, and your ending will be a swift one – and painless."

Alessandra glanced around, searching for a way out. But shadows clung like oil to every wall and hung in every doorway. Jaws snapped and indistinct faces pressed against the obsidian surface, mouthing curses, or perhaps pleading with whatever force held them. "A tempting offer, but how do I know you will hold to your end, eh?"

As she spoke, she took a step back. She hadn't brought her revolver; nowhere to hide it, and it hadn't done much good before, but she dearly wished she had it nonetheless.

But perhaps the Key might prove some use. She extended it toward the nearest clump of shadows and saw it contract and retreat, as if frightened. Her gaze flicked toward the Man and she saw his eyes narrow. "It will do you no good," he said. "There is nowhere you can go that it cannot follow."

"There is one place I can think of," she began. If she could use the Key to get past him, and down the stairs, she had a chance. Thorne would have some tricks up their sleeve, no doubt. She wondered if they had noticed how long she'd been gone yet.

The shadows began to shift and coil, drawing closer to her. Closer than she liked. She turned, swinging the Key about like a torch. Wherever its eerie radiance touched, the blackness retreated, but not for long. The Man approached her slowly, his hand still extended. "You will never reach it. Your time is done. Make your ending a gentle one, at least."

Alessandra was about to reply when she felt something brush her ankle with a feather light touch. She looked down and saw that the shadow was covering most of the floor. Things that might have been hands pressed against it, as if trying to reach up toward her. As she watched, one rose higher than the others, withered fingers twitching. She stared at it in horrified fascination, unable to look away. She realized her mistake almost too late, and managed to duck aside as the Man suddenly charged toward her. His fist narrowly missed her head, and she instinctively jabbed at him with the Key. He made a shrill sound, like a falcon sighting prey, and caught her wrist in an unyielding grip.

He squeezed and she felt the bones of her wrist grate together. She couldn't prevent a cry of pain from escaping her lips and her knees bent. The Key slipped from her numbed grip, clattering to the floor. The shadows swirled up around them, like eager beasts circling injured prey. He looked down at her, his eyes glowing with a sickly fire. "Your pain will be written into the stars," he said, softly. "Your passing will be recorded in the annals of the world to come. Such is the fate you have earned."

"Sounds… ducky," she hissed, through gritted teeth. She caught at his forearm, but couldn't break his hold. "All a- a girl could ask for."

He tightened his grip and she wanted to scream. If her wrist wasn't broken yet, it soon would be. She thought he was smiling behind his ghastly mask; he and Zamacona had that in common too. All of them were sadists, whatever form they took. "Yes," he said. "Ducky. Now, I will–" he began, but the threat was lost in a gurgle of pain. He dropped her, and as she fell, the shadows abruptly retreated. She saw the Man sink to one knee. He had a sword thrust through his back.

A ghostly shape stood behind him, dressed in archaic, almost medieval fashion. Something about it was familiar, however. "Pepper?" Alessandra said, softly. The shape flickered and turned at the sound of her voice. Pepper's face, but not. Camilla. The Man groaned and began to haul himself to his feet, and the apparition turned back, sword raised high to finish what it had begun. All around them, the shadows began to wail.

"No," Carla cried, from the other end of the hall. She had the Key in her hand, though where she'd gotten it, Alessandra couldn't say. Maybe the shadows had given it to her. But as she raised it, the shadows contracted and lost their color. Camilla stiffened, her eyes widening in what might have been fear – or frustration. Then, she was gone… and Pepper with her. Carla lowered the Key and gave Alessandra a hideous smile. "She is ours," she said. "She has always been ours. As are you. This time, you will not escape."

"Oh, I wouldn't be too sure about that, kitten. Play's not done yet." Thorne stood at the end of the corridor, surrounded by a ruby shimmer that kept the squirming shadows at bay. The Man peered at them in evident consternation.

"This does not concern you, magpie," he said.

"Magpie? There's a new one," Thorne shot back. They held out their hand to Alessandra. "Time we were off, Countess. I think we've worn out our welcome here."

Alessandra hesitated, her eyes on where she'd last seen Camilla and Pepper. Then, with a muttered curse she sprang toward Thorne. As she did so, they drew a circle on the air with a finger, and the world turned watery and cold as she plunged through and…

… crashed down into Giovanni's gondola, causing it to buck in the water. Selim and Giovanni stared at her in shock as she picked herself up. Thorne was sitting behind her a moment later. "Well, that didn't go according to plan, did it?" they said, adjusting their cufflinks. "What now, kitten?"

"Home," Alessandra said, as she picked herself up. She felt a churning in her stomach as she thought of Pepper. Something had happened – something bad.

"And quickly."

CHAPTER THIRTY-TWO
Greater Good

Thorne climbed the steps to the palazzo, staying a safe distance behind the countess. Her shock had turned to rage as they drew near home. By the time poor Giovanni had been tying up his gondola, she'd worked herself into a right state.

Alessandra's voice, raised in fury, carried back to them. They smiled thinly. She'd done well, given what she'd been facing. Most mortals broke at the sight of something like the Man in the Pallid Mask, but she'd given him a few wallops to remember her by. She and her little charity case.

Of course, however satisfying in the short term, bopping a creature like that on the snoot inevitably came with a price attached. Case in point: the situation as it stood. Said charity case was lost in Carcosa. Or, at least her spirit was. Her body was safe upstairs, dreaming but not dead, as the saying went.

Thorne entered the dining room, following Alessandra's voice, and winced as a flurry of invective raced by them to freedom. The Cavalier stood stiffly near the window, one hand braced on the back of a chair. The nun, Allegria, sat nearby, a scowl on her face. Alessandra faced them both. "How dare you endanger her like that?" Alessandra shouted, waving an accusing finger in the Cavalier's face. "And for what? Now she is trapped!" Thorne watched in some amusement. It wasn't every day that they were the ones getting yelled at. They glanced at Selim, looming near the door and raised an eyebrow. The big man ignored them and Thorne sighed.

"Cut off, not trapped," the Cavalier said. *You would think of it that way,* Thorne thought, in grim amusement. They'd never pegged the Cavalier as capable of such ruthlessness, but it seemed there were surprises yet in the world.

Alessandra was pale and shaking with fury. "You left her!"

"Not willingly, I assure you," the Cavalier protested. "Her connection to Carcosa prevented me from bringing her out with me. If I could have, I would have. It is true she is behind enemy lines, but not their prisoner. If we secure the Key…"

"There is no if," Alessandra said. She turned to Thorne. "These allies of yours… I want them here tomorrow morning."

"What are you thinking, kitten?" Thorne asked. But they already knew. When pushed into a corner, even the meekest mouse could bite. And Alessandra was by no means meek.

Alessandra ran a hand through her hair, her eyes narrowed in concentration. "That tomorrow will be our last chance. Our enemy won't miss us a third time. So if these allies of yours truly intend to help, it is time they showed willing, yes?" She swayed slightly, and braced herself on the table. The Cavalier made to help her, but she tersely waved him back, even as she rubbed her face.

Allegria stood. "You are tired, Alessandra, as am I. We should all get some sleep while we can. Tomorrow promises to be a busy day." Alessandra protested, but she was clearly exhausted and allowed Allegria to maneuver her to the door. Thorne watched as the abbess led her out of the room, grateful.

"Got bored, did you?" they said, after a long moment of silence. "Decided to see it for yourself?" They clucked their tongue mockingly.

"If we hadn't, you both would have been killed – or worse. She saw that creature about to kill Alessandra and acted... even as I would have, in her place."

"Maybe," Thorne said, not about to acknowledge the point. "The fact remains, the girl is lost in Carcosa and they will hunt her down, sooner or later. Alessandra will not be best pleased by that."

The Cavalier grunted. "Was Lagorio there?" he asked, not looking at Thorne.

"He was."

"And?"

"He as good as declared war on them."

"You still have not told me what you promised them," the Cavalier said. Thorne nodded and stripped off their cravat. It was red silk; expensive, like everything they owned. Only the best for them.

"My little secret."

"I do not like secrets."

"And yet you have so many," Thorne said, pointedly. The Cavalier did not look at them, clearly unwilling to rise to the bait. Thorne almost frowned, but managed to turn it into a sneer. "Lagorio will aid us, because it is in his best interests to do so. He's a monster, but a territorial one. While he's worrying their haunches, we'll strike at their vitals."

"And how do you intend that we should do that?"

"I was rather hoping you had some ideas on that score, old chum."

"Do not call me 'chum.'" The Cavalier paused. "And I might, at that. Earlier today, I had Matteo dig out the plans for the theater they are using." He produced a set of rolled up diagrams and deposited them onto the table. Thorne carefully unrolled the brittle paper and studied the plans as if they knew what they were looking at.

"How clever. And how does this help?"

The Cavalier tapped a point on the diagrams. "There is a cellar, with its own water door. It was all but submerged during the last flood, and never pumped dry. But still accessible to those gondoliers who know of it."

"Like your man, Giovanni?" Thorne patted a stray hair back into place. "How convenient for us."

"Not at all. It will be difficult – and messy. But it is unlikely that they are guarding it." The Cavalier looked at them. "Not impossible, however. We will need to be on our guard."

"Always," Thorne murmured. They hesitated, not wanting to say something to give themselves away, but unable to resist a chance to show their cleverness. "Lagorio hates you, you know. Treachery is almost a certainty."

"Which is why Allegria is here," the Cavalier said, in grim satisfaction.

"I had wondered about that," Thorne admitted.

"Just as Lagorio and his ilk are connected to Venice, so too is she. Like them, she draws on the elemental strength of this place, though she believes it to be the hand of God." He paused. "Perhaps it is, at that."

Thorne snorted. They had met gods before; be-tentacled

horrors, the lot. It was enough to make you agnostic. "So, her presence will keep them sweet, is that it?"

"Indeed. It may even make our enemies hesitate."

"And what about dear little Pepper?"

The Cavalier paused. "I will see to that."

"How?" Thorne asked, mildly curious. The Cavalier was silent. Thorne's eyes widened. "You intend to enter Carcosa yourself? Oh, that is the height of foolishness, man. Especially now. You'll be ripped apart before you even catch a glimpse of her." Riding along with someone who had a connection to Carcosa was bad enough, but to go in cold, as it were, was insanely dangerous, even for someone as formidable as the Cavalier.

"That is a risk I am willing to take. I got the girl into this and I will get her out of it. It is the least I can do for her."

"Who? Pepper – or Alessandra?"

The Cavalier gave Thorne a hard look. "And what is that supposed to mean?"

"I think you know." Idly, Thorne added, "Speaking of which, I'm surprised you haven't yet told her the truth." The Cavalier looked at them, eyes narrowed. Thorne smiled. They wondered if some part of the old fool knew what was coming, and perhaps even welcomed it? The Cavalier had been waging a war without end for so long; perhaps he was looking forward to the rest.

"And what would you know of it?"

"I know enough. What were you looking for in the Rue d'Auseil that night?" Thorne laughed at the Cavalier's sudden stiffening. "Oh yes, I know you were there with them. You went to Paris in search of something and took two of the greatest thieves in Europe with you. And their darling daughter as well. But only you and she came back. Funny that."

"I did not find it so amusing."

Thorne smiled. "No, I expect not. Still, you should probably tell her that her mother's alive, and in the Dreamlands."

The Cavalier was on his feet in an instant, free hand on the head of his cane, ready to draw his blade. "How do you know that?" he hissed.

Thorne's smile widened. "I know so many things; my head is chockablock full of dark secrets, my friend. I know you went somewhere, with the help of a poor old musician. Three of you stepped into the dark, and only one came back. One went sideways, but where did the other go? Did you put that sword of yours through his back?" Thorne leaned close. "Was it on account of the woman? You've always been the romantic sort, admit it."

"Be silent," the Cavalier said, in a grim tone.

"Or else what? You'll serve me the same as you did poor old Ferro?" Thorne sat back and spread their arms. "Well come and try it, old man. I'm no mere thief. I – *awp*!" The tip of the Cavalier's blade rested against their throat. Thorne hesitated. "Well. I saw that going somewhat differently, I admit."

"You are trying to provoke me. Why?"

"Would you believe me if I said the greater good?"

"No," the Cavalier said.

Thorne gave a bark of laughter. "No, I didn't think you'd buy that." A flick of their fingers brought forth a sudden snap of fiery light. The Cavalier shied back instinctively. Thorne struck, fingers weaving an ugly sigil on the air between them. There were many gestures one could make, in order to affect reality. Most were subtle things, quickly made and soon forgotten. Others were more crude; brute force by any other name. This was one such.

A prismatic lance of calcified air formed, piercing the Cavalier's chest with a harsh, tearing sound. His eyes widened and he fell back into his seat with a wet groan. He tried to raise his blade, but it slipped from nerveless fingers. Thorne caught it before it hit the floor. No sense waking everyone up.

The lance faded into dusty motes, leaving only a gaping wound in its wake. The Cavalier wasn't dead yet, but he soon would be. Thorne felt a flicker of regret as they eyed the dying man. It was no easy thing to kill a fellow traveler. It wasn't the first time, but it was never a cause for celebration. Thorne caught the back of their chair and pulled it over to beside the Cavalier's. "For what it's worth, I wasn't fibbing. This is for the greater good."

The Cavalier muttered something beneath his breath. Thorne, incapable of ignoring the melodrama of the moment, leaned close to better hear his last words. The Cavalier's hands snapped up and caught his killer's head. Thorne mewled like a startled cat, but couldn't pull themselves free of the dying man's grip. "Let me go," they hissed, struggling against the Cavalier's hold. "Let me go!" They could feel the air gathering about them. The house had gone quiet. The Cavalier was doing something, but they didn't know what. Whatever it was, they didn't like it. It crawled along their spine like an itch they'd never be able to scratch. Not painful, just persistent.

"No. You are mine until this is done… *kitten.*" The Cavalier pulled them closer. His voice sounded somehow stronger – as if the pain were fueling him. "Venice must survive, Thorne. Alessandra must survive. Or you will not. This I promise you."

Then, message delivered, he slumped back. His robes rustled slightly, as if something were leaving him. Thorne stumbled back, still feeling the pressure of those fingers on the sides of their head. Then, with a muffled snarl, they gestured and soft, pale flames enveloped the body. The Cavalier was consumed in moments, leaving only a few ashes floating on the air. These Thorne swiftly ushered out through the open window.

"Thus passes Caesar, and good riddance," Thorne muttered. Then shivered as they caught sight of the sword-cane still on the table. They reached for it, to hurl it out into the canal... but hesitated. Something told them that if they attempted such an action, there would be repercussions – though what sort, they could not say. Thorne lowered their hand and turned away. They bit back a startled yelp as they saw Allegria standing in the doorway.

"Where is he?" she asked, softly.

"Gone."

She glanced past them. "Without his cane?"

"To bed," Thorne said, with a quick smile. "He is an old man, you know. Needs his sleep." She frowned at this. Thorne knew she didn't believe them. But what did it matter? The deed was done, and her suspicion was irrelevant. "As do you, I expect." Thorne glanced at the cane again, sitting silent on the table like an accusation. They shook the thought off and forced themselves to continue smiling.

"After all, as you said, tomorrow is going to be a busy day."

CHAPTER THIRTY-THREE
The Plan

Alessandra awoke suddenly to the sound of gondoliers singing. Outside, a red sun wavered in the pastel light of morning. For a moment, there seemed to be two of them. She blinked until the discrepancy resolved itself and one sun hung in the sky.

Rubbing her eyes, she sat up. She'd taken her parents' room – or what had been their room – and she sat for several moments, reacquainting herself with its contours. Oddly, it was the smallest room in the palazzo. The walls leaned precariously, giving the impression of a paused collapse. Murals depicting the history of Venice decorated the walls, and exposed beams ran along the ceiling; another oddity. She stood and reached up. The tips of her fingers could just graze the underside of the beams.

She felt the strange markings carved there; at first she'd thought it traces of woodworm, but in the daylight she realized they were sigils of some sort. She wondered if she ought to ask the Cavalier about them, then dismissed the idea.

She splashed water from the basin near the window on her

face, trying to clear the last tatters of sleep from her mind. Her dreams had been confusing things; she'd imagined Pepper, but changed… twisted into an almost unrecognizable form. The Pepper-thing had pursued her through corridors of marble, warbling in alien tones. She'd heard the Cavalier as well, calling to her as if from far away… or deep below.

Not a pleasant slumber, all things considered. She pulled the drop-cloth from the mirror mounted on the wall, and studied her own haggard expression for several moments. "You are looking old, Comtesse," she murmured. There was a sudden fluttering motion in the corner of the mirror and she spun toward the window. Nothing there. Slowly, hesitantly, she looked back at the mirror.

The reflection of a pigeon sat on the sill, a yellow string tied about its leg. The bird eyed her pinkly, and its beak fell open. Something moved within. She turned back to the window, heart pounding. The only sight that greeted her was a sudden flurrying of shadow that was gone almost as soon as she looked at it.

Almost against her will, she turned back to the mirror.

The glass had gone black… a black leavened by an eerie, ugly radiance as of stars of obsidian spinning in an ebon sky. The darkness seemed to press itself forward, and she felt an awful gravity reaching from the glass to grip her limbs, her mind…

And then it was gone. The glass was just glass, reflecting her frightened face back at her. "Enough," she murmured. Then, more loudly, "Enough." She took a deep breath and straightened her shoulders. "You have picked a fight with the wrong thief, my friend. I have bested worse things than you."

It was sheer bravado, of course. But it made her feel better to say it. In the right circumstances, a boast was as good as a prayer.

When she got downstairs, Selim sat at the table, a selection of firearms and knives spread out on a cloth before him as he cleaned and assembled a revolver. He looked up as Alessandra entered the room. "You're awake," he said, slowly spinning the revolver's cylinder with the palm of his hand. He set the weapon down and looked at her. "It is going to rain today. A bad storm, I think."

Alessandra nodded, thinking of the red sky. "Yes. If we are lucky, it will hold off until we are finished with this business."

Selim grunted. "I think we are running short on luck, at the moment." He sniffed and looked around. "This place reminds me of the estate," he said, referring to the d'Erlette chateau. Alessandra had inherited it upon the death of the Comte, but she still wasn't sure what to do with it. She pushed the thought aside; a problem for a later date.

"I grew up here."

"That explains many things," Selim said, absently. He paused. "That was a joke."

Alessandra patted his shoulder. "Yes, you are learning. Very good." She leaned over him and picked up an American-made automatic. The pistol was heavy, but in a comforting way. She checked it over with a practiced eye; she preferred revolvers, and had ever since the war. They didn't jam quite so much, and could fire even after being dunked in water or mud. "When did you acquire all of this, pray tell?"

"I know a man."

"I know many men. That is not an explanation."

Selim sighed. "The Comte saw to it that we had contacts in most major cities. If we needed guns, explosives – someplace to hide – they would provide it."

"Henri was more thorough than I imagined," Alessandra said, setting the pistol back down. The thought was far from pleasant. She was still getting to grips with the extent of the former Comte's organization. Henri had intended to go to war with the gods, and had been in the process of building an army to do just that. Now, what was left of that army was hers… not that she had the first clue what to do with such a thing. A problem for another time. She looked around. "Have you checked on Pepper?"

"She looks as if she is asleep," he said. "But not a pleasant one."

Alessandra gnawed her lip. "No, I expect not." Her eyes flicked to the table again, and she noted the Cavalier's cane laying there. "Hunh. How long has that been there?"

Selim frowned. "Since I came downstairs. Why?"

She picked up the cane and partially unsheathed it. The Cavalier would never have left his weapon here, not unless something had happened to prevent him from taking it. She thought of her dreams, of his voice echoing up, as if from a grave… in the time since she'd visited Arkham, she'd begun to trust such ephemera more. Not every dream was a prophecy; but neither were they simply her subconscious at work.

She had always trusted her instincts when it came to the job; but now she was learning to trust them for other things. Looking at the cane, she knew without a shadow of a doubt that the Cavalier was gone… and it hurt. Why did it hurt? Who was he to her? Just a friend?

Alessandra pushed the thoughts aside. There would be time later – if there was a later – to answer those questions. For now, she had a job to do. Even so, she found herself weighing the weapon in her hands, wondering whether her father had ever done the same thing. Then her fingers curled about the cane and tightened on the lacquered wood. Later.

"I am going to check on her. Is Thorne here?"

Selim shook his head. "They went out last night. I heard them depart. Should I...?"

"No. Come and get me when they return." She wished she sounded more confident of that than she did, but thankfully, Selim gave no sign that he'd noticed. "I will be with Pepper until then." She paused. "Breakfast?" she asked, hopefully. Selim smiled and gestured to the kitchen.

"Pastries, and fresh coffee."

"You are a darling, Selim. Let no one tell you otherwise." Alessandra scrounged a pastry and a mug of coffee and made her way to her old room, the Cavalier's cane tucked under her arm. Pepper lay on the floor, in the center of a sigil-marked circle, twitching slightly in her sleep. Allegria sat nearby, her rosary in her hands, and her eyes on Pepper.

"I warned them," she said, as Alessandra entered.

"I assumed so." Alessandra sat on the bed and tore her pastry in half. She handed one part to Allegria, who took it with a nod of thanks. She looked out the window, at the red sky and slate-tinted clouds. "The calm before the storm."

"In more ways than one." Allegria tapped the edge of the circle with her foot. "This will protect her, but not for long... and if we fail, she will die."

"Where is she?"

"In her dreams. In Carcosa. I think – I fear – that she is trapped within the play."

"Last night, I saw… I am not really certain what I saw. Pepper, but not. Camilla. Two faces, one person. She – they – saved me. Perhaps…" She trailed off. Pepper was tense, quivering. Like a hound, dreaming of the chase. Or dreaming of being chased. She thought of the Pepper-thing in her dream and took a quick, burning swallow of coffee. "This is my fault. I brought her here. Brought her into this world."

Allegria was silent for a moment. "I do not think you can bring this one anywhere, Alessandra. She goes where she wishes, much as we did. Much as we do." She glanced at the cane lying beside Alessandra on the bed. "Was that on the table, still?"

"Yes, why?"

"I saw it last night. Thorne was… looking at it. As if it were a snake, preparing to strike. The Cavalier is not here."

"I know."

"He would not leave so potent a weapon behind. Not today."

"I know."

Allegria hesitated. "Do you think … ?"

"I do." Alessandra sighed and hefted the cane. "I also think that there is little we can do about it, at the moment." She frowned. "Later, yes. But not now. We need Thorne, and we need these allies of theirs if we are to have any hope of success." Gripped by a sudden impulse, she stood and placed the cane in Pepper's hands. Pepper clutched the item instinctively. Alessandra felt a calmness. She looked at Allegria. "Thank you. For sitting with her, I mean. I do not know that I could bear it."

Allegria smiled. "What are friends for?"

Selim coughed politely from the doorway. "Thorne is here," he said, "and a woman." He averted his eyes from Pepper, as if feeling guilty for not taking better care of her.

Allegria frowned. "Red-headed? Tall?"

Selim nodded. "I do not like the look of her."

"Not a fan of gingers?" Alessandra asked, trying for levity. It came off sounding forced. Selim shook his head.

"She stinks of dark magic."

"Elisabetta Magro," Allegria said, harshly. "One of Lagorio's creatures."

"She was at the party," Alessandra said. She dusted crumbs from her hand and knocked back her coffee. "Fine. Let us go speak with our allies, shall we?"

She led them downstairs, back to the dining room. Thorne sat at the table, alongside Elisabetta. Both of them looked inordinately pleased with themselves, which filled Alessandra with not a little foreboding.

"How's the gal Friday?" Thorne asked, giving Allegria a wink. Her expression of mild contempt didn't so much as flicker. Thorne frowned, clearly annoyed by having garnered no reaction. Alessandra sat.

"Sleeping," she said, tersely.

"Like the dead, one assumes," Elisabetta said. Alessandra glanced at her.

"Not quite yet."

"You are an optimist. Good." Elisabetta sipped her coffee and smiled ingratiatingly over the rim of the cup. "Hope is the most potent magic available."

"Debatable," Thorne said. They glanced at the table and frowned. Alessandra wondered if they were worried about the absence of the cane. If so, good. Let them wonder. "Hope won't be much help in this endeavor, I fear."

"Luckily, we have other means at our disposal." Alessandra sat back and glanced at Allegria. The abbess had informed her of the Cavalier's plan the previous night. He'd shared it with her after Pepper had become trapped, as if worried he might not get the chance otherwise. "Speaking of which, is Giovanni here?"

Selim nodded. "Outside. Want me to get him?"

"No need to inform the chauffeur, I think," Thorne interjected quickly. "He already knows his part in my plan."

"Your plan?" Allegria said, from the doorway. "It is the Cavalier's strategy that we will follow this day, Thorne. Claim the glory if you must, but not authorship as well."

Thorne paused, clearly taken aback. Alessandra smiled to see them discomfited. Thorne grunted and said, "Still here? I'd have thought you'd be talking to the Almighty or some other such nonsense."

Alessandra glanced at Allegria, suddenly glad of her presence. "She is my friend." Her tone made it clear there was no argument to be had.

"I'm your friend," Thorne said, in half-hearted protest.

"No, you are not," Alessandra said, pointedly. "We are, all of us, allies of convenience. We have a common enemy and common desire to see them vanquished, but after that... well. It gets complicated, does it not?"

Elisabetta applauded mockingly. "Very good, Countess. Yes. But complexity is the spice of life. Isn't that so, Thorne?"

Thorne didn't reply. Instead, they stared at Alessandra as if puzzled by something. Then they shook their head and said, "Fine. I assume if the esteemed abbess knows, then you know as well. The Cavalier's plan is a risky one, but I do not see where we have another choice…"

Alessandra nodded. "Giovanni will take myself, Selim and Thorne to this forgotten water door this afternoon, while Znamenski is busy with today's rehearsal. We will enter, locate him and disrupt whatever it is that they are planning." She looked at Elisabetta. "While we are doing that, I presume your lot will be causing trouble outside the theater."

Elisabetta smiled prettily. "Oh, we intend to raise quite the ruckus, you can be sure. An army of the faithful awaits our signal and… well, I might have murmured a few choice words in the ears of certain individuals of… questionable political affiliation."

"Fascists," Alessandra said, in displeasure.

"Cattle," Thorne corrected, smoothly. "Willing to helpfully stampede in whatever direction they are aimed."

"I was under the impression that the cast and crew were used to such… stampedes," Alessandra said. The thought of using Fascists to do their dirty work made her feel ill. Then, at least they were a human evil.

Elisabetta nodded. "Oh yes, but our agents will be scattered among them." Her grin was savage. "They have orders to set fire to the theater. No site, no ritual. We will launch the attack in the late afternoon, during the rehearsal." She laughed. "The Fascists will be blamed, of course… which suits all of us, I think."

"Will that work?" Alessandra asked.

Thorne laughed softly. "Sometimes. Assuming it even works. They will be watching for such… hijinks. But that means that they won't be watching us."

"In theory," Alessandra said.

"But how do we know the Key will even be there?" Elisabetta asked.

"Thorne here as good as told me that the Key was integral to the performance," Alessandra said. "For our foes, the play is the thing. They will summon this King of theirs onstage. That means it will be in the building. So, while they are distracted, I will steal it."

"What makes you think you will succeed this time?" Elisabetta asked.

Alessandra smiled, coolly.

"Because, signora, I am the best thief in Europe."

CHAPTER THIRTY-FOUR
Final Rehearsal

Znamenski stood on stage and gazed out at the empty seats. In the gloom of the silent theater, it seemed as if there was an audience there, watching him – waiting. A spasm of pain rippled through him, and he moaned softly, tugging at his necktie with bloody fingers. His hands and arms were red to the elbow and for once, it wasn't paint. Something was growing in him; he knew that now. Something of Carcosa was trying to come through, using his flesh and bone as a medium for its message.

He had no doubt his coming apotheosis would be fatal. Something of him might survive, but then possibly not. He welcomed it either way. The artist consumed by art... was there any greater climax to a career such as his?

He took a deep, shuddering breath. He'd hoped, at least, it would delay itself until after the performance in a few days' time. He so wanted to see his masterwork in full, just once. He loosened his tie and swallowed down the pain.

Alas, alack, such was not to be.

Then, were not the best endings those that weren't?

The day was half gone already. Inside, his crew and actors readied themselves for a dress rehearsal. This was the calm before the storm. No one was in the auditorium, but that would change in a few minutes when the orchestra took their seats. When the crew began to set up the scene for the first act. This was the golden time, before it all crashed together. A moment when all the potentialities – good or ill – were in play.

Outside, the campo was full of bodies as always. But today it was like a nest of hornets. Some message had gone among the Fascists and agitators and now they were talking amongst themselves in loud voices. A sign of things to come? Or simply scavengers smelling the change on the wind?

Either way, he thought today would be an interesting one. It was not going to go as anyone had planned, he thought. But then, that was the beauty of art – of theater.

"You left early, last night," Carla said, from behind him.

He almost asked her as to what she was referring to, but settled for a simple, "Yes."

"Ashamed of yourself, I hope." Carla came around him, trailing her fingers across his arm. "You almost ruined it, you know. By inviting your little thief to our party. She almost got away."

"She did get away," he said, forcing a smile. Was he pleased by that? He couldn't say with any certainty. Something in him was, perhaps. "Slipped right out of your trap."

"We will deal with her, in time. When the King sits upon the throne of the world, all of his enemies will fall before the scythe. Zorzi, Lagorio… even the Red Coterie will fall." She smiled and looked out at the empty seats. "And I will sit at his side and rule well and true in his name."

"And what of me?" Znamenski forced himself to ask. But he already knew the answer. His fate had been decided the moment he set foot in Venice. Carla had strung him along, teasing him just enough to keep his interest. He saw that now.

She looked at him, still smiling, and touched his cheek. "You will be remembered. I will see to it personally, my sweet Jan."

"Cassilda," he murmured. She frowned.

"Cassilda is a fool. She is blinded to the glory that awaits us, seeing only the horror that masks the truth. But I have looked deeper and I know that horror is merely the fire that cleanses, and when it is ash... only truth will remain."

Znamenski didn't reply. He'd given Alessandra a similar speech, and she hadn't been impressed. It was only now he was realizing how ridiculous it sounded. Truth was merely a lie told earnestly. Alessandra knew that. He undid the knot of his tie and stripped it off. "Did you bring the Key?" he asked.

"Of course. I cannot risk leaving it for your little thief to steal. It will stay on my person, until the time comes to use it."

"How practical." Znamenski studied his tie for a moment, and then thrust it into his pocket. Carla's eyes followed his hands.

"Why are your hands red?" she asked.

"I want to show you something," he said, ignoring her question. He led her toward the wings, where props and costumes for quick changes awaited the cast. On a tall mannequin hung the raiment of the King, complete with a diadem. All finished at last, and gleaming oddly in the low light of the stage.

At the foot of the mannequin, something lay crumpled and

broken. Carla hissed in recognition. "Giocondo! What have you done, fool?" She sounded more angry than afraid.

"I need a more vibrant red to complete our potentate's ensemble," Znamenski said, circling the mannequin. He'd opened Giocondo up like an oyster with a palette knife, after enduring one complaint too many. A shame, but there it was. Needs must, and the muse could not be silenced. "What do you think? Magnificent, eh?"

Carla stared at him. "You have gone utterly mad."

Znamenski draped his arms over the mannequin and gave her a toothy grin. "No. Madness is an illusion – even yours, sadly. I have seen the truth, dearest Carla. And a mighty truth it is!" He reached up and plucked the blood-encrusted diadem from the mannequin's head. "When I called you Cassilda I was correct, you know. Whatever you might wish, that is your role and it is a fitting one… the queen who sought to wed a king, and in doing so, turned her city over to him. Of course, in the play, Cassilda has the good grace to realize the enormity of her betrayal, but you… you are too blinded by your madness to see what is right in front of you."

He placed the diadem on his head at a rakish angle. "What do you think? Does it suit me?" He laughed at the expression on her face. "Oh, if only Hildred could see you now."

"My husband…" she began. Hildred was undoubtedly still sitting in his chair, in his palazzo, utterly disconnected from the proceedings he had helped bring about. A bit character and nothing more. Forgotten until the curtain call.

"Is nothing. Was nothing. You married him, thinking him a king. Instead, he was just another serf." Seeing her eyes widen, he nudged Giocondo's body. "Oh yes, Giocondo told me everything, the poor fool. The girl who wanted to be queen and had to settle for regent… so sad." He gave the mannequin a twirl, as if it were his dancing partner. When he'd finished his spin, he stood facing Carla. "My Key, please."

"What are you talking about?" she demanded, even as she stepped back.

He took a sliding step toward her. He felt boneless; light as air. "You made the fatal mistake of assuming that the King – your King – has need of anything so puerile as a queen, Carla Mafei. The play whispered to you and you listened, like all of us. And like so many of them, you only heard the parts you wanted to hear."

Carla slid the Key of Ys from her coat, as if without thinking. It shone softly, and the light danced across the backdrop, illuminating the painstakingly painted archways and falls of ivy. "The Key is mine. It belongs to my family. It is a sign of my birthright. Carcosa will be mine. The King has chosen me…"

"Did he tell you that in your dreams?"

Carla paused. "No." She shook her head, but he saw the hesitation there and his smile widened in amusement. "Take that crown off. You look a fool."

"I am a fool. A jester, a clown. All artists are. We perform for the masses, we show them things they wish to see – or would rather not." He turned to the backdrop and stretched out his arms. He fancied he could almost see something moving in the misty whorls of paint that marked the indistinct background beyond the archway. Perhaps it was merely the glow of the Key playing tricks on his mind. He tipped back his crown and stripped off his jacket. Giocondo had insisted he dress up. "Have you ever wondered why the King dresses in tatters? Such a costume is traditionally the raiment of a fool, after all. The clown, at midnight."

Carla stared at him, and he almost felt sorry for her. She had been in charge for so long that she had forgotten whose bidding she did. She thought the King was coming for her, but Znamenski knew the truth. The Living God was more egalitarian than that.

He was coming for everyone.

There was a distant clamoring, as of many voices raised in argument. Doors slammed. Feet pounded the boards. He tossed his jacket over Giocondo's body. Was it his imagination, or was the dead man becoming something else? He turned as a theater page ran onto the stage, in search of him. "Signori, signori," the young man shouted.

"Yes, Luca," Znamenski replied, calmly. He could see the yellow maggots burrowing in Luca's brain. They had all seen the sign, from the lowest page to the actors and actresses. Carla had ensured it. She had taken their will, and made them props.

"The… the Fascists," Luca panted, glancing over his shoulder.

"Ah. Of course." Znamenski took the young man by the shoulders and patted his cheek. Then, with a flick of his wrists, he snapped the youth's neck. He let the body dangle from his grip for a moment and then dropped him to the stage. "He dreamt of treading the boards, this one. Before you took those dreams, and filled his mind with Carcosa."

Carla stared at the body in bewilderment. Another crash sounded, making her flinch. "What have you done?" she snapped.

"Not me," he said, though he thought that wasn't wholly true. He'd brought Alessandra here, however unwittingly. He'd led her on, taunted and teased her. Set her against Carla and the others – why? He still didn't know. Maybe she was right, and a part of him was attempting self-sabotage. Was that not the hallmark of the true creative? The ineffable yearning to slash a knife across a completed portrait, to smash a sculpture… to murder the patron.

Carla shook her head. She looked at the Key in her hand, as if seeking answers. Her eyes drifted to the backdrop, and widened. Even as Znamenski pulled the necktie from his pocket and slipped behind her, he wondered what she saw there. He had it wrapped around her neck before she realized what he was up to.

He slowly tightened the necktie, cutting off Carla's air. "You know, if you'd let me show the play on the island as I wished, this would not be happening. Or maybe it would. Maybe this is the way the story is supposed to go, hey?"

When he was finished, he laid her gently on the stage. He knelt over her for a moment and then lifted the Key from her slack grip. When he looked up, the Man in the Pallid Mask was watching him. The Man tilted his head in the curious way of his, studying the scene before him. "Are you pleased, artist?"

Znamenski rose, Key in hand. "No. Then, what artist is ever truly satisfied?" He could hear the sounds of invasion now; the crashing had a more permanent quality than previous occasions. "I suspect the performance will be cancelled."

"Possibly," the Man said. He didn't sound worried by the prospect. "Then, the required elements are all here. Perhaps a special early performance – for an audience of one?"

"That sounds delightful." Znamenski smiled. His teeth ached, and he could taste blood. At his feet, Carla's body was starting to twitch, as was Giocondo's and poor Luca's. Death was not the end, in the Kingdom of the Living God. He went to the mannequin and began to unbutton his shirt.

If he was to play the lead role, he would need to dress the part.

CHAPTER THIRTY-FIVE
Water Door

"Almost there," Giovanni said, as he poled his gondola along the Fondamenta Bonlini. Alessandra scanned the buildings that rose on either side of them, noting how the afternoon shadows seemed deeper and longer here. The sun overhead was not the right color for the time of day, and clouds the color of ashes swirled above the city.

"I can taste rain on the air," Selim murmured. He nervously touched his revolver – one of several he was armed with. "It will be a bad storm." Giovanni nodded in agreement. The two seemed to have put aside their dislike in the face of a common foe.

"All the better, given that our allies intend to set a fire," Thorne said. They seemed studiously relaxed, Alessandra thought. Perhaps they were meditating. "From what I've read, Venice and fires don't mix."

Alessandra didn't bother to reply. Her mind was not as calm as she might have wished. She kept thinking about Pepper, trapped in some other realm. Twice now that had happened, and it was becoming a habit. Perhaps after this was done, she and Pepper ought to return to Arkham and see if something could be done… some spell, some protective gewgaw that could keep this from happening again.

As if reading her thoughts, Thorne said, "You shouldn't be so hard on yourself, you know. The Outside finds its own footholds, whatever fools like to tell themselves. No cult has ever summoned something that wasn't already shoving against the door from the other side. Whatever name it uses, whatever form it takes, it is always waiting, always hungering. Always taking. It'll have us all, eventually."

"Then why fight it?" Alessandra heard herself ask. Thorne laughed.

"Ask a fish why it struggles against the hook. Ask a stag why he runs, with a hunter's bullet in him. Our instinct for self-preservation is often stronger than our despair. That is what they do not understand, these ancient horrors. They see us as ants, building temples in the dust. They see only how easy it is to crush us… not what we might do, if they stumble."

Selim perked up. "Listen – I think it has started."

Alessandra could hear it now as well. Shouts and chants; not the ritual barks of religion, but the staccato pulse of politics and demagoguery. Thorne leaned close. "See?" they whispered. "Whatever madness they hope to inflict, we can do it to ourselves just as easily."

"Shut up," she said. "Giovanni…?"

"There." Giovanni pointed. The water door was boarded over, but a few minutes effort on Selim's part saw it open, courtesy of a pry bar. The bottom half of the door was rotted to pulp, and the upper half was soon to join it. The step was gone, crumbled away in whatever storm had seen the bottom of the theater flooded. Giovanni had thought ahead, however. He brought up a flat plank and extended it across. Other boats passed along the canal, but no one was paying attention. Whatever was going on in the campo was clearly preoccupying everyone in the immediate vicinity.

Thorne got to their feet. "Lagorio's connections in the police will keep them from responding too quickly. They'll think it's just another political demonstration until they see the smoke. By then, it'll be too late."

"For whom?" Selim muttered. Alessandra patted him on the shoulder as she stepped lightly across the plank and stopped at the doorway. It had been storage once, and now the degrading remnants of boxes and crates sagged unpleasantly in the skim of *acqua alta*. Milky mold clung to the stone walls or clung to the broken wood that floated atop the water. There was a sour smell on the air; standing water and something else. At the far end of the cramped space, a set of stone steps rose from the water to an old wooden door – no doubt swollen shut by the damp. But Selim and his pry bar could handle that.

Alessandra gestured, and Selim passed her another plank. Giovanni had secured a dozen slats of tough timber from a renovation project somewhere in the city. The water wasn't deep – only a few inches. But the planks would keep them dry. She set the board down at the doorstep and crept across it. She heard the drip of water and the echoes of whatever was happening above. Then, all at once, the sudden patter of rain.

Selim followed her, carrying another board. He passed it to her, and as she bent to set it down, she felt the water ripple. She motioned silently to Selim, and he drew his revolver. Thorne, in the doorway, said, "What is it?"

"There's something in here," Alessandra said, not looking at them.

"Ah." Thorne stepped lightly across the boards, hands in their pockets. "Probably our little shadowy friend from the palazzo. A dweller from deep Demhe, broken to the service of the Pallid Banner." They didn't seem too concerned.

"Our friend in the mask called it the Thing That Follows," Alessandra said, idly. She straightened on her board and signaled to Giovanni, waiting at the doorstep. He nodded. His face was pale, but she was confident he'd stick it out.

The whispering started then, as it had in the palazzo. A child's voice, then a man's. A wasp-hum of murmurs that flitted at the edges of her hearing. The gloom of the cellar seemed to gather itself and she swallowed, ignoring the urge to flee. The darkness deepened, crowding out the tepid light from the doorway.

The thin carpet of standing water began to swirl like a whirlpool, shaking the planks. Alessandra drew her revolver from her coat. Selim had his out as well. Thorne paused, smiling. "Ain't this a pickle? We try and make a run for the stairs, it'll chase us down. And we can't retreat. So what's the play, kitten?"

"Giovanni," Alessandra called. "Light us up, if you please."

Giovanni whistled sharply, to show that he'd heard, and fired the flare pistol Alessandra had asked him to acquire. It was an old model, meant for the trenches, but it did the job. The flare popped and bounced, momentarily driving back the darkness and illuminating the awfulness within, before it retreated into the shadows.

In the spitting light, she saw a kaleidoscope of yellowing

bones, shifting and spinning like a mandala... skulls and femurs and spinal columns lashing like the tails of serpents. Fleshless hands reaching up through the waters, as if to drag them down to untold depths. It was many things and one thing all at once. A horror comprised of the dead. But it hated the light. Maybe it didn't fear it, but it hated it and that was good enough.

She tore her eyes from the horror and started for the steps. "Come on. The flare won't last forever. Selim, get the rest of the boards." He holstered his weapon and hurried to obey. Thorne moved closer to her, still smiling.

"Clever. When did you...?"

Alessandra didn't look at them. "When I saw your light show at the palazzo. And the effect of the Key. Demhe is very dark, I am guessing."

"Abyssal," Thorne said. Alessandra's gaze flicked to them and the barrel of her revolver drifted toward their chest. If Thorne noticed, they gave no sign. Shooting them now might save her a good deal of grief later. But she had a feeling that they still needed Thorne. If nothing else, they were the only one who knew how to rescue Pepper... now that the Cavalier was missing in action.

"Funny, is it not?" she said. Thorne looked at her.

"What is?"

"The Cavalier going missing on the eve of battle. If I were a suspicious woman, I might wonder if you had something to do it."

Thorne looked at her. "And are you suspicious?" Their smile was lazy, but she saw a hard glint in their eyes. A warning – or perhaps a challenge.

She was saved from answering by the fading of the flare. The plank beneath their feet was jostled as something massive moved beneath; an impossibility, but all too real. She caught a flash of bone – snapping jaws and a bristling mane of fingerbones.

Something surged up out of the dark behind Thorne and she shot it. Bone burst and the shadow-stuff fell away. "Selim," she called out. "Hurry!" Thorne turned, muttering something beneath their breath. Light blazed between their clenched fingers and fiery motes danced across the wet air, dispersing the gathering gloom.

Selim reappeared, a trio of planks across his shoulder. In his hurry, however, he slipped and went to one knee in the water. Darkness rose to envelop him as the sunlight faded and the storm rose. At Alessandra's cry of warning, Selim swung the planks around, but they did nothing to deter his attacker. Glistening shadows crashed into him, momentarily submerging. "Selim!" Alessandra cried, taking a step toward the fallen man. Thorne caught her wrist.

"Leave him! He's dead already…"

Alessandra swung her revolver around and aimed it at Thorne, who hastily released her. When she turned back, she saw Giovanni fumbling a new flare into his pistol, and Selim floundering in the water. He'd sunk up to his waist, as if it were a millpond rather than a sludge. She raced toward him, almost falling several times. Tendrils of greasy water snatched at her ankles.

Selim clung to the plank with desperate strength, but was clearly straining against something that sought to pull him under. She reached him just as he sank to his neck. Tendrils of oily black caressed him, and coiled about his arms. Fleshless jaws snapped soundlessly in the waters around him, as if waiting impatiently to welcome him. "Leave me," he gasped. Alessandra ignored that foolishness and grabbed his hand, unwilling to see him die in front of her if she could prevent it. She fired her pistol into the water, but it had no effect. She glanced back to Thorne and saw that they were already climbing the steps. No help there. "Go," Selim pleaded.

Alessandra thrust her pistol into her coat and extended her free hand toward Giovanni. "Giovanni – the flare gun!" The gondolier tossed her the gun and for an instant, she thought she'd missed it as her fingers scraped the butt and it seemed about to spin away. Then her grip tightened and she swung the flare pistol down to aim at the swirling dark that sought to consume Selim. She fired.

Something screamed. Not a cry of pain, but perhaps surprise. Whatever it was, it wouldn't last. Selim scrambled out of the water, coughing. Alessandra shoved him toward Giovanni. "Go, get out!" She tossed the empty flare gun aside and turned to run – but too late. It smashed upward, shattering the plank in front of her, and then the one behind. In the blink of an eye, she'd been cut off.

Past the heaving column of darkness, she saw Thorne standing at the top of the steps. They were gesturing, but not to her. A moment later, the remaining planks save the one she stood on, burst into flame. The darkness retreated with a raucous snarling, as if of a pack of wolves. Thorne made a sharp motion to her. "Hurry, the flames won't hold them back for long. Get up here!"

She ran, water splashing with every step. It wasn't ideal,

but better wet feet and ruined shoes than being swallowed by a living darkness. She reached the steps even as the flames faded. As she quickly ascended, she felt a bloom of relief as she spotted Selim and Giovanni standing helplessly in the doorway. They were alive. That was more than she'd hoped for. "Go back to the palazzo," she called. "Look after Pepper for me."

Thorne was waiting at the door. "A ridiculous display, kitten," they said. "Next time, I'll leave you to your fate."

"Promises, promises," Alessandra said. She shot the lock off the door and gave it a thump with her shoulder. It gave way, and she stumbled into a darkened room. A quick glance told her it was the same storage room where they'd met Znamenski last time. Only now all the costumes were gone... including the tattered mantle of the King in Yellow. There were bodies, though. She didn't look too closely at them, however.

Thorne closed the door behind them and marked a strange sigil on the wood with a fingertip. At Alessandra's quizzical glance, they said, "The Sign of Koth. It will keep our darkling friend down there for the time being."

Shouts echoed outside the room, and running feet. She sniffed the air, catching the tang of smoke. Logorio's servants were hard at work. Thorne met her gaze and nodded. "Looks like the final act has begun."

Alessandra hefted her pistol. "Then let us go find our seats."

CHAPTER THIRTY-SIX
Black Stars

Pepper ran, pursued by dogs with her father's face. Or maybe their faces were Alessandra's. It was hard to tell, in the confusion. They were the color of soiled hospital bedsheets and their howls were like the cries of the lost and the despairing. She ran, and Camilla ran beside her, their breath mingling in a harsh rhythm.

They occupied the same space, the same steps, but were somehow separate even so. It was as if one were a shadow of the other, with each taking turns. It wasn't a good feeling. It made her feel sick; like she was caught in a riptide and the shore was shrinking in the distance. But there was nothing to be done, except flee.

She didn't really remember what had happened… just vague notions of movement and agreement; of swords flashing and dancers dancing; of spinning lights the color of sour butter and the sound of ripped cloth flapping in a wind. Camilla remembered a garden… a masquerade… and a great silence falling over the noble families of the Hyades even as they celebrated Cassilda's ascension.

Pepper still wasn't certain what the story was, there. Camilla had tried to tell her, but they could only communicate in fits and starts, when one of them bled into the other. It was like neither of them was quite real to the other. Or maybe it was the play, trying to pry them apart and make the story go the way it was supposed to.

They'd missed their chance. That was all she knew for sure. Skipped ahead to Act Two, and now Carcosa was on fire and coming apart in an orgy of madness. Buildings frayed like threadbare cloth, revealing an eerie shimmer in the holes. The sky was pallid, pierced by black pinpricks that grew ever wider with each passing step. "Black stars rising," Camilla muttered, in her ear. Whatever that meant.

"Yeah, thanks for the update, I got a peeper-full earlier," Pepper muttered. She wondered why she wasn't more frightened. She liked to think she was hard as nails, but this – she should be terrified. But instead, she just felt *angry*.

Maybe it was because she wasn't really altogether here. In some ways, this was still a dream and used dream-logic. She wasn't afraid because it wasn't – couldn't be – real. She held onto that like it was a spar of wood and she was caught in a maelstrom.

"No mask, no mask," Camilla whimpered, stumbling. She kept trying to gouge out her – their – eyes, which seemed dumb given that they were trying to run away. Even Camilla seemed to agree, because Pepper could feel that she wavered between fear and rage, just as Pepper did. She was acting afraid because something told her she was supposed to, but she didn't want to. She wanted to fight.

"Who gives a holy whatsit?" Pepper snarled. "So what if

he ain't wearing a mask? So what? That just means he's uglier than we thought. I seen ugly before, sister – and damn near got eaten by it! This ain't nothing! You hear me?" Her words sounded hollow, rather than insistent. "Nothing…"

A hound leapt from a crumbled archway and nearly collided with them. Only her – their – instincts saved them from a messy fate. The hound, like all the rest, had a human face albeit one all stretched and twisted out of proportion. It moaned hungrily as it took a step toward where they crouched. "No mask," it tittered. "No mask."

Camilla went for her sword, but it was not there. They'd left it behind when they'd been forced to flee. She screamed in frustration and Pepper screamed with her. More hounds were circling now, human faces twisted in madcap glee. Their babble sounded familiar, and she thought it must be lines from that stupid play. They were reciting it as they prowled, some loudly, some softly. All with an arrhythmic enthusiasm.

She spat a few of the more memorable obscenities Alessandra had taught her. They didn't seem impressed, but it made her feel a bit better about her impending demise. She snatched up a rock, saw that it was encrusted with a colorless fungus and almost dropped it in disgust. Chittering things rode the night-wind high above. She turned, trying to keep all the dog-things in sight. She thought of Alessandra and Cassilda and couldn't decide who she'd miss more. Maybe herself.

The hounds closed in slowly, enjoying her fear. And she was afraid now, though she wished she wasn't. Camilla was murmuring in her ear, pleading for her to run, but to where? Where was safe in an alien city gone mad? Where was home?

Pepper shook her head. "Nuts to that. We got to fight." She slung her rock, the way she had as a kid in Boston when the rats got too close. It bounced off a hound's noggin and made the animal jerk back in pained surprise. She immediately stooped and reached for another rock. Camilla jerked her arm, forcing her to run. "We must flee," she urged. "Find a weapon – find help…"

Pepper figured those for good sentiments, but unlikely to result in anything. She forced them to stand still, to face the enemy. In her head, images of war and bloodshed rose. Battlefields, not of Earth, but of some other world, filled her mind's eye. Camilla, realizing she wasn't going to move, showed her what she had to do. She began to retreat down a shattered cul-de-sac, drawing the hounds after her.

"Narrow street. They can only come at us one at a time. Find a weapon." Camilla spoke in breathless bursts. "If we kill enough of them, the rest might flee."

"Great. Then what?" Pepper asked, snatching up a chunk of rock.

"We keep moving."

"And go where?"

"Anywhere," Camilla said, her voice edged in hysteria. "Away from him!"

"Good plan," Pepper muttered. There had to be some way to get back, to get home. If she could get home, she could help Alessandra. The thought held her, as she raised her rock and the first hound bounded toward them, howling eagerly.

Stand and deliver.

Silver, bright and sharp, flashed across her vision. A hound fell, wailing. A second leapt and was cut from the air.

Then a third. A black shadow stood between her and them, something that might have been a cloak roiling in the wind. She caught a glimpse of a square bauta mask and a tricorn hat, and then the shadow was moving again, too swiftly for her eye to follow. Silver and steel parted the air, as something Latin pattered down like rain. A prayer – an oath – an incantation.

The hounds circled and surged as the fight raged across the broken ground. Pepper felt a burst of adrenaline, and Camilla directed her to a broken slat of wood. She tore it free of its pile of rubble and gripped it like a sword. A hound darted past the newcomer and loped toward her, froth gathering on its jaws. The face was unfamiliar, wide eyes and a blunt nose and fadeaway hair, animal fangs crammed into a human jaw.

She hit it across the jowls with her makeshift weapon, knocking the creature sprawling. It struggled to right itself, and, at Camilla's urging, she stabbed the splintered end of the wood into its throat. Its eyes bulged and it writhed for a moment before expiring. She tore the wood loose and readied herself as the hounds gave voice to a communal shriek of frustration. Relieved, she watched as the survivors of the pack slunk out of sight.

"They're leaving… we beat them," she panted.

No. Merely frustrated them. They will be back, and I can no longer protect you.

She turned. The Cavalier looked like a black shroud on a scarecrow. There was a cold light on him, and she thought that if she tried to touch him, she'd feel only cloth, or worse – nothing at all. "What do you mean? Aren't you going to bring me home?"

I wish I could. But alas, I am only an echo of myself… and a fading one at that. He held out his hands, and she saw that he was coming apart, like a sand sculpture at high tide. *It was all I could do to find you, and tell you where you must go...*

"Yeah, where's that?"

The Cavalier extended a crumbling hand toward what she thought must be the center of the city, where a vast column of light rose into the sky. She hadn't noticed it before – she'd been preoccupied, but still, it seemed like the sort of thing a gal would notice.

Camilla quailed inside her at the sight of it, shuddering and muttering. Pepper wondered how much of that was from having seen all of this happen again and again. What must it be like to live the same horror over and over? She knew she didn't want to find out. She had to get out of here.

"That light – like it's cutting through the city... what is it?" Pepper asked, shading her eyes. The light was ugly; painful. It was like looking into a car's headlights as it sped toward you. It promised bad things. As such, she already knew the answer to her question. "It's him, ain't it? He's... coming onstage or something, right?"

Yes. The Cavalier extended his blade. *One last gift, Miss Kelly. Wield it, until it is time for its proper owner to take it up.*

"Alessandra," Pepper said, as she took the sword-cane. Things were starting to click into place. Alessandra hadn't wanted to talk about it, but Pepper had kept her ears open. You learned to listen for what people didn't say, being a cabbie. "You're more than just a friend of her parents, ain't you?"

I was. Now I am only another memory. He doffed his hat and bowed low, and came apart all at once. What was left of him blew away on the wind.

Pepper looked down at the blade in her hand. "I don't suppose he counts as a dragon?" she asked, hopefully. The only reply was a fading chuckle. The Cavalier was gone, as if he'd never been. Her grip on the sword tightened. "Yeah, that's what I thought," she muttered. She glanced at Camilla. "I'm going. What about you?"

Camilla lifted a shadow-sword in silent salute. Pepper took breath.

"Right. Let's go ruin us a play."

CHAPTER THIRTY-SEVEN
Backstage

Smoke wafted through the backstage area when Alessandra and Thorne emerged from the storage room. Alessandra could hear the sounds of panic and fighting. Glass shattered and wood splintered – a gunshot? She dismissed the thought. Whatever it was, it would no doubt keep Znamenski and his patrons busy.

Thorne smirked. "Looks like we backed the winning side," they murmured. Stage hands ran past, clearly frightened of something. Men dressed like laborers pursued them, shouting. One of them, a sallow, saturnine looking fellow, paused and glanced at Thorne as if recognizing him. A sneer spread across his unlovely features.

"Don Lagorio told me to thank you if I saw you, Thorne," he called, ignoring his fellows' urgent calls to follow. "He hopes you and he will have a fruitful partnership."

"I don't recall saying anything about a partnership," Thorne said, eyeing the man distastefully. "Be off with you, Savio. I'm sure you have actors to terrorize."

Savio grinned, and for an instant, Alessandra saw something feral lurking behind his eyes. Then, he was gone, chasing after the others. Alessandra glanced at Thorne, wondering, not for the first time, about the nature of their bargain – and whether it had something to do with the Cavalier's absence. Seeing her expression, they shrugged. "One of Lagorio's lurkers. Undoubtedly the one responsible for the fire. Savio always was a bit of a pyromaniac."

There was a crack from somewhere above; the sound of wood succumbing to heat. It wouldn't be long before the theater was completely aflame. They had to hurry. "We have to find Znamenski," Alessandra said. Thorne shook their head.

"No. We have to find the Key of Ys. It's the – if you'll forgive the expression – key to this whole mess." Alessandra frowned, and Thorne tittered. "Oh that was funny, admit it. Lighten up, kitten. It only gets darker from here."

"Znamenski might have the Key," Alessandra said, slyly. Thorne peered at her.

"You think, do you?"

"Oh yes. Jan is very good at taking what does not belong to him. If he wants it, as I believe he does, he will have taken it for himself by now."

"A bit like some other people I could name," Thorne muttered, not quietly. Alessandra smiled prettily at them and drew her revolver.

"Shall we go find him, then? As you keep saying, time is of the essence."

Thorne extended their arm. "*Apres vous, mes amis,*" they said. "Where do you think he'll be, then? Cowering in a dressing room, I expect. Or already out the door."

"No. He'll be backstage." Even as she said it, she knew she was right. Znamenski had invested too much of himself into this, just to flee. No, he'd be at the heart of it all – fighting to save his creation, or maybe just watching it burn. Either way, he'd want good seats.

Thorne frowned. "Bit out in the open, is it not?"

Alessandra paused. "As you said, this is the final act. Where else would he be?"

Thorne grimaced and followed her. "Oh, of course. It's a bloody play, isn't it? I hate this. So claustrophobic. Give me a good old fashioned abstruse, frenzied ritual any day."

Alessandra ignored their muttering. The route to the stage took longer than she remembered. Perhaps it was the fire – perhaps something else – but her perception of the corridor shifted and sloped in odd ways, like it was being bent out of shape by the hands of an unseen giant.

The dressing rooms and storage areas were full of chaos. Ransacked by the barbarian invaders; down a side corridor, she saw a group of looters kicking in a door and coming out with armfuls of silks and costume jewelry. Elsewhere giggling Fascists pummeled unresisting stage crew, the latter of whom resembled zombies – unaware of what was going on around them, or perhaps simply resigned to the tiny apocalypse taking place.

Contrary to her assumptions, there were no guards, no phantom protectors. If Znamenski's patrons had hired security for the performance, they were otherwise occupied. An actress prowled by, clad in a dressing gown. She wasn't screaming, and her arm was red to the elbow, as was the knife she carried. Ahead of her, a man stumbled down a side passage, clutching a spurting wound in his neck. Alessandra couldn't say whether he was a Fascist or just unlucky, nor did she have time to worry about it.

Somewhere behind them, a salvo of gunshots sounded, and someone screamed. The cry degenerated into shrill laughter that was then all but swallowed up by the growing crackle of flames. They passed a dressing room where two men, dressed as medieval courtiers, did a stately dance in the cramped confines, fingertips pressed together. A makeup artist smeared their tools across a section of plaster, painting smiling faces atop ungainly, inhuman bodies. A woman dressed like a queen sat in a corner and barked at the approaching flames like a dog, her eyes wide and eerily luminous.

"It's all breaking down, kitten. If I didn't know better, I'd say they wanted this to happen." Despite their words, Thorne sounded nervous. Alessandra understood. It was too easy. The thing in the cellar had been dangerous, but not enough to stop someone like Thorne. Was it simply hubris, or was something else at play?

In a moment, she had it. "The play," she murmured.

"What?"

"You said it yourself. So did I. What happens in the final act of this bloody play?"

Thorne paused. "Damn."

"I am guessing there are similarities, then," Alessandra said. She shoved Thorne back against the wall as a form lurched past, barely human in the thickening smoke. It muttered lines of dialogue she assumed were from the play, and was dressed in an outfit that resembled a cardinal's robes.

Acting on impulse, she reached and grabbed the scarecrow

figure and pressed the barrel of her revolver under their chin. "Znamenski – where?" she asked. The figure – man or woman, she couldn't tell beneath the thick pancake makeup and half-mask – gurgled in reply.

"The King is come," they mumbled. "Rejoice, for the fire of revolution burns bright!"

"Yes, up the people, huzzah," Alessandra said. She cocked the pistol. "Znamenski."

"Easy, kitten," Thorne warned. "I don't think there's much going on in the ol' noodle there. Here, let me…" They gestured sharply in the captive's face, and there was a spark of light, and then the individual slumped. Thorne touched their flutter-ing eyelids and turned to Alessandra. "Close your eyes for a moment."

"What are you–?" she began, but Thorne jabbed her eyelids. She cursed and when she opened them, she saw a faint, gossamer trail of dust-like motes rising from her captive and stretching away down the corridor. "What is this?"

"Magic," Thorne said. "They've seen the Yellow Sign. All of them. It connects them. Binds them to the play. What you're seeing are the tatters of the King, stretching from each victim to the – the original source of infection, for lack of a better term. Follow it, and we'll find Znamenski." Thorne grinned at her expression of disbelief. "Trust me, kitten."

"Not likely," Alessandra said, but set off following the trail of motes. It gleamed against the smoke, winding through the backstage area, tangling with other trails, like a knot of unraveling threads. Eerie figures danced in the corners or crawled across the floor; some in costume, others completely nude. All were connected by the strands.

When they at last found themselves at the stage doors, the air was thick with smoke and Alessandra's eyes were beginning to water. She'd been in burning buildings before – fire made a good cover for theft – but this would be cutting it close. Despite her stinging vision, she saw someone on stage, perched on a throne of wood and paper.

Znamenski.

He was clad in glittering robes of gold, and wore the crown she'd last seen decorating a mannequin's head. Before the throne, two broken forms swung about in a wild dance and Znamenski applauded vigorously. "Giocondo always did fancy you, Carla," he called out. "It seems only fitting that you give him the honor of a dance, before the end."

Actors and crew knelt to either side of him; some were blistered from the fire, others soot-stained and sweaty. All bore makeshift weapons… props, tools and debris. Bodies hung from the structures overhead, some still twitching.

Alessandra stared aghast at the scene, not quite able to process the grisly horror of it. Znamenski turned lazily and fixed her with a smile. "And there we are, right on the mark. Punctual as ever, Alessandra."

"Jan. What is this?" Alessandra took a step toward the gathering, keeping her revolver out of sight.

"Just a brief rehearsal," he said. He had the Key in his hand and he waved it like a scepter. The dancers ceased their whirling. Alessandra recognized them both. The man, she'd seen at the party. The woman was Carla Mafei, or what was left of her. Both looked as if dogs had been at them, and there was no life in the eyes of either.

"What have you done?" Alessandra asked. She could see

the tatters rising from everyone on stage, all stretching up to entwine Znamenski in their sickly radiance. "I knew you were mad, Jan, but this..."

"You sound disappointed. Did you come alone?"

Alessandra didn't turn or show surprise. Thorne had obviously made themselves scarce, hopefully in order to enact some cunning plan. "I did. Surprised to see me?"

"No. Grateful, though. Your little speech last night was... edifying. I've been lying to myself you see. Telling myself that this is simply art. But you are right. It is more than that." He leaned forward on his creaking throne. "You showed me the way, and I'm grateful. So for that, I absolve you of your sins against the throne." He gestured with the Key. "Go, and sin no more child."

"Very nice. Hand over the Key." Alessandra pointed the revolver at him. A murmur ran through his gathered court and she was suddenly all-too aware of how many of them there were. Even the corpses swung around to face her. Her skin crawled as she took in Carla's ruined features, and the necktie dangling from her neck like jewelry.

Znamenski frowned. "How sad. You know, despite being a wonderful thief, you utterly lack any appreciation for those artifacts you stole. You're a craftsman – worse, a stagehand, in this great opera we call life."

"Jan, over the last few days you have led me on a merry chase, and nearly gotten me killed more than once. Worse, you put my friend in danger. Forgive me, but I am not in the mood for a lecture on aesthetic appreciation. All I need from you is the Key."

"No." Znamenski spread his arms. "Shoot me if you must, but I cannot–"

Alessandra shot him. Znamenski stared at her for a moment, as if perplexed. Then, he toppled backward, throne and all, falling into a set of scenery with a crash. The crowd rushed her then, with a great howl. She retreated, but before they'd gotten more than a few steps the whole lot stiffened and collapsed, like puppets with cut strings.

Thorne stepped into view, a smirk on their face. "Ruined minds are the easiest sort to switch off. Cut the instinct to kill, and there's nothing keeping them upright."

Even Carla and her dancing partner were down, but as Alessandra stepped over them, she noticed that they were still twitching... as if something inside them were trying to tear loose. In fact, the others were the same. Their bodies convulsed and jerked like a sack of eels. Thorne saw her look and nodded. "We should be quick."

Before she could reply, Thorne stepped lightly over to Znamenski's body. "I never imagined you might be so pleasantly callous. I'm starting to enjoy our little partnership, I must say. I – *awp!*"

Znamenski's hand fastened itself around Thorne's throat. Thorne clawed at the offending digits, to no avail. Znamenski sat up with something that might have been a sigh, and then rose to his feet, dragging Thorne with him. Something flashed in Thorne's grip – the Key. They sent it skittering toward her and she snatched it up.

"Alessandra, Alessandra... how unbelievably uncouth of you," the artist wheezed, his crown askew on his head. He glanced at Thorne. "Then, you have fallen in with bad company." He flicked Thorne away, as if they weighed no more than feather. Alessandra heard them crash down somewhere on the stage, but didn't take her eyes off Znamenski.

She wasn't surprised. That was the worst of it. The utter lack of confusion. It made her sick to realize that she'd expected something like this. "You are not Jan Znamenski, are you?" she asked, readying herself to fire again, even as she thrust the Key into her coat. She had no idea what to do with it, but better she had it than Znamenski.

"Oh, I am, yes indeed, I am he. The very same! But I am also part of something greater now. Much like your little friend." Znamenski smiled and the edges of his mouth peeled and split, revealing an excess of teeth, rising upward in scimitar curves almost to the lobes of his ears. He flicked his fingers, and the flesh ruptured as gleaming claws slid into view. "The Living God has blessed me not just with talent, but with power as well…" As he spoke, he used his new claws to tear away his robes, exposing a torso that flexed and pulsed in a sickening fashion, as if his insides were being rearranged by an indecisive hand. He groaned, whether in pain or pleasure, she couldn't say.

She shot him again. And again. She fired until the revolver went dry. The impacts staggered him, but he didn't fall. Instead, he shook his head, the crown still firmly in place, and gave forth a full-throated bay of anger.

As she took a step back, she saw his scalp ripple on his skull, puffing up and wrinkling back as his head expanded and flattened. She heard bones clicking and cracking, and felt her stomach twist into a painful knot as he fell onto all fours. His arms and legs twitched, and convulsions ran through his now utterly inhuman frame.

He bayed again, and was echoed by the twitching bodies scattered on stage. Alessandra looked around and saw that they too were changing. She felt her insides turn to water as she realized that she was surrounded by them. Or would be, in a matter of moments.

Then – a flash of light from behind the backdrop. No, from the backdrop itself. She saw that it emanated from a meticulously painted archway. A shimmering gleam that caught and held the eye. She didn't know what it was, only that it was a way out.

She sprinted for it, closing her eyes as she dived through. And behind her, the thing that had been Jan Znamenski howled and gave chase.

CHAPTER THIRTY-EIGHT
Twin Suns Setting

Alessandra came to her senses in a senseless place. The sky was broken into jigsaw hues – striations of red and black that formed no perceivable pattern. The ground looked like shattered glass and the buildings that rose on all sides did so from a hundred different angles. It was like looking at London or Paris through a broken spyglass; a thousand reflections, distorted and pushing against one another in a queasy fashion.

There were fires between the buildings, and elongated shadows danced on the flat walls; celebration or conflagration, she could not tell which. She found herself clutching the Key of Ys tightly, as if it might provide some measure of safety from the madness around her. "Where...?" she began, her voice echoing oddly in the space.

"Carcosa," a mild voice replied. She turned to see the Man in the Pallid Mask standing at ease behind her, his hands behind his back. "The first Carcosa. The heart around which the stories wheel and dance. The true Carcosa." He flicked a speck of ash from his shoulder. "Or perhaps not. Even I cannot say with any certainty."

"Because you are just a part of the story," Alessandra said.

He nodded. "I am. I had another name once, I think. Or maybe I had many. Now I am simply a servant, as are all who come here. As you will be, if you are wise." He held out his hand. "The Key, please."

"Why?"

"Why what?"

"Why the Key, what does it do?"

He kept his hand extended. "Nothing I am aware of. It is merely an object of potency. Such tools are useful, for they allow a focusing of the mind and will. In some versions, it is a different key. In others, a crown… a scepter… a mask. Just… props."

"Props," she repeated, with a sinking sensation. "This is all just a game to you."

"No. Not a game. A performance. One that has been going on for as long as there has been an audience to appreciate it." His gentler tone here, his lack of aggression, all unnerved her more than his previous behavior. It was as if he thought he'd already won. "Just as it will continue until the final curtain falls."

Alessandra shook her head. "What was the point?"

"To show. To teach. The more who know, the better the play." He traced the edge of his mask with a finger. "The King is here. Would you meet him?" He indicated a towering, circular stairway that stretched up into the clouds above.

Alessandra hesitated, unable to answer. She could hear a distant howling on the wind. Znamenski and his pack were close. "Does he wish to meet me?"

"He wishes to meet everyone," the Man said. He gestured

upward. "See – he stands above, waiting patiently. If you go to him, he might be merciful."

Unable to help herself, she followed his hand and saw – Awful – Terrible – Wonderous – Powerful.

The King in Yellow stood on a rocky parapet far above and looked down at her, twin suns positioned as if resting on his shoulders. A stately figure, haloed in a colorless, dolorous radiance; tall in one moment, and winged in the next; human of shape, but inhuman of proportion. Tattered streamers of yellow damask unfurled from it, wafting and snapping for leagues on end, each fold containing all the hues of sickness and decadence.

It – he – wore a hood with a pointed tip, hideous lemon robes, and a golden mask on its face. Golden armor was visible through the frayed patches on the robes, but armor unlike that worn by any human in all of history. A sword was belted at its waist and a basalt throne rose behind it, towering over all existence below.

She wanted to kneel, to abase herself before such awful majesty. To swear fealty to such a king was only natural; man was meant to serve, after all. And to serve a Living God was surely no sin.

But such feelings receded as she tightened her grip on the Key. Its warmth flowed through her, cutting the chill that threatened her bones. She raised it, as if in challenge. The Man sighed. "Disappointing. Znamenski so wished that you would see reason."

As if saying his name had been a summons, Znamenski bounded into view on all fours, followed by several other hounds. They slid to a halt at a gesture from the Man. The beasts paced around her, cutting her off from all possible routes of escape.

"Jan," she began, wondering if there was anything left of the man she'd known in that malformed body. But Znamenski only growled, slaver dripping from his fang-studded maw. He still wore his crown, though it hung awkwardly from his strangely shaped head.

The Man was still talking. "You have stopped nothing. To delay one performance merely lends strength to the next. Indeed, you have done us a service, of sorts. Word will spread of what happened today, and when next the play is performed the audience will be all the greater, and the message more potent." He extended his hand once again. "Give me the Key, Alessandra Zorzi, and learn your place in the story of things."

"Good luck with that," Thorne called out. They strolled through the hounds, who gave way for them, however grudgingly. "I suspect our Alessandra is not one to be taught anything." They stopped in front of the Man and looked around, studiously avoiding the presence far above. "Can't say I like what you've done with the old place, but then we have different ideas of fashion, I suppose. You like yellow, I like red. I have a sense of style, and you… dress like that."

"Thorne," the Man said. "You should not be here."

"There we agree. I do not want to be here, yet here I am. The Key is mine, I claim it by right of the ancient compacts. Don't like it, take it up with those who wrote them." Thorne turned to Alessandra. "Key, please."

Alessandra took a step back. "What about Pepper?"

"I'm sure she'll be very happy here. Key!"

The Man grunted and caught Thorne by the collar. "Are you

so arrogant as to imagine that you can dictate terms here of all places?" He snapped his fingers, and Znamenski leapt with a gleeful howl, bearing a startled Alessandra to the ground. His claws tore her sleeves and his jaws snapped shut, too close to her throat. She twisted around, trying to free herself, and slammed her elbow into Znamenski's face. He jerked back, but grabbed her ankle as she tried to crawl away.

"The Key! Throw me the Key!" Thorne wailed, as the Man slowly lifted them from their feet. Alessandra hesitated, but only for an instant. She hurled the Key toward them, and Thorne snatched it from the air. Unintelligible syllables burst from their lips and a silvery light swelled in the pallid gloom, driving back the writhing shadows and forcing the Man to release Thorne and cover his eyes. Znamenski and the other hounds shrieked in pain.

Pepper... Camilla... raced through the light, sword in hand. Where she had come from, Alessandra couldn't say. But she was glad to see her, and she cried out in welcome. Pepper met her eyes, but only for an instant as Znamenski rounded and swiped at her with his free claw. She ducked beneath the blow and drove her weapon into his belly.

Znamenski fell back, screeching, releasing Alessandra in the process. Pepper ripped the weapon free and sent it spinning toward her mentor. For a moment, a shape so red it was black seemed to follow the weapon's trajectory... a ripple of a cloak, the gleam of a mask... then her hand was on the blade and she was racing toward the Man in the Pallid Mask. He wheeled to face her, but not in time.

She lunged, even as she had been taught so many years ago. The tip sank into the Man's chest – and then through. His eyes widened and his words were lost in a sudden rush of air, whirling upward toward the corona of the twin suns.

The shock of it was so sudden that they both stopped and stared at one another. The Cavalier's blade hummed in her grip, and the metal sizzled where it touched the Man's flesh. Smoke spewed from his pores and his body began to shrink in on itself as she watched. He caught her arm with a withered grip, his mask slipping. "Bravo," he whispered. Then, something foul slid from her sword and collapsed in a heap on the street, a pallid mask laying atop it. Alessandra stepped back, unable to quite believe her eyes. She looked up.

The King in Yellow was gone.

The play was ended, and the curtain was falling. The wind rose and became fierce; howling. It lifted the struggling, blinded hounds and yanked them upward as if they were nothing more than errant leaves. Znamenski, who still lived, clawed at the ground, his eyes no longer mad or feral; once more the eyes of a man. A man who understood what fate awaited him. His gaze met Alessandra's and, improbably, he winked. Then he too was gone, spinning upward into the black eternities above.

Thorne staggered toward her, the Key shining like a torch in their grip. They caught her arm. "We have to go – now!" they shouted, pausing only to glance in startlement at the Cavalier's blade in her hand.

Alessandra nodded and looked around for Pepper, but all she saw was an unfamiliar woman. Camilla, she thought, but not the Camilla of Pepper's dreams and visions. Rather, the woman as she had been, in the primordial city they now knew as Carcosa. She stood serene in the howling wind, arms raised.

Her expression was peaceful; content. She met Alessandra's gaze and nodded, as if in benediction.

A moment later, she too was gone, drawn upward. The city itself was following; it crumbled and the loose parts were dragged upward toward the suns, which blazed more brightly now, like a newly-stoked flame. Tiny figures that might have been people were caught in the updraft, and the ground buckled beneath Alessandra's feet as she ran after Thorne.

"Where's Pepper?" she cried, but Thorne either didn't hear her – or didn't wish to. The stones beneath her feet heaved up, nearly knocking her to her knees. Towers twisted off their bases and hurtled upward like javelins. The noise became overpowering; it slammed into her from all directions, threatening to turn her insides to jelly.

Ahead of them, past toppling columns and rising statues, was the archway she'd come through. The watery light was fading now, guttering like a candle consuming its wick. Thorne went through first. Alessandra paused, and against her better judgement, looked up.

The suns over Carcosa were blazing white. She didn't know what that meant, if anything. What had any of it meant?

It means the play is done, child. Now all that is left is to take a bow and cede the stage for the next performance.

She looked up, and saw a shadowy shape watching her from a distance. "Wait…" she began, but it was gone a moment later. She turned and leapt through the portal, leaving Carcosa to its fate.

CHAPTER THIRTY-NINE
Consequences

Alessandra hit the stage and rolled awkwardly to her feet, sword-cane still in hand. Thorne, standing nearby, backed away. "Easy there, kitten. No need for bared steel." Flames crawled up the walls and licked across the auditorium.

"We shall see. What about Pepper? Did we – did we free her? Is that what happened?" She advanced on Thorne as she spoke, still holding the blade extended. Thorne retreated with their hands raised. There was no sign of the Key. No doubt they'd hidden it away about their person somewhere.

"Maybe we should go check on her, eh? At the very least, get out of this theater before it collapses atop us." Thorne hurried off the stage, heading for the doors at the far end of the auditorium. Alessandra followed silently. The fire was spreading quickly now, eating away at the backdrops. Thorne was wrong, the theater wasn't going to collapse. But it wouldn't be much use to anyone for a long time.

No one tried to stop them. There didn't seem to be anyone left in the theater or the campo at all. Carabinieri whistles sounded in the dusk, and fire boats drifted toward the campo, water pumps at the ready. She spied Giovanni at the far end of the campo, waving desperately. She and Thorne hurried toward the gondolier. "Is it done?" he asked, his face pale in the smoky air.

"It is," Alessandra said. Giovanni spotted the blade in her hand and crossed himself in recognition. She wondered if he understood what it meant.

"I dropped Selim off and came back. That blade…" He trailed off and looked away. "Come. My gondola is just here. We must be away before the police arrive."

The ride back to the palazzo was a quiet one. Smoke hung over the city, made worse by the thin drizzle of rain that spattered down. The clouds no longer looked so threatening, but only time would tell. She pretended not to notice how Thorne's eyes kept straying to the blade sitting across her lap. Did they feel guilty? Or were they worried? She hoped the answer was yes either way.

When they reached the palazzo, Allegria hurried to meet her, even as Giovanni tied up his craft. "She is awake," the nun said, grabbing Alessandra's hands. "God be praised, she is awake!" Alessandra felt suddenly light-headed as she looked past Allegria and saw Pepper running toward her, Selim following in her wake.

Alessandra embraced the younger woman. "Pepper, I…"

"Guess it wasn't a dumb idea to go to Carcosa after all, hunh?" Pepper said, stepping back. She looked unduly smug, given the circumstances, Alessandra thought. "Seems to me, I was right where I needed to be."

"That damn play," Thorne muttered.

Pepper gave them a glare, then turned her attentions back
to Alessandra. "Camilla…did you see…?"

Alessandra paused, wondering how best to explain. "She's
gone, I think. I do not know if it was to a better place, but she
seemed… content." Pepper nodded.

"I guess maybe that was the best she could hope for. At
least we stopped them, right?"

Thorne laughed. "Delayed, maybe. Inconvenienced,
certainly. But stopped? That's a bit much to ask for. The King
is still on his throne, his kingdom is still there. All we can hope
for is that he stays there for the time being."

"Ain't you cheerful?" Pepper said. Thorne laughed again.

"Survival is winning, kitten. Get used to it."

"Wise words," a familiar voice said. Alessandra looked
toward the quay and saw Elisabetta Magro standing in the
entrance to the courtyard, a smile on her face and an umbrella
in her hand. "Survival is all that we can hope for, in these
trying times."

Selim drew his revolver and cocked it. Alessandra raised
her blade. "I did not come to fight," Elisabetta said quickly,
hands held out as if to show she was unarmed. "Merely to
bring you the gratitude of Don Lagorio."

"I am sure that is unnecessary," Alessandra said. Allegria
stared at Magro as if she were a viper. For her part, the red-
haired woman ignored the abbess.

"The bargain is fulfilled and the truce ended," Elisabetta
went on. "Don Lagorio thanks you for your help in disposing
of his enemies." Her eyes flicked to Thorne. "All of them. Red
and yellow alike."

"Judas," Allegria said, softly. Alessandra felt a cold chill grip her as her suspicions were confirmed. Thorne had done away with the Cavalier to secure Lagorio's help. She'd known, but had hoped otherwise. Elisabetta, she noted, seemed inordinately pleased by their reactions to the news.

Thorne glanced at her and then away. "Tell Lagorio his thanks are unnecessary and unwelcome. I merely did what I had to."

Elisabetta smiled and looked at Alessandra. "As to you ..."

Alessandra lifted the Cavalier's blade. Elisabetta hesitated, eyeing the weapon warily. "Ah," she murmured. "I see. I was going to offer you a place in our Order, but I do not suppose you are interested."

"Not in the least. Now leave my home."

Elisabetta frowned but retreated nonetheless. As she climbed into the waiting gondola, she looked back. "Venice is no longer your home, Countess. I advise you to leave and never look back. Don Lagorio's generosity is not without limit."

When she was out of sight, Alessandra turned to Thorne. "You killed him."

"It was necessary. Lagorio..." They smiled, or tried to. Alessandra wasn't having it.

"He did nothing we could not have done ourselves," she said, flatly. "The truth was, you knew that the Cavalier would never let you leave Venice with the Key, so you found a reason to remove him. One that justified your crime."

"And so? I have my Key, you have your friend, and Venice is still here. And it cost us nothing save one unhappy artist and a used up old man. Drinks all around, I say." They patted their jacket as they spoke, but frowned as they didn't find what they were looking for.

Alessandra held up the Key. "This Key here?" She'd filched it as they left the theater. Thorne had never noticed. They frowned and she said, "Never let a thief get close, darling."

"Don't play the comedienne, kitten, it doesn't suit you. Hand it over and we can go our separate ways." Thorne's smile faded. "Or you can be difficult about this, and I can go with my original plan." Their eyes gleamed in the dim light. "And after you, well, one can hardly leave Miss Kelly all by herself in a strange country. I'd have to top her as well, wouldn't I?" They clucked their tongue in evident disapproval and snapped their fingers. "The Key, please. Before I lose my temper."

Alessandra tossed the Key onto the ground at their feet. Thorne grimaced. "Such childishness," they said, as they bent to collect their prize. Alessandra pivoted and kicked Thorne in the jaw, knocking them sprawling. Thorne cursed shrilly and clutched at their face.

Alessandra pressed the tip of the Cavalier's blade to Thorne's throat. Thorne froze, eyes wide. "You won't kill me," they said, in a tinny voice.

"People keep saying that," Alessandra said in an absent tone. "Znamenski was once a friend, and I shot him. You, I do not even like."

Thorne swallowed. "What – what do you want?"

"I want the Key. I want you to leave Venice and never return." Alessandra twisted the blade lightly, drawing a thin trickle of blood. "More importantly, I want never to see you again, Thorne. If I do, it will not go well for you."

Thorne closed their eyes. "We had a deal…"

"I am a thief. Deals are more like suggestions." Alessandra smiled, mirthlessly. "Make your choice. One wrong word, one twitch of a finger and I will take your pretty head, Thorne." She stepped back, careful to set a foot atop the Key. Thorne rose, eyes burning with hatred. They straightened their cravat.

"At least you think I'm pretty," they said. They hesitated, and she wondered if they intended to try their luck. Thorne was nothing if not bold. "We could try another deal, if the old one doesn't suit you. I know things… things that might interest you." Thorne smiled. "About your parents."

Alessandra hesitated. "No. I am not interested." The words hurt to say.

"You heard her. I think it's time you leave, pal," Pepper said, arms crossed. "You ain't got to go home, but you can't stay here."

Selim grunted his agreement, and lifted his pistol. "We should shoot them now."

"I agree with the Turk," Giovanni said, fondling his knife. "There are places we could sink the body that no one would ever find it."

Thorne glanced at them, and then back at Alessandra. "You know this isn't the end, kitten. You're out of your depth and you'll only keep sinking until you see sense." Thorne clapped their hands and smiled, though there was no mirth in it. "But if you insist on dealing yourself into this game, I'm happy to oblige. The more the merrier, I say." They stepped past her, and headed for the canal.

Thorne paused at the doors, turned and gave a jaunty wave. "Be seeing you, kitten."

Then, they were gone.

Alessandra lowered the sword-cane, and nodded her

thanks to the others. Pepper came down the stairs to join her. "They really killed him, hunh?" she asked. Alessandra nodded.

"Yes."

"Maybe we should have returned the favor."

Alessandra smiled, sadly. "You sound like Selim."

"Because I am wise," Selim said. "That one will be trouble down the line."

"He is right," Allegria said. "Creatures like Thorne rarely take defeat well. They are spiteful and determined. A bad combination."

"Yes, but that is a worry for the future," Alessandra said. She looked at the others. "For now, I am satisfied that we are alive." She hefted the Cavalier's blade and, after a moment's hesitation, handed it to Allegria. "I think you should take this."

Allegria took the sword-cane and slid it into its sheath. She cradled it as if it were a holy relic. Maybe it was, given what it had accomplished. "I think he meant for you to have it."

"Maybe. Maybe not." Alessandra looked around, and then back at Allegria. "Look after the place for me, will you?"

"You are not staying?"

Alessandra smiled. "No. I have something that needs returning to its rightful owners." She thought of the Zanthu Tablet, safely hidden in Selim's luggage. And the Key of Ys as well. She wondered what Armitage might make of it. "Besides, Selim has never seen America. I would hate to deny him that pleasure." Her gaze found Pepper. The younger woman looked as if she were describing her adventures for Selim and Giovanni. Allegria followed her gaze.

"She did well," the abbess said.

"Yes."

"So did you, cousin."

Allegria paused. "He meant well, whatever you might think of him. Everything he did, it was all for the benefit of others... including you."

"He never told me why," Alessandra said.

"No. Me neither. But I am sure he had his reasons."

"Let us hope they were good ones," Alessandra said. She smiled and, yielding to impulse, kissed Allegria's cheek. "You will look after Venice for me, I hope. Do not let it sink into the lagoon before I return, eh?"

Allegria returned her smile. "I will do what I can." She gave the sword-cane a tap. "And when you return, this will all be waiting for you."

Alessandra nodded. She took another look around at the palazzo. For a moment, she thought she saw someone standing at one of the windows... a tall figure, clad in robes and wearing a mask the color of blood. Then the light changed and she saw that there was nothing there at all.

Nothing, save shadows and ghosts.

EPILOGUE
Claret and Cinabre

"A toast, to our departed comrade in crimson," the Claret Knight intoned, raising his glass high in salute. Cinabre followed suit, smiling crookedly. His guest was distinguished, and dressed to the nines. The Knight was old, but hadn't lost a step. He was one of the most influential of the Red Coterie in Europe. A good friend to have and a bad enemy to make. Even Thorne stepped lightly around him.

"And how did you come to know this sad news?" Cinabre asked.

"Thorne, of course. They've been hinting at it since they departed Venice. I suppose what's the point of murder if no one knows about it?" The Knight frowned. "The way I hear it, you sent them there."

"Did I?"

"Thorne claims it's all your doing."

"Is that who I have to thank for this unannounced visit, then?" Cinabre murmured. He gave his drink a swirl, inhaling the bouquet. Only the best for the Knight. "I shall speak most sternly with them, when next we meet. Where are they, by the by?"

"The Himalayas, last I heard." The Knight paused. "Did you?"

"Did I what?"

"Send Thorne to eliminate our recalcitrant comrade." The Knight studied him. "I know the Cavalier had become a bit of an embarrassment, but I cannot bring myself to believe that you would do such a thing."

Cinabre lit a cigarette and inhaled. "As a matter of fact, I did."

The Knight frowned. "Why?"

Cinabre paused before replying. "How long had he been fighting his war? How long since he last collected anything of value, my friend? How long since he contributed to our great work in any fashion?"

"How long since you have done so?" the Knight countered.

Cinabre smiled. "I am a machine of perpetual effort. Everything I do is in service to a great cause. The Cavalier was lost. Broken. A new bearer of his Keys is needed."

"And you chose Thorne of all people?" the Knight asked, with a slight sneer.

Cinabre laughed. "No. Whatever they claim, no. I have someone else in mind. As did, I think, the Cavalier." He leaned forward. "He chose an heir, you see. It was only when I discovered this that I decided to… tip the board, as they say."

The Knight sat back and sipped his wine. "The woman. Zorzi."

Cinabre nodded. "I believe so, yes."

"She's left Venice as well."

"Yes."

"But you think she will return, and take up the Cavalier's mantle."

Cinabre nodded. He had wagered much on that very thing. "Yes." Things were coming to a head. He could feel it, building in the distance. A storm of such fury and power that only a rare few could stand against it.

"Why choose her?"

"Who can say?" Cinabre shrugged. "Some connection we are unaware of, perhaps. Thorne might know, but Thorne lies."

"Thorne lies," the Knight agreed. "A vote must be taken, Cinabre. The others will not like this. Unilateral action upsets their digestion. Frankly, it upsets mine as well." He stroked his well-trimmed beard. "But maybe you are right. Maybe it is time for some... new blood."

"I think so."

"Thorne will vote against her nomination, of course."

Cinabre's grin was predatory. "I am aware. I am also aware of how many of our comrades bear Thorne a grudge. They will vote in opposition whatever Thorne insinuates."

The Knight chuckled. "I start to see now why you had Thorne do the dirty work."

"Thorne is reckless. They make bargains without heed of the larger consequences, trusting that they will never suffer them. The Cavalier was the opposite... so fearful of making another wrong move that he could make no move at all."

"You are referring to Paris..."

"I am. That was the last time he left his beloved lagoon. Whatever occurred that night broke him. But now, his powers and responsibilities will fall upon another. One who might put them to better use, if she can but be shown the way."

"By you," the Knight murmured. Cinabre sniffed.

"Who better? I am the one who saw her potential." He

reclined on his couch and scratched his chin. "That said, we can but hope this is all not in vain."

"She owes you a debt, does she not?" the Knight said, after a moment. Cinabre nodded. The Knight grunted and sipped his drink. "Will that make her more open to the idea... or less?"

"She is a pragmatic woman. She will see the benefit of membership and join us."

"You are certain of this?"

Cinabre sighed. "I am certain that the day is fast approaching when we of the Red Coterie must put aside our differences and align once more in the grand design which is our purpose. The war we have been preparing to fight for centuries is brewing." He set his glass aside and looked into the fire crackling in the fireplace. He could almost make out monstrous shapes in the writhing flames; unnamable and indescribable. He blinked the thought away and looked at the Knight. "And when that day comes, Alessandra Zorzi will either fight alongside us... or she will be dead, and of no consequence."

The Knight considered this. Then, he raised his glass. "Another toast then. To making the wise choice."

"To wisdom," Cinabre said. And smiled.

ABOUT THE AUTHOR

JOSH REYNOLDS is the author of over thirty novels and numerous short stories, including the wildly popular *Zombicide, Legend of the Five Rings, Warhammer: Age of Sigmar* and *Warhammer 40,000*. He grew up in South Carolina and now lives in Sheffield, UK.

joshuamreynolds.co.uk
facebook.com/joshua.m.reynolds.3

THE DEFINITIVE GUIDE TO THE WORLD OF ARKHAM HORROR

Venture deeper than ever before into the legend-haunted city of Arkham and its neighboring towns of Dunwich, Innsmouth and Kingsport. Explore 115 fabled locations with more than 500 illustrations in this gorgeous, full-color hardcover guidebook.

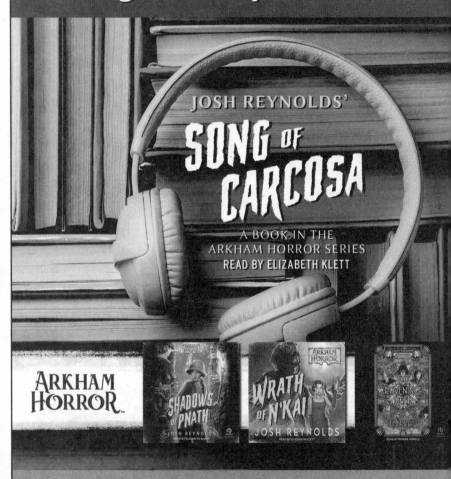